THE LAND OF THE

VOLUME FIV

Open Secrets

Emyr Humphreys was born in the Welsh seaside resort of Prestatyn and educated at the University College of Wales, Aberystwyth, where he began to develop his lifelong interest in Welsh literature, language and politics. He has worked as a teacher in London, as a radio and television drama producer, and as a lecturer in drama at the University of Wales, Bangor.

A highly acclaimed novelist, Emyr Humphreys has won the Somerset Maugham Award and the Hawthornden Prize. He has published books of poetry, and his *Collected Poems* appeared in 1999. He is a productive and greatly respected television dramatist and has produced works of non-fiction in both English and Welsh. His recent novel, *The Gift of a Daughter*, was awarded the Arts Council of Wales Book of the Year Prize in 1999.

THE LAND OF THE LIVING
VOLUME FIVE

Open
Secrets

EMYR HUMPHREYS

UNIVERSITY OF WALES PRESS • CARDIFF • 2000

British Library Cataloguing-in-Publication Data.
A catalogue record for this book is available from the British Library.

ISBN 0–7083–1626–3

First published in Great Britain by J. M. Dent & Sons Ltd., 1988
Reprinted by Sphere Books Ltd., 1989

Published with the financial support of the Arts Council of Wales

Cover design by Olwen Fowler, The Beacon Studio

Typeset at University of Wales Press
Printed in Great Britain by Dinefwr Press, Llandybïe

The Land of the Living

Diffygiaswn pe na chredaswn weled daioni yr Arglwydd yn nhir y rhai byw. *

The seven volumes of this series observe a mainly chronological order. It reads as follows:

* Author's note:

This is the penultimate verse of Psalm 27: '*I had fainted* unless I had believed to see the goodness of the Lord in the land of the living.' It was the word '*diffygiaswn*' that attracted me, and I took it to mean that the poet would give up without the hope of a meaningful destiny for his people. I am aware that the word has been omitted in more recent translations: but it remains apposite to a sequence of stories drawn from the life of a society under siege.

The remaining titles in this series will be reprinted in 2000 and 2001

1

JOHN CILYDD WAS GROANING IN HIS SLEEP. HIS FACE WAS GREY ON THE pillow and the strange sound rose and fell between his parted lips, part moan, part whimper, as though from another spirit trapped somewhere in the depth of his material being. The noise was enough to wake his wife. She lay on her side listening. The bay window of the second-floor bedroom was no more than eighteen inches from the floor. Without moving her head, Amy could see the dawn light spreading over the silted harbour into which a silent tide was running through a veil of mist. She appeared to believe the unearthly sound she could hear came from outside the window. In the first light the leaves on the tops of the trees that lined the wide pavement across the street had been distorted by the salt winds into withered shapes that bore only a faint relation to their original form. They were brown and lifeless and should have fallen. Beyond the harbour the black silhouette of a railway engine shunted into sight. Its whistle was faint but reassuring. A column of steam billowed up to a great height in the still air.

Amy turned to touch her husband lightly: enough to release him from the grip of his dream. Her touch seemed to intensify it. He groaned more helplessly. A film of sweat covered his face. Amy was obliged to shake him by the shoulder.

'John,' she said. 'John! For heaven's sake!'

He shuddered and sat up suddenly. She protested at the draught of cold air as the bedclothes were drawn away from her. With a trance-like motion Cilydd passed the palm of his hand down his chest and found it soaking wet. Amy was already laughing at her own imaginings.

'I thought it was some awful bird outside the window,' she said. 'The noise you were making. I thought I saw it landing on top of that tree; a big black thing. With a long neck. And all the time it was you.'

He sighed and shuddered again.

'Oh dear,' Amy said. 'Did you have a bad dream?'

'Not a dream. A nightmare.'

His voice was so sepulchral it made her smile.

'All over Europe people are having nightmares,' she said. 'No question about that.'

She lay with her hands behind her head apparently contemplating the grim realities of the international situation. He bid more urgently for her attention and sympathetic understanding.

'But this was so real.'

'In that case it wasn't a nightmare.'

Amy yawned and closed her eyes. On a Saturday morning they could stay in bed a little longer.

'Children have nightmares.'

She murmured restfully to herself.

'Don't you remember Bedwyr when he was delirious with a high temperature? Staring straight through you. No idea who you were. Screaming the moon was on fire.'

Cilydd became intent on recalling images, conjuring them up before his eyes.

'Cattle trucks. An endless train of cattle trucks. On the line from Rouen to the Western Front. Only families this time as well as soldiers. I saw one truck filled with ministers going over the Presbytery accounts. They had no idea they were being transported. The treasurer was chanting the balance sheet and he had the ledger open on his knees.'

'Your guilty conscience,' Amy said. 'You're forever forgetting to contribute to church funds. Isn't there something called lapsus-something-or-other? You forget because you don't really want to remember and you don't want to remember because you really don't want to belong. You just go to chapel for the sake of your family and for the sake of appearances and for the sake of Welsh culture or whatever, not because you believe in the stuff. And so on. There you are. I can interpret it all for you. Free, gratis – and for nothing.'

He was unwilling to treat his dream so lightly. His fists were clenched with the effort of recall.

'In my truck it was different. In my truck I was completely trapped and there was no escape. It was bitterly cold and yet it stank of excrement. All my effort was put into a desperate attempt to pull the doors open. Outside fields of white cabbages like skulls

2

were flashing by and behind them hills were rippling up and down like someone shaking a carpet. Somehow I had to get out.'

'Too much cheese for supper,' Amy said. 'That's what my aunt always used to say.'

Cilydd shook his head.

'It was real,' he said. 'Like a warning. Or a message anyway. Most of the men in the truck were already dead. I knew their faces.'

'Or those cartoons you were looking at,' Amy said. 'They were horrible enough.'

He sank down under the bedclothes to stop himself shivering.

'There was a corporal using his bayonet to punch holes in a bucket to turn it into a brazier. Each time it came out like a human shriek. I knew that when he was finished he would start thrusting the bayonet into me. That's why I was struggling to open the door. So that I could throw myself out. I couldn't open it.'

His head was still on the pillow and he spoke in an intense whisper.

'The train was moving and no one could stop it. That was the meaning. It's coming and no one can stop it.'

'Oh I don't know . . .'

Her inclination was to dissent.

'It was a strange effect,' Cilydd said. 'As if the Front was also moving closer. There was no way a collision could be avoided and yet no way of knowing what would happen.'

'They're still talking anyway,' Amy said. 'Where there's life there's hope.'

'And the corporal had blue eyes. They flashed like steel in the sun.'

He murmured in a melancholy trance.

'I don't think anyone can stop it. It's the price we shall all have to pay.'

'What "price" for heaven's sake?'

Amy was impatient with the lugubrious satisfaction he appeared to derive from delivering the verdict.

'What they call Progress. We've constructed a vast industrial complex and it's grown of its own momentum into a monstrous machine with an appetite that will devour the world.'

3

' "We"? How can you say "we"? It was never anything to do with us.'

He shook his head with irritating certainty.

'That was the meaning of my dream.'

'Dreams don't have any meaning.'

Amy gave up her attempt at further rest. She was ready to sit up and register protest in one way or another.

'Mine don't anyway. I'm quite sure of that. Just bits of memories and fantasies jumbled together. Very boring too if you asked me. You shouldn't take so much notice.'

'There are demons.'

He persisted with his grim exposition.

'You are inclined to attach too much significance to every notion that floats through your head, if you don't mind me telling you.'

'Angels of chaos. You can see them quite plainly. Elevated by the collective delusions of the masses into the seats of unlimited power. In that sense the instincts of the cartoonists are correct. The hands of demons on levers, and no one else. Hell is empty and all the devils are here.'

'Oh rubbish.'

Amy could not lie still in bed a moment longer.

'You are just transfixed by your own fears. That's no good at all. I know things are bad, but after all you can still say what you like in this country. You can still act.'

Cilydd gripped her arm.

'I could see their faces. They were all dead. Men I had known. Friends and comrades. Owen Guest. You've heard me talk about him. Second Lieutenant Guest. His uniform covered in shit and blood. And Frankie, Frankie Angelis. And Pen was there too. Pen Lewis.'

Amy shook herself free. She sat on the edge of the bed.

'I wish you'd shut up,' she said.

'Why?'

His question was suddenly sharp, forensic.

'Because the dead are dead. We've got to face that. You're a grown man.'

In her own defence she was ready to attack him. With his hands

4

behind his head he watched her drift about the bedroom undecided whether or not to get dressed.

'You shouldn't attach so much importance to childish fancies. The dead are dead. We've got to face that. We've lost them for ever. All we can do is make the best of what's left to us. You know that as well as I do.'

'They never leave us.'

She dropped her dressing-gown on the foot of the bed. She made an effort to smile, if not for his comfort at least to persuade him to turn his mind to something else.

'It's going to be a nice day,' she said. 'We ought to take the children to one of the quiet beaches. Why don't you go out for a walk? I'll have the boys ready for breakfast by the time you get back.'

'The process has begun,' Cilydd said. 'There's no turning back. The whole machine has been devised to transform people into able-bodied automatons. Whole populations trained to respond like Pavlov's dogs to work, to reproduce, to kill and to die to order.'

'All right. Go and write a poem about it. Do something positive instead of lying there making yourself miserable.'

'What's the point? I'd only be repeating the same thing over and over again.'

He was inclined to ramble on as Amy searched impatiently in the drawer at the bottom of the mahogany wardrobe for old clothes to wear. He began to quote scripture.

' "Death is come up into windows . . . my tabernacle is spoiled and all my cords are broken." '

'Honestly. You and your words. Sometimes I get sick of the sound of them.'

She drew an extra jersey over her head as she passed through the door. In their rooms on the floor below, both boys were still sleeping. In the cot, Gwydion's arms were flung out but the blanket bag she had made him was firmly buttoned on his shoulders. Earlier she had potted him. Now he could sleep until his brother woke him up. She turned down the wick of the small lamp out of child's reach on the landing wall.

The fire in the Triplex grate of the basement kitchen was already laid. All she had to do was put a match to it. While she laid the

5

table for breakfast, picked out socks that needed darning from a heap of washing, moving back and forth between two basement rooms, the flame consumed the crushed newspaper and dried sticks and the inert black lumps took on a satisfying incandescence. Any task, no matter how trivial, was preferable to brooding stillness. There was sunlight in the garden: enough to show the windows needed cleaning: and enough to make too conspicious the sterile fig tree spreading itself untidily at the end of the strip. It had been battered by a recent storm and there were still streaks of sand on the sagging leaves. If she armed herself with a hand-saw plus the large secateurs that hung from a rusty nail in the outside water closet at the end of the lean-to conservatory, she could take the untidy tree in hand. There was no one about to interfere with the process. She could shape it according to her liking or even remove it altogether so that when they came down to breakfast the family would be faced with an accomplished fact.

As her face tightened with a resolve to act a curious figure appeared under the stone archway that framed the door between the narrow garden and the lane. Menna Cowley Jones's ankles were white and naked above her pink fur-lined bedroom slippers. Her overcoat hung open over the flannel nightdress. A hat with a feather in it was balanced precariously on her head. Even in her excitement she was conscious of the comic figure she presented. She carried an open newspaper in her hand and raised it for Amy to see as an explanation for her unorthodox behaviour. She began to gesticulate in a manner that suggested she did not care if all the windows in the massive rear wall of Marine Terrace were occupied by neighbours watching her as they rose from their beds on this Saturday morning. Amy went out to meet her on the garden path.

'Dear Mrs More.'

Menna Cowley Jones swallowed in an urgent attempt to suppress her giggles so that she could be deeply serious.

'I had to tell you if you didn't know already. Thinking of our boys. As I said to my sister Flo. We have to think of our Clemmie. And little Bedwyr next door but two. Little friends. Little comrades. They have a right to their future. That's what I said to Flo. And for once she had to agree with me.'

Her moonlike face expanded in a joyous smile.

'There isn't going to be a war!'

Her plump body was shivering with excitement inside her night-dress. She shook the newspaper to evoke a response from Amy who stood as immobile as a pillar of salt trying to absorb the news.

'The darkest hour before the dawn. That's what I said to Flo. "Don't be so daft," she said. All day she'd been wrapped up like an old blanket in the dark folds of her own foreboding. I'm an optimist you see and she's a pessimist. That's how it's always been. "You have to have faith," I said. "What's that when it's at home?" she said. But I was right wasn't I? They've signed an agreement. This country and Germany will never go to war again!'

'Is it true?'

Amy's voice was strained with incredulity.

'Of course it's true. "Peace in our Time." It's such a lovely phrase. "Give us peace in our time O Lord." I don't know why we don't have it in chapel quite honestly. As a regular part of the service. That's what I said to Flo.'

She was disappointed with Amy's lukewarm reaction.

'Whatever you say about Mr Chamberlain, Mrs More, he's saved us all from the horrors of another Great War.'

Menna chewed her lower lip. In her excitement she had been more outspoken than was her wont. She looked startled by her own daring. She had followed Amy in protests against the government in the past. Now she had to demonstrate quickly that her devotion to Amy and her family remained totally unimpaired.

'It was such a load off my mind, do you know what I mean?'

The feather in her hat drooped as she appealed for Amy's sympathetic understanding.

'The news has been so awful for so long now I just couldn't sleep. And I'm a poor sleeper at the best of times as I must have told you more than once. I think sometimes it's what makes me talk so much. It affects my nerves. "You're not the only one with nerves," Flo says. Well of course I'm not. But I'm the one that can't sleep. I can hear her snoring across the landing. What I'm trying to say is I was thinking of the boys you know. Not just for our Clemmie, but for your Bedwyr and your Gwydion too. Are they supposed to have another Great War to look forward to? I mean, I know your good husband is telling us that it's Wales that counts and who is to stand up and speak for her in the Day of Wrath? But what I'm thinking is that another Great War would finish her off too. So let's take it as a blessing. Don't you agree?'

The flow of her discourse seemed to have passed by Amy's ear, leaving her preoccupied with some interior calculation.

'Flo says I don't understand a thing.'

A note of self-disparagement might have a better chance of gaining Amy's attention.

'Well maybe I don't. But who else does? That's what I say to her. Everybody says they're against war, but until yesterday everybody was making a noise and saying it was inevitable. That's the way Flo talked. Always reading the paper and listening to the wireless. Couldn't bear to do that myself. But I was right, wasn't I? I said, "I'm right, aren't I?" And she was just as ready as I was to jump for joy.'

Menna shook the panels of her overcoat in a muted symbol of the act of jumping. Somehow or other she had to make Amy smile.

'I must go and get their breakfast ready,' Amy said.

Before closing the conservatory door she turned to call out.

'Thanks for telling me. The good news.'

Instantly encouraged, Menna shuffled forward in her slippers, eager with suggestion.

'It's going to be a lovely day,' she said. 'Why don't we take the boys to Abercregin beach? You know how they love it there. Safe and private. And perhaps we could gather some blackberries. There's a place in the hollow where they grow like grapes.'

She thrust her face forward to influence Amy's decision.

'We'll see,' Amy said. 'I'll have to talk to John Cilydd. I know he's got an anti-conscription meeting somewhere. We'll see.'

In her kitchen Amy sat down at the table, her impulse to work evaporated. It was here that Cilydd found her, motionless and staring into space. He stood on the last step of the short flight of uncarpeted stairs. It could have been a stranger he saw seated at their breakfast table.

'Amy. What is it?'

Before she spoke her lips twisted into a sarcastic smile.

'They've signed an agreement. Tweedledum and Tweedledee. Mr Chamberlain and his Herr Hitler. There isn't going to be a war.'

Cilydd plunged his little finger into his right ear and shook it vigorously as if to disturb the wax. It was his turn to be perplexed. Amy slapped the table jumping up to fill the kettle and put it on the fire.

'Marvellous isn't it?' she said. 'Now we must all troop out to the cathedrals of this world and sing a *Te Deum*. As if God had anything to do with it. As if he'd taken Adolf and Neville to one side in the playground and said, "Now boys. Make peace and shake hands." '

Cilydd was pulling faces as if thought processes were attacking his head like a swarm of insects.

'I should go out and get a paper,' he said.

'Yes. Why don't you?'

He became increasingly attentive to Amy's sceptical behaviour.

'It will all be there, won't it?' she said. 'The accurate account. The impartial comment. The this of it and the that of it.'

He moved closer to his wife. He had sympathy for the anger that mingled with her sense of relief.

'It's as if the whole tide of History were running against us,' he said.

'What's that supposed to mean?'

'The Republic's going down. And the Wales we want is going down with it. Like two people who can't swim choking each other. The lostness of lost causes.'

Cilydd stood rigid in the middle of the kitchen floor. Whatever he said tended to reverberate in the basement.

'They'll call it peace,' he said. 'Peace in our time. Pen died for nothing.'

The last statement fell from his lips like a cold fragment of the truth. Pen Lewis had died in Spain for nothing. The Republic was going down and nothing could save it. It became so quiet and still in the kitchen they could both have died momentarily themselves. Amy made a determined effort to break the spell.

9

'It was his own fault,' she said.

'All he went through,' Cilydd said. 'Just for nothing. When I saw those pictures of corpses in the olive grove. It looked just as useless as the Western Front. A fight for nothing. Legalised murder.'

'It was what he chose to do,' Amy said.

The palm of her hand was pressed against the chimney breast as she stared down into the fire.

'It's only the war machine that wins,' Cilydd said. 'It's so obvious really. The biggest, most efficient war machine always wins. So they will go on making them bigger and bigger and bigger . . .'

'Oh, don't go on about it!'

She was shouting at him. He looked at her with dazed surprise. She tried to modify her outburst.

'If there's nothing we can do about it, at least we can stop ourselves going on about it. That's what I meant.'

Her reproof echoed in the quiet. It imposed a silence that became difficult to break. The kettle began to boil. He raised an arm to indicate he was willing to take charge of it. She made the tea with precise economical expertise that made his inactivity somehow culpable and his presence superfluous until she had made him sit down to drink it.

'I suppose I am obsessive, aren't I?' Cilydd said.

She smiled at him forgivingly.

'You can't help it,' she said. 'You can't help your nature.'

'You are history, you are legend.'

He repeated the phrase as if he were trying to attach to it an ironic undertone. Amy was ready for some form of conversation that would re-establish calm in their relationship.

'I never did like history,' she said. 'It was always my worst subject at school. I loved geography and biology and similar things that offered you the world if only you could make the effort to understand it. But history . . . yuk. The past creeping around in your brain, disagreeing with itself and making ridiculous demands. Why should it?'

'I did as you told me,' Cilydd said. 'Like an obedient husband.'

'You did what?'

She was making an effort to restrain her impatience. He ventured to tease her a little.

'I listen to every word you say. I weigh every word. Like gold dust in a balance.'

'What gold dust?'

'I wrote a poem,' he said. 'Just as you told me to.'

Amy smiled with relief.

'Oh John,' she said. 'You poor old thing. I do treat you badly don't I? You are a poet after all. A real poet. A real poet should never have a nagging wife.'

'Well, I started one anyway. As usual. I'm always starting one. Every other hour of the day. Even in the office. I'm ashamed to say.'

They were able to laugh easily together.

'Miss Pearse comes in, just like a school teacher. And I push the piece of paper out of sight, under the blotting paper.'

'She's a dragon,' Amy said. 'Your office dragon.'

'She is rather, isn't she? Still she keeps me up to the mark.'

'And she's in league with your sister Nanw. Nothing goes on in there without your sister knowing.'

Cilydd breathed deeply. It wasn't a fact of life with which he was entirely happy. Miss Pearse was a fiercely loyal person who kept the office in order with a perpetual frown on her face and a crown of frizzy hair.

'What about the poem?'

Amy's interest excited him.

'It's only a start,' he said. 'It's only in my head. Not on paper . . .'

She was gazing at him sympathetically. He began to recite his opening lines.

> 'The dawn after the third day the torturers
> In gym-shoes slide like shadows through the soldiers' gate
> They carry instruments beyond discipline
> To carve graffiti on soft human flesh
> And sign their warrants with the general's name –
> On such a dawn . . .'

Amy held up her hand.

'I'm sorry,' she said. 'Was that the boys? Gwydion can climb out of his cot . . .'

11

'It's not any good,' he said. 'I know that. But it helps to get the damn thing out.'

Amy nodded comfortingly.

'It's the theme I really want to get to grips with. Of course it's beyond me. But I have to try.'

'What theme?'

Amy was determined to be helpful.

'That you cannot overcome evil with evil. I'm more convinced of it now than ever. But how can I prove it poetically? Do you know what I mean?'

'I think so,' Amy said.

'If you can't prove it poetically either you're not a real poet or it can't be true. And if it's not true, then you yourself are not true either. And that is terrible. You are just a pretence. You are just another self-absorbed failure dribbling your life away in a waste of words. Do you know what I mean?'

'I think I do,' Amy said.

She was listening for more sounds from the children upstairs. Cilydd attempted a fresh approach. He sounded desperate with the need to be honest.

'Suppose you were the puppet master, Amy, instead of one of the puppets.'

The mere notion was abhorrent to her.

'I'm nobody's puppet,' she said.

'I mean in the broadest, widest sense. Suppose you had the power. The real power. And you are in charge of the great good anti-Fascist cause. There they are. The enemy line upon line. Attacking or defending. It doesn't matter. Who will you kill? Not the real enemy. Not the evil men in power. Only row upon row of mother's sons lined up and conscripted into uniform. The same old cannon fodder. And the means of killing this time are even more indiscriminate. They don't distinguish between soldier and civilian, they don't know the difference between Fascist beasts and milk-fed mother's darlings.'

Amy waved her hand at the sounds she could hear upstairs.

'Why don't you see what those two boys are up to? I'll get their breakfast ready.'

12

2

MRS ROSSETT'S CAT RUBBED ITS FURRY FLANK AGAINST AMY'S LEG.
Mrs Rossett lifted her gloved hands, as if on the point of
clapping her delight.

'She remembers you! Dear Mrs More. Beauty Puss remembers
you.'

She laughed at herself as she uttered the cat's absurd name. Her
affection for the purring beast, like the pink washable collar she
had placed around its neck, was ridiculous but pardonable because
she was a middle-aged widow confined to keeping house for a
brother crippled by arthritis.

'My brother Nathan says that Beauty Puss is the centre of my
universe. Isn't it dreadful? But what can you do?'

They could hear the Reverend Nathan Harris shuffling about his
bedroom and humming sporadically to himself as he went through
the painful exercise of completing his toilet. Mrs Rossett herself
was already dressed to go out when Amy arrived. A square hat and
a fur-trimmed collar made her look taller than ever. As she opened
the door and then preceded Amy down the narrow corridor of the
terrace house to her kitchen, her stately figure might have looked
more at home in a rambling vicarage or even a country mansion.

' "Every universe needs a centre",' Mrs Rossett said.

She was quoting her brother. It was an old habit of hers to repeat
the more memorable things her brother Nathan said. She even
raised her voice now to give a faint impression of the clarion note
in his piercing tenor.

' "Relativity isn't relative" ' she said. ' "And existentialism isn't
experimental." I don't know what on earth he means most of the
time. But it keeps him happy. "Philosophical investigations" he
calls it.'

Beauty Puss was looking up at her longingly. She wanted to leap
into her lap, but Mrs Rossett shook her head sternly. She did not
want cat's hair on her overcoat.

'The fact is,' Mrs Rossett said, 'he thinks even more of the c.a.t.
than I do. Do you remember how he used to nurse her sitting in
that chair? The warmth of her fur was good for his rheumatism he

said. And do you remember how she used to jump down when you came home from school? Just to rub against your legs?'

Mrs Rossett smiled blissfully into the fire. Amy had once been her lodger. Now, another young teacher from the County School, a man this time, occupied the middle room that had been Amy's. The details of the interior of the house were stubbornly unchanged. The kitchen range had been polished with blacklead to remove rusty blemishes and reflect an immutable perfection. Even the flames of the fire contained themselves to an accustomed height. Dressed to go out, Mrs Rossett sat upright in her chair, calmly dissociated from that dedicated power which polished and preserved all the floors and the furnishings, keeping the habitat minutely intact. She possessed two distinct selves. One that got up at six o'clock in the morning, summer and winter, and worked itself methodically through household chores while brother and lodger were still abed, and a more public persona ready every afternoon to receive visitors and dispense hospitality with regal amplitude.

'You remember how he used to philosophise, Mrs More? Especially if you were listening to him.'

Mrs Rossett made a gesture with her hand to conjure up a vision of the time when Amy lived under her roof. Merely to speak of it brought back something of the comforting warmth she and her brother had derived from the young teacher's glowing presence.

'I should have listened more closely,' Amy said. 'Then I would have learnt more from him.'

Mrs Rossett accepted the tribute to her brother with a graceful sigh.

'He's always in pain,' she said. 'And the years roll by. We are not getting any younger. One thinks sometimes, "What does it all mean?" One can't help it. I asked him the other day, "Are we being tested?" I could see he was in such pain. And do you know, he just smiled at me. You know, in that way he has. The way his poor mouth stretches. And he said as brightly as anything, "Perhaps we are, Nel," he said. "It's as good an hypothesis as any other." '

Mrs Rossett waved a gloved finger to suggest a vague apprehending of concepts far beyond her powers of verbal expression.

What she could enunciate was a benevolent interest in Amy's family.

'Those lovely little boys,' Mrs Rossett said. 'Growing day by day. A wonderful thing. How are they?'

She made a brief but elegant settling motion in her chair to show that she would accept with gratitude any amount of detail of their upbringing that Amy might care to share with her.

'Gwydion can be difficult,' Amy said. 'He's an affectionate child. But so headstrong. Bedwyr of course is an angel. He gives in to the little monster when really he shouldn't. They say boys are more difficult than girls. Still, you need look no further than their respective mothers. Bedwyr takes after Enid. An absolute angel. He really is too good. Just as she was. But Gwydion is a little devil. Just like me.'

Mrs Rossett's head and hat sloped back in a modified rendering of a hearty laugh. She had always found Amy's frankness so engaging. But there was sadness and even tragedy in the fluctuations of fortune since the carefree days when Amy had been Miss Parry, the teacher from the County School, lodging at number seven, Eifion Street. Mrs Rossett's manner glided gracefully into an elegiac mode.

'Ah, Mrs More . . . dear Mrs More . . .'

How could such a happy issue from affliction be celebrated in commonplace, everyday words: Amy's providential marriage to the sad widower of her departed friend; Amy's loving concern for the helpless child baptised on his mother's coffin.

'My dear, we get more old and withered day by day . . . but just to glimpse your happiness, from a decent distance of course, you know it brings a blush of springtime to our dry season!'

She raised a hand to restrain her own enthusiasm but her fingers fluttered inside her glove with a continuing desire to express her admiration more fully. John Cilydd More, solicitor and poet, sensitive protector of the weak and champion of unpopular causes, was Amy's husband and she was his consort and helpmate: and this had to be some form of triumph over cruel adversity. He had lost one exemplary wife to gain another. For a woman alone in her kitchen with only the cat for company, it gave rise to difficult questions concerning the nature of Providence. But such questions could be dissolved if not resolved if the sweet nectar of goodwill were allowed uninterrupted flow like the beguiling melody of a hymn in the minor key.

'Ah, Mrs More . . . dear Mrs More . . . "We have a friend beyond compare, this world cannot contain" . . . One has these rash presumptuous thoughts, prodigal expectations.'

Her brother had begun to sing on his way downstairs. He was laughing at his own eagerness to enliven the monotony of the descent. Amy and his sister waited for him at the bottom of the stairs. Mrs Rossett had his dark overcoat and Amy held his scarf and hat. They were grey to match the profuse curls on which he balanced the familiar Homburg.

'The same old hat, Mrs More!'

The formality of address did nothing to impede the warmth of his manner. Being in Amy's company was one of life's pleasures for Nathan Harris and he did nothing to conceal the fact. He pointed at the door of the middle room, which was closed. It had been Amy's room where they had respected her privacy and cherished her presence. It had even been something of a shrine.

'Mad about football.'

Mr Harris was referring to their present lodger. Adequate but not in Amy's league. He and his sister could hardly 'think the world' of a young man mad about football.

'Plays outside right for his home team, Llanrwst United.'

He chuckled at the incongruous association of the two worlds in the two words.

'Very decent lad. No harm in him. But mad about football.'

He shifted about stiffly as his sister helped him put on his coat. With the same clockwork movement he led the way outside and waited as she locked the front door. His face tilted up slowly until his hat was in danger of falling off.

'"*Der bestirnte Himmel über mir*",' Nathan Harris said. '"The starry heavens above me and the moral law within me." You know, when I was a young man I always wanted a telescope. I really lusted after one. And do you know what my father said to me? I suppose he was right but I was quite hurt at the time. "It costs far less my boy, to look inside yourself." '

16

He laughed cheerfully.

'I don't think it's going to rain, do you? A close ring around the moon. People are inclined to snatch at the least excuse for not turning up to a meeting. I know I do.'

He remained silent as Amy started the car for fear his talking would distract her from the mysteries of the operation. He was intent on enjoying the trip. Short as it was, it demonstrated so much power and potential compared with his own limited resources of locomotion. He could no longer contain himself once the engine had started.

'I was reading you know about light from the stars. There are galaxies so far away from us the astronomers reckon their light began their journey to our field of vision before our sun or our earth were even created.'

'Really,' Amy said politely. 'Is that so?'

She leaned slightly towards him as she held on to the steering wheel to indicate she was giving him concentrated attention. Mrs Rossett, sitting in the dark of the back seat, smiled at the resonant note in her brother's voice.

'Doesn't help the world situation in anyway at all,' Nathan Harris said. 'And if we say it lends a certain perspective, does that mean anything more than indifference, in practical terms?'

He stared through the windscreen as Amy drove through Pendraw. He gave a troubled sigh as though riding through the deserted streets in the motor car gave him more detachment than he was entitled to. He was not a tourist passing through, or a disembodied visitor from another planet. These were his own people, sheltering in their modest dwellings from the gathering cold. Even a crippled shepherd should foster the habit of concern for his flock. My people, thy people.

'We have to persuade people, don't we?' Nathan Harris said. 'It's not easy. "Whom will ye that I release unto you? Barabbas, or Jesus which is called Christ? . . . and the chief priests and elders persuaded the multitude that they should ask Barabbas and destroy Jesus." Dear me, how, many times I have tried to compose a sermon on that text. And failed every time.'

'Don't say that, Nathan.'

His sister raised her melodious voice to encourage him from the back seat. The minister was set on rigorous self-examination.

' "Then answered all the people and said His blood be on us and on our children." That's what's so terrible, you see.'

Amy showed her readiness to catch on to what he was saying.

'Our capacity for self-deception,' Nathan Harris said. 'Limitless. For example, the church through the ages using verses like that to condemn and persecute the Jews. "The people," means us. "Israel," means the church itself. It's we ourselves that crucify him from one generation to another.'

'Don't excite yourself, Nathan,' his sister said. 'Or you won't sleep a wink tonight.'

'Do you know what illness teaches you?' Nathan Harris said.

He made an effort to laugh at himself. He was stimulated by Amy's presence.

'If it teaches you anything that is . . .'

He raised his forearm to prescribe a stiff elliptical motion.

'We each of us possess our little planetary system of concerns and it revolves like the hands of a clock for twenty-four hours a day around the burning sun of self.'

'Nathan!'

His sister administered a gentle reproof.

'I have never known a more unselfish man than you.'

He would not allow her to interrupt his delight in speculation. It was Amy he most wished to impress.

'This is what I would call the force of gravity. You can go against it momentarily when you laugh at yourself.'

'Mr Harris . . .'

He held up his hand to show Amy he hadn't finished.

'Self is almost a synonym for sin when it becomes selfish. That's obvious enough. But a sick man can see it more clearly. It stands out like bones under starving skin. But this is what I wanted to say and this is what alarms me, Mrs More, in political terms you see, in practical political terms. And I can't tell you how much it goes against the grain for me to have to say this, me of all people. It means you cannot base a political policy on any foundation except enlightened self-interest.'

Mrs Rossett sat back and beamed at the prospect of friendly conflict. She was listening to pleasing echoes of past debates and affectionate encounters between an ageing cripple and a lively young woman.

'How you always argue, you two,' she said.

She spoke so softly they did not hear her.

'That's all right,' Amy was saying. 'That's fine. That's perfectly all right.'

'Oh? Is it? Is it? Here and now? At a time like this?'

'Especially now,' Amy said. 'We can demonstrate that a Popular Front against conscription would be in everybody's best interests.'

'Opportunism you mean?'

'You can call it that if you like,' Amy said. 'I call it a Popular Front. The working class. The young. Socialism. The Welsh language. Welsh culture. Your chapels, your religion, conscience, the family, our way of life. Everything.'

'Well, well . . .'

'Well what?'

She was smiling at him.

'You amaze me,' Nathan Harris said. 'But then you always did. Didn't she, Nel?'

He raised his voice to obtain confirmation from his sister. Now he would demonstrate how much pleasure it was to give way to her.

'I bow to your better judgement,' he said. 'Even if it means old preachers like me taking a back seat.'

'There you are,' Amy said. 'That's not self-interest.'

'It could well be,' Nathan Harris said. 'These speculations of mine are always so inconclusive. "What shall it profit a man . . ." ' Gaining his own soul is the ultimate self-interest! Better than gaining the whole world! We have His word for it.'

'You must tell Hitler and Chamberlain that,' Amy said.

They laughed together. The lights in the Calvinistic Methodist chapel were visible from a distance. The place of worship and the nonconformist graveyard which surrounded it was isolated in the countryside in a central position to serve a community of farms and villages.

'Old Tasker, bless him.'

Nathan gave sympathetic consideration to the problems of Tasker Thomas, the prime convener of the public meeting.

'He expects too much of people. And they always let him down. I sometimes wonder if a man like that should dabble in politics. I've always felt he was cut out to be a saint.'

'He leads by example,' Amy said.

'Does he? I suppose he does. Self-sacrifice. Idealism. In your Popular Front he'll have to restrain himself, Mrs More. Let it be enlightened self-interest tonight and let lay people take the lead. Men like your good husband.'

'A Broad Front,' Amy said.

'Broad and Popular. Let the small countries and the little people unite! In this day and age they have a mission and a message.'

Nathan raised his voice to pulpit pitch. Amy was allowed to drive slowly through the graveyard so that Nathan Harris could get indoors with the minimum of effort. Other cars were left in the road. People stood by ready to help Nathan. His jokes reverberated in the frosty air.

'The halt, the blind and the lame,' he said. 'They're not likely to conscript me, are they? Mind you, they shoot horses in this condition.'

Their arrival was greeted excitedly by Tasker Thomas. He was a minister of the most unconventional sort. Even in the cold weather he wore an open-neck shirt. His head was bare and the light from the vestibule sprinkled frostily on the fringe of untidy ginger hair around his bald pate. The floor level of the chapel was almost full and there were men sitting in the gallery. He rubbed his hands and repeated to Amy and Mrs Rossett what he had already said to John Cilydd standing in the shadows behind him.

'I've made a rough calculation,' he said. 'There must be over forty per cent of the adult population within these walls tonight. And what can that mean except mass conversions! If the spirit is with us, who shall stand against us! There are young men up there in the gallery, you know, determined to defy the government.'

He turned his attention to Nathan Harris. Tasker's solicitude tended to slow down his progress.

20

' "Not by might, nor by power, but by my spirit, said the Lord of Hosts . . . For who hath despised the day of small things?" Zachariah chapter four, part of the sixth to the tenth verses. What do you think?'

Tasker was uncertain of himself. He needed Nathan Harris's advice. Nathan removed his Homburg hat. His grey curls flourished in a way that drew attention to his stiff wasted frame.

'The folly of preaching?'

He managed to raise his eyebrows and smile. Tasker nodded eagerly.

'Not a sermon,' Nathan said. 'I don't think so. No.'

'I agree. I agree. But I thought, should I share an experience? Is that possible? In the trenches you know. I've told you this before. That young lad from the valleys dying and asking me to whisper a prayer in Welsh in his ear. And that strange purple sunrise. Piercing the mists and the stumps of trees and showing up a tank stuck tail up in the deserted trench. The boy dying at my feet. And the conviction that came over me at that moment. We must never let it happen again. As warm as a conversion. And my heart filled with a joy I thought I'd lost for ever.'

He peered into Nathan's sallow face. The inner door was open and the people turned around to mark their approach. They both became acutely aware of row upon row of expectant faces.

'If we can't learn from experience . . .' Nathan said. ' "Feed my lambs" . . .'

Tasker accepted the remark as a sign of approval. In the dimmer light of the vestibule, Mrs Rossett took hold of Amy's arm. John Cilydd had paused to study the church notice board in order to give the infirm minister more time to proceed down the aisle. Mrs Rossett whispered in Amy's ear.

'I do wish Tasker would wear a tie. It doesn't matter to me of course: but it does turn some people against him.'

21

3

CLINGING TO THE RADIATOR, AMY LISTENED TO CILYDD'S VOICE echo in the empty school hall. He was standing on the dais, his dark overcoat open, his arms stretched out. Behind him the memorial window to the pupils killed in the Great War was like the negative of a giant photograph: the lead was more conspicuous than the stained glass, the *dulce et decorum* inscription barely visible around the outlined feet of the angel of victory. A north-west wind driving sleet in gusts against the windows obliged Cilydd to raise his voice.

'It's the figure I want. It's the way I see it!'

Alone on the dais with arms outstretched and no one to hear him except his wife he could exercise absolute bardic authority. There was an image he had to impose on the society to which he belonged.

'A boy stripped to the waist. Little more than a boy. A sacrificial figure lashed to the wheel of a gun-carriage. Field punishment number one. In cruciform. Can you imagine a more powerful image?'

Amy shook her head. The triumphant note in Cilydd's voice seemed to reverberate in her head matching the echo in the empty hall. Her body leaned towards the dais as she clung to the luke-warm radiator. She raised an arm.

'In front of that window,' she said. 'My God, the power of it! I see exactly what you mean.'

Her approval made him masterful and confident.

'They want something from me,' he said. '"Would you compose something for the school's Golden Jubilee?" So what am I supposed to do? The local tame poet. Make a work. Bear witness in one way or another.'

'I think you are absolutely right,' Amy said.

'Do I have a contempt for people, or do I try and communicate with them? It's a straight choice. And if I communicate, it can only be the truth as I saw it and as I see it.'

'Well of course,' Amy said. 'They have no right to ask for anything else.'

'I saw it with my own eyes,' he said. 'More than once.'

He knelt on one knee with the urge to confide in her. She came towards him and sat on the steps of the dais. During the war, when she had been a small child, this man she had married had been an under-age volunteer in khaki on the Western Front. The fact was as familiar as lichen on a tombstone. A grim catalogue of events in which she had no part still exerted power over this man. He was also a poet, capable at this moment of filtering through his presence past experiences painful enough to disrupt the inanimate stillness of the school hall.

'We all hated it. Hated it. I saw two Red Caps tying a poor lad to the wheel of a limber in the main street of Lillers. Outside an estaminet, the lads were playing housey-housey. "The more you put down the more you pick up! Pay the man his money!" Two of them pretended to start a fight. The others piled in. They were drawing off the Red Caps so that the others could loosen the bonds and give the poor bugger a few swigs from a bottle of wine. We all hated it.'

Amy shivered.

'Terrible,' she said. 'Terrible.'

'Humiliation,' Cilydd said. 'In all that death and destruction. It seemed to say to us as we stood watching, "This is what you get for surviving. This is your reward for not being blown to bits."'

'I never knew,' Amy said. 'I never really understood.'

'Did I ever tell you about a chap from Birkenhead called Arty? Artful Arty?'

He held his head to one side to show he knew it was possible he might have done. Memories of the war came and went like a weather system in the unconscious mind. Amy shook her head.

'You might have told Enid,' she said. 'She was always a better listener.'

'He was older than the rest of us. We were so young I suppose he looked terribly old. He had false teeth. They didn't fit properly. He had this belt he'd made for himself with a row of little flasks hanging from it. Filled with rum and whisky. Always wore it under

his tunic when we went up the line. Nobody really liked him. Arty-
Artful-rob-all-my-comrades. Gave the unit a bad name. He tried to
attach himself to me because I was Welsh. "I'm a Taff," he used to
say with a heavy Scouse accent. "I'm a Taff. Did you know that?"
Always used to sound as if he were on the verge of bursting into
tears. "I shouldn't be here by rights," he used to say to anyone who
would listen. One day I heard him say to Jimmy Flynn, "I'm a
Paddy you know. My mother was Irish. Did you know that?" The
same accent. The same whine. The same whinge. It was so funny.'

Cilydd wasn't smiling. Amy was puzzled.

'Was he Welsh or wasn't he?' she said.

'I didn't mind him. The other lads couldn't stand him. Told him
he was a scavenger to his face and told him to bugger off. Oh he
was Welsh all right. One day they picked him up dead drunk on the
floor of a support trench. He could have suffocated in the mud.
The moment we got back to the rest area he got field punishment
number one. He should have been tied up near the main gate, but
the King was in St Omer so they stuck him on a limber on the way
to the latrines. Whenever I passed he used to call out, "Cofia
amdan'i. Cofia amdana'i – Remember me." Once he did it
and the Red Cap struck him across the mouth. Broke his false
teeth.'

Cilydd's tongue passed over his own teeth as he relived the
incident. To show her sympathy and understanding Amy reached
out to touch his knee.

'Do you know that was the exact moment I became a Welsh
Nationalist, an irreversible Welsh Nationalist. It wasn't Arty mind
you. It was the "cofia amdana'i" that did it. Just the sound of the
words.'

His eyes shone with the desire to communicate even more
closely with her.

'That's what I want to bring out you see. The word and the
image. Like one of those Renaissance pictures of the agony in the
Garden. But particularised. The figure stands for Wales as well as
for suffering humanity. The implication would be that small
countries can be crucified just like individuals. War machines are
juggernauts that destroy everything in their path. You can't make

24

an elegy or a requiem about that. You have to have individual suffering and make it visible. Indelible. You have to . . .'

He was lost for words, overcome by the urgency and enormity of the task he was imposing on himself.

'You do it, John Cilydd,' Amy said. 'You do it exactly as you want it.'

They stood together on the dais. Their large gestures reflected their sense of command over the empty hall. The apsidal area behind them would provide a perfect stage setting.

'The window could be lit from the outside,' Cilydd said.

'And the voice and the singing could come from up there.'

He pointed towards the narrow gallery at the back of the hall.

'Only mute figures on the stage,' he said. 'A dumb show. And the centre piece this helpless youth tied to the wheel, a representative figure in front of the angel of victory.'

He held her hands tightly in his, but released them when they heard voices at the back of the hall. Mr ap-Vychan, the headmaster, still wearing his MA gown, was talking in a worried undertone to Mr Samwell, the Welsh master, who wore his overcoat and carried his hat and attaché case ready to go home. It had gone five in the afternoon. There was no one else about, except the caretaker and his wife, shifting desks and coughing in the dust of a distant classroom. The headmaster's gown fluttered behind him as he hurried down the empty hall. He was a large man who cultivated a benevolent but bustling manner. Cilydd and Amy occupied a station on the dais that belonged to him and the exercise of his appointed office. Had they been children they would have been ordered off in peremptory fashion. The smile on Mr ap-Vychan's plump face as he approached them was conciliatory. At the foot of the dais he turned sideways and rubbed his hands like a referee before kick-off.

'So good of you to help us out, Mr More,' he said. 'Much more than that of course. As we celebrate our golden jubilee we want to show that we are not content to rest on our oars or on our laurels. We want to be modern and go-ahead in the arts. It's a great piece of good fortune that Mrs More, a former member of staff – before my time of course – should be married to a national winner. As I was saying to Mr Samwell and he agreed with me wholeheartedly, if we have a distinguished poet in our midst it is our bounden duty to listen to what he has to say. Education means nothing without a firm cultural base. That's always been my view!'

He glanced at Mr Samwell for some gesture of support. Mr Samwell hurriedly nodded. Mr ap-Vychan's lips parted before he spoke to show he was conscious of approaching delicate ground.

'But I must tell you,' the headmaster said. 'I have reservations about a young lad on a wheel. Stripped to the waist.'

He paused for Cilydd to speak. Only when it became certain that nothing would be forthcoming did he hurry on.

'I can see the dramatic force,' he said. 'I can quite see that. I just doubt whether this is the appropriate occasion.'

He glanced up to see whether Cilydd and Amy appreciated his doubts or at least accepted their validity and sincerity. They both remained expressionless and rigidly silent.

'I don't want to be over-literal,' Mr ap-Vychan said. 'God forbid. But am I not right in thinking this barbarous custom was done away with in 1917? Were there not protests in Parliament?'

He raised his eyebrows, pleased with the shrewdness of his point. Cilydd tapped himself hard on the chest.

'I saw it myself,' he said. 'With my own eyes. I saw it more than once.'

His voice trembled with suppressed emotion.

'I have to look at the problem from every conceivable angle,' Mr ap-Vychan said. 'There are parents who lost brothers and relatives for whom the loss is still an open wound. That sort of thing.'

'Well they should be the first to appreciate the work.'

Amy's face grew red once she had blurted out her comment. Cilydd seemed to have no objection to her speaking.

'If it gives offence,' she said, 'well, modern art always does, doesn't it? If we want to be up-to-date it's a risk we have to take. And in any case the whole point of the thing is to make people think, isn't it? To think deeply, and feel deeply. That's what I think anyway.'

The headmaster was more perplexed by Cilydd's silence than Amy's argument. He was confronted by a larger problem than he had anticipated. He had no prepared response to the poet's sphinx-like silence. If some kind of a compromise had to be reached there was nothing in this mute confrontation to contribute to it.

'Well, at least let us think about it, shall we? I'm sure we shall find a solution. With a sprinkling of goodwill on all sides. Let me leave you to consider the problem further with our genial producer.'

He was referring to Mr Samwell. He encouraged the Welsh master to approach the dais before sweeping out of the hall. Mr Samwell listened to the firm tread of the headmaster's footsteps as he made his way back to the seclusion of his study. He gave Amy a tentative smile. They had been colleagues. They had produced school plays together in the past.

'I'm awkwardly placed,' Mr Samwell said.

Cilydd and Amy relented sufficiently to show that they could see that.

'He's not a bad chap.'

Mr Samwell gave his assessment of the new headmaster as quietly as he could so that his voice would not pick up the reverberation in the empty hall.

'He has a certain sympathy. With the Cause.'

Mr Samwell left the exact nature of the Cause unspecified. It was a polite amalgam of pacifism and Welsh nationalism to which he himself owed a certain allegiance.

'Old Pierce would never have entertained the idea,' Mr Samwell said. 'Not for one second. His wife would never have let him.'

He essayed a smile in the hope that they would be amused by a reference to the former headmaster's hen-pecked condition. He resumed his considered appraisal of the new regime.

'He's very go-ahead. Full of new ideas. Most of them very good ones. He's ambitious too. In a perfectly healthy way. A bit unlucky perhaps, with everything so unsettled. These are nervous times. We feel the tremors, even in a school like this. Is the world about to come to an end? All that sort of thing. Is this the right time or even the right place?'

Cilydd became suddenly vehement.

'There never is a right time,' he said. 'Reform, revolutionary change, they are always scheduled for indefinite postponement.

27

That's how the aggressive and the reactionary can always combine to seize the initiative. Not now. Never now. Always later. Always too late.'

Mr Samwell gave a deep sigh.

'Oh, I take your point,' he said. 'Of course I do. I'm just a timid school teacher, afraid of putting a foot wrong. Falling over himself to please and placate those set in authority over him.'

Amy gave him the friendliest smile.

'That's not true Mr Samwell,' she said. 'You know it and I know it. When I was on the staff here you stood up to old Pierce every day of the week. And to his wife.'

They were able to laugh with each other: both warmed by the recollection of old staff-room battles they had shared together. Mr Samwell shifted closer to the dais steps to bask in Amy's approval and possibly acquire even more.

'Let's do it,' he said. 'Just in the way Mr More suggests. A little shorter perhaps. With the precise aim of sharpening the impact. I've been thinking about it. I haven't been altogether idle. I have some ideas I'd like to offer.'

He was ready to go beyond mere acquiescence. Cilydd's vision would be realised through wholehearted collaboration. Mr Samwell grinned as he tied his scarf around his neck. They would enjoy working together and their collaboration would be spiced with a trace of conspiracy. Cilydd offered him a lift home. In view of the weather Mr Samwell confessed that he was glad to accept.

'People don't realise do they,' he said, 'the extent to which the Great War still casts a shadow over our lives.'

The car was parked near the rear entrance. Mr Samwell called out a cheerful goodnight to the caretaker and his wife. There were lights still on in the headmaster's study. They illuminated a diagrammatic timetable that covered half a wall and a plaster cast of Socrates on a plinth. Mr ap-Vychan himself was seated at his large desk absorbed in writing letters. Amy insisted that Mr Samwell sat in the passenger seat while she sat in the back.

'My older brother was killed on the Somme,' Mr Samwell said. 'My mother, you know, she's never got over it. If I'm late coming

28

home from school she's at the front door to meet me. It's quite suffocating at times. But there we are.'

Mr Samwell nursed his attaché case on his knees and sighed. It was a testimony of patience and resignation. He turned in his seat to smile shyly at Amy.

'It could be the reason why I'm not married,' he said. 'Apart from the fact that no one would have me.'

Amy was ready to respond.

'Now I'd say any girl who captured Mr Samwell would be a very lucky girl indeed.'

'Hear, hear.'

Cilydd called out with unexpected vigour as he changed gear to descend the steep hill. The prospect of active partnership brought all three closer together.

'I have an idea for the voice,' Mr Samwell said. 'The invisible narrator. Unless of course you want to do it yourself, Mr More.'

'Oh good heavens no,' Cilydd said. 'Not me. You are in charge Mr Samwell. You are the producer.'

'It could be a good tactical move.'

Mr Samwell extended his jaw to emphasise his shrewdness.

'You know the absurd struggles that go on among people with a thirst for power. Pendraw I think sometimes is a microcosm, an epitome, of this particular form of human folly. Politics seem to penetrate into every crack and crevice of our corporate existence, like rising damp in an old house.'

'Very good,' Cilydd said.

His approval of the simile encouraged Mr Samwell to further heights of analytical speculation.

'It goes far back,' he said. 'Well beyond denominational and sectarian differences. It could be an endemic divisiveness in the Celtic temperament. A natural tendency in a mountain race exacerbated by urban settlement. The old enmities of a hill people cramped and confined in sectarian side streets . . .'

His inspiration gave out abruptly.

'That sort of thing,' he said.

Amy leaned forward to redirect his train of thought.

'What was your idea for the voice, Mr Samwell?'

29

'Forgive me,' he said. 'I'm always trying to fathom the mysteries of Pendraw politics. You know Meredith the Workhouse has been appointed a school governor? In the Alderman Llew interest of course. But he has his own underground British Legion line to Doctor D.S.O. Not so much a foot in both camps as a finger in both pies . . .'

Mr Samwell held on tightly to his attaché case as he shook with gentle merriment. He cleared his throat as he made the effort to restrain himself.

'The voice from the balcony,' he said. 'The invisible narrator. One of the school's brilliant old boys. E. V. Meredith. What about Eddie Meredith?'

Mr Samwell's smile was mischievous and gleeful.

'He's such a show-off,' Amy said.

Then they giggled together when she realised she had unwittingly taken his point.

'Mr Samwell,' Amy said. 'I had no idea you could be such a Machiavell.'

'The "Oxford Man", not the Foreign Correspondent of *The Willesden and Kilburn Herald*?' Cilydd said.

He sounded keen to join in the fun.

'Is that what he's doing now?' Mr Samwell said. 'I thought he was in the film business.'

'It's not easy to keep up with him,' Cilydd said. 'He might turn out to be one of nature's penny-a-liners after all. Do you think he'd do it? Pendraw County School Golden Jubilee. Very small beer for him surely.'

'Oh, I don't know,' Mr Samwell said. 'Most men like to cut a dash on their home patch. His father of course would be immensely pleased. Shall I make the approach? Or will you?'

'From you,' Cilydd said. 'It had best come from you. As formal and as flattering as possible.'

The car drew up alongside the house in the Victorian terrace where Mr Samwell lived with his mother. The terrace possessed slate-roofed verandas and narrow front gardens filled with evergreen shrubs. The beating of the rain on the hard leaves mingled with the noise of Cilydd's motor idling. Across the way the slate facade of one of Pendraw's larger chapels was gleaming wet.

'Won't you come in?'

Mr Samwell's invitation was pressing.

'That's most kind of you,' Cilydd said. 'But my sister Nanw is looking after the boys for us. Baby-sitting as they say.'

'Bedwyr. Gwydion.'

Mr Samwell savoured the legendary names. On the strength of a sense of mutual esteem, he ventured a fresh line of speculation.

'You know, if I may say this, you have no idea how envious it makes an old bachelor like me to see a happy marriage. Shall I tell you what attracts me most of all about the married state?'

He saw them both smile but refrain from irreverent or frivolous comment.

'It's the idea of partnership,' Mr Samwell said.

He spoke with an air of daring frankness.

'To have a partner multiplies life's possibilities. A real partnership can transform the most humdrum routine into sparkling adventure! Am I right, would you say?'

He clutched his attaché case more closely as he prepared to get out of the car. He had to expunge an impression of having taken advantage of their goodwill.

'Listen to me pontificating,' he said. 'It's hardly an area in which I can display special knowledge. Oh dear. There she is.'

The front door of Mr Samwell's house opened sufficiently to show the outline of an anxious figure against the economically dim light in the corridor behind her.

'Please don't think I'm ungrateful to my mother.'

He unburdened himself in a rapid undertone. A personal confession would in any case be some sort of restitution for his audacious observations on the merits of marriage.

'I'd be quite lost without her. I may as well admit it. She sees to my every little need. Clean shirts. Clean collars. Always there. Ever faithful, ever sure. Goodnight both.'

They watched his mother open the door wider to allow Mr Samwell's unimpaired progress into the depths of her house. The door closed. Amy thought the better of climbing into the front seat.

31

'My goodness,' she said.

'What is it?'

'Can't you smell? Poor old Mr Samwell.'

'He's younger than I am,' Cilydd said. 'Although he doesn't look it.'

'She may keep him in clean shirts, but I don't think she ever washes under his armpits. He always smells when he gets excited. I remember that from school. Poor old Mr Samwell.'

Amy lay back. Cilydd was worried.

'Do I smell?' he said.

Amy laughed.

'Of course you don't.'

'You would tell me, wouldn't you?'

'Of course I would.'

Cilydd's anxieties were still unassuaged.

'You would tell me, wouldn't you? If you found me repulsive.'

Amy leaned forward to tickle the back of his neck.

'Well, we'll have to see about that, won't we? Now get moving. Or your sister will be pulling a face as if she'd swallowed a mule.'

~ ii ~

In the room below them, Gwydion was whimpering in his sleep. Their bedroom door was wide open. The light from the night lamp on the landing threw shadows of the bannister rails like giant prison bars on the pink and white wallpaper. Amy raised herself on her elbow, undecided whether or not to get out of bed. The north-west wind blew around the terrace: but inside a column of silence reached from the basement to the top of their tall house. It was this rule of silence that magnified the little boy's moans. Amy listened intently then buried her nose in her pillow.

'He's always like this. When your sister's been with them.'

Her voice was muffled as she talked to herself.

'I don't know why she makes such a difference between them. I don't. He's only small I know, but he's perfectly well aware of it. It registers. Even the smallest baby knows how the arms holding him feel about him. Right from the start.'

32

Cilydd's hand slid quietly under the bedclothes in search of hers.
'I thought you were asleep,' she said. 'I didn't want to wake you.'
'Can't you sleep?'

He whispered affectionately and squeezed her hand.

'I've been thinking about you in the war,' she said. 'And I've been thinking how selfish I've been too.'

She breathed into the pillow like a penitent in a confessional.

'Oh rubbish.'

She heard his quiet laugh. She could see his profile but not his smile. His head was as still as an alabaster effigy on a tomb.

'I'm trying to be honest,' Amy said. 'We've both suffered. I think it is right we should have to comfort each other. You know when I saw you standing on the dais in the school hall, with your arms stretched out. It went right through me. As if everything was my fault.'

'Well it isn't, my dearest, is it?'

'Unless you want to sleep,' Amy said. 'Tell me about it. Tell me everything.'

'You've heard it all before,' Cilydd said. 'It's ancient history.'

'I haven't,' Amy said.

She turned to lie on her stomach. Her face was close to his, eager to listen.

'Or if I have, I wasn't listening properly. I'm like that sometimes. I listen but I don't hear.'

The sash window rattled in its frame. Beyond the clamour of the wind, the ebb tide was sucking pebbles down the shelving shore. Amy snuggled further down into the warmth of the bed. Her voice became sweet and plaintive like a child's.

'We hardly ever get a chance to talk properly. Your practice. Your clients. The boys. Your family. This cause and that. Tell me everything. Absolutely everything.'

He reached out in an attempt to draw her body closer to his. She resisted. Her overwhelming need was to talk and if possible to talk as they had never talked before.

'Make me understand,' she said. 'I know I'm stupid. I know I'm down to earth and insensitive. Your sister thinks I treat you badly. I know she does. Perhaps she's right. Maybe I do.'

'I'm not complaining,' Cilydd said.

'That's not the point,' she said impatiently. 'I ask myself the most ridiculous questions. "What is a poet?" I ask myself. Now this minute. And I just don't know the answer. You mustn't laugh at me.'

'I'm not,' Cilydd said. She could feel his body shaking.

'Of course you are. Don't make me cross.'

'I'm laughing because I love you,' Cilydd said.

'It's a funny way of showing it.'

'It seems the only one available to me at the moment,' he said.

Again his hands reached towards her under the bedclothes. She caught them and held them firmly in her own.

'I don't know what a poet is either,' he said.

'John, I'm serious.'

Her voice was tense with a desire to understand.

'Tell me . . . What was the worst thing. In the war. Did you kill anyone?'

She held her breath as she waited for his answer.

'Not as far as I know. If I did, it wasn't intentional.'

'I've told you I'm serious.'

She shook his hands in reproof.

'Tell me about when you were wounded. Tell me every detail. I want to know.'

'Best thing that could happen,' Cilydd said. 'To be wounded. To get out of it and still be alive. I was lucky. In one piece. Really lucky. You've seen my little scars. My battle scars. The words we use to glamorise our miseries.'

When Amy fingered the scars at the back of his neck as if she were touching them for the first time, Cilydd became comfortably morose. Amy listened like a child unable to sleep and eager for a long story. He spoke in a soft monotone that suggested a soothing process. He would unburden himself, he would lighten the load of memory, even recall old suffering, in a way that would not offend the woman lying at his side.

'Gas was much the worst really. Horrible stuff. They dumped me alongside a ruin. It had been a lock-keeper's cottage alongside the canal before it was shelled. I could still hear the guns. I thought I

34

was blind. And I thought I was going to die. The whole earth was trembling with the thunder of the guns, but I don't think I was afraid. Maybe I was beyond that. The last object I saw was a swan on the canal. A swan in the middle of it all. The image was fixed on my eyelids and wouldn't move. The swan wanted to move but it couldn't. I thought it was death.'

'You poor darling. They left you there . . .'

Her hand touched his face. He turned to touch it with his lips. Her sympathy was a benediction: but he had a committment to the truth of the experience.

'Oh, they were absolutely right,' he said. 'Not to move me. They were rough I suppose, but how could they not be in the middle of a battle. I passed out anyway. I can just about remember a hospital train and a hospital ship. And one enormous vomit. And sleeping. Always sleeping. And a funny dream of sliding down the side of a mountain lying on a tin tray. I must have done that sometime when I was a boy.'

'A boy.'

Amy repeated the word as though she had never thought of her husband as a boy before. The way she listened stimulated his urge to recall.

'I'll tell you the funniest thing,' he said. 'This was really funny. I think I must have been in some sort of coma and yet I remember it so well. I think I must have trained myself to be still and silent. Maybe I thought if I was still and silent enough, the whole war would go away. There was a staff officer standing at the foot of my hospital bed. All polish and glitter. Like a dummy in a shop window with the sun on it. I could barely open my eyes. But I could see him so I knew they were all right. He was holding a letter in his hand and asking me if I could hear him and if I wanted him to read it. He thought my sight was more or less gone. He was a proper shit. "Welsh is it?" he said. "I thought you might have been Irish with a name like More. One of those Sinn Fein bastards." I was lying there, utterly helpless and that was the way he talked. I think he was showing off in front of a pretty nurse.'

Cilydd stopped talking. This fragment of his past was emerging from the shadows into a new clarity as hard and as clinical as hospital daylight. The officer was still at the foot of his bed and the nurse close by: but now it was the victim who sat in judgement to appraise the significance of an incident of twenty years ago.

'What letter?' Amy said. 'What letter John?'

'About my discharge,' he said. 'It was so ridiculous. Our minister, father of the famous Alice, he had written to the War Office, requesting my discharge on the grounds that I was under age.'

'Alice who?'

'Alice Breeze. You've heard me talk of Alice Breeze. My calf-love.'

'Never mind about her. What about the letter?'

'That was really funny,' Cilydd said. 'My grandmother must have put him up to it. And they hated each other.'

'What was in it? In the letter?'

Amy was impatient until Cilydd seemed to quote from memory.

'"From the Colonel in charge of Records, Hounslow, to the Reverend Goronwy M. Breeze, The Manse, Glasfryn Uchaf, Caernarfonshire, North Wales." My goodness that spit-and-polish creature made a meal of the address. "With reference to your letter regarding number 87144 Private J. C. More" . . . that sort of thing. "I beg to inform you that this man's age on attestation was nineteen years one month and that therefore is his official age. It is regretted that your request for his discharge cannot be acceded to et cetera et cetera . . . somebody or other on behalf of the Colonel in charge of Records, blah, blah." My grandmother must have bullied Breeze into sending the letter. Can you see her at it?'

'Yes I can.'

Amy's assent was so heartfelt they both started laughing. Cilydd saw his grandmother shake her umbrella over the minister's head. He spluttered as Amy put her hand over his mouth. The doors were open and their noise could disturb the sleeping children.

'I know now why he did it,' Cilydd said. 'The immaculate Mr Breeze. The climate of opinion was changing. In 1918 they couldn't wait for the bloody war to come to an end. No more fiery sermons about the beauty of sacrifice. Now it was all "the best interests of our boys at heart" and "a welfare" and "home fires burning" and chapel-welcome-homes.'

36

'How old were you really?'

Amy already knew. Her whisper was to demonstrate a fresh upsurge of pity and compassion.

'Seventeen years, one month . . .'

'Silly little boy.'

Her lips touched his cheek.

'Silly little boy who ran away to war . . .'

She would make it her business to console and comfort him. Shyly she undid his pyjama buttons and slid her hand across his chest in a tentative embrace that still warned him not to move. He had to remain still and disciplined to please her. Only his head moved on the pillow. Frankness and honesty could bring them closer. His lips moved as though they were giving up a guilty secret.

'In war the bravest and the best get killed. I wanted to salute my friends. I wanted to celebrate their memory. That's a poet's job.'

'Of course it is,' Amy said. 'I can see that. I really can.'

'Pay tribute. That means pay debts. That's what a poet does.'

'Of course. Of course.'

He shivered as her hand passed lower down his body. They confined themselves to close intense whispers. No sound they made should be allowed to disturb the boys. The communication between them would be as secret and as silent as the flow of an underground river. He still wanted to express the remorse and self-reproach of a survivor enjoying life denied to his comrades and companions.

'They were all so young . . . Boys and yet men. Brave men. Living a whole lifetime in the space of a few incredible weeks and months.'

Suddenly he found it impossible to convey to her the grim experience: a phase in his early existence he hesitated to share even with her.

'To live through it, to escape it like I did was a kind of disgrace. The best ones went. It . . .'

When words failed him Amy became intent on reassuring him.

'You have as much right to live as anybody,' she said. 'Of course you have. It would be ridiculous to assume anything else. It would be like saying nobody has the right to survive.'

He lay as still as a patient under sedation.

'There is this aura attached to death in battle,' he said. 'It was the same when Pen Lewis was killed in Spain.'

'You were wounded,' Amy said. 'You have as much right to be alive as anybody and far more than most. You have a right and a duty to speak out against war. I don't need to tell you surely?'

'It's not rational,' he said. 'I know that. But it's there. I feel it and I don't even know what to call it. It's too simple to call it guilt and yet that must be what it is. A sort of ghostly guilt that can come back to haunt you without any warning at any time.'

'Don't talk about it any more. Don't talk.'

Amy pressed her fingers against his mouth.

'It's not wrong to be alive. I'll show you. I'll make you well.'

She stopped whispering before mounting him with a resolute skill that made him moan with pleasure. With the gratitude of a blind suppliant his hands moved carefully over the shape of her body that was in itself a life-giving protection. Her rhythmic movements became a lesson in love that bound them closer than they had ever been before. The sound Gwydion made as he whimpered in his sleep was as distant as the inhalation of the tide as it drew contours of pebbles down the beach. For Cilydd and Amy to be absorbed in each other was to reinforce their courage; an act of defiance against the new threat of war and death.

~ iii ~

Eddie Meredith observed his reflection in the window pane with evident satisfaction. He wore the uniform of a second lieutenant in the Territorial Army. The faint image in the glass of clouds moving majestically across a blue sky enhanced the theatrical effect of his costume by supplying a backcloth of limitless space. Cilydd sat behind his office desk, slumped with the effort of withholding his approval. Eddie shifted in sprightly fashion on the stained floor-boards of the bay window as though he were about to invite an invisible partner to dance. He was an attractive figure and his flushed face suggested he had drunk enough to be unable to conceal the fact that he knew it.

The uniform was well cut. Its elegance drew attention to Eddie's practised charm. His dark curls had been disciplined, but his dimpled smile radiated more mischievously than ever. He tucked a silver cigarette case into the breast pocket of his tunic. Holding an unlit cigarette between his fingers, he sloped his wrist in the direction of the narrow street below. It was market day in Pendraw and the pavements were crowded. There were still farmers who came in with horse and trap and slowed the traffic down to a crawl.

'What a hole,' Eddie said.

His voice was loud with cheerful contempt. Cilydd's response was swift.

'It's the hole you crawled out of,' he said.

Eddie laughed delightedly.

'Good old Cilydd,' he said. 'You haven't changed one bit. And I love you for it. All the same, I still think I was right and you were wrong.'

Cilydd stared at Eddie's uniform with unremitting distaste.

'The English may be pretty unbearable at times,' Eddie said. 'But at least it's a great big world outside. The one thing you're not likely to die of is suffocation. Just look at it. I don't know how you can bear it. Honestly I don't.'

'Why bother to come back?'

'To see you of course.'

Eddie gave him a direct and dazzling smile that seemed to bring Cilydd to his feet to avoid its unsettling impact. In the outer office, Miss Pearse was hammering at her typewriter with determined vigour. The noise suggested somehow her disapproval of Eddie Meredith's unscheduled visit.

'At a time of crisis,' Eddie said, 'and what time isn't a time of crisis these days? A chap is keen to know what his closest friends are up to. I think I'd look rather good like this. On the stage. For your anti-war epic. Mind you, the whole world will be in uniform soon. It's coming as sure as night follows day and there's not a damn thing you can do to stop it.'

'Oh yes there is.'

Cilydd rubbed his fist in his hand as he stood alongside Eddie in the bay window.

'Your mind doesn't have to be in uniform,' Cilydd said.

'Look down there.'

Eddie nodded down at the street.

'The hungry sheep are not even looking up,' he said. 'They haven't got two notions to rub together. Just look at them. Shuffling around like sheep in boots. Waiting for something to happen to them. That's not a people. That's not a nation. You're banging your head against a wall, J.C. And I wouldn't be a true friend if I didn't tell you you are wasting your time. All this Welsh nationalist stuff. It's such small beer. And pacifism is no better. Mix them together and it must make the most innocuous and ineffective brew ever concocted by the mind of man. That doesn't mean to say that I don't love you.'

He grasped him suddenly around the waist and with surprising ease lifted Cilydd's feet from the floor.

'You're a marvellous old bugger!' Eddie said. 'But being a poet these days is like aiming a pea-shooter at the moon.'

Cilydd struggled ineffectively to free himself from Eddie's grip. The younger man took delight in exerting his power. His face was close enough to Cilydd's to kiss him.

'Put me down, you idiot.'

Cilydd became anxiously aware that they were visible from the street. The more he struggled the more likely their pantomime would attract attention.

'Please Eddie.'

A note of pleading was enough. When he was released Cilydd moved away from the window.

'You know as well as I do that a power struggle between great empires has damn all to do with the well-being of small nations like ours,' Cilydd said. 'They call it "the international situation". But all it amounts to is a vicious power struggle between the hegemony of an English-speaking *Herrenvolk* and an up-and-coming German-speaking *Herrenvolk*. Between two rival power complexes that couldn't care less about the small and the helpless that will get crushed to death once their tanks and juggernauts start moving. Are you one of us or aren't you? What are you doing in that uniform?'

40

Cilydd stabbed an accusing finger in Eddie's direction. Eddie pressed his fingers to his breast and assumed an expression of mock alarm on his face.

'It fits quite nicely,' Eddie said. 'And it pleases the old man no end to see me in it.'

'I thought you couldn't stand the sight of your father,' Cilydd said.

He was very ready to remind Eddie Meredith of the harsh things he had heard him say about the Master of the Workhouse.

'Adolescence,' Eddie said airily. 'I don't know whether you've noticed J.C., but I've mellowed considerably. That's one thing you do realise after you've knocked about a bit in the great wide world. There aren't that many people who give a damn whether you're alive or dead. At least the old tin-pot workhouse despot thinks the world of me. And that's not something to be sneezed at in this cruel day and age. But I'll tell you one thing J.C. and I wouldn't tell you if I didn't love you in my fickle fierce fashion. You want to watch out.'

Cilydd took a deep breath.

' "Watch out",' he said. 'For what?'

'There are tough times coming,' Eddie said. 'I can see it all with prophetic clarity. And not through a glass darkly, old fruit. You are in line to lose one job after the other. They won't have a Welsh Nash and a potential conchie as a prosecuting solicitor for a start. Once the emergency comes. And it's coming fast. My old man is a magistrate now, thanks to the Liberal network and the machinations of Alderman Llew and the I-won't-stand-in-the-way-of-a-good-man, Doctor D.S.O. So you watch out. The best thing for your brilliant anti-war tableaux would be to have E. V. Meredith in his shining uniform recite your lines like John O'Gaunt on Judgement Day before the assembled faithful. I'm here to help you, old boy.'

'I don't need any help,' Cilydd said.

He sounded stubborn and sulky.

'And I certainly don't want the protection of an alien state. I don't want to be overwhelmed by it and I don't want to be absorbed by it. I'll stand on my own feet, until I drop.'

41

'Oh dear.'

Eddie raised his arm to lean against the window frame and gaze down at the people in the street.

'The last of the Welsh Puritans if not the last of the Mohicans. You're worse than dear old Tasker in a way. At least he's got his simple faith to keep him trotting down the beaten track to oblivion. You're not even a Christian for God's sake. You don't believe a word of all that comfort and consolation. You are standing on your bits of principle like a man on a raft made from a box of matches. Shall I tell you my new motto?'

He smiled at Cilydd in search of his sympathy. Cilydd came to his side and placed an arm over his shoulder.

'It's not very elegant, but it's the best I can do under the circs. "Stop worrying, do as you're told, and enjoy yourself when you can."'

Eddie lowered his head overcome with sudden gloom.

'Can't help getting the jitters sometimes. It's like something bloody horrible that can't be averted. Who can guess what it will be? Not like the last one I hope. What do you think?'

His brown eyes were as round as a dog's begging for comfort. Cilydd squeezed his shoulder, but when Eddie tried to touch his cheek he moved his face out of reach. As he glanced down at the street he saw Amy bending over the pushchair in which Gwydion was squirming restlessly. Alongside her, Bedwyr held his Aunt Nanw by the hand. Nanw had already seen the men standing in the bay window. She saw her brother with his arm around the shoulder of a young man in a lieutenant's uniform. She swayed and for a moment it looked as though she was going to faint. Bedwyr called out. Amy straightened herself quickly and took hold of Nanw's arm, shaking it with what appeared from the first-floor window as impatience more than concern or sympathy. She bent over Gwydion again insisting that he bent his legs and sat still as they crossed the street.

'Here they come,' Eddie said.

He pulled a face of mock alarm.

'The advance guard of the future. You can never tell can you? Little Adolf was once an infant in Mrs Schickelgruber's pushchair.

42

Straining and stranking inside his harness. And now he's big enough to swallow Danzig for breakfast.'

Cilydd returned to his desk. He fingered documents that awaited his attention.

'Should I make myself scarce?' Eddie said.

He moved about the sparsely furnished room and returned to the window to inspect his reflection. The light had changed and it was only dimly visible.

'I don't think she approves of me, does she?'

Eddie sounded in need of reassurance.

'Not that I do myself, if it comes to that,' he said. 'But I'm the only self I've got, so I've got to put up with it. I was going to suggest something, J.C. Why don't you invite Hetty and Margot down to see the show? They'd be thrilled to bits.'

'They wouldn't understand a word,' Cilydd said. 'Not one single word.'

'Ah yes but they'd see me, wouldn't they? Resplendent on the stage. At my best and most glorious. I think it would do me a bit of good. They've rather gone off me, you know. To be perfectly frank. I'm not turning out to be the brilliant young working-class boy they rather hoped I would. They think I'm sinking into a morass of petty-bourgeois reaction. Just because I couldn't work up a proper head of enthusiasm for their Scarlet Pimpernel exploits with German refugees.'

Eddie gave up talking. Cilydd was listening to the commotion in the outer office. His son Gwydion was crying. When his mother reproved him the two-year-old cried even louder. Cilydd stood by his desk, holding papers as though to protect himself. Amy looked exasperated as she entered the room. She drew the door behind her to speak more freely and reduce the level of Gwydion's unreasoning howl. Amy pointed accusingly at Eddie.

'That stupid uniform,' Amy said. 'And your sister. I thought she was going to collapse on the street. All she kept murmuring was, "Owen, it's Owen".'

'Where is she now?' Cilydd said.

He had to show concern for his sister.

'In the lav,' Amy said. 'Where else? My goodness. Highly-strung spinsters. She's got all the artistic temperament you should be entitled to.'

'Owen Guest.'

He was ready to explain his sister's behaviour.

'Second Lieutenant Owen Guest. Killed at Pilckem Ridge. Aged nineteen years, one month. I suppose you could say she never got over it.'

'Well that's cheerful,' Eddie said.

He gave an exaggerated shudder.

'What's the expression about walking over my grave?'

'Go and see if you can calm Gwydion down,' Amy said. 'And your sister too while you're about it.'

Cilydd closed the door carefully behind him. Gwydion's howls took time to subside. Miss Pearse was being as helpful as she could be. It was her voice that Amy and Eddie could hear as they stood at some distance from each other in Cilydd's office.

'It seems the dead are walking quite a lot these days.'

Eddie spoke as confidentially as he could. Amy was watching him suspiciously.

'Old Nij,' Eddie said. 'You remember Margot's cousin Nigel. He was rather gone on you too, wasn't he? He's joined the Regular Army. I see him from time to time. He's going to put me up for the Travellers'.'

'That will be nice for you,' Amy said.

'I'm quite thick with old Nij. I was telling John Cilydd I think Margot and Hetty have gone off me a bit.'

'Surely that can't be possible.'

He winced to show her sarcasm was not lost on him.

'They suspect me of petty-bourgeois reaction. They could be right too. But I was telling you about old Nij. He's taken it into his head to start a collection of souvenirs of the Spanish War. He's quite obsessive about it. Do you remember his ridiculous ambition to drive his taxi in every capital in Europe? He's that kind of chap. Once he sets his mind to it he'll pick up everything like a vacuum cleaner. He's got letters and notes from Pen Lewis. From when he was a battalion commissar on the Jarama. I thought you'd be interested.'

He smiled in a friendly fashion, but a cold silence grew in the room

44

as he waited for her to speak. Through the closed doors they could hear Cilydd's sister Nanw excusing herself in a fluid discourse that took into account an apology for disturbing the conscientious Miss Pearse in the execution of her many duties. The street noises were distanced by the sheer length of Amy's silence. She spoke at last.

'I'm not a collector,' she said. 'I must see to the children.'

She left Eddie alone in Cilydd's office.

4

THE KITCHEN TABLE AT GLANRAFON WAS LAID FOR A GENEROUS Sunday tea. Mrs Lloyd was already seated at the head of the table. Her elbows rested on the polished arms of her chair as she watched Amy strapping Gwydion into his high chair. She was also lending an ear to the conversation between her grandson, John Cilydd, and her youngest son, Tryfan the shoemaker, who still had to take their place at the table. Her daughter Bessie and her granddaughter Nanw were busy transporting plates of home-made white and brown bread and butter, of scones, and of cakes from the back kitchen and the scullery.

'I hate to see a good man abused.'

Uncle Tryfan's high-pitched voice rang out so loudly that Gwydion stopped struggling against his mother.

'That's what it amounts to.'

Tryfan's spectacles glinted as he moved his head to defy anyone to contradict him.

'There's no one here to disagree with you,' Mrs Lloyd said.

She waved her hand impatiently.

'Take your places won't you,' she said. 'This isn't a public meeting.'

Tryfan stood behind his chair at the bottom of the table. He had more to say and he was determined to say it.

'I don't know what a saint is,' he said, 'but if I did I would venture to say that Tasker Thomas was the nearest thing to one that I have ever encountered.'

He spoke with the solemnity of a confession of faith. But having made the pronouncement his face was wreathed in smiles and he winked at Bedwyr who sat perfectly still in his place between Cilydd and Amy exuding his own aura of good behaviour.

'Look at him,' Uncle Tryfan said. 'He looks a bit of a little saint too, doesn't he?'

'He is.'

Nanw breathed her conviction as she set the last plate of thinly cut brown bread and butter within her grandmother's easy reach.

'He has to make a stand,' Cilydd said.

He was still concerned with Tasker Thomas's problems with his deacons and his church.

'He has done in the past,' Tryfan said. 'And there's no doubt he'll do it in the future.'

Cilydd closed his eyes and waved his hands above his plate in order to make the subtlety of his argument more manifest.

'He mustn't let them ease him out,' he said. 'That's my point. He's such a soft-hearted chap in so many ways. And he's always so eager to please. He wants to love everybody. But I don't believe you should love the human race to the extent of allowing it to trample all over you. I really don't.'

'Well now then . . .'

Mrs Lloyd interrupted in a manner designed to bring their discussion to a temporary close. She leaned towards Bedwyr before giving him a rewarding smile.

'I understand we have someone in our midst who will recite a new grace before food.'

Bedwyr looked up at his mother in search of a nod before pressing the palms of his hands together and closing his eyes. His voice emerged in a clear piping note. It was a grace composed in *englyn* form. The innocent rendering of the sophisticated prosody in the silence of the kitchen was like the song of a choirboy in a cathedral. Mrs Lloyd was so pleased she opened her eyes, raised her eyebrows and smiled before Bedwyr had finished. In simple justice the warmth of her good opinion had to include Amy. The little boy's second mother had gone to the trouble of teaching the child a grace his great-grandmother had never heard before. It was in a new style but its orthodoxy was impeccable. The grace could only be understood as a token of a general desire for reconciliation. Mrs Lloyd addressed her grandson Cilydd. She was reopening the subject of support for Tasker Thomas.

'You can tell him if you see him,' Mrs Lloyd said. 'He will always be welcome in this house.'

'Hear, hear.'

Tryfan banged his hand on the table until the cups rattled in their saucers. Bedwyr looked alarmed but his brother Gwydion gurgled with delight as if he were being entertained by a clown in a circus. Tryfan picked up a spoon and pointed it at Bedwyr in a gesture of goodwill and unstinting approval. Bedwyr smiled shyly and shrank lower in his seat between John Cilydd and Amy. Gwydion's response was more boisterous. He banged his spoon against his enamelled feeding plate and his food was in danger of spattering in his great-grandmother's direction. As if at a given signal Amy and her sister-in-law Nanw across the table rose in their places to stretch out hands to restrain him. Nanw gave way to the natural mother and sank back in her seat. She contented herself with smiling approvingly at Bedwyr, clearly commending the example he set his unruly brother. Uncle Tryfan, at the bottom of the table, laughed loudly until his mother advised him to restrain himself.

'Don't be hard on him,' Mrs Lloyd said. 'It's all his Uncle Tryfan's fault.'

'Yes indeed.'

Auntie Bessie was very ready to echo her mother. If the presiding deity at the head of the table was in the mood to unbend sufficiently to urge Amy not to discipline her offspring she in her turn could indulge her inclination to dote equally on Bedwyr and Gwydion. Like her brother Tryfan she was unmarried, living under her mother's roof and for this reason perhaps was all the more devoted to the cult of the family.

'The precious thing,' Auntie Bessie said. 'The precious little thing. Both of them I mean.'

She was on her feet, hovering between her mother and the home-made high chair in which Gwydion went on pushing his food dangerously near the edge of his plate.

47

'This was your chair, you know, John Cilydd,' Auntie Bessie said. 'I can remember you in it as if it were only yesterday.'

Uncle Tryfan was amused by the notion of his tall nephew in a baby chair. He leaned sideways to push Cilydd's right arm so that he could share the comic vision.

'I made it,' Uncle Tryfan said. 'With a little help from your father. Mind you, he was a better sailor than a carpenter, poor fellow.'

'I was thinking,' Auntie Bessie said.

Her cheeks flushed at her own temerity in proposing a course of action.

'There are four generations present at this table. Four generations.'

Her lips tightened in awe at the magnitude of the concept.

'I just thought Amy dear, if you had your camera, it would be nice to take a picture of the occasion.'

She held her breath as she waited for her mother's consent. It was after all a Sunday. Perhaps taking photographs on the Sabbath would relate too closely to making graven images. The worried frown on Auntie Bessie's homely face suggested a vague recollection of her mother's disapproval of Amy's camera. She could see John Cilydd and his second wife, and even the two boys, sitting on one side of the long table like delegates at a peace conference. Her nephew looked like a spokesman poised between a desire to please and a resolve not to make superfluous concessions.

'It could be done,' Mrs Lloyd said. 'At the bottom of the old garden perhaps. Or the orchard. After tea of course.'

This gracious consent brought a general measure of relief. The family was able to concentrate on eating. There were further expressions of support for Tasker Thomas, a chosen person surrounded by the hosts of Midian in increasing numbers. John Cilydd was encouraged to speak his mind on the ever present issue of peace and war.

'Once a war starts,' he said, 'it will be impossible to stop it.'

Tryfan was so alarmed and impressed that he stopped eating. His mouth hung open.

'It will be a case of war without end and no amen,' Cilydd said.

He raised his voice to resume the rôle of *enfant terrible* he had so often exercised at this table. But now his family listened with a certain respect. He was an accredited correspondent from the outside world bringing back reports on an increasingly incomprehensible situation and they had need of his comments.

'We mustn't, at any point, lose sight of our own values,' he said. 'I mean values more than beliefs. You all know me as a bit of a heretic. But that doesn't mean that I don't value what this place stands for. This way of life. The more it is threatened, the more faith we must have in ourselves.'

Tryfan, Bessie and Nanw were ready to agree. Mrs Lloyd grunted her inclination to dissent.

'What about faith in God?' she said.

It was a question none of them were eager to answer. In the polite silence Gwydion took a growing interest in the subdued clatter of cutlery. He began to add to it by banging out a basic form of syncopation on his feeding plate. Amy restrained him by squeezing his right arm and whispering in his ear. Mrs Lloyd watched her with favour. She recited an adage in support of the firm line Amy was taking: to the effect that an infant's rule extended beyond the first year and a day would ruin him for life. Cilydd frowned as though he found the piece of folk wisdom of dubious value but refrained from comment. Gwydion dared to challenge his mother. He waved his loaded spoon again. Nanw watched him, chewing her food with a jaw that had become temporarily rigid. When she realised Amy was looking at her, she stared with sudden and yet impersonal interest at the framed aquatint of 'The Broad and Narrow Way' which hung in the position where she had always seen it, above her brother's head. Amy was cross at having to shake Gwydion's arm again in full view of her husband's family. Mrs Lloyd was sympathetic. She made a positive attempt to lighten the atmosphere.

'It reminds me of my grandmother,' she said. 'Whenever one of my children misbehaved she always used to say, "Now who is this one taking after?"'

Tryfan laughed expansively as if his mother had made a joke. He thumped his end of the table to give notice that when she had quite

49

finished, he himself might well have something to contribute to the gaiety of the occasion. Gwydion's mouth hung open as he stared warily at his great-grandmother. She spoke to him in the most intimate manner.

'Now who is it you take after, young man? I don't recall anyone in our family with lips like Cupid's bow. Indeed I don't.'

Cilydd was amused to hear such an expression coming from his grandmother. Mrs Lloyd, too, was ready to laugh to herself and repeat it boldly.

'Black curls and Cupid's bow,' she said. 'Like those silly magazines we used to read when I was a girl.'

Everyone looked at Gwydion. He was a pretty child; dark blue eyes, a mass of black curls and cherry red lips so precisely carved as to give a hint of mischief even at this early age. He revelled in the wealth of attention. Amy was obliged to put in a word of restraint.

'He knows we are talking about him,' she said.

She murmured under her breath and smiled and, in the interest of demonstrating impartial affection, ran a hand evenly through Bedwyr's less spectacular hair.

'And this one certainly does. Takes in everything. Misses nothing.'

Amy was touching lightly on the mysteries of childhood. To Tryfan and Bessie her words carried melodious echoes of how once things had been with them. They gave her the rapt attention of exiles filled with nostalgia for a land for ever out of their reach.

'He's so sensitive,' Amy said. 'As if he wants to make himself responsible for the good behaviour of the world around him.'

Both Bessie and Tryfan showed how well they understood that condition.

'Well that's his conscience, isn't it?' Mrs Lloyd said.

She had no hesitation in isolating an attribute powerful enough to have descended directly from herself. Amy had not finished her diagnosis.

'Enid was just the same.'

She continued her rapid murmur, her eye fixed on Nanw as if insisting on her attention if not her whole-hearted concurrence.

She had to sustain the impetus of her remarks through lips that barely moved in order that they should skim along outside the range of Bedwyr's comprehension.

'She was the same at school, the poor little angel. Ready to bear the sum of the world's ills on her little shoulders.'

Amy was carried away by the desire to celebrate the virtues of her dead friend in the presence of a family some of whose members may not always have appreciated them when she was alive.

'She was even then a child of sorrows and acquainted with grief. Mostly other people's of course. She was always so ready with her help. More than anyone I've ever come across, to be quite frank. Never hesitated to take on other people's burdens, bless her.'

The response around the table was not enthusiastic. Even Tryfan was smiling absently into space. It was in some obscure way indelicate for a second wife to be so insistent on the excellences of her predecessor. Cilydd was disturbed and shifting uneasily in his chair. What Amy was saying could be interpreted in so many ways. Were they to imagine that she had married her dead friend's husband in order to take up the burdens the departed one had left behind her, such as the obedient little boy who now sat between them? There was a muscle twitching visibly high up in Nanw's right cheek. Amy had ventured too far into the region of things best left unsaid. Could she have been so unfeeling as to suggest there had been a lack of warmth and considerate affection in the reception Enid had encountered when she arrived in Glanrafon as Cilydd's first wife? Or was she even complaining obliquely of her own treatment? Amy ruffled Bedwyr's hair once more before she fell silent. However generously honest she had intended to be, she had spoken out of turn and come close to giving offence among a clan where this was not so difficult to do.

Neutral topics at such a juncture were hard to come by. Uncle Tryfan clapped his hands and then waved them in the air, but said nothing. Gwydion had become dormant. Slumped in his high chair with his mouth open and his plump arms hanging loose over the sides, he offered no immediate topic for comment. Mrs Lloyd, however, did not give up. Amy was her grandson's wife and her offspring would in their turn carry on her honourable lineage. She pointed a friendly and approving finger at the latest addition to her family.

'I suppose he could resemble your father,' she said.

Amy moved her head to get Gwydion's appearance into clearer focus.

'I honestly don't know,' she said. 'I never saw my father. Except in a photograph.'

Mrs Lloyd looked put out. This young woman sitting at her table with such ease and confidence and so fashionably dressed that her presence made the kitchen at Glanrafon appear more antiquated than ever: this former County School teacher who used to drive her own little car with such an air of independence: this pretty girl who had married her brilliant but erratic grandson in some dingy London Registry Office, who had appointed herself the little Bedwyr's second mother and had given birth to the recalcitrant infant strapped down in John Cilydd's old highchair was admitting that she had never seen her own father except in a photograph. Here she sat at table giving out information that should have been made available long before any form of marriage was allowed to take place. Disapproval more than curiosity began to cloud Mrs Lloyd's face. Marriage was a sanctified bond between families, it was a serious piece of social management that should never be undertaken lightly in a well-ordered civilised community. What kind of an antecedent was this unknown father?

Amy was prepared to provide all the information she could with bright disarming frankness.

'I used to have a photograph of him in a white suit,' she said. 'I think it was a white suit. It was a bit of a secret really. My Uncle Lucas couldn't stand the sight of him.'

She laughed, but Mrs Lloyd could not accept such disturbing information as subject for laughter.

'I used to hide the photo under my mattress when I was a little girl. What happened was, after my mother died, my father went off to sing with the Carl Rosa on a tour of Canada.'

Tryfan leaned over his hands on the table, eager to hear every detail of an intriguing story.

'I was no bigger than little Gwydion here when my aunt and uncle took me in. I must have been like a little orphan in a storm.'

'Dear heaven . . .'

Auntie Bessie was so moved she was lost for words. Amy smiled to reassure her.

'I don't remember anything of course. Not a thing. But apparently he turned up in uniform and then my Uncle Lucas found out he was claiming maintenance for me, so he wasn't very welcome. I shouldn't be saying all this should I? With little ears listening.'

She turned to Cilydd and he nodded in sober agreement.

'It's always money, isn't it? That causes the trouble. So sordid somehow. No wonder we don't talk about it.'

Tryfan leaned even further over the table, borne down with curiosity. A story had to have an ending.

'What happened to him?' he said.

'He was killed in the war,' Amy said. 'Like so many others. My Aunt and Uncle never talk about him. I sometimes feel I'd like to know more about him. And yet I do nothing about it. Connie Clayton – housekeeper of the illustrious Duff-Plunkets of Culpepper Square. You've heard me talk of Connie? Poor old Connie. She knew him. She's such a terrible snob. She lives and breathes in their reflected glory . . . Oh, what a gorgeous smell.'

Auntie Bessie pushed back her chair and hurried to the oven. When she opened the oven door and brought out two gooseberry tarts, one after the other, the aroma generated a fresh outburst of geniality and goodwill. The tart was served with fresh cream and eaten with universal murmurs of appreciation.

'Your pastry,' Amy said. 'It melts in the mouth. What's the secret?'

Auntie Bessie smiled shyly. The praise was as sweet as honey.

'A pair of cold hands,' she said. 'All the better if they are rough as well.'

Tryfan waved his hands for silence although no one was speaking. His mouth was full and he pulled a funny face. Watching him from the high chair, Gwydion was reactivated. He waved his spoon about.

'There was a preacher,' Tryfan said. 'He ate so much of Bess's delicious tart, he fell asleep in the parlour while he was looking over his sermon. He arrived at the chapel just as the congregation was coming out.'

The anecdote was untidily told, but the family shook with polite laughter just the same. Amy turned her attention to Gwydion.

'He's getting restless,' she said. 'Does anyone mind if I turn this little lion loose?'

She untied his straps. He looked up at her gratefully as she did so. Feeling his feet on the kitchen floor he trotted around the table to get as close as he could to Tryfan, who was delighted to claim the little boy who had made a bee-line for him.

' "Suffer little children",' he said.

He cut the quotation short when he caught his mother's warning glance from the top of the table. He leaned over to clap his hands and encourage Gwydion to do the same in a mirror image of innocence.

'They are all right in their place,' John Cilydd said.

His tone was deliberately devoid of sentiment.

'But when they are transported in their thousands, when they become the unwilling agents of a totalitarian war agency, the angels will become devils as far as our way of life is concerned. They will be an invasion that will obliterate our national being more effectively than bombs or bullets.'

'Dear heaven.'

Tryfan paused in the process of extracting his spectacle case from his waistcoat pocket. He would entertain Gwydion by opening and shutting it before giving it to him to play with.

'Do you really think so?'

Cilydd clenched a fist with the effort of making his uncle and other members of his family understand a complex argument.

'It's all part of the strategy of an air war,' he said. 'Do you follow?'

Bessie and Tryfan both shook their heads. His grandmother transfixed him with an unblinking stare as though seeking in vain to account for Cilydd's character. He was her daughter's son. His father had been a worthy member of the congregation, a first mate lost at sea: and yet there were moments when this one appeared like an alien presence in the body politic of her family.

'Hiding the children of English cities in Welsh villages so that the English air-force can bomb Cologne and Berlin and Munich and Hamburg with impunity. That's the lesson of Guernica. Do you follow?'

'He's right,' Nanw said. 'Of course he is.'

She wanted to show active support for her brother.

'I don't take the same view as Tasker on this issue,' Cilydd said. 'I'm sorry to differ, but there we are. The facts are staring us in the face. We have to be realistic. I've said as much to him. He says we can conquer by kindness. Wave a magic wand and turn them all into little Welsh children overnight. It isn't going to happen. It's no part of the Government's plan.'

'Of course it isn't,' Nanw said.

Cilydd frowned as if to signal that her supporting echo gave more irritation than comfort. Gwydion had dropped Tryfan's spectacle case on the stone floor and Tryfan was glad of the diversion. The problems his nephew insisted on elaborating were too enormous and painful to contemplate. He passed a hand over his furrowed forehead before replacing the spectacle case in his waistcoat pocket. There was so much more the family at Glanrafon needed to know from John Cilydd who was a practising solicitor actively engaged in public affairs, as well as a poet. In a world confused with rumour and propaganda and the constant threat of war, they had to rely on him for a proper interpretation of events and a form of comment that would take into account their values and vital interests. But it was an uncomforting process. There were times when they could even suspect him of taking a perverse pleasure in disturbing the tranquil waters of their existence. Mrs Lloyd's eyes were shut as she concentrated on digesting the latest instalment of her grandson's independent point of view. There was a polite silence while the rest of the adults at the table waited for her to speak. Bedwyr wriggled in his chair as he tried to locate the whereabouts of his little brother. He tugged anxiously at Amy's sleeve.

'Mam,' he said.

Amy motioned him to keep quiet. In the still silence they all heard the shattering of glass echo in the front parlour. Seized with a premonition, Nanw was instantly on her feet. Cilydd and Amy looked under the table where they expected to find Gwydion playing. When she saw he had gone, Amy turned pale. With her hands flat on the table she waited with everyone else to hear what had been broken in the parlour. Nanw was already on the spot; the first witness of the accident.

'Oh, you little monster.'

Out of her initial wail there was no mistaking the expression Nanw was using.

'You little beast. You wilful little monkey. You knew you shouldn't touch those things. You've heard me say so before . . .'

'I can't bear it.'

Amy struggled to her feet. John Cilydd followed her to the parlour. They found that Gwydion had grasped a tassle just within his reach and brought a small assembly of ornaments crashing to the floor. He was squinting up at his Aunt Nanw, a little frightened but even more intrigued by the symptoms of her distress. She was nursing fragments of a glass swan in a way that emphasised the priceless irreplaceability of the original object. Her face, normally so pale and impassive, was twisted with anger and dismay.

'You come here!'

Amy snatched up Gwydion sternly enough to begin with. She was prepared to slap him. Even as she raised her hand the expression on Nanw's face forewarned her it would not be punishment enough.

'He's allowed to do whatever he likes,' Nanw said.

The boy's parents stared at her without saying anything, trying to establish the exact nature of the indictment. Nanw was addressing herself directly to her brother. This implied at once that she was laying the major part of the blame for the child's misbehaviour on his mother. She was appealing for some form of judgment and even satisfaction. Their continuing silence obliged her to explain herself still further.

'He has a wilful nature. Anybody can see that. It's in him and it has to be curbed. Why should I have to say this when it's obvious to everybody? He's a wilful child. Everybody knows a wilful child has to be disciplined. It's the only way.'

She lapsed into a mournful contemplation of her own loss. It was plain that she wanted to remind her brother of how much the glass swan had meant to her and how delicate and precious an object it had been. Now it was worthless and there was no way it could ever be repaired.

Without any warning, Gwydion suddenly burst out crying. He had been placid enough when his mother picked him up. Now he sensed some impending catastrophe: his best defence would be to howl. He did this with a will. His screwed up eyes opened momentarily to gauge the effect before the tears were propelled outwards and began to roll down the creases in his plump cheeks. Whatever reproof Amy had in mind was abandoned in her effort to pacify him and bring him comfort.

'As if the little mite knew what he was doing. Honestly.'

She glared uncompromisingly at Nanw. Her sister-in-law stepped back into a shadowed corner of the room. There was no one to comfort her. Her sorrow was a solitary pain. It was an old wound never completely healed. Breaking the ornament had been enough to reopen it.

'I can't bear it,' Amy said.

She breathed deeply and clasped her son closer. For her husband's sake and for the sake of family harmony she had spent the afternoon suppressing her opinions and her natural instincts. Now she needed immediate release.

'What can one say?'

Amy stared despairingly at John Cilydd.

'It's impossible. I can't bear it.'

Getting out through the front door into the fitful sunlight in the garden brought her some relief. She was able to stride about with Gwydion in her arms. He was still sobbing, but also aware that the immediate danger had passed. The garden was an unsatisfactory refuge. It was entirely overlooked by the house. Any member of her husband's family could move to a window and observe her movements with critical eyes.

A small iron wicket gave access to the old stackyard alongside the outbuildings. She carried Gwydion across to the hay barn. Here she could let him loose. The smell of hay made him smile. He knew how to scramble up the side of what was left of last year's hay and if he slid down there was no danger of him hurting himself. He was strong enough to establish his own routine without his mother's help. Each time he gurgled with laughter she smiled. Watching his uninhibited activity seemed to offer her solace. It was some time before John Cilydd found them.

'This is where you are.'

She turned at the sound of his voice, but eyed him coldly. If he had been engaged in a vigorous defence of her behaviour back in the house, her silence suggested it was an activity of questionable validity. A devoted husband would have made a more effective protest by leaving immediately at the side of his wife. And there was the question of where he had left Bedwyr. Nothing he had done so far had contributed towards preserving a united family front in such an unsympathetic environment. For the moment, Cilydd stood stock still with exemplary paternal benevolence, watching Gwydion enjoy himself. A hen disturbed in its nest in the hay made off, flapping its clipped wings and squawking indignantly. Gwydion paused in his play to watch it with his mouth open, uncertain whether to laugh or cry.

'Treating a little child like that . . .'

Amy sounded indignant but she had made a concession in being the first to speak.

'I know,' Cilydd said.

His voice was mellow with the desire to sympathise.

'What on earth has she got against the poor little mite?'

They both looked with equal affection at the little boy playing in the hay.

'An old maid.'

Cilydd offered this as an interim explanation.

'Where's Bedwyr?'

Amy tried to suppress the element of reproof in the question.

'Uncle Tryfan has taken him to his workshop. Bedwyr loves being in there.'

'She was never like this with Bedwyr. Never.'

Amy could consider Nanw's behaviour more rationally, knowing that Bedwyr was in Tryfan's care and not Nanw's.

'I find it incomprehensible,' Amy said. 'Imagine her saying to me, "What a time to bring another child into the world." Imagine her saying that.'

He had heard it before: but now Amy wanted him to consider the awesomeness of the statement in the context of Nanw's outburst in the parlour.

'There I was,' Amy said, half amused by the recollection in spite of herself. 'Lying absolutely exhausted in a nursing home bed, still not totally unmindful of the fact that poor Enid, poor chick, had virtually died from the after-effects of childbirth, and there was your sister perched at the foot of the bed like a great big bird of ill-omen. "What a time to bring another child into the world." That was all she said. She was muttering but she intended me to hear it. And she didn't even look at poor little Gwydion. Barely glanced at him.'

'That uniform,' Cilydd said.

'What?'

Amy showed her displeasure. Cilydd had not been listening as closely as she would have liked.

'That's what set her off,' Cilydd said.

He knelt alongside his wife eager to account for his sister's unstable emotional condition.

'Seeing Eddie was like seeing the ghost of Owen Guest.'

'That show-off.'

Amy was ready to vent her anger on Eddie Meredith.

'He ruined everything,' she said. 'He turned the whole show into a circus. An absolute circus. And that man Samwell was totally weak. I mean, he should have stopped him. He had no control over the creature whatsoever. There was no anti-war effect at all. He turned the whole thing into a recruiting rally.'

'Owen Guest gave her that glass swan,' Cilydd said.

He was prepared to explain patiently.

'Or at least she believes he did. I'm not so sure myself. I can't tell you how complex it is. Her emotional outlets have always been severely restricted. At one crucial moment she settled all her affections on Owen Guest. She lost him. The truth is she would never have had him in any case. But he was killed. So there was nothing to contradict her romantic illusion.'

Amy was drawn into the analysis in spite of herself. It would have been more pleasant for her to go on watching Gwydion displacing the hay and burbling joyously to himself.

'As a matter of fact she went through a less intensive version of the same infatuation with old Val.'

'Good Lord.'

Amy was genuinely surprised.

'I never knew that. I never noticed.'

'It was before your time,' Cilydd said. 'When I first knew Val. He came here a week before the Summer School in Coleg y Castell. You and Enid would have been still in Llanelw County School. She was completely bowled over by him. Very quiet of course. But I could see it.'

'Good Lord!'

For a moment it appeared that Amy had begun to sympathise with the depth of Nanw's disappointments.

'So you see, she's jealous,' Cilydd said. 'I don't like saying it, but in a sense, it is the dominating emotion of her life. I don't know what the devil we can do about it. Except understand.'

'She's no cause to be jealous of me,' Amy said. 'None at all.'

'You used to be so good with her, Amy. I mean you used to manage her so well. Far better than I ever did.'

'She makes me so uncomfortable,' Amy said. 'As if she's watching me all the time, waiting for me to slip up or give myself away or something. It's pretty unbearable.'

'She was the same with poor Enid.'

Cilydd was intent on comforting Amy as well as uncovering the mysteries of his sister's psyche.

'She sees a figure move closer to me, with more title to my love and affection and she immediately resents it.'

'It's unhealthy,' Amy said.

'Of course it is. I am her one and only brother. Since our father was lost at sea and our mother was a useless invalid and our grandmother so authoritative and distant, I became her principle object of affection.'

'My goodness.'

He ignored the mockery in Amy's voice in his determination to complete the analysis.

'There was a merging of the maternal and the natural outgoing mating instincts in their stereotyped romantic forms. The images of Owen Guest and the young Val, they merged into my image, if you see what I mean. In this poor repressed creature, crouching like a nervous rabbit in a hutch behind the wire netting of the Post Office section, waiting for a message that will never arrive. You can't help being sorry for her.'

Cilydd looked at Amy, eager for her approval.

'Well I'll try anyway,' Amy said.

He clasped her in his arms.

'Amy,' he said. 'You're marvellous. You really are.'

Even if the problem could not be solved, it was a burden they could share together. Gwydion was beginning to tire. Climbing the hay was beyond his strength. For each step upward he slipped two steps down. Cilydd kissed Amy tenderly on her cheek.

'My marvel!' he said. 'My miracle!'

He felt her give a profound sigh. Gwydion had begun to whimper and snivel.

'Do you know what I think we need, more than anything,' he said. 'A little holiday. A nice little holiday. It seems sometimes as if we are condemned to live in an impenetrable forest of other people's concerns. How much more can we take on, for God's sake? There must be some minimal entitlement to selfishness.'

Amy smiled and struggled to her feet.

'Come on,' she said. 'We've got to take this one home anyway, before he disgraces himself again.'

5

CILYDD RAISED HIMSELF SUFFICIENTLY IN THE LOW-SLUNG DECK-chair to watch Bedwyr trundle his toy wheelbarrow along the gravelled drive. The small boy was absorbed in transporting bricks from a heap behind the empty coach-house to a den he was constructing with exemplary patience among the azalea bushes beyond the western fringe of the Old Rectory lawn.

'He's a builder,' Cilydd said. 'Maybe he'll be an architect one day.'

Amy adjusted the tattered straw hat that shaded her eyes. Cilydd studied her with indulgent admiration. Her cotton skirt was hoisted well above her knees to expose her bare legs to the sun. She was sniffing a pot of white vanishing cream before applying more of it to her face, her arms and her legs.

'I must admit the world looks different from here,' Cilydd said.

His pipe had gone out. He examined the tobacco-stuffed bowl without attempting to relight it. An old Ward Lock guide book for Sheringham and District lay abandoned on the grass. He wore an old-fashioned alpaca jacket and dark trousers. His one concession to the warm weather was an open-necked cream-coloured shirt. Colonies of midges rose and fell under the spreading branches of the ancient yew tree among the elms and hornbeams planted to hide the lawns and gardens of the Old Rectory from the parson's meadows and the country road.

'I quite liked old Parker's story about the mad Rector,' Cilydd said. 'Didn't you?'

'I wasn't listening,' Amy said.

'The old man had a phobia about trespassers. Ready to shoot at them from his bedroom window. Got up one morning and saw a group crossing the meadow. Fired a warning shot and then discovered he had been aiming at the old King and one of his mistresses. Lady Something or other. He was so appalled at his own sacrilege he spent three successsive nights kneeling in the church on his bare knees. I thought it was a lovely story.'

Amy rose from her garden chair and walked towards the house.

Gwydion was asleep in the bedroom above the drawing room with windows overlooking the lawn. She listened intently for any sound and then strolled back to the cast-iron table. The ice in the glass jug was melting fast. She put it on the grass in the shade under the table. A wasp was invading the sugar bowl she was using for making pressed lemon drinks.

'It's such a relief when the little monster stops screaming,' she said. 'He gets over-tired, trying to keep up with Bedwyr. That's the trouble.'

'Must be marvellous to be English,' Cilydd said. 'I mean you can afford to be as eccentric as you like if you are convinced that the entire globe regards you with esteem and affection. "Best in the world", whichever way you turn. That's what it means to inherit the earth.'

He stretched himself on the faded canvas of the deck-chair and raised a hand to tilt back the tassled shade above his head. He picked up the guidebook and dropped it again. He was in the mood for speculation but Amy was still absorbed with the problem of Gwydion's difficult temperament.

'I hope to goodness he doesn't develop a screaming temper. I don't think I could bear that.'

'Oh, I shouldn't think he would,' Cilydd said.

His remark was too objective, too comfortable and complaisant. Amy waved the pot of vanishing cream at him.

'Why don't you discipline him sometimes?' she said, 'Why should I have to do it every time?'

'Well, I will of course,' Cilydd said. 'I'll do whatever you say, Amy, you know that.'

This did nothing to assuage her indignation.

'Men have the remarkable gift for distancing themselves from the sordid trivialities of the domestic scene,' Amy said. 'It's wonderful really. The way they can turn up at home from work like weary travellers from another country arriving at the first convenient hotel and be quite put out when the antics of squabbling children interfere with the service.'

Cilydd smiled uneasily. Had Amy allowed it he would have laughed, but she was still frowning. He extracted a penknife and began to ease a hole through the too tightly packed tobacco in the bowl of his pipe.

63

'I'm not that bad am I?' he said. 'I hope I'm not that bad.'

'Why should I feel guilty when Gwydion misbehaves?' Amy said. 'Why should it always be me?'

She stood up again and walked back towards the house. They had the place to themselves. An old rectory in the depths of East Anglia. There were so many sights and sounds they still had to see and absorb. Cilydd struggled out of his deck-chair. He picked up the guidebook to glance at it again and confirm that it did not include their immediate area.

'Amy!'

He called out her name. Her gesture demanded that he lowered his voice. The loudest sound that she could permit was the rumble of the single wheel of Bedwyr's wheelbarrow on the gravel. Against her will Cilydd drew her back from the wall under Gwydion's window to the middle of the lawn.

'It's a lovely afternoon,' he said. 'We're on holiday after all. The guidebook says that East Anglia has a greater wealth of superb medieval buildings than anywhere in the world. "Best in the world", Amy love. "Best in the world."'

She wasn't in the mood for enjoying one of their established jokes. He persisted in his attempt to cheer her up.

'There's your Old Buckenham and your New Buckenham. There's your Methwold and your Hockwold. Or shall we settle for your Long Melfords and your Lavenhams?'

He stretched out his arms to indicate the great range of natural phenomena he was ready to respond to: not merely late medieval churches and houses but hedgerows rich in wild flowers and birds they might not have encountered before, village greens, farms, cottages, dew ponds, old inns they could enter freely if they felt so inclined, fields of waving corn and above them the incomparable breadth of sky.

'We've come to enjoy ourselves and forget our load of cares!' he said. 'Let's explore this Anglo-Saxon paradise.'

'You go,' Amy said. 'I'll stay with the children.'

'I wouldn't dream of going without you.'

'I suppose I'm a rotten mother,' Amy said.

She looked down at her toes as though she were on the brink of self-reproach.

'I never wanted to be one,' she said. 'I know that much. I had my own career and I wanted to follow it. I wanted to have a hand in the way things went. In education. More than that. In the way society developed. And here I am . . .'

She made a helpless gesture in the direction of the bedroom where Gwydion was sleeping. Then her arms hung at her sides and she looked so solitary and helpless, Cilydd was completely at a loss to know how to console her.

'I'm impossible aren't I?'

Her eyes filled with tears as she looked up at him imploringly.

'Of course you're not,' Cilydd said. 'The boys adore you. I adore you. You mustn't worry about Gwydion. He just takes longer than Bedwyr to get used to strange places. Takes after me, I suppose. Rigid and unadaptable. You are a perfect mother, Amy. Everybody says it's marvellous the way you never make one iota of difference between the two.'

'Everybody? Who's everybody?'

The relief his words had brought her seemed only temporary. She began to prowl around the edges of the lawn unable to respond to his urges that she should relax, take it easy and seize the opportunity to enjoy herself.

'Once he wakes up,' Cilydd said, 'we could put them in the back of the car and motor as far as Lavenham.'

Amy shook her head.

'He'd probably be sick in the car,' she said. 'Or he'd scream his head off in the church. You can't take him anywhere. The fact is we shouldn't have brought them with us if we really meant to take advantage of this place. If only your sister were a bit more reliable. Do I mean reliable or stable? Both I suppose. I don't know what she'd do to the little mite if she had him to herself for ten days.'

Amy became aware of the look of misery on her husband's face. He gave a profound sigh. She took his arm and led him back to the chairs in the middle of the lawn. She stirred the red guidebook on the grass with her foot.

'We've come all this way to escape from the clutches of your family Mr More and I can still hear their voices buzzing like hornets in my head. Does that mean I've got bees in my bonnet?'

'Who hasn't?' he said.

Amy poured cold water on some lemon juice. Cilydd added sugar himself.

'Poor old Nanw.'

He allowed himself to sympathise with his sister as he sat back in his deck-chair.

'Poor old Nanw indeed,' Amy said. 'What about your grandmother's will?'

'Well what about it?'

Cilydd's voice hardened as he asked the question.

'Not that I care two hoots about wills and property and land and all that. As I told your sister, "The land belongs to the people," I told her. "So when the just society comes along it will have to be nationalised in one way or another. We are living at the fag end of a decaying social order," I told her. "Things have got to change," I said, "otherwise the human race is finished."'

'What have you got against my grandmother's will?'

'Your sister is as wily as the serpent in the Garden of Eden,' Amy said. 'I'm sure she put her up to it.'

'Up to what?'

'You are a lawyer,' Amy said. 'You can tell me. Why is everything tied up in your grandmother's will so that everything eventually ends up in the lap of little Bedwyr, and little Gwydion as far as I can make out gets virtually nothing? Isn't that your sister's doing? It looks typical to me.'

Cilydd smiled and shook his head.

'Not that I care tuppence,' Amy said. 'As I told your benighted sister, "The only legacy my boys need is health, strength, and intelligence. And I'll see to it they get them."'

Amy looked disappointed at the sound her phrases made on the Old Rectory lawn. They had lost the resonance they seemed to have possessed in front of the Post Office section at Glanrafon Stores.

'There is no knowing what making such a difference between them will do to their relationship in the future,' Amy said. 'And that's what I really care about. If I don't make any distinctions between them, I'm quite sure they shouldn't.'

Cilydd studied his pipe and nodded in a sage fashion.

'I agree with you,' he said

'Well in that case why don't you do something about it?'

'At this stage there is very little I can do,' he said.

'Why not?'

'My grandmother is the kind of ruler who wants to impose her stamp on the future after she has gone.'

'A bossy old woman,' Amy said. 'That's what she is.'

Cilydd was surprised by the vehemence of Amy's attack.

'I've learnt to get on with her.'

Amy hastened to define her position more precisely.

'And that wasn't easy. I know she's unwell, and she's old and all that sort of thing. But you've got to admit, old age has done nothing to impair her willpower.'

Cilydd smiled and pointed the stem of his pipe at her. He was daring to tease her.

'You are surrounded by love and affection,' he said. 'In the long run, love is more powerful than willpower or law and order. Stronger than edicts and acts and last wills and testaments.'

'I have to say this,' Amy said. 'In the interests of truth or whatever. Maybe you can't see it because it's too close to you. But just look at your uncles. The three of them. Simon, Gwilym and Tryfan. Tryfan has the sweetest nature I know but he's not a complete man. Any more than the other two. I don't want to sound melodramatic, but in one way or another, she's managed to emasculate the three of them. I don't think it's an accident at all that the three of them haven't produced any offspring between them. She's always ruled them with a rod of iron. Simon's wife and Gwilym's wife are so different, but they're both equally terrified of her. And Simon and Gwilym seem to hate each other's guts. And look at your poor old Auntie Bessie. She treats her like a skivvy. And she's tied your sister to the Post Office section like a nanny goat to a post. You are the only one she's spoilt. And you escaped. Maybe because an unexpected emotion, an untoward affection, broke the iron circle of her will.'

'Amy,' Cilydd said. 'It's having a drastic effect on you! You're breaking out into poetry!'

'You listen to me,' Amy said. 'I'm serious. Maybe this distance is a help to see things in their proper perspective. You escaped and you went back.'

'Wait a minute. Wait a minute. You brought me back, Amy. Kindly don't overlook that. You brought me back. And I'm eternally grateful.'

'Just listen,' Amy said. 'You fell from grace. Only temporarily maybe. But you fell. And now you have a successor. An heir apparent at the very centre of her scheme of things. Little Bedwyr. And he has the added qualification of not being the fruit of my womb. I dare say she gave poor Enid quite a hard time of it. But all that is forgiven and forgotten now. Poor Enid fulfilled her function. She produced an heir to the throne and my God, the whole thing sounds like the rise and fall of some ramshackle empire!'

'Amy. Darling. Listen to me. There's nothing to worry about. I'll see to it that Gwydion doesn't suffer in any way at all from this will. I am a lawyer after all. I understand these things. Be assured.'

'You think I'm losing my sense of proportion?'

'Not by any means,' Cilydd said. 'In the real world inheritance is very important. You led me back to mine. Nothing grand. Nothing spectacular. But it's all we've got so we'd better hang on to it.'

'I never said that.'

'It's not what we say, it's what we do that counts.'

He smiled at her confidently as he made the pronouncement. Amy looked as if she were searching about for grounds for disagreement and failing to find any. Cilydd leaned back in the deck-chair ever ready to proceed from their particular circumstances to more general propostions.

'When empires are about to crack up,' he said, 'and if bourgeois society is doomed and civilisation swamped by the titanic struggles between communism and fascism and so on, surely it's a good thing to have a stake in our own little corner of the globe, a legitimate claim on our own thin soil, a grip and a title to our own land . . .'

When he saw Amy's body begin to shake he lost the elusive thread of his discourse.

'What's the joke?' he said.

'Something your Nain told me,' Amy said. '"That boy could never bear to get his hands dirty." '

'Did she say that about me?'

Cilydd sounded indignant as if he had been slandered. Amy held out both her hands in a limp gesture.

'She said when you were a little boy you would hold out your hands like this until someone came along to wipe them.'

'I don't believe it,' Cilydd said.

'And she said when you were a big lad you hated working in the fields. And that's why you went for a lawyer.'

'Did she indeed.'

Cilydd was ready to smile.

'Yes. That's what she told me. And when you went for your articles or whatever they call it, her parting shot was, "And if you keep your hands clean in that job, my boy, you'll be the first one ever to have done so."'

They laughed together. It was a pleasant sound in the quiet of the afternoon. Bedwyr lowered the shafts of his wheelbarrow, shading his eyes with his right hand to see what was amusing his parents. They were happy figures on the lawn. This was enough to make him smile himself. Until he heard the telephone bell ringing inside the house.

'Mam!'

Bedwyr called out like a sentry on duty.

'Damn!' Amy said. 'I told Margot not to telephone at this time of day. That stupid bell is enough to waken the seven sleepers.'

She sprang to her feet and rushed to the house. Cilydd began to follow her and then decided to converse with his son.

'Bedwyr,' he said.

Bedwyr looked up obediently.

'I meant to ask you. What exactly are you building down there?'

Bedwyr's face creased with thought as he squinted up at his father.

'A prison,' he said.

'Dear me. Why are you building a prison?'

'To lock up all the bad men,' Bedwyr said.

Cilydd restrained himself from smiling too broadly.

'But there aren't any bad men here, are there?' he said.

It was a difficulty Bedwyr had already considered and overcome.

'I can put Gwydion in there,' he said. 'When he's naughty. He won't mind at all.'

Cilydd met Amy as she emerged from the house. She looked put out.

'I don't believe it,' she said. 'That's what comes from accepting favours from people. Margot was absolutely explicit. She said we'd have this place to ourselves.'

'What's happening?'

'That was Margot on the phone. From Harwich. She and Hetty are picking up four refugees from the boat. She wants to bring them here. A professor and his wife. A painter and a Countess something or other. She says would we mind? Well what could I say?'

'Good lord.'

'She told me they wouldn't be down until the weekend after next. And now they're going to be here for supper. Six of them for heaven's sake. There's absolutely nothing here for them to eat. Nothing.'

Cilydd made helpless gestures that suggested he should drive down to the village shop four miles away.

'Do you realise we came here for peace and quiet so that you could plan your book. It was their idea for goodness' sake. Hetty's anyway. She thinks you're a raving genius.'

Cilydd looked mildly embarrassed.

'Not that you've done much,' Amy said. 'Not to my knowledge anyway. Have you done much?'

'Not much.'

Cilydd stood rebuked in front of the Old Rectory.

'I didn't really want to come here.'

Amy looked cross at being unable to contain her irrational resentment.

'I wanted a break of course. Whatever that means. I needed something. To get away certainly. And you needed a holiday. You needed a chance to think. Put some order into that book dear Hetty is so determined you should write. I'm not against it mind you. I'm all for it. You should write it. She's quite right. All I'm saying really is, if you can't afford a jolly nice hotel and total independence, it's not worth the trouble. Truly it isn't.'

They both turned to watch Bedwyr trundle his wheelbarrow around the side of the house.

'Gwydion's woken up,' he said. 'I can hear him crying.'

The cars signalled their approach by blowing their horns as soon as they turned into the drive. Amy had put the boys to bed. She rushed out to greet the arrivals in the gravelled space in front of the house. She turned around like a forlorn dancer on an empty stage before retreating to stand alongside John Cilydd under the iron work veranda that gave a more fanciful air to the austere facade of the Rectory. Their stance had to be a quiet reflection of their status. They were in temporary possession: Margot the true owner was about to make her presence felt.

The red sports car and the black saloon came to a halt away from the house. Margot was being thoughtful. She waved at Amy and Cilydd with apologetic cheerfulness before putting her head through the open window of the Lanchester saloon to consult with her friend Hetty whose hands still gripped the steering wheel as though in readiness for any sudden change of plan. Margot stepped over the gravel towards the veranda. One white-knuckled fist was pressed against her asthmatic chest. The beret she wore allowed a lock of hair to hang roguishly over her right eye. Her breathing suggested she was struggling to remain calm, but her eyes glittered with excitement.

'My dears . . .'

They heard the wheeze in her whisper as she approached them.

'Are you sure it will be quite all right? Because if not, at a pinch we could put the four up at "The Maid's Head" or "The Swan" .'

'I've got some stew ready,' Amy said. 'And the beds are aired.'

Margot took hold of her arm and shook it to express admiration and affection.

'You're marvellous,' Margot said. 'Isn't she marvellous J.C.?'

John Cilydd smiled, very willing to agree.

'I think she is,' he said.

'Of course you do. Where are those delightful little boys?'

'Asleep, I hope,' Amy said.

'Oh God, I do hope we haven't woken them up.'

Margot lowered her voice to speak at great speed.

'Now where shall I start? We have here four smouldering brands, just snatched from the Nazi Fascist flames. And when I say smouldering, I mean smouldering. Skin of their teeth absolutely. Out of the jaws of hell. What they need most urgently at the moment is rest and regroup. I hated the thought of disturbing you, I really did, but they need some kind of special attention and poor old Het and I need time to think.'

Margot's breath gave out again. She gestured towards the saloon.

'In the depths of the Lanchester, under dear old Het's watchful care, Professor and Frau Eisler. He's a Professor of Philology I think and she's just about as upset as can be. Which is a problem.'

Margot pressed her fingers hard against her chest as if the pressure she exerted would provide her with the extra puff she needed. There was so much to explain and it was so difficult to condense the essential information.

'First of all come and meet the younger set,' she said. 'In my vicious little red roadster. That's the Countess for you. Sitting in the front, the Red Countess according to the genius flopping in the back. She says he is a genius, and he seems to agree with her. His name is Carl Hans Benek and hers is Erika von Tornago, I think. She wants us to call her Erika and call him Hans. She may be red but she's very well connected. Otherwise they would never have got out. She isn't Jewish, but he is.'

Margot frowned as though she had run out of the ability to discriminate between degrees of information. Her fingertips tapped on her forehead and then on her lips in a way that suggested she was about to exercise the maximum discretion.

'Their nerves are on edge,' Margot said. 'And so are mine. I just keep telling myself to remember that their world has come to an end – in a sense. Fact is they don't like each other. My lot and Het's lot. Thank God we've got two cars. I know it's unfair our disturbing you like this. But we need moral support among other things. I'll say not one word more and you two can behave as if you know nothing.'

'We don't really,' Amy said.

Her manner was cheerful. Margot was reassured. As they moved towards the sports car she began to make semaphoric gestures intended to put everyone who could see them at their ease. In the case of the young woman in the passenger seat of Margot's sports car, this seemed hardly necessary. She was wearing sports clothes and a blazer with polished brass buttons. She could have been on her way to a tennis tournament except for the exotic stole of scarlet around her neck. Her eyebrows were plucked, her straight hair dyed blonde. She stared at Amy without blinking. Her protégé had adopted an embryonic posture on the back seat and appeared unwilling to meet anyone.

'Here we are,' Margot said.

Her voice wheezed with unspecific geniality.

'Our good friends all the way from Welsh Wales. You've heard all about them. Of course you have. This is Erika. And that's Hans, down there.'

Curiosity made Hans turn his head. Black hair stood up straight on his neat small skull. His eyes were large and suspicious. His nose twitched above a querulous mouth. As between forest tribes unsure of each other's rituals there was a hesitation long enough to rule out handshakes. Hans raised a limp hand and waved it. He gave a smile of brief and unexpected brilliance.

'There you are, you see,' Margot said. 'Hans is a genius. He has promised to give the world something that will last for ever. Am I right Erika?'

Margot giggled in order to diminish the sententiousness in her pronouncement.

'Sure.'

Erika's voice was deep. This and her self-assurance made Amy and Cilydd observe her with absorbed intensity. Hans stretched himself and yawned. He seemed to have decided it was both safe and worthwhile to draw attention to himself.

'Hans Benek,' he said. 'Degenerate artist.'

It was a phrase he had learned. He delivered it with such formality he might have been bowing and clicking his heels. Then his thin form began to shake inside the blue serge suit that seemed two sizes too big for him. His open-necked blue shirt was crumpled and grimy. He gripped the back of Erika's seat and leaned forward to recite with a precision that stretched the sinews in his neck.

73

'O Welt ich muss dich lassen
Ich fahr dahin mein strassen
Ins ewig Vaterland . . .'

'Shut up, Hans. You can be such a bore.'

His mouth trembled at Erika's rebuke. He went on muttering the words as he curled up on the back seat. Erika looked at Amy as though she owed her in particular an explanation.

'He has given up alcohol,' she said. 'But somehow the effect is still there. Especially when he is disturbed. It is strange.'

Amy's lips parted in mute assent. She was plainly intrigued by Erika's deep voice and cool authoritative manner. Erika gave her red stole a levelling tug before bestowing upon Amy a gracious smile.

'It could be chronic.'

She raised her voice to address Hans.

'And I tell you this. You must talk English. Or you will be arrested as a spy.'

He turned on his side and exhaled a profound sigh. Margot looked at Amy making a face to show that she was combating a pity that could easily overwhelm her.

'A cup of tea,' Amy said.

Margot seized on the suggestion.

'Of course,' she said. 'What else, my dear?'

They both laughed, attempting to include Erika in their appreciation of the miraculous powers of a cup of tea. She did not respond. She sat in the passenger seat of the sports car with the stillness of an automaton that had switched itself off. A first move had to be made, but Erika was not disposed to make it.

Margot shuffled about in a fresh effort to initiate cheerful confusion. Hetty Remington and Professor Eisler had climbed out of the Lanchester. Their intention was to begin unloading a surprising quantity of luggage: also to persuade the professor's wife to emerge from the back seat of the saloon. Hetty raised a hand briefly to salute John Cilydd and Amy. John Cilydd hurried across to help her. Hetty was tall, and unloading luggage gave her a legitimate excuse to stoop. She greeted Cilydd shyly like an old friend, uncertain how much pleasure to display at seeing him. She managed to introduce the short professor without straightening up to hover above him. The professor offered Cilydd his hand gratefully. He appeared to be conscious of having more benefactors than he could ever repay. Hetty spoke softly to keep him calm. Her American drawl, slight as it was, contributed to the soothing effect.

Inside the saloon Frau Eisler was applying her husband's purple handkerchief to her eyes. Cilydd's presence made her even more unwilling to stand in broad daylight. Her husband's body swayed from one side to another as he divided his effort to appear agreeable with his concern for his wife's distress. Hetty drew quiet attention to their specialities in order to encourage possible interest the two men could take in each other.

'Now Professor Eisler. I should tell you Mr John Cilydd is writing a key book on the medieval poetic tradition in Wales. Or at least we hope he is.'

She gave Cilydd a shy smile.

'And Professor Eisler is preparing the definitive etymology of Bavarian dialects. Have I got that right, Professor?'

'Alas,' he said. 'That won't be so easy now.'

The melancholy note in his voice brought a fresh bout of weeping from his wife. He stood still, his hands dangling at his sides, his head held to one side mutely pleading for understanding. His clothes were old-fashioned. One of the buttons of his spats was missing.

' "Why fret?" I say to her.'

The professor spoke in an urgent undertone.

'We escape. We are lucky. We are very lucky. She will fret for our house in Hanover. So big and so full of beautiful things. "What is it now," I say to her. "I think of my Brandenburg porcelain," she says. "What is all that?" I say. Pots. Just pots. But that makes her worse. So what should I say?'

Cilydd could not help him. It was Hetty who managed to persuade Frau Eisler to step out of the car. She was a stout lady. Her hands plucked nervously at the lace trimmings of her plum-coloured dress as she blinked in the afternoon light. She saw Hans perching on the folded hood of Margot's sports car like a man at a race meeting. He waved at her and sang out in German. She froze at the sound.

' "I'm nice to people. I wear a bowler hat. If people smell I say well so do I . . ." '

Erika emerged from the rectory. Once again she ordered Hans to shut up. He threw back his head, emitted a thin imitation of a wolf howl and sank out of sight on the back seat. Only then did Frau Eisler shift.

~ iii ~

Professor Eisler had to coax his wife to eat. They sat a little apart at the end of the bare table. They were isolated figures caught in a pool of purple light filtered through panes of coloured glass above the kitchen windows in the Old Rectory. Frau Eisler shut her eyes and shook her head with a theatrical emphasis that much embarrassed her husband. He lectured her in a subdued but sustained recitative that fluctuated between entreaty and reproach. At the other end of the table Amy paid close attention to Erika and Hetty in order to avoid observing the foreign woman refusing her food. Hans with his mouth open was gazing at the kitchen ceiling as though the patterns of discoloration would offer up more secrets of English domestic life than struggling to keep up with the exchanges around the table. Margot was questioning Erika about the state of affairs in Germany. Erika's command of English was good and she took particular pleasure in exercising it. Her blonde hair swung about as she demonstrated an aristocratic resolve not to give a damn for critical reaction to anything she chose to say.

'Somebody will kill him,' she said. 'I am sure of it. That is what will happen. Otherwise he will be after us. Like an ogre in a nightmare. Fee-fi-fo-fum.'

No one laughed. Hetty was particularly intent on extracting some fragment of information that might offer a clue to what could possibly happen next.

'But the people,' Hetty said. 'The more educated and intelligent people?'

'Useless.'

Erika was categorical.

'My sister is in Berlin. Loving every minute of the great adven-

76

ture. With my best friend at school. My closest friend. My beautiful Liesel.'

Erika turned to address Amy.

'Like you she looked. Liesel-too-good-to-be-true, I used to call her. Are you too good to be true, Mrs More?'

'Amy,' Amy said. 'Call me Amy.'

Erika bowed to show her gratitude.

'Liesel struts about in her smart Red Cross uniform. Her horrid brother Konrad is in the SS. Konrad always hated me. If you want to get on, you join. In the modern mechanised state, always the opposition is never more than a handful. Good people like you. Or rejects, like that pathetic little Jew there, with nothing to lose.'

Her attitude spoke more of arrogance than affection as she pointed at Carl Hans Benek. He continued to study the ceiling as if it were a great canvas on which he contemplated composing a picture.

'They call him a virus. They have sunk that low. The German people, my dear, are so hard-working and so stupid. They are drugged by military discipline. They march and sing. March and sing! They march up and down and salute each other all day long! *Heil Hitler!'*

Erika thrust out her right arm in an assertive Nazi salute. It was so convincing it caused Frau Eisler to burst into tears. The professor sprang to his feet and stood behind his wife so that she could rest her head against his waistcoat. He gazed reproachfully at Erika.

'Countess,' he said in German. 'Again you upset my wife.'

In the same language Erika's reply sounded brusque and uncompromising.

'Your wife upsets too easily, Herr Professor. I have told you, you must stop her or she will drown you in her tears.'

'Countess, please . . .'

The professor appealed to Margot and Hetty.

'Ladies . . .'

Hans pulled out a large red handkerchief from a jacket pocket. He waved it helpfully in the air and pulled a long face before applying it to his own eyes. Frau Eisler had watched his antics through half-closed lids. She began to cry more loudly than ever.

'Do you think your wife would like to go to bed?' Amy said. 'I'm sure she must be very tired.'

The professor was both eager and grateful. Amy came to his side. Together they brought the heavy lady to her feet. Hans stuffed his handkerchief into his mouth to stop himself laughing. Erika turned her frustration and anger against him.

'Stop it you stupid creature,' she said. 'We are in another country. Do you realise that? Do you want to be arrested as a foreign spy? Learn to be quiet. Learn to behave.'

As Amy led the professor and his wife out of the room, Erika lapsed into despondency. She hung her head over her plate so that her face was hidden by her hair.

'You think I'm awful,' she said.

She raised her head to stare at Margot across the table.

'You know why that woman is crying? For her villa. For her stupid bourgeois villa in Hanover. I said to her on the ship, "Leave it to Adolf," I said. "He will paper it for you." She has no sense of humour. She cries for her house, for an empty house. On the day before the streets are running with blood. And you look at that academic fool. Rubbing his hands like a pedlar. What does he sell? Bits and pieces of Bavarian dialect. God help us. Fools like that have brought a great country, like a ransom in a bag, to the feet of barbarism.'

She spoke to Cilydd.

'Have you got anything to drink?'

Cilydd scrambled to his feet looking around the kitchen, shaking his head and mumbling his apology.

'Children!' he said.

He muttered the only explanation that occurred to him. The Countess said she would be satisfied with a glass of water. She looked up challengingly when he set it in front of her.

'This Welsh,' she said. 'What is it? Are the Welsh racially inferior to the English? Like the Jews as we say?'

She laughed at his embarrassment. It seemed to bring some relief to her pent-up feelings. There were creases in her sunken cheeks as she leaned towards Hetty and displayed her strong teeth.

'This is a poet?' she said. 'In an unknown tongue. This is a genius who will write a book to tell us all the wonderful things we are missing?'

Hetty began to blush, overcome with shyness.

'Come off it Erika,' Margot said. 'We know you've had a bad time. But cool down a bit, won't you?'

'Cool down.'

Erika savoured the phrase.

'Cool down. That is very English. Cool down. Keep cool. Cool. Coo like a dove in a tree.'

She turned her hand in a menacing gesture letting a crooked index finger symbolise a gallows.

'If he gets here,' she said. 'Every one of us will hang. Except perhaps for that fat woman crying upstairs. Each one of us a dead body twisting in the wind.'

She pushed back her chair, no longer able to sit still. She left the kitchen. In the dim passage she stood next to the grandfather clock, her head lowered, listening to the measured tick as though it contained a message. When Amy came down the stairs she went to meet her reaching out her hands in a gesture of apology.

'I am sorry,' she said. 'You think I am difficult. Impossible?'

'Good heavens, no.'

Amy's sympathy was generous and unstinting.

'We understand,' she said. 'You have lost everything. It is terrible for you. I know that.'

Erika looked ready to embrace Amy as she stood on the stair above her.

'I had great wealth,' she said. 'Perhaps I will have it again. I would share it with you.'

Amy was staring at her gravely, intent on exercising sympathetic understanding.

'I knew, here was a girl I could talk to,' Erika said. 'When I first set eyes on you. Out of all the confusion, I felt so. How does one know such things?'

They stood in silence listening to the murmur of voices in the kitchen.

'We disturb you here,' Erika said.

Her determination to be frank now appeared like a mark of respect.

'It doesn't matter,' Amy said. 'Honestly.'

She became mildly embarrassed by the importunate directness of Erika's stare.

'I tell you this,' Erika said. 'I tell you a secret. I have jewels hidden. In Umbria. Do you believe me?'

'Of course,' Amy said.

'I got them out,' Erika said. 'They are hidden in a Castello near Todi. The old man is my uncle by marriage. I went there for holidays every September when I was small. Will you come with me to collect them?'

Amy laughed at the spontaneity of the offer.

'I will leave that Hans here, or maybe with your husband. And we will go and collect my jewels, you and I. Then I shall have proper money again. Listen.'

Erika lowered her voice.

'This Frau Eisler – she is an impossible woman. How could I stay here and try and share a kitchen with that incompetent fool shuffling about and sobbing with self-pity? Your good Margot thinks I should look after her. She has not said it, but I know it is in her mind. I could not bear it.'

She grasped Amy's arm.

'How could I live in the same house. She hates Hans. And Hans hates her. He says she smells. She does too. How can I make the good Margot understand this. Will you help me?'

'I'll do what I can,' Amy said.

'And you will come with me to Italy,' Erika said. 'I will look after you. A short but wonderful holiday. An adventure in the sun.'

'Well,' Amy said.

She showed that she was tempted.

'In this world,' Erika said. 'At this time we must seize every moment as it comes or it will be too late. Do you understand?'

'I think I do.'

Erika was so delighted with her new friend, she grasped Amy's hand and raised it to her lips.

6

CILYDD LEFT HIS CAR OUTSIDE THE DESERTED SMITHY JUST A hundred yards up the country road from Glanrafon Stores and farm and the surrounding outbuildings. He turned off the engine. There was an abnormal silence about the place. The doors and windows of the smithy had been painted recently in red lead. The absence of noise was unnatural. It was all too tidy. The bellows were cold and lifeless. Harrows and ploughshares leaned against a fallen wall gathering rust as they waited attention. Grass grew between the cobbles. An August stillness pervaded the place like the respectful quiet preceding Sunday afternoon service in chapel. Cilydd took his time. He walked towards his old home and the ringing of his footsteps was louder than the range of mellow sound that had been the breath of the solid world of his childhood.

Uncle Tryfan's workshop was silent. The half-door was open. The room had once been an outside kitchen and was still furnished with a fireplace, an oven and a boiler. He saw his uncle seated on his bench facing the low window. Instead of working, the shoe-maker nursed a woman's boot in the lap of his leather apron. The boot had buttons on the side. Through the window a pair of rooks were winging around the top branches of the isolated oak in the field behind the outbuildings. In the same bright light Cilydd detected the dried trail of a tear on his uncle's cheek.

It was Tryfan's normal practice to welcome visitors. The workshop had places for them to sit. Discussion and debate and country philosophising could flourish while he continued working, the usual smile creasing his thin face. Today he seemed unaware of his nephew's presence in the doorway. Cilydd was obliged to speak first.

'Don't you feel a draught? With this half-door open?'

Tryfan could not be bothered to consider his own condition. He lowered his head to contemplate the woman's boot in his lap.

'No point in mending them, really.'

He could have been excusing himself for being idle.

'Being a creature of habit I expect I shall mend them just the same.'

Beams of sunlight penetrated the interior. The tools of the cobbler's trade, the trays of nails and fragments of leather looked as if they had occupied the same space since time began. Leather skins, old boots and lasts littered the empty fireplace. An enlarged studio portrait of the young David Lloyd George gathered dust on the chimney breast.

'I can't see her wearing them ever again.'

Tryfan lifted the other boot. The creased leather showed how often it had been polished. Tryfan's oval spectacles glinted in the light as he turned to stare defiantly at his nephew. Without his smile his face was oddly unfamiliar.

'She said when she went upstairs she would never come down again,' he said.

He spoke as though someone was at fault. He set his mother's boots in a neat pair in his lap and bent their soles in unison.

'She's in pain,' Tryfan said. 'She's in pain all the time and there's nothing we can do about it.'

He was a forlorn figure alienated even from the tools of his own trade. Cilydd turned away from such overwhelming sadness.

'I'll go and see her,' he said.

He had begun to move away when Tryfan called him back. He saw his uncle raise one of his grandmother's boots in an oddly commanding gesture. He pointed it at the apprentice bench which was always available for anyone who stopped by for a chat with Tryfan Lloyd as the cheerful shoemaker worked steadily at his craft. Years ago there had been an assistant. The seats were still spaced at a distance to allow sewing arms to be stretched without colliding. Cilydd perched obediently on the edge of the bench and squinted at Lloyd George's youthful image as he waited for his uncle to speak.

'I can't say what it is between you and your sister Nanw,' Tryfan said. 'It's not for me to say. I don't know and I don't want to know. What I do know is that your Nain has taken it in and it is making her most unhappy. She is a woman who has worked hard for everybody all her life. She never spared herself I can tell you. For the benefit of everybody. She was protector of us all. You know that John Cilydd, as well as I do. And now she's wasting away.'

With his head down like a schoolboy suffering a rebuke, Cilydd studied his fingernails with close attention.

'You've gone your own way in the world and we have been proud of every success that has come to you. Very proud if I can say that much. But now it is time you and your sister Nanw approached her bedside together. As close as this pair of boots. I'm not asking too much, am I?'

The trace of a smile showed on Tryfan's thin face. Cilydd cleared his throat.

'No, of course not,' he said.

He remained rigid in his seat.

'But she can be difficult,' Cilydd said.

Tryfan brushed the objection aside.

'You know as well as I do, Nanw would do whatever you asked. As she always has. All you have to do is find the strength to ask her.'

He stared at Cilydd until his nephew rose to his feet, ready for an attempt to approach his sister.

'I'll go and look for her,' he said. 'When I've had a word with Uncle Simon. He wants to talk to me.'

'You won't need to look far,' Tryfan said triumphantly. 'She's never far from your Nain's bedside. There they are the both of them. Nanw and Bessie. Blessed among women I would say, spinsters or not. But of course it's an old bachelor who's talking. Let her see how much you value them. Let her see it. I know she's lying there with her eyes closed most of the time, but she misses nothing.'

Cilydd crossed the farm road and the cobbled forecourt between the outhouses and the stores. The shop was empty, but the door was ajar so that the bell would not jangle. Once inside he could find his way by smell alone: flour and dried fruits to the left: cloth, camphor, polish and ink to the right; straight ahead the antiseptic smells of the medicine section and into the dim interior, hardware and ironmongery. From the warehouse came the smell of cattle food mingled with a faint whiff of paraffin, like a trace of incense in an empty church. His Uncle Simon was waiting for him perched on a stool by the grocery counter. He wanted a word in private.

But he did not turn as Cilydd entered. He could have been a customer in no hurry to be served. His thick fingers were drumming against his bald pate with resentment rather than impatience.

'Yes, well, John Cilydd. I wanted a word with you.'

As he spoke, to avoid looking at his nephew, he fixed his gaze on the word "Dispensary" arranged in a half-moon of clear letters in the frosted glass of the door in the wall between the shelves. Beyond it his mother treated patients suffering from wild warts with a secret remedy that she had passed on to only one of her children, Cilydd's Aunt Bessie. Bessie kept the key of the door.

'About my mother's will. What else?'

He was the eldest son. The reference to 'his mother' rather than 'your grandmother' was plainly intended to establish his degree of precedence. Cilydd leaned back against the counter, folded his arms and crossed one leg over the other in a posture of academic detachment.

'They're gathering around, aren't they?' Uncle Simon muttered.

'The vultures.'

He nodded towards the kitchen.

'Tasker Thomas is in there. And my brother Gwilym.'

Simon shot a malevolent glance at his nephew as if to imply another predator had just flown in.

'Everything cut and dried,' Uncle Simon said. 'That's how it is.'

His resentment at having to express his displeasure seemed even greater than the grievance itself. This nephew of his should know what he was thinking and how he felt without his having to complain openly: just as he should have used his professional expertise long ago at least to put the whole business on a better footing if not to rectify a great wrong.

'It's all settled,' Cilydd said calmly. 'Everyone knows exactly what is in Nain's will. Each one knows exactly where he or she stands. And that is exactly what Nain wanted.'

The even calm of his utterance caused Uncle Simon's head to start trembling, heavy as it was, like a bud in a slight breeze. An obscure heat rose in his thick neck and suffused his face with a rash that glowed in the dim interior of the deserted shop. His powers of speech were inhibited.

'But for me,' he said thickly. 'You would never have become a lawyer.'

Cilydd made no attempt to correct the statement. He carried on as though he had not heard it.

'Her wish is that everything should continue as usual,' he said. 'Whether that is ever a possibility in this world is not for me to say. The function of a testament is to see that the testator's wishes are carried out as far as possible to the letter. Everyone to co-operate to see that a way of life as well as an inheritance is handed down from one generation to another. This place will be in Nanw's name.'

Cilydd made a brief gesture to indicate the shop. He was not telling his uncle anything he was not already well aware of. It was not necessary for him to recite the details like a parson going through a common prayer service at speed. He was attempting to draw his attention to a fundamental principle underlying the settlement.

'Nobody can really legislate for perpetuating a way of life,' Cilydd said. 'I'm well aware of that. But there is an underlying value in the urge to co-operation. And that's really what she wants, more than anything else. And with that I am bound to say I am in full agreement.'

Uncle Simon had found his voice.

'And your son gets it all in the end.'

He glared at his nephew. He was so upset he could not manage his customary sniff. Cilydd remained calm.

'Who can say what the end will be,' he said. 'The great nations of the world are ready to declare war on each other. Anything can happen.'

Simon's calloused finger pointed indignantly at Cilydd and then drummed on the counter.

'I'm the eldest son,' he said. 'I have my rights. What does the law say about that?'

Cilydd tried to reassure him.

'Your tenure, your position, your portion, they are all assured for life.'

This brought Simon no comfort.

85

'I'm being set aside,' he said. 'That's what it amounts to. When I'm gone, Ponciau Mawr and so on all pass to your son and I don't have a word to say about it.'

'You don't have any children, Uncle,' Cilydd said. 'What would you want to do with it?'

'It was the same when my father died. I was the eldest. But I was struggling so hard at Ponciau all the paper work was done behind my back. Nobody ever worked as hard for as long as I have. And what thanks do I get? I was old enough. I could have taken it on. But she had all the reins in her hands and she would never let go. And now it's happening all over again.'

His voice sank to a tragic whisper. His hand thumped on the counter. He was entitled to some sympathetic attention.

'Don't worry Uncle.'

Cilydd obviously intended to comfort him.

'*You* tell me not to worry.'

Simon's face was contorted with an expression of intense dislike which he made no effort to conceal. He repeated the second person singular in a desperate bid to diminish his nephew's importance in the Glanrafon scheme of things.

'You. I don't see you doing any better as a lawyer than you did as a farm-hand. Messing with politics you don't understand. Anti-conscription. Anti this and anti that. What kind of lawyer is that? In the fields you were as weak as an old woman. I tried to lick you into shape: but there was no staying power there. It would be pretty bad for this country if it had to depend on men like you. I never saw a worse attempt at being a farmer.'

Cilydd was unmoved.

'Just as well I got away then,' he said.

'Dodging. Double-dealing. Complaining. Running home to Nain. A would-be poet without a licence.'

Cilydd's cool smile infuriated him further.

'You are no more competent to deal with this estate than you were with a load of manure. Laziness and extremist politics is not much of a recipe for making a lawyer, if you ask me anything.'

Cilydd grinned.

'You can always get yourself represented by another lawyer,' he said.

Simon jabbed a carrot-like index finger at him.

'Don't think I wouldn't do that, my lad.'

Cilydd had his parting shot already prepared.

'Of course you would have to pay him,' he said.

He left his uncle speechless and sauntered calmly down the passage to the deserted kitchen. It should have been full of the family. The firelight polished the vacant seat of his grandmother's Windsor chair. He heard the murmur of men's voices in the scullery. The Reverend Tasker Thomas and Cilydd's Uncle Gwilym had taken temporary refuge in an odd corner where they appeared to imagine they were least in the way. They were sipping hot tea from a matching pair of Edward VII coronation mugs. Uncle Gwilym had his back to the sink and his mug was raised as a partial shield against the innocent earnestness of the minister's discourse. He smiled stiffly at his nephew. A third presence might bring him welcome respite: on the other hand his nephew cherished a range of views that were more extreme than Tasker Thomas's. Tasker swung round to identify and greet the new arrival. His ruddy complexion radiated instant goodwill.

'John Cilydd, old friend.'

Tasker raised his cup as though he were proposing a toast. Cordiality did not deflect him from the thread of his homily.

'I was making the point, John Cilydd, and I believe you would agree with me in this: the initiative is with the destroyer. I concede that history shows that was always the case. But in the next phase, when passive resistance on a sufficient scale, on a disciplined level, is tried out, the forces of goodness would reassert themselves. As in nature, spring in the human psyche as an expression of the divine will would overwhelm the cold armies of cruel winter . . .'

Tasker Thomas paused abruptly and screwed his eyes tightly as if to scrutinise the molecular structure of the rhetoric that gushed out of him. Uncle Gwilym took the chance to shake his head with vigour. He had his weekly column in the local paper to live up to. The least he could do was to support his own written word.

'He must be stopped,' Uncle Gwilym said. 'This is the first

essential. It's what every responsible person is saying, Mr Thomas, not just me.'

'Ah yes, but how?'

Tasker was smiling forgivingly at both of Gwilym's hands clasping his mug to stop them revealing the extent of his agitation.

'"Seventy million Germans curable or killable" – that's what he said wasn't it? All-out war. And what does that mean? Introducing the enemy's methods to defeat the enemy. The destruction of city for city. Million for million. Is that the only way?'

Out of politeness, Tasker stepped back to ease the pressure of his presence in a confined space. It also enabled him to enlist John Cilydd's support.

'There are weapons made now . . . Gas and bombs that can destroy whole cities. How dare we use these weapons? The day will come when any hand will open Pandora's box, not just a dictator's. I'm not so naive as I look, you know!'

The seriousness of the sitation restrained Tasker from laughing at himself.

'Out of the mouths of babes and so on. These are facts for all mankind to consider. The New Testament leaves the children of the Church of Christ, here in Wales and all the world over, with one last great historic mission to perform even if it leads to martyrdom.'

'Martyrdom?'

Uncle Gwilym muttered the word darkly.

'Peace is one thing,' he said. 'Everybody wants peace. Martyrdom is another. Nobody these days wants to be burnt at the stake. Not if they're in their right mind, that is.'

His lips twitched with pleasure at the speed of his own response. Tasker's eyes had widened with childlike wonder. He had a reply ready, but Auntie Bessie was in the doorway bearing an invalid's tray and needing access to the sink. Tasker jostled Cilydd in his haste to make way for her.

'She hasn't touched a thing,' Auntie Bessie said.

She poured the cold broth down the sink. Her face was taut with anxiety.

'This is the third day she hasn't eaten a thing.'

She gazed at Tasker and at Cilydd in turn as if one or other of them could provide an explanation. There was nothing they could say.

Tasker withdrew from the scullery. He was not one of the family. But he was present to bring what comfort he could: to offer effective service on the periphery. He detained Cilydd at the foot of the stairs.

'This is not the time,' he said. 'And yet in a sense it is. Peace and reconciliation were never more urgently needed. Shall we turn your Cae Golau into an authentic field of light?'

Tasker smiled as though the phrase were in itself some consolation in a troubled time. He whispered enthusiastically.

'A community of conscientious objectors, not cut off from the world but bonded together more effectively to save the world.'

Cilydd was uneasy.

'There is a problem,' he said. 'These refugees . . .'

'Evacuees?'

They were speaking in such subdued tones, Tasker was obliged to raise his eyebrows to show he was uncertain whether or not he had heard correctly.

'No, refugees,' Cilydd said. 'Escaped from Germany. Amy thinks we ought to put them up at Cae Golau.'

Tasker struggled manfully to conceal his disappointment. Cilydd touched his arm.

'We'll see,' he said. 'When she gets back. Perhaps something can be arranged. I must go up now.'

'It can be a shock.'

Tasker whispered a last warning close to Cilydd's ear.

'The speed with which they change. She's going downhill. Be prepared.'

When Cilydd turned, half way up the oak staircase, Tasker raised a hand in a gesture of mute benediction. The floorboards creaked as Cilydd tiptoed towards the half-open door of his grandmother's bedroom. He saw his sister Nanw standing in motionless silhouette by the single window overlooking the walled garden. His grandmother was a small shrunken figure lying on a heap of pillows on the right side of the double bed. Her eyes were closed. The pallor of her shrunken face made her difficult to recognise. The ruddy complexion had vanished for ever. The springy red hair which for so long had withstood the ageing process had become a handful of grey wisps.

He had arrived, but there was nothing to say. Nanw ignored his presence. Her shadow supported the ceiling like a caryatid. In the gathering silence, the old woman's breathing increased in rapidity and then stopped as if undecided whether to make the effort to continue. The future of their world trembled in the balance. Auntie Bessie shuffled up behind him carrying yet another bowl of soup, freshly prepared to tempt her mother to eat. When his aunt spoke in his ear she sounded that much more distraught from the effort she made to whisper.

'What am I to do? I don't know what I can do. The doctor hasn't been. He should have been, but he hasn't been. He said he was coming. I don't see why she should be in pain. He said he would see to it.'

Cilydd relieved his aunt of the tray. He placed it on the dressing table. He moved his face so close to the small mirror to study the reflection of his grandmother lying on the regal assembly of pillows that his breath misted the image.

'Who is that?'

Mrs Lloyd's dry voiced cracked the silence. All three turned to look at her in attentive alarm. Her eyes were open. They looked abnormally large in her shrunken face. They swivelled around slowly as she took full account of who was present in the room. Her mouth twisted in an unexpected smile.

'I'm not dead yet.'

Her voice was spirited and clear. She saw her daughter Bessie's grief tremble on the brink of unassuagable despair and she addressed her with all her accustomed firmness.

'Marah,' she said. 'Look it up in Mr Charles's dictionary. And Baca. I'm getting the two confused.'

When she heard Bessie on her way downstairs she raised a finger and beckoned. Cilydd and Nanw stared at her emaciated arm. She motioned them both to stand side by side at the foot of the bed where she could see them together with the least effort. They had to wait while she gathered more strength to speak.

'You know what I want.'

They both nodded, but this did not satisfy her.

'I want no more nonsense from you two.'

She tried and failed to raise her head to glare at them more accusingly. She struggled to breathe regularly, so that she could speak.

'Don't worry Nain.'

Cilydd made his statement.

'We shall take care of everything.'

He made an effort to look at his sister.

'Won't we Nanw?'

Nanw was instantly moved by the unaccustomed note of tenderness in the way he addressed her.

'Of course we will,' she said.

She grasped the brass rail of the bed, leaning eagerly forward to convince her grandmother of her dedicated devotion. Mrs Lloyd managed another phrase.

'I'm depending on you both.'

Silently the old woman's lips formed the words a second time. Cilydd and Nanw were standing side by side in penitential silence when Auntie Bessie arrived in the doorway carrying the leather-bound scriptural dictionary. Her fingers were already inserted in the appropriate sections.

'"Three days after crossing the Red Sea",' she said breathlessly, ' "in the desert of Sur, they came to a place where the water was too bitter to drink . . ." '

Auntie Bessie waited to see if her mother's eyes would open.

Mrs Lloyd's breathing was regular. There was no point in disturbing her. Auntie Bessie sat in a corner nursing the book ready to answer any question if her mother woke up.

7

THE WOMEN IN THE QUEUE FOR THE LAVATORY IN THE LADIES' waiting-room at Dover Priory were all talking at once. Their holidays abroad had been cut short. They were eager to share their experiences with anyone willing to listen. Erika trod on a large woman's sandals as she pushed her way out. She ignored the protests. It was Amy who was obliged to apologise as she followed behind her. The platform was crowded. Trains were delayed. People were sweating in the bright sunlight with excitement and foreboding. Erika elbowed her way to the end of the long platform. She gazed with angry longing at the sea and the white cliffs still shimmering in the morning haze. Seagulls swung about lazily on warm currents of air. Ships in the channel looked like innocent toys.

'The smell,' Erika said. 'The stink of sweaty clothes. And those voices. The English whine. Full of envy and discontent. And now full of fear. I can't stand it. Tourists, God help us. All I want is to hear hens scratching under the olive trees. Just once. Oh God, I can't bear it.'

'I think you should pull yourself together.'

Amy spoke so severely that Erika was obliged to open her eyes and stare at her like a bereaved child. She sat on the edge of a broken baggage trolley. Tears of frustration spurted from the corners of her eyes as she shut them tight to block out the chaos and discomfort of the crowded railway junction.

' "Near and yet so far" . . . Is that how you say it?' Erika said.

She opened her handbag to examine handfuls of francs and lire.

'What use are these?' she said. 'What value? No more than my jewels. They may as well not exist. I'll never see them again.'

'There is still a glimmer of hope,' Amy said.

'Hope? Will they turn back because your Mr Chamberlain lifts his umbrella? This is the war they wanted. Those gangsters. And they've got it. Oh God. Oh God . . .'

She gazed at the childlike expression on Amy's appealing face. In her distress she saw instead of innocence a horrifying ignorance.

'Italy will come in,' she said. 'I told you what Muzio said about when they crossed the frontier from Switzerland. His car in the long queue and the *carabinieri* making the same joke time after time. "Come in and stay in. Mussolini needs you." '

'Well it hasn't happened yet, has it?' Amy said. 'And it's no use getting yourself worked up until it does.'

Erika grasped Amy's hand. In her extremity this attractive young woman appeared as her last refuge, her last hope, at the end of the line. She would vent her anger against the people on the platform. Some of the excitement had subsided. A communal inclination to patience and good humour had asserted itself. The civilian ferry services to Calais were suspended. The travellers and their luggage settled down to wait for the London–Victoria special they had been assured was due to draw in.

'The bloody dull unspeakable English. At any time in the last five years they could have stopped him. And now . . . it is let loose. The genie is out of the bottle! And it is what they wanted.'

'Do keep your voice down,' Amy said.

Erika was bent on being unreasonable.

'You are bloody Welsh,' she said. 'You do not understand any-thing. I do. Their lives are so dull, so boring. All this gives them a bit of excitement. A thrill. They like their thrill. They love their Mister Hitler. He is their lovely bogey man.'

A formation of RAF bombers flying south brought the women rushing out of the waiting-room. They craned their necks at the sky and listened intently to the drone of the mechanical birds set on relentless migration. Some began to count aloud as the planes flew to-wards France. Momentarily Erika was diverted from her own misery.

'Icarus,' she said. 'One has to fall into the sea.'

The train for London–Victoria shunting carriages alongside the platform at first gained little notice.

'They're flying south.'

Erika's voice was thick with envy.

'I wanted you to see it, Amy. Experience it. The grapes ripening. The white oxen. The oxen ploughing. The fruits in the orchard. The September moon hanging over those calm civilised hills. Like a quattrocento painting.'

93

Amy was aware that the scramble for seats had begun.

'Oh, come on!' she said. 'Let's try and get a decent seat.'

In the crowded train no distinction was made between first, second and third class compartments. Erika continued to make loud remarks but Amy did not stop to listen.

' "Keep smiling",' Erika said. ' "Keep your pecker up." The language of a nation of insensitive imbeciles. Are the Welsh like that also? Excuse me, I say . . .'

They found two places opposite each other in a first class compartment where all the corner seats were already occupied. Amy sat next to a middle-aged clergyman who transferred his benevolent smile temporarily in her direction. Previously it had been directed at the flustered young woman whom Erika had settled next to. The clergyman was sharing the contents of the young woman's picnic box and listening attentively to her account of her journey from Brittany where she had been staying for three weeks and three days with a family from Paris in their holiday home. This was the family that had provided her with the generous picnic box including two half-bottles of wine. Her name was Iris Bodley. She taught French and Latin to the lower forms in the Tillotson School for Girls outside Egham. At the moment she was being overwhelmed by her love for Paris.

'My mind was set on it,' she said. 'I had just two and a half hours before the train left Gare St Lazare. I never saw so many taxis, but it was just impossible to get one to stop. I wanted to print the whole place on my mind. Do you know what I mean?'

She turned to smile at Erika, holding out her picnic box and offering her a hard-boiled egg.

'Do have some,' she said. 'I'll never manage it all myself. My French family. They are so terribly kind.'

Erika shook her head and laid it back against the antimaccassar in a manner calculated to demonstrate its delicate state. Miss Bodley inhaled the freshness of the sea air through the open window.

'The flowers in *Le Jardin du Luxembourg*,' Miss Bodley said. 'They were a blaze of colour. I walked down the *Boule Mich* right to the river. I dashed into *Notre Dame*. And I had to cross the island

94

to take a last look at *Sainte Chapelle*. Oh, it was so sad, you know. And I kept asking myself the same question over and over again. When shall I see you again?'

The depth of her nostalgia prompted the clergyman to indulge in a quotation.

' "*Heureux qui, comme Ulysse, a fait un beau voyage . . . Et puis est retourné, plein d'usage et raison . . .*" ' Miss Bodley was delighted. She would have clapped her hands but for the large box on her lap. The clergyman's plump cheeks gleamed as he relished the effect he had made.

' "Du Bellay", ' Miss Bodley said. 'One of my very favourites. And Ronsard of course. One must never forget Ronsard.'

The clergyman waved a finger and raised his voice to a more oratorical pitch. The whole compartment was welcome to hear what he had to say.

'I took a party of Friends of the Cathedral on a tour of Rome in '29,' he said. 'I read *Antiquités de Rome* to them in the evenings. We watched the sun setting from the Palatine hill. Glorious it was.'

He made a gesture that involved vistas and visions.

'To look beyond the grandeur of ruined palaces and forsaken temples,' he said. 'And hear the deathless spirit of the city sighing, grieving for its vanished splendour.'

Erika sprang to her feet so suddenly that Miss Bodley's picnic box was in danger of being overturned. Erika grasped her own head in her hands, mumbled her excuses as she fumbled her way into the corridor. The clergyman's mouth hung open in mild surprise as he watched her go. Amy made an explicit apology.

'Bad news,' she said.

She followed Erika and found her with her forehead pressed against the cool glass of the window of the carriage door.

'Trapped,' Erika said. 'On an island full of creatures like that. "A right little tight little island." You don't know that song? You don't?'

She stared accusingly at Amy.

'I'll tell you something you won't like to hear,' Amy said. 'In English or any other language. You sound just like poor old Frau Eisler.'

Amy wrung her hands in broad imitation of the Herr Professor's wife.

'My jewels!' Amy said, 'My precious jewels!'

'They *are* mine!'

Erika was indignant.

'And they are precious. My tiara. My diamond bracelet. You never saw anything like them. Family heirlooms.'

'Call yourself a socialist,' Amy said. 'If you can't have them, you can't have them. And that's all there is to it.'

'I shall throw myself off this train when the damn thing starts moving,' Erika said. 'Save him the trouble of killing me. I'll kill myself.'

She opened the window as though in preparation for the desperate act.

'All my hopes in a leather handbag stuffed with jewels,' she said. 'What could be more ridiculous. More absurd. I'm nothing. Not even an empty handbag.'

'That's rubbish,' Amy said. 'And you know it's rubbish.'

'My Uncle Monschi shot himself,' Erika said. 'After losing everything at a game of cards. Now I've lost everything. Except I do not have a gun. The best possible way to kill yourself. Did you know that?'

Whatever else Erika had in mind to say was submerged by a curious warble that invaded the late morning sunlight like an unaccountable blast of cold air. The chill wail gathered strength so that there could be no mistaking its message. It came from the siren fixed to the clock tower of the red brick municipal building not far from the station. People shivered as they forsook their places and crowded to the windows to try and make out what exactly was happening. In the street outside there was a shrill blowing of whistles. The siren screech seemed endless. What had long been feared at last had arrived. Erika put her hands over her ears. Her lips moved. They seemed to be saying the noise was like the end of the world.

~ ii ~

Unable to get to his feet, the Reverend Nathan Harris peered down through the bannisters at the two little girls cowering together in the passage of number seven Eifion Street. He could see how tired and bewildered they looked and he was concerned to put them at their ease. But he could not move. Arthritis had locked his joints. His arms were too weak to grasp the hand-rail and pull his body up.

'Do you know this one? I'm sure you do.'

Nathan Harris enunciated his English with cheerful clarity. He began to sing in a piercing but tuneful tenor.

> "Now the day is over
> Night is drawing nigh.
> Shadows of the evening
> Fall across the sky."

He fell silent and waited for their response. Their names and the name of their school were written in bold ink on luggage labels tied to the lapels of their overcoats. Their gas masks in cardboard boxes were suspended from their necks. Their belongings were at their feet. At the end of their journey they were still as closely attached to their equipment as they had been at the beginning. But they had been crying. Grimy tears, stained their cheeks. Nathan Harris was intent on cheering them up.

'I'm trapped you see!'

He pulled a comic face.

'Like a monkey in a cage.'

His loud laugh gave the girls a view of the cavernous interior of his mouth and the poor condition of his back teeth.

'I am stranded and you are landed,' he said. 'I can't get up and I can't get down. Now I wonder if two little girls from Wallasey would like to help me?'

Their response was to draw closer to each other, like children lost in a forest. One was small with a pretty doll's face and flaxen hair. The other wore her school cap. She was tall for her age with thin arms she seemed able to twist like rope behind her back.

'You are safe here,' Nathan said. 'You are young. And I am old. But not as old as I look. Only as old as I feel.'

He was inclined to laugh, but restrained himself in the interest of creating an easier relationship with the little evacuees.

'Two little swallows,' he said. 'Migrating. Do you know about swallows?'

Their considered response to interrogation was to remain silent. Nathan gave a deep sigh.

'You are important little people,' he said. 'The first fruits I understand. The pick of the bunch as they say. "It's nice to be important, but it's more important to be nice." Did you hear that one before? Did you?'

The girls checked with each other before agreeing to shake their heads. Nathan was bent on exercising the practised benevolence of a minister who had always been rated a success with children on every Wesleyan Methodist circuit he had served. Adults listened with admiration to the repertoire of anecdotes he was able to deploy when the children trooped to the deacon's pew to recite their verses half way through the morning service.

'Now then, I must learn your names, mustn't I?'

He poked a bony finger through the varnished rails. The girls glanced nervously at each other. Nathan smiled at them.

'Which is June and which is Lily?' he said. 'I should know but I am silly.'

The small girl's pretty face was contorted with discomfort and grief. Her tall companion was alarmed.

'June wants to go,' she said. 'To the lav.'

Nathan reproached himself for thoughtlessness.

'Well of course,' he said. 'Take her round the back. Through the kitchen. Go on. Through the back door. You can see it straight in front of you.'

The girls hesitated. They were being obliged to penetrate even further into the unknown. The shadows were gathering faster in the back of the house. There was a knock at the front door and Tasker Thomas let himself in. His eyes were shining with excitement. June and Lily drew back as though they were facing yet another threat. Nathan held out his arms. Tasker bounded up the stairs to haul him gently but firmly to his feet. Through the open door Nathan could see as many as dozen tattered evacuee boys. They were plainly a category of rejects: the children that no one would take in during the initial selection process. They were ragged and dirty. They had little or no luggage, although some of them derived some comfort by hugging badly wrapped parcels close to their chests. Many of them did not even have the gas mask issue. Two small ones in the front had a skin condition. They were idly scratching themselves as they shifted closer to peer lethargically into the interior. They gave off an unpleasant smell that could be detected at some distance. June and Lily stepped back. They looked at the ministers on the stairs for some protection and were bewildered by a fresh torrent of Welsh speech breaking over their heads.

' "Come unto me",' Tasker said. ' "Bring me the poor and the starving", and so on. It's amazing what is happening, dear Nathan. If only you could see them. Hundreds of them. Lost. Hungry. Exhausted. We have to improvise. We have to do what we can.'

Nathan looked down at June and Lily.

'They want to go to the lavatory,' he said. 'They're frightened to go round the back. Would you be so kind as to take them?'

Tasker pointed at the boys on the pavement.

'Keep your eye on them,' he said. 'They're always liable to run away.'

Nathan was amused by the directive.

'I hope you don't expect me to chase after them,' he said.

The clockwork stiffness of his descent aroused more interest among the evacuees than anything else they had seen hitherto. The largest at the rear of the group began to mime Nathan's awkward movements. Others followed suit until Nathan arrived in the doorway to look down at them with unrelenting benevolence.

Tasker returned ushering the two little girls in front of him. He gave a warning cry.

'Don't ask them in!' he said. 'For your sister's sake. They are all verminous. I intend to take them to the chapel vestry. I've had the boiler on in the schoolroom kitchen. They need a bath. They need clean clothes. I expect most of what they are wearing will have to be burnt. But what an opportunity, Nathan! Don't you agree?'

'We must do what we can,' Nathan said.

'Troops of hungry children, uprooted from their homes, you know I saw a little girl on the platform, she couldn't have been more than nine years old, carrying a little girl of four. They were both lost. Completely lost. So this is modern warfare, I said to myself. And what is this? A children's crusade? It's no use, Nathan. You can't have a gospel without a political dimension!'

'These little girls are getting nervous again,' Nathan said. 'I'd better say something in English.'

He turned to the girls with a gesture of introduction.

'This is June,' Nathan said. 'And this is Lily. Summer flowers. What beautiful names. Now tell me something, young ladies. Do you like Sunday School?'

The girls hesitated, still uncertain how to react.

'If you stay with us, you'll come with us to Sunday School. And you'll learn Welsh. And then you'll understand every word we are saying. The mission and the message. And we'll have tea and trips. And you'll like that too.'

The largest boy on the pavement had caught the reference to tea.

'Mister,' he said plaintively. 'Can we 'ave summat to eat? We're bloody starvin'.'

Nathan fumbled in the pocket of his raincoat hanging in the hall. There were no more than two or three boiled sweets left in the bag he carried to give to children he might happen to encounter.

'Dividing the need of one between the nine,' he said ruefully. 'It can't be done, can it?'

Tasker wished to convey to Nathan the essence of his policy in as few words as possible.

'We must not lose the initiative,' he said. 'The Lord has delivered them up into our hands and so on. Doctor D.S.O. and the billeting officer are hopping mad with the Merseyside Medical Service for allowing children to be sent away without any medical examination or proper pre-preparing. Very well. Let us keep two steps ahead of the enemy so to speak. We form our own organisation, powered with goodwill, and we immerse these little ones in goodwill and Welshness. Do you follow me? It will be a case of total immersion. Cleansing waters in every sense . . . And the Law of Love will outwit the lovers of the Law. Do you see what I mean?'

Nathan saw what he meant. But he appeared less imbued with civic enthusiasm than his colleague. Tasker had ventured more than once into the public domain, and each time at no small cost to his own ecclesiastical standing and well being. He was sufficiently sensitive now to recognise his friend's anxiety on his behalf. But he had no more time to spend in theoretical discussion. There was work to be done.

'Now let me muster this army of ragamuffins.'

He muttered instructions to himself as he turned a boy's head in the direction he wished him to take.

'Mrs Solomon, "Gwalia", wouldn't let these in the cafe,' Tasker said. 'But there's a binful of buns at the back of the bakery and that's where we are heading. While the water heats up!'

Nathan stood in the open doorway as the tired evacuees straggled down the street towards the bakery. Tasker drove them forward like a shepherd with an assortment of sheep and goats. There was some confusion as they met Nathan's sister Mrs Rossett, accompanied by Menna and Flo Cowley Jones and Nanw More on their way back to number seven from the reception centre. Tasker's genial gestures indicated that he could not stop to converse with the four ladies, but would be in urgent touch with them as soon as his current committment permitted.

Menna and Flo were having an argument.

'Divide and rule,' Menna said. 'That's what it amounts to. That's what it means.'

'You don't know what you're talking about,' Flo said.

Menna was hurt.

'That's what you always say,' she said. 'Even in front of little Clemmie. And now, he's saying it.'

'Now come in everyone. Come in do.'

Mrs Rossett combined the role of peacemaker with that of hostess without any apparent effort.

'I'm sure we could all do with a nice cup of tea.'

Nathan drew her attention to June and Lily. She paused on the threshold and then stood aside so that Menna, Flo and Nanw could admire her new charges.

'Here they are,' Mrs Rossett said. 'My "Lily of the Valley", and my little "June bloom".'

She spoke in English so that the girls should be aware of the affection she was ready to show them.

'Did you give them mintcake, Nathan?' she said. 'I particularly told you to give them mintcake.'

Nathan winced and shrugged his shoulders. He could only speak to his sister in Welsh.

'How could I?' he said. 'I was stuck on the stairs. Like the Bala bell. And there was nobody here to move me.'

Nanw and Menna began to murmur their anxiety on behalf of the crippled minister and his widowed sister. Flo was more detached. She stepped after them into the passage so that she should not be seen lighting a cigarette in the street.

'Mrs Rossett, my dear,' Menna Cowley Jones said.

Her cheeks and her chin trembled as she spoke.

'Are you sure it won't be too much for you. Two little girls. And you already have the teacher and your poor brother to look after . . .'

Her eyes swivelled in Nanw's direction to solicit an expression of support. Nanw's face flushed as she drew their attention to the wider context.

'This is just the point my brother was making all those months ago. The government takes no account of our separate existence as a Welsh nation. We are just another reception area to be made use of. The English in their big cities can choose whether they go or stay. We have no choice. We have to take them. You should have heard those dirty mothers with babies outside the station. Complaining that the public houses were shut.'

Mrs Rossett opened the door of her front room. It was little used. Even on a warm September evening the interior was chilly and smelt strongly of furniture polish. A bold oil painting the width of the sideboard dominated the room. It showed a blue-funnelled ship in full sail and steam ploughing through stylised waves. There was also an enlarged and tinted photograph of Mrs Rossett's late husband in his merchant navy captain's uniform. He stared wide-eyed out of the past into some unspecified future.

'Ladies, ladies,' Nathan said. 'Tasker has taken over the vestry and the schoolroom and the kitchen and so on. Not to mention the official toilets. I don't suppose his deacons will like it one bit.'

'They don't like anything he does,' Nanw said. 'They want to get rid of him.'

Menna Cowley Jones looked deeply shocked by such bluntness. No one sat down. Menna's sister Flo drew on her cigarette and looked away as though her sister's emotional behaviour in public was an embarrassment to her. The shadowy parlour was filled with an uneasy silence. They were a company often drawn together in search of the comfort of improvising some common course of action. Now the dark time had come. There seemed nothing left to say.

'So this is war,' Nathan said.

The statement was obvious and inadequate. They were all frozen figures as inanimate as the mahogany table in the middle of the room. Nathan shifted awkwardly out of his sister's way.

'I must attend to those two little girls,' Mrs Rossett said. 'Bless their hearts. It is no fault of theirs.'

Flo Cowley Jones extended a restraining hand, a lighted cigarette between her fingers. She was a school teacher, experienced with children. She had once taught for two terms in a Birmingham elementary school and she was in the habit of remarking that the experience had marked her for life.

'Dear Mrs Rossett,' Flo Cowley Jones said. 'Don't kill yourself exercising kindness, if I may put it that way.'

Through the window Nanw More saw her brother Cilydd pull up his car alongside the pavement. The heads of a number of children were just visible bobbing up and down on the back seat. She saw her brother give them stern instructions to remain where they were, while he grasped the brass sphinx knocker of number seven and entered the house. Cilydd encountered Nathan Harris turning himself around in the passage. It made him aware of the retired minister's infirmity and of how much his sister had to contend with.

'Look,' Cilydd said. 'If you feel your sister cannot manage, we could appeal for exemption to the billeting officer.'

Nathan raised a calming hand. He leaned against Cilydd so that he could whisper loudly in his ear.

'She's taken to them,' he said. 'June and Lily. And I think I have too!'

'I could take it before the magistrates,' Cilydd said. 'It's quite obvious I will have to in some cases. Davies the Town Clerk is swollen with his new importance. Like a little Mussolini. And of course he's got Doctor D.S.O. behind him. A natural dictator if ever there was one. My goodness they are going to enjoy throwing their weight about.'

Nathan was still thinking about June and Lily.

'We'll take them to chapel,' he said. 'And we'll teach them Welsh. We may as well be truthful. I think we'll enjoy it.'

He remembered Tasker and his platoon of ragged children.

'I'm a bit worried about Tasker,' he said. 'He's picked up the dirtiest to put up in the chapel rooms. The deacons won't like that.'

'People don't realise the full extent of the billeting officers' powers,' Cilydd said.

He raised his voice as he entered the parlour.

'It's a form of dictatorship,' he said. 'You can be fined and imprisoned for resisting his instuctions.'

'There you are,' Menna said to her sister. 'What did I tell you?'

'Oh for goodness sake,' Flo said. 'You didn't say anything of the kind, Menna.'

'I suppose we had better get them all to bed,' Cilydd said. 'They're tired out. Only the big ones won't leave the little ones alone. For you, ladies.'

He addressed Menna and Flo.

'I have Francis Joseph O'Farrell and Dixie Jones. Francis Joseph is a very sober little boy. He's already told me he's going to be a priest when he grows up. Dixie is more lively. But they are both very clean.'

He turned to his sister.

'Would you mind taking the rest? A family of three. Eunice, George Albert and Billie. Eight shillings and sixpence a head.'

He smiled but Nanw was reluctant to treat the responsibility as a joke.

'Now then ladies,' Cilydd said. 'There is such a thing as a black-out. We should move.'

'My goodness,' Nathan said. ' "And Darkness shall reign from Dusk to Dawn and there will be no more light." The chapel windows are so big. How can we black them out?'

There could be no question of waiting for Mrs Rossett's kettle to boil. The Cowley Jones sisters pushed into the back seat alongside the five children. Menna made loud remarks about the tightness of the squeeze until her sister warned her not to make a spectacle of herself in front of the strange children. Nanw sat in the front. She remained silent until they had dropped off the Cowley Jones sisters and their charges outside the front door of the house in Marine Terrace.

Cilydd drove westwards along the promenade. A red sun was setting over the black mass of the headland. The quiet waters of the bay glittered in the oblique light. He took an uneven road between a stretch of gorse-covered waste land and the golf course. The three children in the back dozed as the car bounced over the poor surface.

'Well, it's come,' Cilydd said.

He seemed eager to unburden himself and yet there was little he could say. He turned on the lights of the car and abruptly turned them off again. In the brief beam of light a rabbit scampered across the road.

'It's been coming for so long,' he said. 'There was nothing we could do to stop it. Nothing . . .'

'You did all you could.'

Nanw was prepared to stop him reproaching himself.

'We must take each day as it comes,' he said. 'Each day as it comes.'

It was consoling merely to repeat himself.

'Everything will change,' he said. 'Everything. A whole world will be swept away. But that doesn't mean we have to lose everything.'

This met with Nanw's approval.

'We must hang on to what we have got,' she said.

Cilydd frowned. It didn't seem a phrase he could approve of: and yet he found it difficult to modify.

'Things don't have a divine right to stay exactly as they were,' he said.

This silenced Nanw. There were many practical steps that she should be discussing with him. But he seemed in one of his elevated moods when it would be wiser for her to keep her own counsel.

They were approaching the dark outlines of the buildings of Glanrafon Stores before she spoke again.

'It's a pity Amy isn't here today,' Nanw said.

Cilydd's jaw tightened. He leaned forward to peer more closely through the window.

'She's a free agent,' he said. 'She can go where she likes. She's not my prisoner.'

'I wasn't criticising,' Nanw said. 'Don't think that. It's that there are so many important decisions to be made. By the hour almost. That's what I meant.'

Cilydd responded to her conciliatory tone.

'Are we imposing?' he said quietly. 'Is it too much for you and Auntie Bessie to have the boys? And now these at the back as well.'

'It's not that at all . . .'

'What is it then?'

'These are such difficult times. That's all I meant. Cae Golau for example. You don't want that filled with evacuees, do you? A host of dirty mothers with their babies.'

Cilydd drew up outside the Stores. He was smiling at his sister.

'Don't worry,' he said. 'She'll be back tomorrow. I'm sure. And she's on the new committee to deal with the impact of the influx as they say. They won't be able to tread all over Amy. Margot Grosmont has got her on another committee to help German refugees. You don't have to worry about Amy.'

'I hope you don't think I'm interfering,' Nanw said carefully. 'But I thought the idea you and Tasker had of turning Cae Golau into a self-sufficient retreat for our conscientious objectors was quite wonderful. A small oasis of committed Welshness. The training ground for a peace army. I thought it was wonderful.'

'A bit of a pipe dream,' Cilydd said.

'Oh no.'

Nanw was unwilling to belittle an exciting concept.

'I thought your analogy with the Dark Ages and the monastic life and so on was exceptionally illuminating.'

Cilydd grunted to show that he was inclined now to treat the notion with a degree of scepticism. The children on the back seat were moving about and asking plaintively where they were.

'Amy will be back tomorrow,' Cilydd said. 'We'll see what she has to say about it.'

8

~ i ~

'MY GOD, MY DEARS . . .'
In the unfurnished dining room at Cae Golau, Erika raised her arms so that Cilydd and Amy should give her their undivided attention. She wore a Hungarian sheepskin coat that reached to her ankles and a red cap that she claimed to have made herself.

'I can not tell you what we have been through!' she said. 'I cannot. Me, more, far more, than that one.'

She pointed at Hans leaning against a shutter and staring through the window. His overcoat was too big for him. He shrank inside it as though it offered him spiritual as well as physical protection. The room smelt damp in spite of the spring sunshine. On the bare walls, rectangles of unfaded pink showed where pictures had once hung. Erika's voice reverberated throughout the house.

'The snow,' she said. 'I am used to snow. But not English snow. Not that house. That awful rectory full of Jewish refugees quarrelling all day. And no heat. None. And damp everywhere. And that foolish Frau Eisler always weeping, weeping. "What are you doing?" I say to her, "Adding to the damp?"'

She threw back her head and clapped her gloved hands together.

'What a winter,' she said. 'What a war. I do not imagine things will be worse. It was like a concentration camp. And the English in the village did not like us. Who would blame them? One good thing is that one over there learning English and now here he does good painting. That is good. Now because you are so kind he will learn Welsh. Yes he will. And I too. Do you hear me, Benek?'

Hans was absorbing the sunlight. In the untidy garden daffodils grew in circles around two monkey-puzzle trees. A flock of starlings landed on the wet grass. They rose and fell in balletic waves as though under some invisible apparatus of control, until one, uniform in appearance with all the others, broke away to enter into a skimming flight of its own that disrupted the pattern. The chaos was intense, but momentary. Without any apparent effort a new pattern established itself.

'A second Eden,' Erika said. 'That we can make.'

She lowered her voice to convey sincerity and committment.

'You give him this chance,' she said. 'In your Wales. We are in your debt for ever.'

'He likes it,' Amy said.

'Of course he likes it. I would have killed him if he did not. You take this risk for us. He understands. We are in your debt for ever.'

'No risk,' Amy said. 'No risk at all. Is there John?'

'Of course not.'

Cilydd smiled agreeably.

'The only risk is that those dirty mothers and their babies will come back,' Amy said.

Erika listened to her closely. This was her benefactress and every word she uttered was of special interest and significance.

'I wouldn't have believed it without seeing it with my own eyes,' Amy said. 'Mind you I'm not condemning them. I'm condemning the society that brought them to such a pass. The poverty. The squalor.'

Cilydd showed his support by nodding sagely.

'You should have seen them,' Amy said. 'Bed-wetters all. The mothers and the children. Toddlers would just go into the corner and do their business. The women and the children. You could see armies of lice marching over their heads. With the naked eye. It was unbelievable.'

'It was amazing,' Cilydd said.

He spoke with the objectivity of a scientific observer.

'Can you smell anything?' Amy said. 'Babies? Cats? It may sound selfish but we were so relieved when they went back. We had to burn the curtains as well as the bedding.'

'What are those trees?'

Hans leaned against the window until the fine bone of his nose was bent against the pane. Cilydd was very ready to observe familiar objects through the eyes of the painter.

108

'Monkey-puzzles,' he said. 'That's what we call them. Hideous. I always though so anyway.'

'Why do you say "hideous"?'

Cilydd showed he grasped the searching nature of the question.

'It could be to do with my childhood,' he said. 'My great-uncle lived in this house. Cae Golau. When I was a lad I had to visit him every week. With a basket of groceries and delicacies from my grandmother. He had a hole in his throat. The noise he made used to frighten me.'

Erika was seized with an inspiration.

'You will do things together,' she said. 'Poet and painter. You will stimulate each other. War or no war. Civilisation must go on.'

Hans waited for the echo of her voice to subside.

'Why "hideous"?' he said.

'Depressing,' Cilydd said. 'That would be a better word. They were like warning signals. Sign posts. Families with seafaring sons liked to plant them. His father was a sea captain. Brought the seeds back from Valparaiso. I still think they look odd. When I was a small boy I used to call them Temperance Trees.'

'Now you listen to him, Benek!'

Erika made an attempt to embrace Cilydd. In spite of himself he recoiled from her. He shut his eyes and then opened them to look across the empty room at Amy. He grinned self-consciously when he saw his wife was laughing at him.

'How can I thank him?' Erika said. 'My Welsh Kropotkin! Margot, the good Margot has swallowed the Nazi–Soviet pact. But I cannot. I tried, but I cannot. She attends every meeting of the Labour group on her Borough Council. In shabby little rooms drinking dishwater from grubby cups.'

'That shows how good she is,' Amy said.

'Oh, she is a saint!'

Erika was quick to agree.

'But the Nazi–Soviet pact. I see twin monsters of state power. I see two massive engines of oppression, running on the blood of their own people. But here, here, perhaps we may build an earthly paradise? And my Hans Benek will paint to pay the rent!'

'Take each day as it comes,' Amy said.

'Small societies,' Erika said. 'Communes. True communist communes. Oases of civilisation. Though the heavens may fall.'

Erika could not stop talking.

'Hans will paint better than ever before. Visions. Visions. You know if only that screaming madman had been able to paint. He would not then have to crush up people to find a colour he knew how to use. He looks at the white mountains and someone else dips his brush in blood.'

She held Amy by the shoulder.

'Let me tell you,' she said. 'When that insane Führer, that house-painting pig entered Vienna with his horrid arm stretched out, I was there. I was staying with my great-aunt. And I saw relatives and friends change their shirts overnight. Do you know what my aunt said? My great-aunt. Such a gentle little woman. "What a pity it isn't Bismark in charge." That's what she said.'

Erika gazed searchingly into Amy's face.

'You've no idea what I am talking about?'

'Yes, I have,' Amy said. 'Up to a point. But I've told you, history was never my favourite subject. I don't have a pedigree you see. I think that might be an advantage. My goodness it's cold in here. You'd think the snow was still on the ground.'

A heap of old magazines with pale green covers had been tipped in front of the grate where a paper fire was still smouldering. Amy drew Cilydd's attention to it.

'John. Your fire is going out.'

'Hans is so happy here,' Erika said. 'It is strange really. I have never seen him so happy. He is a bit of a hermit you know. In his own strange way. A night walker. A moon worshipper.'

She stopped talking to watch Cilydd tear up magazines and toss them on to the fire. She bent down to pick up a magazine and examine it more closely.

'Welsh,' she said. 'All in Welsh. How interesting.'

'Temperance magazines,' Amy said. 'That's what they are really. Edited by Cilydd's great-uncle Ezra. The one with a hole in his throat. Not much of a reward for an apostle of teetotalism.'

Erika seemed only to have partially understood. She raised a finger to demand Hans's attention.

'Benek,' she said. 'You hear that. "*Schnapps, Bier, Wein, Nein, Nein, Nein!*"'

'They don't burn very well, do they?' Cilydd said. 'Do you think the content has anything to do with it?'

Once she had grasped the sly reference, Erika laughed out loud and slapped Cilydd on the back.

'That is the joke of a poet,' she said. 'Subtle but brisk. We understand each other. Do you hear that Benek? You must learn this language.'

Erika clasped a magazine to her bosom.

'The omens are good,' she said. '"And after the mist, everywhere was light." The Field of Light, you tell me. "Only the deserted rooms of the court, leaving the four in a world without man or beast other than themselves to inhabit it . . . inherit it . . ." You see how quick I learn.'

She smiled at Cilydd, eager for his approval. Hans began tapping the window. He wanted to draw their attention to a dark figure standing motionless on the drive beyond the monkey-puzzle trees.

'There is a serpent in the garden,' he said.

The others stood behind him. Amy burst out laughing.

'It's Robert Thomas,' she said. 'Robert Thomas the molecatcher. He's probably dying of curiosity.'

'Dying?'

Hans looked to Amy for some explanation.

'Full of,' Amy said. 'Full of curiosity. He wants to know everything.'

'He follows me,' Hans said. 'When I walk at night. Even in the churchyard.'

'Now you make me curious,' Amy said. 'What were you doing in the churchyard?'

Hans placed his hand against his mouth. He seemed to he considering the wisdom of providing an answer to her question. He smiled at her slyly as though challenging her to credit what he had to say.

'I saw a woman there with a white carnation in her coat glowing in the dark. She had a limp. She smiled at me. And then that man threw his shadow towards me. And she disappeared.'

Erika was aware of Amy and Cilydd looking at each other. Constrained by politeness they were plainly embarrassed by the effort of concealing their incredulity.

'That sounds like one of his pictures,' Erika said. 'When he's been alone for some time the veil between imagination and reality melts. There are presences everywhere. I think that is why he loves this place. The presences.'

In the practice of his art, Erika conceded her protégé unqualified authority.

'Now then,' Cilydd said. 'May we see the work in progress?'

Again Hans Benek pointed at the dark figure in the garden.

'He watches me,' Hans said. 'I am painting in the stable kitchen. And I turn suddenly. And I see his face in the window.'

'You should paint him,' Amy said. 'He's got a face like a walnut. And his teeth are all brown from chewing tobacco.'

Cilydd still waited for a reply to his request.

'Now Benek,' Erika said.

Her voice was uncharacteristically respectful.

'You owe it as from one artist to another. And we can come too? Amy and I?'

Erika chattered excitedly as they crossed the stable yard. Hetty and Margot were negotiating with a gallery in Cork Street. If Hans could produce thirty-five canvases by the end of April it was possible he could have a show to himself. Otherwise he would have to wait until the late autumn. The stables at Cae Golau were if anything more attractive than the house. She took Amy's arm, gazing directly into her face in her effort to infect her with the same excitement.

In the stable kitchen, Hans crouched inside the battered grandfather's chair like an outsize domestic animal. He blew absently on fingertips poking out of khaki mittens, and watched the reaction of the others as they studied the canvas on the easel under the skylight. The paint was still wet. Pigments were splashed liberally over the sacking and the old newspapers intended to protect the tiled floor. The painting bore a tenuous relationship to the visual reality around them. This gave them at least the pleasure of recognition. The paraffin lamp, a curtain of cobweb in the depth of the side window, the bent guttering above the water-butt outside the same window, a broken harness, all lived again in an alternative atmosphere of rich swirling colour. Deep in the picture towards the top of the canvas the haggard features of a woman brooded in a blue haze. While they considered his picture Hans studied them with the wide-eyed stare of a child woken from a long sleep.

'Do you see what I mean?' Erika said.

She appeared more proud and confident of the work than the artist himself. A certain anxiety was creasing the skin of his face as he strove to maintain his capacity for seeing the world and the objects and the people in it in a consistently original light.

'This was something that had to be saved.'

Erika was categorical. Cilydd and Amy were very willing to agree. But they found it difficult to make effective comment. Hans had begun to smile at them with the persistence of a wolf posing as a grandmother in a fairy tale. The more canvasses Erika produced for display the more difficult they found it to respond with meaningful remarks.

'It's so different,' Amy said. 'So very different.'

' "Different from", or "different to",' Erika said helpfully. 'Which is correct?'

'This is a field in which we are very inexperienced,' Cilydd said.

He breathed heavily as he spoke.

'You will have to teach us,' he said. 'Mind you, we are very willing to learn. We need to learn. We need to respond.'

Hans had begun to tremble and twitch inside the large overcoat he was wearing. Amy looked at him anxiously.

'Is he all right?'

She whispered to Erika.

'Should we leave him?'

Hans glared at them.

'I need a woman,' he said. 'How can I work without a woman?'

'We'll leave him,' Erika said.

With the calm of an experienced nurse, she placed a new canvas on the easel.

'We'll let him alone,' she said. 'We shall let him fight with his passion. We shall let him have his outburst of creativity. He does not like people watching.'

In the doorway she turned to deliver a final admonition.

'Benek! The world belongs to the Devil. Only colour belongs to God.'

In the yard she shrugged her shoulders inside her sheepskin and gave a conspiratorial chuckle.

'I have to say these things,' she said. 'From time to time. He likes it. It is the Slav in him I think. You know his grandfather was a celebrated Rabbi in Galicia. But I think all the terms and the words mean something quite different to him. Painting is his religion.'

Robert Thomas was still waiting by the field gate. The sack over his shoulders was tied with a large safety pin. The smile on his face was fixed like the sunlight. He was a country man and his place was in the fields in sunshine or shower. The call of a blackbird pierced the undulating countryside behind the molecatcher's motionless figure as far as a fringe of ash trees on the horizon.

'He wants to talk to you,' Amy said to Cilydd. 'He's so polite poor old thing. Doesn't want to intrude.'

It was an opportunity to enlighten Erika about the character of the local people.

'I don't know whether you've noticed yet,' Amy said. 'How polite they all are. Like Chinese, Margot says. Although I don't know what she knows about Chinese. But it's very ceremonial. People come to the shop and inquire about your health before they say what they want. Isn't that so, John? He looks rough, but he's perfectly harmless.'

'Except when he's drunk,' John Cilydd said quietly. 'My sister came across him in a ditch once. Dead drunk. She ran all the way home and locked the door behind her. I don't know what she was expecting.'

Robert Thomas touched his cap as Cilydd approached him.

'The winter is over and gone, John Cilydd More,' he said. 'The voice of the turtle is heard in the land.'

'What can I do for you, Robert Thomas?' Cilydd said.

'I was wondering, things being as they are,' Robert Thomas said, 'if you would like me to set the old kitchen garden here in order. Dig for victory as the saying goes. In addition to my duties catching moles and rats and vermin and so on. I don't want to blow my own trumpet, but I have the reputation of being a good gardener. And now that my own few acres have been taken from me, I am short of a place where to practice Adam's art, so to speak. Time was you know when the walled garden of Cae Golau was famous for its fruit and vegetables. I could pay a small rent or we could divide the produce, as you see fit.'

Cilydd nodded gravely.

'That's something to think about, Robert Thomas,' he said.

To demonstrate his satisfaction with the progress of the negotiation, Robert Thomas stretched his right leg forward, extracted an oval box from his waistcoat pocket, rolled a quid of Amlwch tobacco between finger and thumb and planted it into a corner of his mouth that would not impede his utterance. He had a hymn to quote.

> ' "In Eden which was love's abode
> I lost my crown and found the load
> I'll carry to my grave . . ." '

He chewed his tobacco and smiled. John Cilydd was a national winner fully capable of appreciating the aptness of the quotation.

'Let me give it a little more thought,' Cilydd said. 'There are other considerations, Robert Thomas.'

'Of course. Of course. In one sense there is no hurry at all,' Robert Thomas said. 'But it should be turned, if I may say so. I have already sown my spring onions. May I suggest without any obligation and without pressing towards hasty conclusion, that I be allowed to start digging? It will have to be dug, and if you can't see your way to letting me rent the place, you could pay me some reasonable sum for my labour and perhaps I could help with cultivation in some general way. Labour will be scarce as you no doubt appreciate with this conscription and the war and so on.'

'Thank you very much, Robert Thomas. I appreciate the offer. I'll be happy to take you up on it, when the time comes. But I must ask you one thing. Don't pay too close attention to Mr Benek the painter.'

It was a mild rebuke, but enough to make the molecatcher shift his leg and chew more rapidly.

115

'He doesn't like being watched you see,' Cilydd said. 'He's an artist. He's a very sensitive creature.'

Robert Thomas turned his head so as to spit gracefully into the laurel hedge behind him.

'I don't know if you know this, John Cilydd More.'

He lowered his voice to put the matter as delicately as he could.

'The foreigner walks abroad at night.'

The molecatcher seized upon the emerging comment he read on Cilydd's face to answer it before it even took shape.

'As I do myself in the course of my profession. The night is important for me. I am one of those creatures condemned to wander the woods after dark. And I have to admit secret pleasures derived from the rivers and the streams in the moonlight. But this fellow, forgive me for saying so if he is a friend of yours. There is no one to take precedence over my loyalty to the old Glanrafon family, the golden corn of the country and particularly your sacred grandmother of blessed memory, this fellow, he is a German and people are talking you see. They are chattering and murmuring about spies and lights and all that sort of nonsense.'

'Mr Benek is a Jew,' Cilydd said.

He spoke with deliberation and Robert Thomas listened with studious attentiveness.

'Driven out by the Nazis,' Cilydd said. 'And the Countess von Tornago whom you see talking to my wife is also forced into exile for her anti-Fascist views. Do you follow me, Robert Thomas? They are very important people.'

Robert Thomas's mouth hung open. He was stirred by a memory from the distant past.

'Do you remember that strange woman who used to talk to the spirits of the dead soldiers killed in France? In that bald house near mine on the estuary. She was a foreigner. She was Jewish.'

Cilydd allowed himself a smile.

'The world is full of foreigners and Jews, Robert Thomas.'

The molecatcher chewed more rapidly. His eyes shone with excitement.

'She had a son who was a deserter,' he said. 'He was shot back in

France they said. Don't you remember, John Cilydd? It was a big trouble at the time.'

'I would prefer to forget,' Cilydd said.

'And now it's all happening again.'

Robert Thomas gave a deep sigh.

'God protect us. Nobody knows what will happen. A man knows no more than a maggot.'

Robert Thomas was resolved to offer some consolation for their condition: even as the threatening shadows gathered, his vigilance would be undimmed.

'Don't worry, John Cilydd More. I'll keep an eye on the poor fellow. For his own good.'

ii

Amy's Aunt Esther sat by the window of the bungalow staring at a rear view of the uncompleted amusement park between the coast road and the undulating sand dunes. Puddles had accumulated around the pile of building materials in the corner of the car park and rain glistened on the surface of the stretch of new road that swept up to the gap in the dunes before petering out in trampled sand. Behind the nearest shelter overlooking the empty paddling pool, children's paddle boats were stacked under a flapping tarpaulin. The shutters were up on the snack bar and the ice cream kiosk. Esther Parry looked capable of dashing outside to tie down the tarpaulin. From force of habit she sat on the edge of her chair, as if her sleeves were already rolled up to respond to any one of a myriad domestic tasks that might present itself. Her body was tense with unaccustomed inactivity.

'He never liked it here,' she said. 'Never. I should never have made him move.'

Her voice was thick with grief and self-reproach. Amy rested her hand gently on her aunt's shoulder. She wore a new black costume with a white blouse.

'It wasn't you, Auntie,' Amy said. 'It was me. I kept on nagging you.'

Together they listened to a blowing of bugles being scattered by the west wind. Low clouds scudded overhead. A roll of drums broke off in the middle of a crescendo. The avenue of bungalows with red tiled roofs was wedged tightly between the unfinished amusement park and a large holiday camp, with white walls still uncamouflaged, requisitioned by the army.

'He didn't ask much,' Esther said. 'His bowls and the Public Library: that was all he wanted.'

She looked up at Amy in search of comfort and guidance.

'Do you think I ought to go and give Connie a hand?' she said.

Her cousin, Connie Clayton, was in the kitchen washing and drying up after lunch. Amy shook her head.

'Funny isn't it?' Esther said. 'They never got on. And now here she is. Down from London. Ready to cook for his funeral.'

Amy drew up a chair so that she could sit facing her aunt and command her attention.

'I wanted to talk to you about that, Auntie,' Amy said. 'When you've had time to think about things. And decide what you're going to do.'

Esther gave a deep sigh and shook her head. Haunted by the immediate past she was incapable of contemplating any form of future. What she might do was of no importance compared with trying to understand what had happened. She was unable to restrain herself from going over the details of Lucas Parry's death yet again.

'He didn't need to go out,' she said. 'I told him. "You don't need to go out, Lucas." He was always so conscientious. Some deckchairs had blown over, "What does it matter," I told him. "They're all broken anyway. They're only waiting for somebody to come and cart them away." But he insisted on going. That's how he was. The job was far below a man of his ability as I've told you before; but having taken it on he did it as well as he could. He even did little repair jobs for them. They never paid him for them. But that's how he was. He liked being a watchman. "I'm the watchman of Happy Acres," he said. "You couldn't have a better title for a failed preacher than that, could you? The watchman of Happy Acres." We used to laugh about it. Such an intelligent man, your uncle. He didn't want to come here at all. He only came to please me. "If it makes things a bit easier for you, Est," he used to say. You'd be surprised you know to see how free and easy he had become. Being philosophical he called it. Do you remember last summer when you dropped in with the boys, you caught him washing and drying the dishes. He never washed a dish in his life until we moved here. All by himself. Washing up. And you said, "Uncle, what on earth are you doing?" And he said. "I'm laying the plates out so they can breathe." '

This made them both laugh until Esther's brow furrowed as she considered the course of her husband's life that had come to such an abrupt end.

'People used to tell him to his face his sermons were too long. He never really had a chance, did he? He never had a proper chance in life.'

'He had you, Auntie,' Amy said.

She reached out to take her aunt's rough hands in hers. Esther Parry's head oscillated as she contemplated the extent of her own inadequacies.

'You were the perfect wife,' Amy said. 'I heard him say so myself. I heard him admit it. And you were too.'

'He never had what he wanted,' Esther said.

She could have been intoning a litany.

'And all he wanted was to do good. To be a preacher and to make people see the light.'

Amy ventured to smile.

'That was asking a lot, Auntie,' she said. 'It's the last thing most people want to see.'

Even though Amy spoke softly the trace of cold truth in her generalisation made her aunt shiver as if 'seeing the light' was linked in some disturbing way with the shock of Lucas Parry's accidental death.

'He went straight out after the news. He never misses the news. He sits with his ear glued to that little box. Getting a bit deaf you see. Listens to every bulletin. Grunting his responses as though that man in London could hear him. Sifting the grain from the chaff he called it. Scratching around like a hen in a heap of progaganda he called it, to pick up grains of truth. He was always keen on the truth.'

Esther stared sternly at Amy in order to convey the depth of Lucas Parry's dedication.

'Out he went. The wind was blowing. Those army lorries for ever turning and reversing around the place. Up and down Happy Acres just as they please. Training they called it. "And to think we moved here for peace and quiet," we used to say. His leg was bad. Because of the weather. He limped more than usual. And in the wind he couldn't have heard it coming. They say the lad driving put his foot on the accelerator thing instead of the brake. This great lorry going backwards. It just went over him. Crushed the life out of him.'

She was beyond tears. She frowned and closed her eyes.

'I can't understand it,' she said. 'I just can't understand it. I try as hard as I can. But I can't.'

Connie Clayton tapped the door before limping in with a tea tray. She continued to wear her jaunty black hat to denote her visitor status, but she wore one of Esther's pinafores to protect her black dress.

'I've brought a cup and saucer for Mr More,' Connie Clayton said. 'He should be back any minute, shouldn't he?'

She smiled with nervous affability. Under this roof Amy became a more volatile and unpredictable person: the rebellious child of her long-dead cousin Grace, the residual legatee of a complex Welsh nonconformist family inheritance and not the urbane and polite collaborator and friend of Miss Margot who stayed at 43 Culpepper Place. She was faced with Amy's devotion to Esther and what was left of the young woman's outspoken critical attitude towards Lucas Parry. She placed the tea tray on the table and moved cautiously around it as though stepping through a minefield.

'The officer whatever his name was offered to take the service in hand,' Esther said. 'I told him we were perfectly capable of looking after our own dead.'

'Quite right, Auntie,' Amy said.

Connie Clayton smoothed the tablecloth with her left hand.

'I expect he meant well,' she said. 'The young officer.'

The way Esther and Amy both looked at her discouraged her from pursuing that line of speculation.

'This war,' Connie Clayton said. 'It upsets everything. I think I told you that Lady Violet has decided to remain in Canada for the time being. In North America anyway. For the duration of hostilities as they say.'

Esther's reaction was a brief snort. The shock of her husband's death had damaged the censor which normally governed her social responses. A primordial prejudice against English aristocracy shot to the surface. To close her own ears against any unconsidered blasphemy, Connie hastened to give Amy news of 43 Culpepper Place.

'Miss Margot wants to turn over half the house to the Refugee Children's Committee. I suppose you've heard that, Amy? I'd still be there of course. To keep an eye on things. It's a worry of course. An added responsibility.'

Connie Clayton sighed gently to indicate that she fully understood Amy's desire to concentrate on her aunt's condition. At the same time, prolonged silence could create discomfort. The war was a topic like the weather upon which it was safe to dilate in general terms, after a decent interval.

'Mr Chamberlain says that this Hitler fellow has missed the bus.' Connie said. 'I do hope he is right. We had the most terrible winter in London. Did you know the river Thames had been frozen over?'

However amazing this appeared to Connie, Esther was determined not to attach any importance to the fact. The Thames was not a river she would ever want to have anything to do with, however hard Connie Clayton tried to invest it with prestige and glory. Connie resorted to pouring out tea. Holding her cup and saucer, Esther neglected to drink. She was staring so intently at the wet amusement park, the awful accident could have been re-enacting itself before her eyes.

'People get killed in the black-out,' she said. 'They say that. But this was broad daylight. It was stormy. I'm not saying it wasn't stormy. He shouldn't have gone out at all. And I suppose that boy was too stupid to see what was right behind him. The weather was too bad to be teaching soldiers to drive great lorries. What use is it? Except to kill people. Is that all we are here for?'

Her cup was in danger of toppling out of its saucer. Gently Amy relieved her of them. Esther's back stiffened as she looked up again at Amy.

'Do you want to see your uncle?' she said.

Some form of movement was preferable to witnessing a trance of grief. Esther had to lead the way. Connie offered her arm to support her. Esther ignored it. Lucas Parry was laid out on the single bed in the spare bedroom. His body had been dressed in a white dressing-gown instead of a shroud. Esther held on to the edge of the coffin and gazed admiringly at the dead man's features. His narrow face was like carved ivory, already old and yellowing, his lips yellow-blue.

'I know he's dead.'

Esther was talking to herself. Her lips were close to smiling.

'But I could stand here all day and talk to him,' she said. 'I don't know about the spirit or things like that. But I have this feeling as if a whole time of life all the years had rolled back to sink themselves in him, so that he would remember every little thing for ever. I'm silly I know. Ignorant.'

Connie shifted about in the open doorway. The room was too small to accommodate the three of them.

'He's at peace,' Connie said.

'I want to talk to him even more than when he was alive. That's funny, isn't it?' Esther said.

A gust of wind swept the front door out of John Cilydd's hand as he opened it. He held on to his grey Homburg hat as he closed the door against the wind so that he looked as though he had spun into the vestibule. Connie Clayton made a particular effort to receive him graciously. She took his raincoat and hat and urged him to take tea in the living room. He was polite but morose and distant; a lawyer unwilling to speak until his client was ready to give him her full attention. Amy led her Aunt Esther into the room. The bereaved woman looked suddenly exhausted. Amy made her sit down with her back to the window. Cilydd closed his eyes and cleared his throat.

'They've admitted liability,' he said. 'That's the first step.'

Under more favourable conditions it could have been a matter for quiet congratulations. Amy showed her guarded approval.

'Whom did you see?' she said.

'I saw the colonel,' Cilydd said. 'I wasn't going to be fobbed off by some half-baked junior officer just out of Sandhurst.'

He could be seen making an effort not to look too pleased with himself.

'The army,' he said. 'Doesn't change. Bureaucracy on wheels. Red tape. Tidying and toadying. My God. Just the smell of the place. Spitting and polishing. Brought it all back to me.'

Amy was hardly in the mood to listen to reminiscences of army life.

'What did he say?' she said. 'Will Auntie get compensation?'

Cilydd's head jerked up.

'Of course she will,' he said. 'The only question at issue is how much and how long will it take us to get it. We have to find a way to settle out of court that won't be disadvantageous to your aunt. And this is war-time. Men and units are shifting all the time. The secret is to be quick and efficient about it.'

Cilydd sounded quite pleased with his own progress until Esther Parry interrupted him with an outburst of indignation.

'I don't want to be beholden to them,' she said. 'I don't want their charity. On any account.'

Cilydd was taken by surprise. He jumped to his feet as if to repulse an attack.

'Good heavens,' he said. 'It's not charity. It's yours by right. You must understand that.'

Esther became sullen and nibbled at the back of her thumb.

'I don't want to have anything to do with them,' she said.

'Of course you don't,' Cilydd said. 'And you won't have to. But there is such a thing as natural justice. And it still has some bearing on the law of England, thank goodness. And since that is the law we are obliged to live under, it is only right and proper that we should make use of it.'

Esther was unconvinced. Cilydd made a greater effort at patient explanation.

'Listen,' he said. 'A man does a day's work and he gets paid for it. Through no fault of his own he has an accident at work. The law says he is entitled to compensation. Now that is a right, an elementary human right that reformers along the years have had to fight for. To fight tooth and nail. Now that right is enshrined in the law. By the same token, your breadwinner has been snatched away from you. Not by his employer but by the army and therefore by the state. The law decrees that you are entitled by right to compensation. Do I make it clear?'

Esther was on the verge of tears but still uncertain about what course she should take.

'Don't shout,' Amy said. 'Don't raise your voice, John Cilydd.'

Cilydd apologised. He clasped his hands together and let them hang between his legs like an accused man waiting for a verdict.

'So long as I don't have to do anything about it,' Esther said. 'So long as I don't have to go cap in hand and begging.'

Amy rubbed her aunt's back to comfort her.

'Now don't you worry, Auntie,' she said. 'We'll take care of you. Just don't worry.'

~ iii ~

The old bicycle creaked and groaned as John Cilydd struggled to ride up the hill. He raised himself from the shrivelled seat to bring all his weight to bear on the pedals. He wobbled on a zig-zag course until the sheer steepness forced him to dismount. He removed his hat to mop the sweat from his brow and wipe his spectacles. He frowned at the view. There were ships on the distant horizon making for Liverpool. Shadows of clouds on the shifting sea were like memorial traces of the long winter. Through the bare branches of the trees on his left he could see sunlight glitter on the river as it meandered towards the estuary and on the roof of the Pleasure Pavilion that dominated the promenade at Llanelw. He trudged up the hill until he came across a lady's bicycle abandoned in the grassy ditch beneath the stone stile leading to the path into the wood.

The sunlight had difficulty in penetrating the wood. The trees looked black and the bird song was intermittent. Cilydd climbed uphill through the blue shadows and threaded light until he saw Amy, shrunk inside her winter coat, sitting with her back against the bole of a mountain oak, her shoes buried in a shoal of withered leaves. Opposite her, below the moss-covered remnants of a wall, a bank of primroses squinted out of their green shadows. He saw tears still wet on her cheeks. He threw himself down beside her, exaggerating his exhaustion. He tried to tug her hand out of her pocket to take it in his own.

'How was he?'

Amy freed her hand to search for a handkerchief. Cilydd sighed.

'He looks so thin,' he said. 'He's wasting away. And yet he's so serene. So calm. He looks at you and you feel you are the invalid and he's somewhere beyond and above you. On another plane of existence.'

'Val.'

She managed to mutter the name and it sounded like an incantation.

'What did he say? About me?' Amy said. 'What did Val say?'

'He understood,' Cilydd said. 'He understood perfectly.'

'He understood perfectly that it was an excuse.'

Amy was not prepared to forgive herself.

'Because I'm ashamed to go and see him. And I don't even know why I'm ashamed. It's not just that I can't bear to see him suffer. To see him wasting away.'

'He understood you had to stay with your aunt,' Cilydd said. 'He fully appreciated that.'

From their vantage point in the high wood they considered the future of Esther Parry like a distant prospect that would become more visible the longer it was studied. Amy stirred inside her thick coat.

'I pressed her to come and live with us,' she said. 'I really pressed her. But she won't leave. She has all sorts of reasons and excuses. But the real thing, the real reason is she wants to be near his grave.'

Cilydd watched Amy's face closely, concerned to make his own reaction harmonise with hers.

'It's so stupid,' Amy said. 'You can just see her. Week after week. Taking flowers to the cemetery and sitting there and talking to him as if he could hear her. When you're dead, you're dead and that's the end of it.'

Amy pointed vigorously at the earth. She kicked at the dead leaves.

'She's ridiculous, but she's right,' Amy said.

She leaned her head against Cilydd's shoulder. Her body shook with a bout of emotion that was laughter as much as tears. Cilydd held her as tenderly as he could. He found a clean handkerchief in his pocket and opened it so that she could blow her nose.

'You know something?' Amy said. 'Her love shaped his face. Do you know that? Gave it as much dignity as it ever had. And I never saw that until he was dead.'

She sighed deeply and her body trembled as she recovered her breath.

'That's what I've been thinking up here. It's so useless to go back over the years. I never liked him. I used to think he was a tyrant. And yet they doted on me as if I was their own daughter. Their one and only daughter. I never gave Lucas Parry anything except rebellion and suspicion and dislike. And all the time she managed to love him and to love me. She managed it. But that's not what's making me cry. Do you understand that?'

She stared defiantly at Cilydd.

'Tell me,' he said. 'Tell me.'

'I've been thinking all the time. I could have done the same for Val. I should have. I should have. Instead I'm crouching up here, ashamed to go and see him.'

In spite of himself, Cilydd looked hurt. He stood up and moved away as if to gain a clearer view of the sea through the trees.

'You see, you see.'

Amy was resolved to think aloud and make him follow her thoughts wherever they led her.

'We watch others,' she said. 'All our lives we watch others. And you would think we would learn something. But we don't. I said horrible things to her. To try and make her see sense. I said, "You'd rather be with him dead than with me living." I must have wanted

126

to hurt her. "You're upset," she said. And she smiled as she said it. "You don't mean it. You don't know what you're saying." And I knew exactly what I was saying. And now I've hurt you.'

Cilydd turned to look at her shaking his head.

'I'm not jealous,' he said. 'Not any more. I used to be. It used to eat me up. I was so jealous of Val. Perhaps I still am. But in a completely different way.'

'Come and sit here,' Amy said. 'Come and hold me. Babes in the wood.'

She held up her face so that he could kiss her.

'We have to keep each other warm,' she said. 'Or we'll die of cold.'

He was encouraged to make love to her. Inside her overcoat his hands explored the shape of her body as if they were trembling with a fresh discovery. She took his head in her hands to gain his attention.

'John,' she said. 'John. What did Val say? I want to hear every word.'

He buried his head in her breast.

'Now I am jealous,' he said. 'In the old way.'

They laughed together. She stroked his face to show how ready she was to be kind to him.

'What was the different way?' she said. 'What was the different way of being jealous?'

Cilydd leaned back to stare at the fragments of blue sky between the topmost branches of the trees.

'That serenity he has,' Cilydd said. 'It's more than detachment. It's as though he were looking into another world. It's as though nothing any more could disturb him. It's like an aura.'

'What did he say about the war.'

'Nothing really,' Cilydd said. 'Nothing new.'

'Did you tell him about me and the Red Cross and the WVS and so on?'

'Yes I did.'

Amy wrapped her coat about her person.

'Did he approve or disapprove?'

Cilydd shook his head at a loss for an exact answer.

127

'Did you tell him I wanted to know what he thought,' she said sharply. 'Did you tell him that?'

'Yes I did.'

'Did you tell him my motives. Did you tell him I was getting into position. Ready for the revolution. I'm serious now. Did you tell him? I want to be in a position to have some influence on the course of events. However small. And whatever I do I want him of all people to understand why I'm doing it. Did you tell him that?'

'Yes I did.'

'And what did he say, for heaven's sake?'

'He told me to love and protect you, whatever happened.'

'Is that all?'

Cilydd laughed as he pulled her to her feet.

'It's quite a lot,' he said.

He embraced her tenderly and she submitted until she became restless again with the desire to talk.

'We used to listen to every single word he had to say. He was our oracle!'

Amy raised her voice. A startled thrush flew off the branch above their heads and skimmed through the trees like a stone on the water.

'And now you mean to tell me he has been struck dumb,' she said. 'About this huge shadow hanging over the whole of life, he has nothing to say.'

They made their way downwards through the trees. At one point the angle was so steep they allowed their legs to give way in the knowledge that their hands would save them as they tumbled against the trunk of a tree.

'I can't really describe it,' Cilydd said. 'You couldn't say he was dead to the world. Or even removed from it in some mystical way. And yet the only thing he had to tell me really was to go on looking after you, whatever happened.'

'Why shouldn't it be me looking after you?' Amy said.

'Loving you was what he said in actual fact,' Cilydd said. 'Go on loving you. There was a bowl of red tulips in his room. The sun was shining on them. The stems were bowing like swans' necks. I had a feeling he was perfectly content to spend hours looking at them.'

128

'Loving them do you mean?'

Amy breathed deeply, throwing her head back as if she were prepared to face any truth, however stark or disturbing, however unpleasant.

'No. I don't mean that,' Cilydd said. 'I don't exactly know what I mean. Something to do with inner peace, being reflected in the world around him. The small world. A shrinking world perhaps. Oh, I don't know what I mean.'

'Well I can tell you one thing I've decided,' Amy said. 'Whatever happens, I'm not going to take this war lying down. Do you understand me?'

At the end of the path they sat on a stone stile together to contemplate the view as far as the horizon.

'You don't want me to get involved,' Amy said. 'The war effort. Sounds awful I know.'

'I want you to do whatever you like,' Cilydd said.

'Miss Eirwen put my name up,' she said. 'For the County Committee. That means the Regional Committee as well. She's obviously forgiven us. For our extreme views and so on. She obviously wants us to have a place in the hierarchy if that's what you can call the scheme of things. But I won't do it, John, if you don't want me to. I won't touch it.'

'You are a free agent,' Cilydd said. 'You know that. You must do what you think is right.'

Amy pushed her fist under her chin. She wanted him to appreciate how much thought she had been giving to practical politics: the courses of action that had to be followed once a period of theoretical detachment had come to its appropriate end.

'I meant what I said about being in the right place at the right time in a period of revolutionary change,' she said. 'Nobody knows just how all this war business is going to end. I mean, if there were a total collapse of the capitalist-imperialist system, there must be key positions that will have to be occupied. Do you know what I mean?'

Intent on her exposition she was slow to recognise the expression of gloom gathering on Cilydd's face.

'I know your sister Nanw won't approve,' Amy said.

She tried to make light of the matter.

'She never approves of anything I do. But how do you feel? Tell me what you're thinking.'

His first answer was a single word.

'Isolated,' he said.

She nudged him to make him say more.

'Like a single stone,' he said. 'Like a pebble on a beach. On an island. That's what isolated means after all. Surrounded by a vast grey-blue indifferent sea. With ships on it. A liquid element sparsely populated with men for ever on the move. A great traffic on the sea, the great traffic on the seas of the world that has nothing at all to do with me.'

He waved a hand at the great stretch of ocean they were looking at.

'I'm sinking deeper and deeper into my isolation. Just waiting for the sea to come up and swallow me. Whatever the world does or decides to do seems to have less and less to do with me. I don't count and I can't think of any good reason why I should.'

When he stopped speaking the silence between them was heavy with melancholy in spite of the sunlight.

'Oh John, don't sound so miserable. Please. I know it's a terrible time we're going to have to go through. I can see that. But don't say we count for nothing. Never say that.'

He looked at her tenderly. There were tears balanced delicately on her eyelashes.

'Except to look after you, my darling,' he said. 'Old Val was quite right about that.'

He kissed her eyes and transferred the taste of salt to her lips.

9

~ i ~

PROFESSOR GWILYM HAD DIFFICULTY IN CONTAINING HIS DISTRESS. Underneath his ancient MA gown he was dressed as smartly as ever: a dove-grey flannel suit with a double-breasted waistcoat and a pale purple bow tie. His dark hair with the discreet streak of white was smooth and glossy, but there were fresh lines of care on his elastic features and the pallor of a sleepless night on his skin. His face twitched as he greeted John Cilydd More and Miss Sali Prydderch, the Inspector of Schools. In spite of the bright sunshine there was an atmosphere of gloom and foreboding in the college cloister. Undergraduates congregated in groups around the doors of the lecture rooms, apparently unwilling to part from each other and yet deriving no comfort from their sporadic conversations. Professor Gwilym observed their behaviour with helpless compassion.

'What can one do?' he said. 'There is nothing one can do. And that's the sum of it. They can't concentrate. Just over a fortnight until the exams start. But life is already preparing a gigantic final examination for all of us. Eh?'

He glanced at Cilydd and Sali Prydderch for some brief sign of appreciation of the metaphor. Out of the shadowed cloister he pointed at the sunlit terraced garden. The lawns were trimmed. Ordered ranks of aubrietia and alyssum hung over the parallel lines of dressed stone. The birds were still singing in the warmth of the morning sun. The sheer wall of the college tower was less oppressive under the strong light. Traces of white cloud high in the sky underlined its blue serenity.

'A telegram was delivered,' Professor Gwilym said. 'In the middle of my lecture. He had to go. Just look at the poor things. They stand about all day. As we all do. From bulletin to bulletin. I was telling Hector Powell as we came out of Faculty yesterday afternoon. It's like waking up and discovering that life is the real nightmare. Holland over-run in a matter of hours. Rotterdam bombed to pieces. What's happening I say to myself? What's happening? How can lightning strike out of such a blue sky?'

Cilydd and Miss Prydderch followed the professor up the wide stone staircase to the top corridor where the heads of departments in the Faculty of Arts had their rooms. The echo of their footsteps and her innate inclination towards diplomatic delicacy compelled Sali Prydderch to reduce her inquiry to little more than a whisper.

'How is my darling little Bedwyr?'

She smiled hopefully at Cilydd.

'I know I'm a doting aunt,' she said. 'I daren't say great-aunt, heaven forgive me. But he does seem to me the most perfect child ever created. I can't help it, can I?'

'They are fine,' Cilydd said. 'Just fine.'

'And of course our pretty little Gwydion. They are so beautiful. There is nothing, is there, when all is said and done, more beautiful in the whole wide world than little children. Is Amy coming? Dear Amy. I was so sorry to miss Lucas Parry's funeral. But the meeting at the Ministry. It was something I just couldn't get out of. Goodness, I hope she understands.'

Miss Prydderch paused on the stairs to regain her breath and demonstrate her undeviating sincerity.

'This petrol business,' she said. 'One can't get about in the same way.'

'She will pick me up at one o'clock,' Cilydd said. 'That's our arrangement.'

'Will she bring Bedwyr?'

Miss Prydderch's face lit up at the prospect. Professor Gwilym had reached the top of the stairs. He looked down with a degree of disapproval at the confidential exchange between his visitors. He delayed interrupting their conversation as if he were making an effort to allow for their family relationship: Miss Sali Prydderch was the aunt of John Cilydd More's first wife. A doting aunt who had transferred something of her original affection for the mother to the child. He could hear Bedwyr's name recurring and it was sufficient to encourage him to exercise additional patience. When Sali Prydderch raised an apologetic hand for him to witness, he smiled and nodded his head with avuncular approval.

'The call-up business,' Miss Prydderch said. 'They must realise all your family responsibilities.'

In spite of himself Cilydd was blushing.

'Deferred,' he said.

He seemed to have difficulty in enunciating the word.

'I have an indefinite deferment,' he said. 'I wasn't sure about it. But my sister has pushed me into it really. She has registered the farm at Glanrafon in my name, And Cae Golau of course. But I was extremely dubious about it. My age group isn't likely to be called up at all. Thirty-nine next birthday. But I should have registered as a conscientious objector. I should have.'

Miss Prydderch frowned as she considered the problem.

'I'm not sure,' she said. 'What does Amy think?'

Professor Gwilym raised a hand in a manner that implied that it was time and not his patience that was giving out. They hurried up the stairs to join him.

'I've asked Hector Powell to join us. And the Bishop. And Sir Watkin Llewelyn. I thought if we could have a brief confab before they arrived. So that we are agreed on our general strategy. Our plan of campaign. Oh dear, these military metaphors. They seem so inappropriate somehow applied to our modest little aims. The important thing is that we stick together. "Stick" isn't the right word either. At a time like this even every day speech seems under attack. As if the hurricane brewing up will blow clichés as well as people to smithereens. Oh dear. Oh dear.'

Miss Prydderch placed a soothing hand on his sleeve. The top corridor was long and narrow. Cilydd was obliged to walk behind them. Sound reverberated from the marble floor to the high ceiling, prohibiting any speech that was not of a quasi-public nature. They were stopped in their tracks by the clatter of high-heeled shoes and a woman running to catch up with them and calling Professor Gwilym by name. All three turned around with the startled expression of people being accosted in a church. Light fell from a sequence of arched windows so that the figure of the fashionably dressed woman fleeing down the corridor was more visible in the shadow than in the radiant dazzle.

'Mademoiselle Fougère.'

The professor murmured the woman's name.

'Monique Fougère.'

Sali Prydderch's back stiffened. Professor Gwilym had a reputation as a ladies' man and this woman was calling his name with an urgency that proclaimed her right to his immediate attention.

'She lectures in French here,' Professor Gwilym said. 'A very cultivated woman.'

Mademoiselle Fougère pushed past Cilydd in her effort to reach the professor. He saw black hair parted in the middle, large spectacles, and skin blotched with emotional upheaval.

'They have broken through!'

Mademoiselle's hands rested on the professor's shoulders. Her thin body was shaking.

'They are bombing Paris!'

'A rumour,' Professor Gwilym said. 'Only a rumour. You know what they say about alarm and despondency.'

She swept aside his attempt at a jovial manner.

'I must talk to you,' she said. 'I must see you. Come to my room. Now, at once!'

'My dear Mademoiselle Monique . . .'

The professor smiled with the effort of pacifying her.

'I have a meeting. We have a meeting.'

'*Est-ce que vous avez un revolver?*'

'My dear Mademoiselle . . .'

The French lecturer glanced at Sali Prydderch and Cilydd in turn. She was ready to throw restraint and discretion to the four winds.

'This place is full of traitors,' she said. 'I say it. I see it. Three quarters of my students are conscientious objectors. Enemies of France. My own colleague is an enemy of France. *Mon dieu, quelle idée de venir ici!. . . Forcée a vivre parmi des gens dépourvus de toute culture . . . Ma douce France! Mon cher pays . . . dois-je en finir?*'

The professor was unable to provide any answers to her urgent questions. He could only ask Sali Prydderch and John Cilydd to excuse him while he escorted Mademoiselle Fougère back to her room. They watched their slow progress down the corridor. The woman's body was shaking as she wept openly. They saw the professor place his arm over her shoulders to comfort her.

'No sense of proportion!'

Miss Prydderch muttered disapprovingly.

'No restraint. Taking advantage of his goodwill. Gwilym is such a lover of France. She knows that. So she takes advantage of it.'

'What do we do?' Cilydd said. 'Wait for him here or go to his room?'

Miss Prydderch was decisive.

'Go to his room,' she said.

The green linoleum on the floor of the professor's study and the wide window set in carved stonework gave an impression of elegant austerity. The bookshelves, the table and chairs were made of the same light oak. Green tiles surrounded the fireplace. The rail of padded leather was too low to sit on. Miss Prydderch made her way to the window to admire the view: the harbour and slate quay in the foreground bathed in sunshine and beyond the long bay the outline of the limestone headland shimmering on the horizon.

'Her notion of culture is rigid to say the least.'

Sali Prydderch was still concerned with Mademoiselle Fougère. Part of her mind appeared divorced from her discourse, as if it had been detailed to compose a hypothetical picture of what the professor would be doing with the Frenchwoman in her room at any given moment.

'I had it out with her once about the Bretons,' Sali Prydderch said. 'The French treat their culture like dirt. At least the English leave us alone to our own cultural devices. I put that to her and she didn't like it one bit. What a time this is. What a terrible time.'

She looked around for somewhere to sit. The seminar chairs were too low to allow her to look through the window. Perched on the edge of the professor's desk she could still see the view.

'I've never been a one for this pan-Celtic business,' Sali Prydderch said. 'We're neo-Hebrews from nonconformity and we are or should be the direct British heirs of Classical Tradition. Hebraeo-Romano-Britons so to speak. And yet when I look at that view I sense the inward pull of Celtic magic. Do you know what I mean? It is important. It's like the language, if we lose it, we lose something precious and priceless, something of paramount importance. If we lose it, we become units, we become less than a genuine people. Isn't that what you feel?'

Cilydd looked as if he wanted to agree with her without sharing her enthusiasm. She was quick to latch on to his attitude.

'You are one of these "Wales neutral" people of course,' she said. 'I can't go as far as that. It's all right for the Irish maybe. They have an ocean to wrap around themselves. But what have we got? Nothing. I know it sounds ignoble. But we live in a state of

perpetual grace and favour. Principality means dependence in the
last resort. And what is this except the Last Resort?'

'Peace is our only chance.'

Cilydd sounded morose and stubborn.

'It's too late for that.'

Sali Prydderch flushed with sudden anger and distress.

'It's too late! It's much too late!'

'Once the world gives itself over to violence, it will never stop,'
Cilydd said. 'And what chance will we have then? A defenceless
minority clinging on to the very fringe of existence. We'll count for
nothing. Unless we make the effort to stand on our own feet, we'll
be swept away!'

He stopped speaking abruptly when he caught himself making
angry gestures. Miss Prydderch HMI had gone pale as she considered her own outburst. In this confrontation he was Bedwyr's
father and she was his great-aunt. She was in the act of shouting
down the man Enid had loved so much: and had Enid been alive in
this room at this moment it would have been his sullen and
uncompromising outlook she would have shared, not her aunt's: it
would have been a lifetime of love that her niece would have spilt
in this man's defence, all the love that she had lavished on her as
long as she lived. Even if this was a time of the breaking of nations,
they were both better advised to keep silent. Cilydd looked at the
bookshelves. She looked at the view.

When he opened the door, the professor was too absorbed in his
own disquiet to notice the depth of the silence.

'The Bishop can't come,' he said. 'Or more exactly, the Bishop
won't come. Or even more exactly the Archbishop won't let him:
i.e. advises him not to come. At a time like this, wiser not to get
involved with any schemes sponsored by notorious Welsh
nationalists. This is a nation divided.'

Professor Gwilym shrugged in Gallic fashion and held out both
hands palm outwards.

'And what are we doing?' he said. 'Planning a news sheet, a mere
monthly news letter for our own young people in the armed
forces.'

He made a signal to anticipate an objection from Cilydd.

136

'Or any of our young people sent, driven, scattered abroad, dispersed by the emergency, shall we say?'

'What did you do with Mademoiselle Fougère?'

Miss Prydderch smiled sweetly as she asked the question as if to differentiate between polite concern and vulgar curiosity. The professor frowned like a man exercising his powers of recall. He had so much weightier things on his mind than a spinster's temporary loss of self-control.

'Do?' he said. 'I managed to soothe her with honeyed words.'

He slumped into the swivel chair behind his desk and adopted a pose of gloomy thoughtfulness that could have suited a pre-Raphaelite portrait of some great captain facing the prospect of defeat.

'Is this one of those terrible turning points in history?' the professor said. 'One of those cataclysmic upheavals we are able to read about so calmly in our history books. Is that what we are living through?'

Neither Cilydd nor Sali Prydderch could provide him with an answer. He sat up, suddenly resolute and prepared to give a lead. He let his fist fall on the desk with a muted thud.

'Certain things we shall have to do,' he said. 'This war may be repugnant to our nonconformist pacifist tradition, as modern warfare is repugnant to any person of sensibility in this day and age. What I'm saying is we must act! We must see to our defences – you see the language I am using?'

He smiled at them both to make them appreciate the ambiguity of his phrases.

'We are called upon, called up, conscripted, compelled, summoned to the defence of England and her empire. That is what it amounts to. Let them call it the defence of freedom and democracy if it makes them feel better. But the point is, surely these large phrases, these generous concepts, entitle us also to defend and safeguard the culture and language that gives us our own national identity. Do you take my point?'

He leaned forward with the resolution of the experienced committee man determined to carry the meeting with him however difficult the exposition of his point of view.

'We must use their terminology in our own defence. This we

must agree on. And we must be united as we do it. All shades of opinion. We must not allow political or sectarian divisions to blind us to this absolute necessity. Otherwise everything we treasure, all we have in this world will fall into the capacious coffers of the English exchequer as unclaimed inheritance, as has been allowed to happen so many times, so many times in the past.'

'Exactly.'

Miss Prydderch HMI demonstrated her complete agreement. Her eyes shone with admiration for the professor. Whatever his shortcomings and weaknesses, his powers of exposition and expression had her total support. He was in earnest and he was disinterested. He exercised his taste for stylish language as a healing function: and for this alone she could give him total allegiance. John Cilydd on the other hand had still to be convinced. Professor Gwilym made a concentrated assault in his direction.

'We have our language to persuade us, John Cilydd. *Yr iaith. Yr iaith.* By the mere act of being its practitioners, we make submission to its power. And this power speaks to us in our inward being and in our inmost heart. And what I hear it say at this terrible moment in time is that we should not allow this European crisis to divide us. Even in the execution of a great war in which we will suffer more than we shall act, it demands our devotion. The words of our language remain miraculous because they create a unity where there would otherwise be nothing but dissent and discord.'

Footsteps and voices were reverberating boisterously in the corridor. Other members of the committee were approaching in their own good time. The professor stopped to listen and identify the newcomers.

'Sir Watkin,' he said. 'Hector Powell. And I think Judge Bryn Morgan. Excellent. Now, John Cilydd, my dear fellow, are we agreed?'

Cilydd permitted himself a quiet smile.

'You've convinced me,' he said. 'At least for the time being. And what other time is there?'

All three appeared in cheerful accord when the door opened.

Hans Benek paused by the sagging gate to observe the scene at the bottom of the meadow. Three young men stripped to the waist were toiling in a ditch intended to save the meadows from the encroaching scrub. Beyond the young brushwood lay a marsh streaked with rusty reds and dark greens. A sluggish stream snaked through the reeds. There were yellow iris in flower. Vapour rose from stagnant pools in the rays of the morning sun. Benek's grey shirt dangled outside his trousers. He clutched a sketchbook but he seemed to have no intention of opening it. Behind him Amy and her two little boys put down the picnic basket. Amy had to restrain Gwydion as he struggled to squeeze himself between the standing stone and the gate in order to roll about in the flood of glossy green hay.

'The conscientious objectors,' Amy said. 'They look just like white slaves, don't they? My goodness, Uncle Simon is enjoying himself.'

The tenant of Ponciau was striding stiffly about, pointing with a long stick, apparently as unrelenting as an overseer of slaves in some silent film. A period of prolonged agricultural depression was coming to an end. For the first time since the last war a third of Ponciau fields was under the plough. This same free labour had finished planting two acres of field potatoes. Now there was time for ditching, for reclaiming land, restoring wild hedgerows, repairing and white-washing outbuildings. One of the young men in the ditch straightened his back and shaded his eyes to make out the figures at the top gate. Uncle Simon turned himself when he saw this. He raised his stick in a gesture that was more a summons than a greeting.

'That man wanted me to work for him,' Hans said.

He grinned at Amy.

'I have work, I tell him. I paint.'

Hans gave a wristy flourish with his right hand.

'I am degenerate artist. I do not think he understood.'

The path wound upwards between two overgrown hedges. It was made narrow by grass and wild flowers, mostly cow-parsley, campion and vetch, growing the length of an arm from either bank. They walked in single file shaded by hedgerows but with the sun hot on their backs. A lark's song trilled high in the sky above them. Amy told the little boys to breathe deeply and tell her what they could smell. Bedwyr said, 'buttercups', Gwydion said, 'bees'. They ran ahead skirting a patch of nettles thrusting higher than the soft grass. 'Bluebells,' Amy called out. 'Can't you smell them? Bluebells.'

She sounded as young as they were. In the bright sunlight the slope and the wood that surmounted it stood out with magical clarity. Like unleashed puppy dogs, Bedwyr and Gwydion scampered towards the trees. They both yelled as they trampled among the bluebells but the noise they made was softer than the piercing birdsong that surrounded them. There were so many bluebells and their feet were so small, their diagonal passage made no difference to the drift of colour that saturated the slope. Unsmudged blue and green mingled miraculously without merging; like everything else on this May morning they proclaimed a joy of rebirth.

'There you are, degenerate artist!'

Amy put down the picnic basket and stretched out her arm, making Hans a gift of the landscape. She was as proud of the pale gorse blooms, the gold of the straggling bushes of broom, of the tender edible brown of the myriad leaves that had settled on the single oak tree on the slope, as if she had invented them; or at least, as if they were her own private property, her domain, her renewed inheritance in which she had an inalienable right to rejoice. With her arm still outstretched she looked at Hans and waited for an appropriate response. She was willing to share with him the wonder of a corner of Coed Ponciau that she particularly loved. He tugged at the tail of his shirt to wipe the sweat off his brow. There was a black stubble on his chin. He had not shaved for two or three days. It disconcerted her to see him screw up his eyes and shake his head.

'What's the matter?'

'Too much green,' he said. 'Too much green.'

'What do you mean, "too much"?'

Amy was indignant. How could a painter not respond as she responded to so much loveliness?

'Go back to the ditch,' Amy said. 'You'd be better off in the mud.'

Hans sank to his knees and rolled his thin body into the shade of a spray of golden broom. He raised his hands on either side of his eye sockets to black out an excess of light.

'Colour is a cage,' he said.

Amy frowned. She listened moodily to the voices of her children playing in the wood. The sound intensified the enchantment of the place. Hans had nothing to say to children. He looked at them as if they were a rival species. Once he had asked her when they were going to learn English and that had seemed the limit of his interest. It was also possible that he considered her incapable of comprehending the delicate perceptions with which his mind was perpetually engaged. He was muttering now like an internal combustion engine refusing to start.

'We see,' Hans said. 'I see. I want you to see, through bars of colour.'

He was so pleased to have completed the sentence that a quiet smile illuminated his thin sallow face. His teeth shone conspicuously amid the stubble and the shade of the broom.

'But I don't.'

Amy was emphatic. Hans screwed up his features for a renewed attempt to break through the barrier of language and disparate experience.

'Inside nature,' he said. 'I find my way there. I work there. The force in the rock. The feel of the stream. The touch of the leaf.'

His urge to communicate gave out. He lay on his back and studied the light through his fingers. Bees flew sideways as they worked among the flowers. The sound they made wove an atmosphere of quiet serenity. Amy's gaze followed the shallow shadow the broom bush threw across the slope.

'I don't understand your pictures,' she said. 'You may as well know it.'

'Understand?'

Hans turned his hand in order to watch the filtered light move across his skin. He repeated the word 'understand' as if to show his contempt for it. Amy would not allow her difficulties to be summarily brushed aside.

'I suppose you think we are all ignorant around here,' she said. 'Because we don't understand your pictures.'

She knelt on the far side of the picnic basket.

'All that splashing and slashing of colour,' she said. 'I don't understand it. Tell me. I want to know. Is it because you find the world so awful that you distort so much?'

Hans wriggled in the shade of the bush. His manner implied that her question touched on problems that were far too complex for his inadequate English to deal with.

'When colours are splashed all over the place . . .'

Amy sounded more confident.

'It suggests the violence of the spoilt child. It is childish, isn't it? Or childlike. Do you know the difference? Childish and childlike. It looks as if you had something inside you that wanted to explode. Is that right?'

He stared at her calmly until she began to blush.

'I ask you a serious question,' she said. 'About your art. You should know what you are doing, surely. You should be able to explain to some extent anyway.'

'Come down here and I will show you,' Hans said.

There was no mistaking his suggestion. Amy lifted her head to oblige him to take notice of the children shouting in the wood.

'I paint you,' he said. 'My colour will overcome fear. I paint you naked. And behind you red and gold circles. And a red sun. A world subdued by the female form.'

With his thin hands he sketched voluptuous strokes. His gestures left her more embarrassed than amused. He began to crawl towards her.

'You just stay where you are,' Amy said.

From the wood the children's voices merged with the more insistent warble of the skylarks. The day was still in perfect balance between earth and sky. He watched her intently as she absorbed the warmth of the sun.

'You know "*carpe diem*",' he said.

'Just about.'

Her sarcasm went undetected.

'"*Carpe diem quam minimum credula postero*," Hans said. 'There will be no tomorrow. Believe that.'

Amy stared at his foreign gestures with disapproval.

'It is happening. The Fascists will conquer Europe. Then they will come here. This little Welsh world. Easy to break. Like a green eggshell.'

Amy's fists were clenched.

'I'll fight them,' she said. 'I can tell you that much. Even if I have to do it by myself.'

Hans stretched his arms eagerly towards her.

'I wish to feel that strength,' he said. 'I want to feel it from the inside. It is what matters. It is what will be left. The life source. A source of Life. A life source is a colour source. I need you. Do you understand what I am saying. I worship colour. I worship you.'

He was staring at her with a degree of devotion that made her uncomfortable.

'You don't know me at all,' Amy said. 'You don't know anything about me.'

Hans began to shiver as if he had been cut off from the warmth of the sun.

'They will come here,' he said. 'Where will I hide? I need a quick poison. When they come, I swallow it.'

'It's no use being afraid,' Amy said. 'That's no use at all.'

Hans looked at her intently and raised a clenched fist.

'It is happening,' he said. 'But you are there. You let me worship you.'

'Don't talk such rubbish,' Amy said.

His smile was at its most exposed and wolfish.

'You want to be worshipped,' he said. 'And you want to be mastered. He does not do this for you. In the way you want. I could. I could do.'

Hans patted himself comfortably on the chest. Amy's cheeks were burning.

'You talk about snakes in the grass,' she said. 'That is exactly

143

what you are. You are ready to betray your benefactor. At a time like this.'

'I only face the truth,' Hans said. 'You are not right for each other. I see that.'

'You see nothing of the sort,' Amy said. 'You see just what you want to see. Like a greedy snake.'

He took her anger lightly, making crawling motions without moving any closer to her.

'What about Erika?' Amy said.

He began to shake with laughter.

'What is so funny? I wish you'd stop laughing. You look so stupid.'

He made an effort to sober himself up.

'You are right,' he said. 'There is no time to waste. You are what you are. I am what I am. We are threatened as the world is threatened. But here, at this moment, the secret of the form lies in the space between us.'

Amy was still cross: but her curiosity was roused.

'What secret?' she said. 'What form?'

Hans reached across to touch her ear. She pulled her head away like a child in danger of being stung.

'With my brush, maybe with my pencil, I possess your ear,' Hans said. 'A hundred times perhaps if there is time. I need every day that is left to possess it, so that I may explore it. I need more. From what is between us, from what you are and what I see and what I feel, there grow shapes, there grow visions, there grow colours and harmonies. You understand. In one way or another, we are together. And we make life together. Like one man and one woman in a garden. And the world begins again. We do not destroy. We create.'

He smiled with triumph at the success of his exposition. He had driven Amy into thoughtful silence. When she looked up from the ground and gazed at him she seemed to be seeing him in a new light. He was encouraged to move closer and to touch her. A new sound from below them made her push away his eager hands.

'For goodness sake,' she said. 'Can't you see there's somebody coming.'

144

Beyond Hans's shoulder she could see a policeman raising his bicycle over the low stile across the path at the bottom of the slope. The machine hung momentarily in the sky. Beyond it across the valley she could see sheep with their bulky lambs grazing in the shade between the rock outcrops on the hillside. The policeman's deliberate actions seemed to bring everything closer. Soon it would be time to dip the sheep before shearing. The policeman would need to find his way to every sheep-dip however inaccessible: no war or state of emergency could alter the unhurried inevitability of the seasons, and the policeman's movements were made to match. Once the bicycle was over, he turned to Uncle Simon who was following him. Amy and Hans stood up on the slope a respectable distance apart.

'I don't know what they want,' Amy said.

She kept her voice down. Hans strained to hear what she was saying.

'He can't force you to work in the ditching,' Amy said. 'If that's what he's after.'

Uncle Simon had raised his arm. His long-sleeved vest was visible under his rolled-up shirt sleeve. His fustian working trousers were held up by both belt and braces. Amy turned her head to call at the boys by their separate names. It was appropriate that Uncle Simon and the policeman should know she had the children in her care. They appeared on the fringe of the trees. They stood there, their legs apart, like a pair of startled fawns. They saw their great-uncle scramble up the slope ahead of the policeman. This in itself was a wonder. He seemed to have lost his usual stiffness in his eagerness to speak to their mother and Mr Benek, the artist. They heard the peremptory nervousness in his voice as he addressed their mother in Welsh so that Benek would not understand what he was saying.

'It's bad,' Uncle Simon said. 'The Germans are burning their way through France. Fire and slaughter. Nothing can stop them. As for this one, he's got to be locked up. He's a spy. He walks in the night.'

'He's not a spy,' Amy said. 'That's utter rubbish. He's a refugee.'

'They've all got to go in,' Uncle Simon said. 'The government says so.'

The pronouncement gave him pleasure. It allowed him to shift his stance and address Hans with unconcealed loathing in rudimentary English.

'You German,' he said. 'In France, German soldiers dropping from sky dressed like nuns. You go with policeman.'

Amy spoke in Welsh to appeal directly to Simon Lloyd's sense of proportion.

'You know it's nonsense,' she said. 'War propaganda. It was the same last time, for heaven's sake. Cutting off nuns' hands and dropping little children in boiling water. Use your common sense, Uncle Simon.'

He was not prepared to take such an open rebuke from his nephew's second wife.

'Oh, nonsense, is it? Nonsense you say. And what about your great movement against conscription? Where are your tens and hundreds of young Welshmen following Arthur and refusing to submit to the Saxon yoke?'

His fixed grin of triumph made her thoroughly uncomfortable. He turned to urge the policeman up the slope. His voice reverberated across the valley.

'Come on Pritchard! This is your man!'

Hans watched the steady ascent of the policeman with increasing alarm.

'The police,' he said. 'What does he want?'

Amy shut her lips tightly. Uncle Simon smiled as he spoke.

'You,' he said. 'Enemy alien. 18b. They lock you up.'

Hans slipped as he retreated backwards up the slope. The soles of his urban-looking shoes were worn smooth and streaked with green sap. Amy could see his mouth hang open and the blood drain from his narrow face. He lay on his back in the attitude of a paralysed insect that would never regain the use of its legs. The scent of bluebells crushed under his body assailed their nostrils. The policeman greeted Amy politely.

'Good morning, Mrs More,' he said. 'It's a lovely day.'

The sound of the policeman's voice in a language he could not understand galvanised Hans. He scrambled with desperate speed through the bluebells. He shot past the children. They were ready

146

to turn and chase after him until they heard their mother call out their names. The policeman and Uncle Simon had no hope of catching up with him. The policeman looked at Hans's sketchbook on the grass but did not pick it up. Uncle Simon's eyes shone with an inspiration as he grasped the policeman's sleeve.

'Look, Pritchard,' he said. 'This is a hunt. You hang on a minute and I'll go back to the house and pick up my twelve bore.'

PC Pritchard tugged thoughtfully at his moustache. The situation was without precedent. He was a heavy man with plump cheeks. Only his eyes darting about suggested his mind was capable of being more agile than his feet. Out of apparent respect for Amy he refrained from picking up the sketchbook to examine its contents.

'It's our only chance,' Uncle Simon said.

His confidence in his own wisdom was growing.

'A gun will bring him in – or bring him down. He is a spy. He is guilty. And so he runs. We know our duty.'

'Simon Lloyd.'

Amy's voice was firm and merciless. The policeman was very ready to give her his close attention.

'Do you want to make a fool of yourself in front of the whole country? Gun indeed. Gun! That creature is as harmless as a baby. Anybody with an atom of sense can see that. He is a Jewish refugee. He is an artist. He is very frightened. He has more to fear from the enemy than any of us. Don't you see that?'

PC Pritchard was glad to agree with her. Uncle Simon took a few steps up the slope as if to show he was ready to undertake the pursuit alone.

'Constable Pritchard,' Amy said. 'My husband will vouch for Mr Benek. He will vouch for his innocence and he will bring him to the police station at Pendraw, before six o'clock this evening. In the meantime the children and I will deal with him. He is completely harmless.'

The policeman looked thoughtful.

'Mr More knows the law,' he said. 'He knows it back to front. I'll say that for him.'

'I will find him,' Amy said. 'Calm him down. Give him something to eat. I could bring him in myself if it came to that.'

PC Pritchard nodded and fingered the strap of his helmet.

'It's going to be hot,' he said. 'It doesn't really agree with me.'

The strap like the rest of his uniform was too tight. He ventured to take the helmet off and mop up the beads of sweat on his pale forehead with a red cotton handkerchief decorated with white polka dots. Uncle Simon looked down on his relaxed behaviour with increasing disapproval.

'I'll sit down if you don't mind Mrs More,' PC Pritchard said. 'I've got this thing they call a heart murmur. I don't expect I'll have to go. It's not a question of going this time though, is it? It looks as if they are on their way here. The sky is thick with them.'

He gazed across the valley like a spectator waiting for a game to start. He was ready to enjoy a short rest.

'It looks black,' he said. 'And on a day like this. Goodness knows what we'll all have to go through. No bells on Sunday from now on. That's definite. I suppose you've heard that?'

Uncle Simon's patience gave out.

'You can't sit there Pritchard,' he said. 'The whole country is in danger. Every second counts. I'm going to get my gun.'

Uncle Simon stumped off down the hill. Amy made no attempt to call him back. PC Pritchard shook his head.

'I said to my wife this morning,' he said. 'Just as we were getting up. "Morfydd," I said. "I fell asleep in one war and now I'm waking up in another."'

Amy knelt to open her picnic basket. She smiled in response to the policeman's droll remark before offering him a drink from the thermos flask.

'Very nice,' he said. 'We've got to make the best of it. You will bring the stranger to the police station, Mrs More. That's the best way we'll do it.'

10

THE WHOLE COMPARTMENT SHUDDERED AS THE WHEELS OF THE underground train clanked and groaned to a halt. The silence was deep and disconcerting. Passengers standing in the central aisle were glued together with apprehension and the taut effort of listening. A burly strap-hanger in a bowler hat wearing an ARP armband stared down at Amy and Margot, a smile sequestered in the corners of his mouth under the aegis of a pencil-line moustache. His steel helmet hung by its strap from his shoulder. He was prepared to dispense comfort and reassurance in the most chivalrous and knowledgeable manner possible. In a train so deep underground there could be no danger from a bomb, even if an air-raid had started, which was unlikely. His smile when it broke would suggest that, at the least, wartime embellished hum-drum routines with the aura of high adventure.

'Poor old Het.'

Margot muttered to herself. In the uneasy quiet it was blurted out like an unscheduled prayer during a memorial service. Amy removed her glove to grasp Margot's hand and bring her some comfort. The strap-hanger raised his eyebrows and leaned more closely over them as though he were entitled to listen in on what they had to say.

'I was thinking of her claustrophobia.'

Margot turned to whisper urgently with her face close to Amy's.

'This kind of thing used to worry her to death.'

Amy squeezed Margot's hand. She gazed straight past the strap-hanger's helmet to study as much as she could see of the coloured diagram of the Piccadilly Line. There were exhortations and advertisements to which she could attach a degree of attention during the unaccountable hiatus. Further down the compartment Erika von Tornago had found a perch where, with her elbow tucked into her ribs, she could read her tiny volume of the letters of Madame de Sevigne. She was wearing a blue cotton overall over her office clothes.

'She was buried alive,' Margot said.

She shut her eyes as she contemplated the horror.

'She was alive when they dragged her out. That's what I find so terrible.'

The strap-hanger was listening to her as intently as Amy. Accounts of casualties were common property; out of catalogues of incidents there were lessons to be learned. The engine started up again and his body swayed in front of them. The train crawled forward. The passengers responded with familiar quips.

'Off we go again!'

The strap-hanger seized the opportunity to smile at Amy and speak to her.

'You can't hit a moving target underground,' he said. 'Now that's a fact.'

Snatches of old jokes, grumbles and even songs caused a wave of long-suffering laughter to sweep through the compartment. Margot was still thinking of Hetty.

'She was my responsibility,' she said. 'She was an American after all. I shouldn't have let her go. But she insisted. She was meeting this cousin. What could I do? I couldn't stop her could I?'

Amy squeezed her hand again.

'Of course you couldn't,' she said.

'She got religious you know.'

Margot's eyebrows raised as she recorded a surprising fact it was as well for Amy to learn.

'I don't know where she got it from, but she got it all right. And it wasn't just fear and worry. And she was all out for the war effort. Absolutely all out. Never saw anything like it really. But there you are. That was Het all over. Ready to starve herself. Giving her rations away. All out or nothing.'

She tugged her hand out of Amy's grasp so that she could steady herself by clasping her hands together in her lap. The shunting motions of the train disjointed her thinking. The engine would lurch forward and grind to another halt. The strap-hanger apologised for bumping into Amy's knee. He looked hurt when Amy ignored him to concentrate on the things Margot was trying to say. They were important but often inaudible. A lock of hair

150

hung over her right eye. Her beret looked as if it was ready to slip off.

'We've just got to win, she would say. Goodness knows how, when or why. But we've got to do it. And that means we've got to believe in miracles. Your John Cilydd wouldn't agree with all that, would he?'

Margot shifted her head to take notice of Amy's reaction.

'She was quite gone on him,' Margot said. 'I used to wonder why. No offence, but they were so utterly different. But she'd caught a glimpse of something. Genius she called it. And he used to talk to her for hours on end. God knows what about. People are mysterious aren't they? I think so anyway. I can't make head or tail of them half the time.'

It was as much of an effort for Amy to adjust herself to Margot's manner as to any of the exigencies of war-time London. The surface of enthusiasm, of eager politeness, even the bouts of asthma had, like the bloom of youth, the petal complexion, gone for ever. Hetty's death in the air-raid had narrowed her face, giving her jaw-bone a sharp and permanent prominence. The only familiar features were the frankness and the residue of goodwill: the urge towards good works; the unquenchable concern for others. She asked about John Cilydd.

'What's he up to? How's he managing?'

Deep in the underground, reality was the condition of being hemmed in by sequences of obstacles that at any moment could become unsurmountable. Margot's thin voice was like a polite request for news from another country. Amy was eager to tell Margot about her husband.

'He's being driven further and further into himself,' she said. 'I don't know what I can do about it.'

It was Margot's turn to offer Amy comfort. She could only do so by listening more intently.

'He thinks people are using words like "traitor" and "coward". Not that they would dare do that in my hearing. Bedwyr came home crying from school. Boys in the playground saying his father was a German spy. That sort of thing. He's taken to working in the office at night, then spending the daytime on the farm. It's as if he can't bear to be in contact with people. I try to impress on him that it doesn't matter what other people think, so long as he is at peace with himself. He just looks at me like an injured animal and says nothing.'

'Does he know about you and Pen?'

Margot's question was so blunt and forthright, Amy blushed to the roots of her hair. In spite of herself she glanced at the strap-hanger standing over them to see if he had overheard the question. The train was crawling forward again. Abruptly the strap-hanger turned his head to avoid Amy's gaze. At a moment when she was least prepared for it, she had to find an argument to counter Margot's demand for total honesty.

'He had his share of suffering in the first war,' Amy said. 'I have to remember that.'

This argument made no impression on Margot.

'Everyone has to suffer,' she said. 'In one way or another.'

'He was no more than a boy,' Amy said. 'He was under age. He shouldn't have been there. It was terrible in the trenches.'

Margot examined the proposition and seemed to find it wanting.

'That was then,' she said. 'This is now.'

'How could I tell him?'

Amy's voice rose in indignation. She no longer seemed to care who was listening.

'Pen is dead. He chose to die. In a way everything to do with him was an accident. John Cilydd is the boy's father in every sense that matters. Why should I give him additional pain? Especially at a time like this. He's down enough as it is, for goodness sake, Margot. What are you thinking?'

'You may well be right,' Margot said.

The train was crawling into Knightsbridge station. Amy placed her hand on Margot's arm to prevent her getting to her feet.

'What are you thinking?' Amy said. 'I want to know.'

'Just that some day perhaps, he'll have to know. And then again perhaps he won't.'

Amy wasn't satisfied. She shook Margot's arm.

'Well if he had to know,' Margot said, 'it would be better if it came from you. That's what I was thinking.'

Erika was at the sliding doors peering through the lozenge of unprotected glass to verify the name of the station. Under the concave protection of a vast poster of warships in battle order, a schoolgirl and a little boy, brother and sister, were staking out an area where the rest of the family could join them after work. With her platform ticket still between her teeth, the girl was lining up suitcases to mark the boundary of their territory. The little boy wore wellingtons and a blue gaberdine raincoat, both sizes too big for him. After an enforced silence, Erika was eager to speak to both Amy and Margot. On the moving staircase there were more people coming down than going up. These were carrying suitcases and bedding. But for the worn expressions on their faces they could have been going on holiday. At the barrier there were more people lined up for shelter for the night. Erika had to express her admiration.

'There it is,' she said. 'There you have it.'

'Have what?' Amy said.

'The hope of victory. I see no other.'

Erika was breathless with the ideas she wanted to express. Her friends were impatient and longing to get home.

'The French and the Italians will never learn how to do it. The Germans will only do it so long as someone yells at them. But here, your people do it of their own record. The ultimate weapon – the queue! It is not sheeplike. It is inner discipline, that is what it is. And where does it come from? The climate perhaps. I do not think so. I say it is the combination of the dregs of puritanism, of piety and justice and a lasting-for-ever patriotism. Do you know what I mean?'

'Oh come on,' Margot said. 'Do get a move on!'

Above ground the setting sun had broken through the cloud cover. There was a fleeting exaltation to be gained by breathing the sharp air. Icicles hanging from the exposed floorboards of a wrecked house were frozen evidence of fire-fighting the previous night. The evening light invested the quiet of the untidy streets with an unearthly beauty. Here the living and the dead could converse more frequently and more fluently than ever before. The ornate facade of a red-brick building reserved for the rich who needed to live near the centre of power had collapsed into a heap of rubble. It had sunk into its own shadow. The whole block was deserted as though inside perpetual night had already fallen. In the broken windows across the square curtains hung out like drab flags of surrender left by occupants who were dead or gone. Above the stark chimney-pots an ungainly barrage balloon was being transformed into a giant goldfish in the last pink rays of sunlight. The cold imposed an ominous silence as the three women hurried towards the shelter of Culpepper Place. Amy paused to look up at the barrage balloon, Margot stamped her feet. The sound rang along the pavement.

'Come on!' she said. 'My feet are like two blocks of ice.'

'I think one of my cousins will be on his way tonight to drop some of his Fuhrer's visiting cards,' Erika said.

Amy paused to listen to her. She looked up at the barrage balloon. The cold seemed to tilt the earth towards a vast indifferent sky, imposing stillness and silence on the city.

'My whole family inside the Greater German Reich,' Erika said. 'My sister in Berlin. And my best friend Lieselotte. Did I tell you about Lieselotte-too-good-to-be-true. Lieselotte the Paragon. My best friend at school. I was always the naughty one. I adored her. She will be with the Red Cross in Berlin. Ever faithful, ever sure. And I am here. Left out. Shut out. Outside Festung Europa. Shall I tell you something, Amy? But for you I would be a ghost.'

Margot stamped her feet on the pavement. Her voice echoed down the deserted street.

'Come on, you two,' she said. 'My feet are like two blocks of ice.'

~ ii ~

The strangers in the seaside town looked like refugees from the weather rather than the war. A chill wind cut into the streets from the sea. When it slackened the rain would fall. An urge to discover convenient and agreeable shelter seemed to govern a pattern of crowd movement that would otherwise be random and aimless. John Cilydd forged ahead up the High Street towards the town clock. His sister had difficulty in keeping up with him and he was

154

not inclined to wait for her; and yet even the way in which they held on to their dark hats proclaimed an umbilical relationship. There were soldiers everywhere. Nanw paused for breath and saw pale youths in khaki calling out to each other across the street. It was a forlorn sound however hard they tried to make it challenging and cheerful. They were even more at a loss than she would have been without her brother to follow. He knew the place so much better than she did. It was here at Aber he had found his first wife: and, by extension his second. There were few undergraduates around now to flaunt their college scarves. So many soldiers at a loss what to do next. They had time on their hands, but few ways of spending it. Gaping at the childlike face of a soldier trying to light a wet cigarette, Nanw bumped against a farmer who stood as solid as a bollard on the edge of the pavement.

He smelt of the cattle mart. He ignored the impact and Nanw's murmured apology. He was spellbound by the presence of so many women in damp fur coats and conspicuously bedecked with a dazzling array of jewels and forms of glittering adornment he had never seen before. These were well-to-do people from the cities who had fled from the bombing. They were on the look out for shops and cafés and hotels they had not frequented before. Only by close observation could a hill-farmer keep abreast of the transformations taking place in the world around him. Standards of human behaviour were shifting. These rich women were inclined to shriek with laughter for no apparent reason except to draw attention to themselves. Within his arm's length two women in fur stopped to greet each other effusively. He saw first one and then the other strip off a glove and raise a white hand to display finger nails painted the same shade of deep purple. He heard them shriek out "snap" at each other. This brief encounter and the stationary bulk of the farmer completely blocked Nanw's progress. She saw the two women claw-shape their fingers at each other in mock attack. Their faces were distorted with enjoyment. The farmer was overcome with the desire to join in the fun. He offered to capture their hands in the crook of his ash stick. In abrupt unison the merry expressions on the womens' plump faces turned to outrage and hostility. As they stalked away one of them elbowed Nanw off

155

the pavement. She called out her brother's name. She dashed after him as she saw him, head down, turn into a side street on the right of the town clock. Nanw caught up with Cilydd wedged in the narrow doorway of a crowded café, scanning the interior with anxious eyes.

'I can't see her in there,' he said. 'Can you?'

Nanw nudged at his side. The rain was beginning to fall.

'Let's get inside,' she said.

'It's so full.'

Cilydd was unwilling to move.

'Perhaps she's gone somewhere else. Perhaps she couldn't get in. The place is so packed.'

'No, it isn't.'

Nanw had seen two vacant places at a small table. Other people had arrived behind her, wanting to get in. She gave Cilydd a determined shove. Even as they edged towards the back of the crowded room, he continued to look around for a glimpse of his wife hidden among so many strange faces. The cacophony of loud voices disturbed him. He murmured something about the Tower of Babel which his sister failed to hear. A pair of diminutive waitresses apparently chosen for their size darted between orders like game dogs in a thicket. There were two places against the long window right at the back of the café. Nanw sighed with relief as she sat down.

The small table already had a solitary occupant. A tall woman knitting a scarf stooped over a volume of the Home University Library open on the table where her plate of beans on toast had been. Her pot of tea confirmed her unobtrusive place in the corner between the window and an angle in the wall. She was absorbed in her reading and knitting. The hubbub in the café did nothing to disturb her concentration. She did not take in Nanw and Cilydd's presence until one of the small waitresses leaned over the table to take their order. The fretted white band around the waitress's hair was askew and her face gleamed with sweat. Her pencil hovered in circles above her pad as she recited in hurried monotone the limited choice available. Nanw strained to catch the items. The tall woman's knitting needles paused and a slow smile broke on her pale face as she restrained herself from offering advice. She had her own request to make once Cilydd and Nanw had decided what they would eat. She knitted more slowly and smiled at Cilydd in particular. When he recognised her the smile would show that she was a woman prepared to transform any petty privation into a source of philosophical amusement. In the meantime her knitting spelt out a pattern of goodwill.

'I'm sure you don't remember me.'

She spoke in a low voice that successfully combined shyness and a need to be noticed. Her pale blue eyes looked up and down from the pages of her book to the faces of Nanw and John Cilydd. As she leaned further forward her beak-like nose shadowed a rapid flow of speech issuing from a wide mouth.

'Of course, I know you, Mr More. And I can guess this is your sister. You look so alike if I may say so. I'm Mabli Herbert, I was here in college with Amy and dear Enid. All those years ago.'

Outside in the lane a sudden gust of wind overturned a dustbin. In an hysterical tattoo the zinc lid rattled out of sight.

'I'm down specially to hear you,' Mabli Herbert said. 'Down from the hills. A rare privilege. And to think I have the pleasure of sitting at the same table . . . You don't mind, do you?'

She closed her book quickly when she saw Nanw was looking at it. 'Philosophy,' she said. 'My WEA class. It's the one chance in the week I have to get out. Mrs Lloyd Jenkins picks me up in her little Austin Seven. I can just squeeze into it, if I bend double. But it's not a long journey. Just down to the Central School. We meet in the cookery classroom. At least it's warm there. But the lighting isn't very good.'

She smiled wistfully at Cilydd.

'I don't think you remember me,' she said. 'But why should you? Life takes charge of us, doesn't it? Like an ever rolling stream and so on. I was the one that pitched a folding stool over the hole on the first green of the golf course and started to paint the view.'

'Of course!'

Cilydd strugged to look intelligent as he ruffled through his memory like a lawyer taking a hurried view of the files of a forgotten case.

'Not that it did much good,' Mabli Herbert said. 'But I look

157

back on it as something of a high point in my not so brilliant career. At least I tried to make a stand, or should I say a sit. I suppose I'm what you could call a failed teacher. I tried it and failed. I couldn't keep order. I suppose my height had something to do with it. Children always making jokes about ladders and stilts and so on. My mother and I live with my uncle Lodwig. Lodwig Herbert. "The old Canon", as they call him around here. The largest vicarage in the smallest parish in the diocese. But that's enough about me. I can't wait to see Amy.'

She shivered with pleasurable anticipation and leaned over the table to smile specifically at Nanw, assuming that Amy was a figure of exciting dimensions in her existence also.

'We were so innocent, weren't we?'

Mabli was eager to include Cilydd and Nanw in her recollections.

'And we meant well,' she said. 'We really did. We were going to make a better world and it seemed such a straightforward task. We had our heroes like John Cilydd More and Val Gwyn to show us the way. Students can't get along without heroes. Especially female ones. Students I mean. Wales seemed ripe for remaking in those days. And now look where we've got to. When I think of all that terrible slaughter and suffering on the Russian Front. I can't sleep at night. I just can't.'

She resumed her knitting at an increased speed. She frowned at the debris spilt from the dustbin across the lane. The needles clicked in a bout of industry that seemed a substitute for going out in the rain and clearing the mess up. The little waitress arrived with two plates of chips and fried spam and a pot of tea for two. Cilydd looked down at his plate with obvious distaste. In a quiet voice Nanw urged him to eat. She had to show a concern for his well-being. He had a poetry reading, an illustrated lecture to deliver. He had unconventional points of view to put across with delicacy and sophistication. There would be academics in the audience as well as ordinary WEA members.

Mabli Herbert observed brother and sister eating. They looked bound by the closest ties, abroad in the cold wilderness of war time in a hostile environment with little else except each other to rely on. The café was stuffed with strangers, who had no idea that this was an important poet, a national winner. Mabli checked her knitting and stretched her neck in a gesture that suggested that with very little encouragement she would get to her feet and from her extra height demand silence so that these strangers and foreigners could listen to Welsh poetry and acquire some notion of where exactly they were and how softly they should tread in their trespass.

'I keep in touch.'

She ventured to address Cilydd and Nanw as they looked at her and chewed in unison.

'In the most round about way actually. I don't know whether you've heard Amy talk about Gwenda G.'

Neither Cilydd nor Nanw indicated that they ever had.

'She was in Col with us. She used to be one of the family as we called it. There was Amy and dear Enid, a saint if I ever saw one, and Gwenda G. and me and one or two others. Gwenda G. was a year ahead but was kept back for not turning up for an exam or something like that. She was a terror. My mother was convinced she was a bad influence on me. But the most amazing thing was she married D. I. Everett! You remember D. I. Everett?'

It was plain that John Cilydd had the greatest difficulty in remembering.

'The college Bolshie, we used to call him. He and Gwenda couldn't stand the sight of each other. They really couldn't. I may as well tell you the whole story. He was mad about Amy. Absolutely gone on her. Did you never hear her mention him?'

Both Cilydd and Nanw shook their heads. Even if they had, they looked so distant and solemn it would have been unlikely that they would admit it.

'The things we had to get up to, to "protect" her. Oh dear. "Battles long ago." It all seemed so vital and important at the time. And now hardly anything seems to matter. We had such high hopes. I just wonder where have they all gone?'

Nanw put down her knife and fork. Her knuckles gleamed on the edge of the table. Reminiscences were as unsubstantial as smoke. To keep in touch with reality there were necessary handrails that had to be held on to and never let go. She spoke rapidly and quietly as if repeating a lesson that had been codified into a litany.

'Wales is an occupied country,' she said. 'Drained of all her young people. First twenty years' unemployment and then conscription. Everyone sent away and the place filled with army camps, bombing ranges, evacuees, war emergencies, war training; you only have to look around you.'

When she had finished she glanced at her brother for some sign of approval. He was the master and she was the pupil loyally repeating the tenets she had learnt at his feet. He seemed lost in contemplation of the row of dustbins standing at intervals in the narrow alley like untidy sentinels of a settlement abandoned by its inhabitants. The rain splashed on the battered lids with anxious persistence, and he looked like a man who longed to be elsewhere, at the same time knowing there was nowhere else to be.

'There seems to be so little we can do,' Mabli said. 'As my poor mother put it. "War is so overwhelming." Sitting up there in that vicarage I can't help asking myself, "Just what is a conscience really good for?" '

Her knitting needles clicked on. It was easy to ask questions: impossible to answer them. Nanw and Cilydd had finished eating. They seemed prepared to sit in silence like poultry asleep in a warm shelter with their eyes half open. There was a short time to pass before the meeting started. The rain beating down on the dustbin lids made the interior of the café a delectable refuge. Mabli Herbert resolved to indulge in the comfort and solace of a friendly chat.

'Gwenda came down for a rest from the bombing,' she said. 'She was full of it as you can imagine. But most of all so pleased to have met up with Amy. Through D.I.E. I suppose. "Die" we call him and everyone thinks it's "Dai". A bit of a macabre joke but Gwenda was always amused by that sort of thing. Die is a member of the Labour group on the Borough Council, although Gwenda says he's still a dyed-in-the-wool Bolshie. Dai-dyed-in-the-wool she calls him. He sits next to an upper-class left-wing Englishwoman called Margot something. You can imagine, his surprise when he finds out Amy is staying with her. Gwenda said he came home looking as if he'd had a heart attack. Anyway, as far as I could understand it, he is absolutely bent on getting Amy on some committee to do with Socialism and Post-War Reconstruction. But I expect I'm just telling you something you know already. It's such a small world, isn't it? Small and yet there seems so little we can do to stop it tearing itself to pieces. That's what disturbs me so much. I just can't stop thinking about it. I knit of course and I read. And I prepare my weekly lecture. I wish I could be a bit more like Amy. I always did you know. Even in college. She was the one for getting things done. I expect if it hadn't been for her I would never have had the courage to park myself over the hole on the first green when we made our famous protest. "Protest." It's a strange word, isn't it? This little protest and that little protest. They all seem pretty futile. And yet we have to make them. That's what I say to my mother anyway. I think she'd much prefer it if I stayed home in the vicarage and did nothing. Absolutely nothing.'

Cilydd and Nanw stirred in their chairs. Nanw bent over to pick up her handbag and prepare to pay the bill.

'I talk too much,' Mabli said. 'I know I do. And if I didn't I'd have mother there to tell me I did. One thing Gwenda said really amazed me.'

She began to put away her knitting in a colourful cotton bag.

'She said D. I. Everett had got Amy's name down on the list of likely Parliamentary candidates. For Labour! For a seat in North East Wales. I couldn't believe it. But Gwenda said it was gospel. That's the way she still talks. I think she was even a little jealous. I think she would have liked her own name to go down. Especially with Die so well in with the Party Organiser at Transport House. I must admit it did surprise me a little . . .'

Mabli was slow to appreciate the effect she was having on the brother and sister across the small table. Nanw's pale cheeks were burning red like warning signals. Cilydd had turned to look at the greasy raindrops on the window pane.

'Unintended words,' Nanw said.

She spoke so sharply Mabli was alarmed.

'I beg your pardon,' Mabli said politely.

She had heard the words but was still unclear about their meaning.

'Ambition,' Nanw said. 'It drives people. Their petty plans. Their ceaseless social climbing. This lust for attention and public honours. This unsatiable appetite for the crumbs of power. If anyone asked me, I would say that was the Welsh curse. The flaw that has kept us down throughout the centuries.'

There was nothing in what she said that Mabli would want to disagree with. What disturbed her was the vehemence with which Nanw had said it. Cilydd was rising to his feet.

'I expect it is time to go,' he said.

Mabli could see how disturbed he was by his sister's anger. It was better they moved as quickly as possible before Nanw said something her brother would prefer her not to say. Mabli squeezed her way between the tables towards the cash desk. There could well be exchanges between brother and sister it were better she should not overhear. She moved clumsily as though the sense of being the unwitting cause of trouble was overwhelming her and threatening every move she made with some untoward physical mishap. Her cotton knitting bag swung about threatening milk jugs, ash trays, cigarettes held back by women immersed in gossip, and a little waitress carrying greasy plates.

'There's none so blind as those who will not see.'

Nanw was challenging her brother, standing in the way of his passage from the table by the window.

'What have I been telling you all the time,' Nanw said. 'WVS, Red Cross, Civil Defence. What a wonderful excuse. Up to London every chance she can get. And now we know, don't we? She's not on our side and I don't think she ever was. And now you know it.'

He had begun to squeeze her arm in his effort to make her move out of his way. She looked up at him imploringly.

'I can't bear to see you being deceived,' she said. 'You're hurting my arm.'

He looked down at her calmly.

'We'd better move,' he said. 'We don't want to be late for the meeting.'

162

11

C ONNIE CLAYTON WAS IN THE OLD BUTLER'S PANTRY AT 43
Culpepper Place, keeping warm and listening to Evensong on
her treasured wireless. The fire in the old-fashioned grate was little
more than a red eye in the cinders: but the room was insulated
with cupboards from floor to ceiling and the thick wooden shutters
were closed. She was clutching a gilt-edged combined *Book of
Common Prayer* and *Hymns Ancient and Modern* as though it had
been her intention to follow the service in detail. Her black dress,
the grey shawl over her shoulders, her hair net and distraught
nervous expression made her look older than her years. She rose
awkwardly to her feet when she heard the basement door open and
Erika von Tornago calling out her name.

'Mrs Connie! Guess who is here. Connie! Are you there?'

The corridor was like a tunnel between the sand-bagged
basement area and the stairs. Erika and Amy had only the chink of
light under the door of the butler's pantry to guide them as they
groped along avoiding the sand buckets and stirrup pumps and a
thick line of outdoor clothing hanging from cloak-room pegs.
Connie did not open her door. They found her with her back to the
wireless holding her prayer-book, her head trembling with distress.
The voice on the wireless was praying in Anglican singsong for
comrades overseas, prepared to risk their lives on land, on sea and
in the air. Erika made straight for the fire to rub her hands.

'Oh, Connie, my dear,' she said. 'You are a marvel. She is a
marvel, is she not, Amy?'

Connie swung around and limped towards Amy. Her agitation
overwhelmed her formal welcome.

'Such a dreadful thing. So terrible,' she said. 'You remember Mr
Eccles. Dear Mr Eccles. The Reverend Donald Eccles. He was
curate of St Stephens. You met him last year. With Miss Margot.
He was here to change my library books when I couldn't go out.
You remember Mr Eccles?'

Her large eyes were fixed on Amy's face insisting that she should
remember. Amy was tired after her long journey. She frowned in a
fruitless effort of recall.

'He married such a nice young person from Purley. Very young but very nice. They were married the day war broke out. It was that terrible night last week. He's moved you see. Curate in charge at St Mark's, Forest Gate. The church was on fire. Mr Eccles rushed into the vestry to save the vestments and the silver and so on. It was bombed. While they were fighting the fire. A direct hit. He was killed instantly. And I've been thinking you know about his young wife. Such a nice person. Such a nice smile. I can't get her out of my mind.'

Connie stretched out her hand to switch off her wireless and save the wet batteries. This was her private property and she could deal with it as she liked. Her attitude towards Erika was one of cautious respect. She shuffled about apologetically in front of this enemy alien warming herself in front of the fire. This after all was a Countess and she was making amends for her foreign origins by contributing to the war effort at Bush House.

'I have some supper ready,' Connie said. 'I didn't know when you'd be back. I made sandwiches and left coffee in the thermos. And in the round tin those Welsh cakes I made with dried egg. I think you like them.'

Erika patted her arm.

'Connie dear. You must not worry. We have eaten. In the great Corner House of Mr Lyon. You have had bad news. You should rest. You should go to bed.'

They persuaded Connie to sit down. She was reluctant to do so. Erika set about making a cup of tea while Amy prepared to talk seriously to the housekeeper.

'Miss Margot is resting,' Connie said.

She wanted to give a dutiful account of herself.

'I made a tray and took it to the library. And do you know, there she was in her working clothes, stretched out on the sofa fast asleep.'

'I'm here for three days,' Amy said. 'Now what I want to say is this. There is no earthly reason why you can't come back with me. I've talked to Margot about it. It's all perfectly clear. There is really no good reason why you should stay on in this house. None at all.'

Watching the kettle boil on a primus stove, Erika called out in cheerful support.

'None at all!'

Connie stared at the small fire in the grate. At the risk of sounding stubborn and disrespectful she recited chapter and verse to justify her staying on at 43 Culpepper Place.

'We must all do our duty,' she said. ' "Stand firm and carry on." That's what Mr Churchill says.'

Amy pressed a knuckle against her lower lip. She was making an effort at patient exposition. There were even alternatives for Connie to consider.

'You know there's a place for you with Aunt Esther in the little bungalow. I know she'd love to have you.'

Connie's eyes swivelled briefly to check the authenticity of the last statement.

'Or you could come to me. I could really do with your help. Or you could even go to Cae Golau. There are those people there who need looking after. They need a housekeeper if ever anybody did.'

'I wouldn't want to let Lady Violet down,' Connie said. 'Or any member of the family for that matter. The last thing she said was, "I'm relying on you to keep an eye on things," and that's what I'm trying to do. With so many people coming in and out. All part of the war effort of course. But I think it helps if I keep an eye on things.'

Amy turned to Erika for support.

'It's not safe for her here, is it?' Amy said.

Erika decided on a clear-sighted and categorical contribution to the discussion.

'You may not like it, Mrs Connie, you may not like it, but if this war means anything it means class distinctions are finished. Are gone for ever.'

Erika made a grandiloquent sweeping gesture. The kettle whistled. She turned her attention to making the tea. Connie resented her own inactivity. She pulled a face at the fire.

'I know my place,' Connie said. 'I may be old-fashioned, but I know my place.'

This made Erika laugh.

'You are lucky,' she said. 'There are not many people who can say that these days.'

Connie allowed her body to lapse into a sulky and resentful silence.

'There was an English hymn,' Erika said. 'I remember. "Here is no abiding city . . ." The whole world is being . . .'

She made a sequence of gestures suggesting machines churning up the land.

'Like I stir this tea. That is this war. Stirring up the whole world.'

Amy stretched forward to make a persuasive assault.

'There is no earthly point in your staying on here,' she said. 'Margot is grateful of course. We all are. I am quite sure Margot's aunt would never want it if she knew the true circumstances. This bombing could go on for ever. Really it could. Like world without end, Amen. The place has its function and it is doing what it can, if you like, but that's no reason for you to go on risking your life to keep it like a pin in paper when everything else is collapsing in a heap of bricks and dust.'

Connie said nothing. The shape of her shoulders suggested that she was hurt. Amy had said more than enough. Erika saw it was time to change the subject.

'Some music,' she said. 'With my cup of tea.'

Connie sat up in alarm.

'Miss Margot is resting,' she said.

'Of course she is.'

Erika reassured her.

'Don't you worry. I'll play very quietly.'

The house was cold but surprisingly clean. Connie Clayton kept herself strenuously busy indoors removing dust and dirt dislodged by the night raids. Erika and Amy spoke in whispers on the broad staircase as though out of respect for Connie's loyal efforts. Amy had to amend Erika's unqualified admiration.

'This isn't her place,' Amy said. 'She doesn't really belong here. I don't know how many times I've tried to tell her, but it never sinks in. She's a colonial appurtenance. Just like one of those ayahs or whatever they call them. Worth and value, measured by their loyalty and devotion to the Raj. The English *Herrenfolk*. I know what I'm talking about you know.'

She could see Erika smile and she supposed she was being mocked. Erika hastened to reassure her.

'My goodness of course you do. This war breaks down classes. For that it is good. It is like shaking the kaleidoscope. The pieces all fall in a new pattern. I write this to poor Hans in Toronto. He has the promise of a place on a Swedish freighter. I tell him to sell pictures to pay the fare. What I earn at Bush House is little. But for Margot where would I have a place to lay my head?'

Amy turned the knob of the library door as softly as she could to peep inside. Most of the furniture was under dust-covers. The shutters were closed and the thick curtains drawn. Margot had left on all the lights. She was sprawled on the sofa still wearing her overcoat and her grimy brogues, her mouth open at a crooked angle as she slept. All the pictures had been taken down so that the white marble chimney breast surmounted with a broken pediment in the style of a doric temple looked more conspicuously theatrical than ever. Amy found a rug and spread it over Margot without waking her. The first notes of a Beethoven sonata rang out in the silence in spite of Erika's foot on the soft pedal. Amy closed the library door. In the drawing-room she put her finger to her lips and Erika stopped playing.

'Are you sorry for her?'

Erika seemed eager to fathom the depth of Amy's attachment to Margot.

'I'm sorry for everybody,' Amy said. 'Do you know I have absolutely no recollection of that curate Connie was going on about. None whatsoever.'

The fashionable lighting gave the chilly room an illusion of comfort. Erika shifted up to make room for Amy alongside her on the long piano stool. She patted the place.

'Come and sing something, Amy,' Erika said. 'Ever so softly. "*Voi che sapete.*" You sing. I play.'

Amy shook her head.

'I don't know how she sticks it,' she said. 'Night after night.'

Erika smiled and touched out *Hearts of Oak* on the keyboard.

'She is English,' she said. 'I tell you. It is their *métier*. Sticking it out. Like God forgiving.'

Amy stared critically at Erika's bright toothy smile. She took a deep breath that indicated both a desire to talk and an uncertainty about the worth of the effort. Erika put her hands together in a mute gesture that asked for absolution. She would dedicate herself to listening with total sympathy to anything Amy had to say.

' "I'll never feel the same about flesh again",' Amy said. 'That's what she said. The way she said it . . .'

Amy tapped her breast bone with the tips of her fingers.

'I understood about poor old Het. I thought I did. But when she told me about that arm. Anybody's arm. Still warm. All sticky at one end. And the ring on the finger. The ring as bright as anything in the dust and the debris. Like opening a tomb, she said. And the arm still warm. She's so sensitive. And she made herself go through with it. Night after night. And when she said, "I'll never feel the same about flesh again. Mine or anybody else's", it made me feel as though she had penetrated to the heart of existence. Human existence. Gone somewhere, been somewhere, where I could never follow. We attach so much importance to flesh. At least I do. Flesh is everything. People are all flesh, nice and nasty. Good or bad. But when old Margot said that about not feeling the same about flesh, "mine or anyone else's", it gave me a glimpse of a totally different dimension. All mind and all spirit. And all mind and all spirit in this war directed against flesh. Like a war within a war. Do you know what I mean?'

Erika got up from the piano stool to place her arm comfortingly around Amy's narrow waist. With gentle pressure she encouraged her to pace up and down the drawing-room like a patient recovering from shock.

'If we are going to die,' Amy said. 'All I am saying is we may as well die for something worth dying for.'

Her body shook with laughter as if she had made a joke. Erika rubbed her back.

'Now tell your ancient Aunt Erika,' she said. 'Post-war reconstruction. When you are in parliament what will you do?'

'If I ever get there,' Amy said. 'If I ever want to get there. If they ever let me . . . I don't give a damn about the British Empire so called. I know that much.'

'Good. Good.'

Erika nodded sagely. Amy ignored her reaction. She seemed intent on making her own position clearer to herself.

'Well what do you want?' she said. 'The monarchy. Rubbish. The City of London. Pernicious. Penny Gehenna. The English class system. Due for demolition. And I'm not a pacifist, you know. Not any more. "All armed prophets have conquered and all unarmed prophets have failed." Who said that?'

'Um.'

Erika made a great pretence of thinking.

'It could be Marx or Machiavelli,' Erika said. 'It could even have been Adolf, God help us. The mighty thinker of *Mein Kampf*. That turgid ignoramus dictating his handbook for gangsters at the top of his horrible voice. Amy! Imagine! The world is within your jurisdiction. How would you have it? Your committee for the post-war paradise. Your Welsh socialism.'

They smiled at each other like children playing a game.

'I want independence and I want equality,' Amy said.

'For yourself? Or for your Wales?'

'For everybody,' Amy said. 'A federation of socialist soviets from one end of Europe to the other.'

'Why not! Why not?'

'I'm serious.'

'Well of course you are.'

'That's the real war,' Amy said. 'Behind this one. The one worth fighting.'

'How many wars?' Erika said. 'One? Ten? A hundred?'

Amy stopped smiling. She glowered at Erika.

'You sound just like John Cilydd,' she said. 'How many wars do you want, he says. As if I were some sort of stupid child. It's terribly difficult to argue with him.'

'He dotes on you?' Erika said. 'Is that the expression? Dotes? It is difficult to argue with someone who dotes.'

'All he worries about is Wales and conscientious objectors,' Amy said. 'I can't even tell him I could become a Labour candidate.'

She sat down on the piano stool with her back to the piano. Erika was ready to comfort her.

'It's so odd,' Amy said. 'I don't know how it happened. We seem to have changed positions. Like playing musical chairs in the dark ... The Spanish Republic. My goodness, he would have fought and

169

died for that. He would. He would have gone with Pen. That war could easily have killed them both! But now . . . I can't describe it. He looks like a wounded animal. That's the only way I can describe it. And sometimes he looks at me as though I were the one responsible. But I can't help it. It's not my fault, is it?'

Erika tried to bring her comfort by placing her arms around Amy's shoulders. Amy's eyes closed as she made her confession.

'I sometimes think I've done him a terrible injustice. I made him marry me. And we are not really compatible. I don't think we ever were. I want to make up for it. I really do. I try. I try. But everything I do seems to make things worse.'

'He loves you,' Erika said.

She spoke as though Cilydd's condition was as enviable as it was inevitable.

'So he has what he wants. That is more than most of us ever get.'

Amy drew herself away to face an imagined accusation.

'You think I'm expecting too much,' she said. 'Asking too much. A woman can't expect to have a family and a career . . . That sort of stuff?'

Erika smiled and reached out to stroke Amy's hair.

'You must not feel guilty,' she said. 'That is all I'm saying. That never . . .'

Their bodies stiffened as the siren at the end of the square began its strident wail. The warning rose and fell with a power and an urgency that penetrated the closed shutters and permeated the house.

'God, that noise . . !'

Erika clapped her hands to her ears.

'I will never get used to it. It is so bloody near!'

Amy was on her way to Margot's bedroom. The wail of the siren was an hysterical accompaniment to every move she made. Connie had been tidying up. The usual confusion of books and clothes and gramophone records was absent. Margot's books that reflected her passionate interest in public health and local government were stacked in two neat piles between her easy chair and the cold fireplace. Her blue dungarees and steel helmet were laid out almost ceremoniously on the oak chest at the foot of her double bed.

Outside, sirens from other boroughs were calling to each other eerily through the cold night. Amy put on the blue steel helmet. She saw herself between the web of sticky tape on the dressing-table mirror. She tilted the helmet back so that some of her golden curls could appear decoratively around her face. Margot, yawning, watched her from the open doorway.

'What are you up to?' she said.

'I thought I'd come with you,' Amy said.

'You stay put and get some sleep,' Margot said. 'You've got committees tomorrow. They're worse than air-raids. I'll take my helmet if you don't mind.'

Amy followed her down the stairs. Now that she knew Margot was awake, Erika was playing the piano as loudly as she could. Margot raised her hand to draw Amy's attention to the music.

'I don't know whether you've noticed yet, but our Countess Erika's nerves are none too good. There's a nasty character in Bush House who's upset her quite a bit. I've offered to look into it but she won't hear of it. Some engineer-in-charge who goes on and on about not being able to understand anybody willing to be paid to fight against her own country. That sort of thing. Did you have a word with Connie? Place is alive with music tonight.'

The door of the butler's pantry was closed and the light under the door flickered. Connie was listening to her wet-battery wireless by candle-light. A cockney voice was carolling 'Lily of Laguna' and Connie's voice was quavering in an oddly ecclesiastical way as she joined in the chorus.

'Let me come with you,' Amy said. 'You know I'm a practical person. There must be lots I could do to help.'

Margot shook her head. From the sand-bagged basement area they could see searchlights crossing the sky, and stars twinkling frostily beyond their reach. Amy's eyes shone with excitement.

'It is beautiful,' she said. 'Really beautiful.'

'Stay inside,' Margot said. 'You may be needed here.'

'I've been wanting so much to talk to you lately Margot. About everything. And we haven't talked at all. We should tell each other what we are thinking and feeling. What else are friends for?'

'I'll tell you what I feel,' Margot said. 'Disgust. Anger. Just

171

enough anger to keep me going. The thought of what human beings are capable of doing to each other.'

From the top of the basement steps Amy watched her dark figure disappear out of the square into the street. A man passed by on a bicycle ringing the bell intermittently as a substitute for a light. The red reflector on the rear mudguard wobbled as the rider meandered on his way. Amy stepped into the middle of the road to take in the silence of the square. The houses seemed to shrink inside their own shadows. Sooner or later the bombers would seek them out. They had no form of defence from aerial attack. When a stray dog howled, Amy became aware of the cold night. She ran indoors hugging her own shoulders.

Inside the house the piano playing upstairs gave an illusion of normality until she climbed the stairs and heard the stumbling urgency of Erika's playing. In the drawing-room she found Erika peering short-sightedly at the notes in the book of sonatas in a pool of yellow light. Erika shouted above the noise she was making.

'I'm trying to leave out the pauses!'

Amy saw her fingers reeling over the keyboard as if they were running away from each other.

'I should be braver,' Erika said. 'But I'm not. He is looking for me. I dream he sends black angels from his Nazi hell to find me and destroy me. He has a special search for German traitors. I have seen myself like a dead fly under his black stamp on my passport. He wants me out of this world.'

'Come on,' Amy said. 'You play and I'll sing.'

Erika scrambled about in the double stool for an aria she knew Amy could sing. They played and sang together with uninhibited gusto until they heard the first crump of high explosive. Erika's fingers fell away from the keyboard.

'Hold me. Hold me.'

Amy sat down beside her. She pressed her brow against Amy's neck. The throb of the engines in the sky was all they could listen to. Erika muttered close to Amy's ear.

'I can hear what those engines are saying. It's worse than, "where are you?" It's, "destroy you, destroy you".'

She brushed Amy's cheek with her lips.

'You are so beautiful. I don't want to die without saying that to you.'

'Oh, for heaven's sake,' Amy said. 'Don't get hysterical.'

'You are life. They are death. And so I cling to you.'

'Erika! Really . . .'

Erika chuckled and shivered with pleasure at the note of reproof in Amy's voice. She held on to her waist and closed her eyes.

'You must hear my last will and testament, my Amy. Everything I have in this world is yours. My jewels. My land. My love, which is all that is left.'

'You do talk a lot of nonsense sometimes.'

Amy scolded her gently. Erika became more coy and childlike.

'I would sing you a love song no one else has ever dared to sing you. In German. Real German. And it will be so beautiful, it will lure you into a new way of loving. Do you hear that, Amy? Even your name is love.'

Amy pushed Erika away and sprang to her feet.

'Connie,' she said.

Her manner was brisk.

'She'll be frightened. I must go down and see how she is.'

Amy listened to the noises of the night. South of the river anti-aircraft fire was punctuating the menacing drone of the bombers. With relentless regularity high explosive was adding to the sinister increase in commotion. Erika held her fear in check by watching Amy with avid concentration. Amy spoke about Connie.

'If she can stick it, I can,' Amy said. 'And so can you.'

'Let it bring us closer,' Erika said. 'That's all I ask. You are so cautious. Your soul is all caution. But this is right. That is proper. When the vessel is so perfect, the spirit inside should be careful and proud.'

'You talk such rubbish,' Amy said. 'And you call it poetry. Just like John Cilydd.'

'Life comes to life near death.'

Erika raised her hands in an ecstatic gesture before they both began to giggle. There was an improvised shelter under the wide staircase. In a cupboard among tins of furniture polish Erika had hidden a bottle of Cherry Herring. She took Amy by the hand and offered to share this last bottle with her. They crouched on the

173

bedding in the shelter and sipped the liqueur together. Erika trembled with nervous excitement.

'What I want are concrete walls so thick no bomb could break through them. It would be wonderful. Inside a warm bunker just you and me and no clothes. Maybe a sheet. Maybe a blanket.'

Amy made a stern effort to sound responsible.

'I'll tell you one thing. Connie will be coming back to Wales with me. There is absolutely no sense in the poor thing putting up with this night after night. No sense at all.'

As the sound of the raid grew heavier they stretched out on the bedding and drew closer to each other for comfort.

'I could stay here for ever.'

Erika whispered as she stroked Amy's hair so lightly that Amy did not shift her head out of reach.

'I am not jealous,' Erika said. 'And I can tell you why. Jealousy comes with possession. No one can possess you. You are beautiful and inviolate. When you want to be free, I will help you. I will do anything you ask. Anything.'

Amy lay quiet, staring at the wall, listening to the raid. Erika leaned over her to brush her lips against Amy's ear.

'We can be frank with each other,' she said. 'I will tell you all and you will tell me all. That is all I ask. I feel better with you.'

'I feel so guilty,' Amy said. 'It is easier to be here. It is as if I were released. Set free.'

She turned to face Erika and found herself in her embrace.

'To me you can say anything,' Erika said. 'All I want is to comfort you. I tell you, if I have to die, I may as well die in the arms of someone I love.'

'So long as you keep your hands still . . .'

Erika whispered urgently as if everything she had to say were a secret. There was a sudden silence. Amy put her hand over Erika's mouth. In the street a man on a bicycle was shouting, 'Lights! Lights!' at the top of his voice. They could hear the insistent ringing of bells as fire engines approached their area from several directions. Amy rolled out of the shelter under the stairs.

'There must be lights showing somewhere upstairs,' she said. 'Or incendiaries. I must go and check.'

The pulse of the bomber engines entered the silence like a cannibal giant in a child's dream climbing the stairs.

'You go down and join Connie. See if she is all right.'

'No. No. Amy stay here. Don't leave me.'

Amy was active and angry.

'Shut up will you! And do as I say.'

She was on the stairs when every light went out. A pressure of air forced her to her knees, with hands over her ears. All the bricks and mortar that surrounded her were being transformed into paper and the paper was being ripped into elongated sheets. The stairs under her feet rippled and rose up to toss her down into a basin of darkness that gave a fleeting illusion of ultimate security. In the distance she could hear Erika screaming her name. Into the basin and the transitory silence great chunks of masonry began to drop in free fall through a cloud of dust that threatened her with death by choking. There was no possibility or point in speech of any kind. She had to remain still and find a way to breathe. As the dust slowly subsided she could make out pencils of light against the open sky. The fire bells were receding. Erika was wailing about being buried alive. She could not have been more than a few yards away.

'Keep still!'

Amy found the strength to speak.

'Don't move. Do you hear? Don't move an inch.'

'I think I'm bleeding.'

She could hear Erika sobbing.

'Keep absolutely still!'

Amy looked up and in a brief flash of light she saw an entire chimney piece of white marble, even the broken pediment in imitation of a doric temple, balanced above them on the flimsy support of hanging lath and plaster.

12

IT WAS SO QUIET IN THE LANE, THE APPROACH OF THE CARTHORSES rumbled like distant thunder. Cilydd laughed to see Eddie Meredith stuff his hip-flask away and wipe his mouth. Together they stood with their backs against the bank to allow the horses' uninterrupted passage to the shore. The boy in ragged trousers, sitting sideways on the lead horse, was singing to himself in piping soprano until he noticed the two men: one in a captain's uniform and the other in a hat and a dark overcoat that reached almost to his ankles. Greetings exchanged were minimal. He was embarrassed by having his singing overheard and Eddie Meredith was clearly not pleased to be seen at such a time in such a place. All the boy used to control the huge horses, there were four of them, were rope halters and the thin leads which he sifted like ribbons in his grubby hands. Cilydd studied the boy and the horses closely. When they had passed he tipped back his hat, opened his long coat and thrust his hands deep in his trouser pockets.

'One of the Cefnysoedd boys,' Cilydd said. 'To judge by the cut of his jib. Their mother is Robert Thomas the molecatcher's first cousin. In which case it won't be long before your presence in the locality is known, Captain Meredith.'

'Damn,' Eddie said. 'Just my luck.'

'Anyway you couldn't possibly expect to come and go without your father knowing.'

They followed the horses down the lane to the beach. They watched the boy lead them to the water's edge to soak their fetlocks in the brine. The scene was idyllic. The beach was deserted. The light of the late afternoon burnished the windows of houses far across the bay. The outline of the mountains was etched with piercing clarity against a pale yellow sky in the east. The boy made the horses break into a ponderous canter through the shallow water so that the splashes shod their hooves with wings of light.

'He thinks I should be put away,' Cilydd said. 'Your father. He thinks men like me should be put behind bars. Or stuck up against a wall and shot.'

'It's ridiculous,' Eddie said. 'When I'm home. If I want a drink, I have to sneak off to the outhouses. And chew shallots before coming back into the house.'

'It's quite possible I would be in prison, but for Amy,' Cilydd said. 'Your father and his friends are quite scared of her, I'm happy to report. Her public work and her heroic experiences in the Blitz have not passed unnoticed in our local rag. I am left in comparative peace. Only partially ostracised you could say. I am at liberty to think my own subversive thoughts.'

'Nothing has changed and everything changes.'

Eddie kicked at a pebble. A return to familiar surroundings filled him with an urge to be frank.

'I feel hellishly guilty,' he said. 'For three months when I was in West Africa I didn't write home. I could have been dead for all they knew. They had no idea where on this earth I was. But what could I say to them? I've always had more to conceal than to reveal as far as my parents are concerned. That's the sad and bloody terrible truth. So my poor old mother can go on believing I'm doing terribly well. And the cuttings about my triumphs can go on getting more and more dog-eared in my old man's wallet. The pangs of remorse in Takoradi. The moans and groans of a self-pitying little shit.'

He paused to look at Cilydd and see whether or not his ruthless honesty was being appreciated.

'And here I am now,' he said. 'At it again. But what can I do? The fact is I have absolutely nothing to say to them. It's shameful, but it's true. They don't know me, so why should they want to know anything about me? What's the point? Better for them to look at the photographs of me in my uniform on the mantelpiece. A glossy little icon. I think that's why photographs were invented. To keep reality at an arm's length. A nice little photo. That's what they need. It's what they like. Not a nasty complicated abnormal human being. Subject for a poem there, J.C.? Shouldn't wonder.'

Cilydd had stopped to look back at the horses. In spite of their size from a distance they looked as if they were gliding over the shallow tide.

'There's your watch-tower,' Eddie said.

He was pointing to an isolated outcrop of rock on the west side of the deserted shore. There they could sit, talk and enjoy a drink and the view. It was a place for reflection where an individual could indulge in a prolonged contemplation of the landscape. It was a bay that could boast legends of sunken cities. There were two mysterious islands beyond the blunt headland that thrust itself southward and behind which the sun would set. This was the basic landscape of their lives. They knew each harbour and estuary, all the old towns and villages and ancient castles, and in the case of some of the farms, they would know the name of every field. They were familiar with a whole range of chapels of varied denominations and with exotic Old Testament names.

'At least I can talk to you, John Cilydd.'

Eddie sounded eager and breathless. The best access to the top of the rock was from the furthest side. Cilydd led the way. Once on the top of his tower he moved to the edge facing the sea. The horses were being led back to the lane. Their silhouettes were a stately antique frieze.

'That is if you think I am still worth talking to,' Eddie said.

They were high enough to catch a fresh breeze off the sea.

'War or no war,' Eddie said.

From such a place of vantage, as though the view had somehow reinforced his understanding of the significance of their existence, Cilydd was inclined to pontificate.

' "War is an extension of politics," as Pen Lewis used to be so fond of quoting. But I would be inclined to change the proposition. I would say, "War is an interruption of politics".'

Eddie made a clear attempt to restrain himself from comment and looked around for a place to sit.

'War is the last thing I want to talk about, maestro,' he said. 'But I'll say this. We're going to win in the end. No question about that. No matter how much blood is spilt. I can only hope it won't include mine. I think I'd better drink to that.'

' "We",' Cilydd said. 'Who's "we"? And what does "win" mean? *Who* is going to win?'

'Oh, God,' Eddie said. 'I don't know, do I?'

He was being drawn into a debate he had no wish to take part in. He sat down on the rock and produced his hip-flask to swallow a comforting drink. He offered Cilydd the flask.

'Go on,' he said. 'I've got plenty more in my briefcase. Neat little bottles. All in a row. What are you laughing at?'

'Sudden vision,' Cilydd said. 'Voice from the past. Chap in the trenches. Archie. He had a belt under his tunic with about half a dozen little flasks dangling from it. "What'll you have, rum or whisky?" He used to ask me what the war was about. I could never really tell him. He would have been too drunk to follow anyway. We now know the purposes of that war was to make sure of this one. And then what?'

'I don't want to talk about the war,' Eddie said.

'I'd like a war to save what's left of Wales being overwhelmed by England,' Cilydd said. 'Bloodless battles, no doubt. "It is permitted to die for everything except Wales." But battles all the same. Endless battles. On and on to the end of time.'

Cilydd swallowed a mouthful of whisky and stared mournfully at the restless light on the sea. He was confronted by a limitless expanse of water, intractable and unchanging.

'There's one thing I've learnt,' Eddie said. 'Since I've been seconded to the Army Bureau of Current Affairs. Not that I didn't know it already. But it confirms what I thought. Advertising and education are closely related. When I see a hut full of ignorant bastards who can hardly read or write, I say to myself, how are we going to educate this lot? And I know there is only one answer. Harness their appetites and you've got access to their perceptions. And from then on, "Presentation is all!"'

He raised his voice, but Cilydd remained unimpressed by the slogan. He muttered to himself.

'Is it true?' Cilydd said. 'That's what counts.'

Eddie produced a silver cigarette case and offered it to Cilydd before selecting one for himself, closing the case and tapping the cigarette on it.

'Look here old chap,' he said. 'I'm relying on you. We've got to put Wales on the map.'

'What map?' Cilydd said. 'And who are the map-makers? I've told you before. Their Annals are not our Annals.'

'Annals! You are talking as if we were still living in the Middle Ages. The Dark Ages I should say.'

'Maybe we are,' Cilydd said.

'Listen now,' Eddie said. 'Let's be sensible. I had a hell of a job selling the notion. You've no idea. There was a snotty little swine from the British Council and he had a lot of influence over the Colonel. I stuck my neck out I can tell you. "Look sir," I said. "It's time we put the original British-ness back in the British Army and the British Council." It was a risk, I can tell you. For a second the whole thing hung in the balance. And then suddenly the old boy laughed and said his grandmother was Welsh and from then on everything went swimmingly.'

'Good job she wasn't Chinese,' Cilydd said.

It was an uncharacteristic attempt at facetiousness and Eddie ignored it.

'A nice little pamphlet about the poetic tradition,' Eddie said. 'Couldn't possibly do any harm and might do a spot of good.'

'I've told you,' Cilydd said. 'Ask Professor Gwilym. He'd do it like a shot.'

'That's just the point,' Eddie said. 'I don't want regurgitated academic clichés that smelt of sick even when I was in school. I want to make it new. Produce something fresh, sharp, brisk, with plenty of bite in it.'

Eddie stood up on the rock and struck an attitude.

'It's my country too, you know,' he said. 'I love it just as much as you do, in my own somewhat erratic fashion. Of course there are all sorts of things I can't bear about it. You know that. But when we get down to fundamentals, I think I'm probably just as aware of bonds of attachment as you are.'

'Good,' Cilydd said.

'I can't write the thing myself,' Eddie said. 'I'm a journalist. A superficial sort of chap. I don't know enough about the subject. But you do.'

'Extraordinary,' Cilydd said.

Eddie turned to eye him suspiciously.

'What's extraordinary?' he said.

'This war is being fought to defend the Welsh poetic tradition. Does Mr Churchill know about this?'

180

'Oh, come off it, John Cilydd.'

'That's what's so remarkable about the English. They do good even when they don't know they're doing it. That's what comes of being the Lord's annointed . . .'

'Oh for God's sake why don't you face up to things as they really are. There is no frontier. We've met and we've mingled . . .'

Cilydd smiled sarcastically.

'Some of us have mingled a good deal more than others.'

'Your attitude,' Eddie said. 'It's several centuries out of date.'

'Like my language. Which is your language.'

Eddie ignored the intervention. He became a man tired of bottling up self-evident truths out of respect for the susceptibilities of an old friend. He spoke in passion.

'The Anglo-American power is going to win this war,' he said. 'No question. It may take a long time but it will happen in the end. Then there'll be a reckoning. And a new world order. And those in power will look in this direction, and they'll be saying, now just what contribution did all this Welsh stuff make towards our final victory? That will be the measuring rod. And the only one for decades to come. Does this ailing little culture deserve support? Left or right, it's exactly the same question the government in power will ask. And Westminster will still be the one and only seat of power.'

'Dear me,' Cilydd said. 'You have thought it all out.'

'Yes I have.'

Cilydd rose to his feet and buttoned up his coat. He scrambled down the face of the rock and Eddie stood on top watching him go.

'What's the use of producing high-class literature if you can't persuade anybody to read it?'

Eddie's challenge echoed across the beach. The shelving shore swept eastwards until it reached the blunt edge of a promenade more than two miles away. Fitful rays of sunlight picked out patches of green high on the rugged outline of the mountains. Cilydd squinted up at Eddie from the base of the rock.

'You are not offering me the kingdoms of the earth again, are you?' he said.

He turned to walk along a line of firm sand through the loose shingle stretching like a narrow highway that led back to where the last of the old sycamores leaned over the lane. Eddie was obliged to run to catch up with him. He was out of breath when he spoke.

'I know you're a fine poet,' he said. 'And so do one or two other people. But out in the nasty great big world there's damn all anybody that's ever heard of you. Have you thought of that?'

'Oh yes I have.'

Cilydd's sardonic smile did nothing to calm Eddie down.

'I repeat my point,' Eddie said. 'Because you can't bloody well answer it. What's the point of producing good stuff if you can't persuade anybody to read it?'

'It's a very good point,' Cilydd said loftily. 'And I doubt if there's an answer to it. Or if there is, I don't know it. But I do know this, in the marrow of my bone. And this is axiomatic, Captain Meredith. A work is a votive offering. And it has value in direct ratio to the amount of truth it secretes. In whatever language let me add. But here, in this place, and now, at this time, our language. And furthermore . . .'

He wagged a finger teasingly under Eddie's nose.

'For the dedicated poet in our tradition, I say dedicated but I also mean "called and designated", it is the language of the tradition that speaks or sings him and not he that makes use or abuse of the language. Hence the civilising power of language. That's all I'm concerned with really. And as for Marxism or what will be left of it when this orgiastic upheaval is over, it may be an excellent tool for dissecting aspects of history. But even when the forensic operation is a success, the cadaver is not obliged to come back to life. And the pathologist is certainly not required to swallow the scalpel.'

It was the coolness of Cilydd's manner rather than what he had to say that irked Eddie.

'Let me tell you something,' he said. 'It's all very well for you to go on philosophising under the local equivalent of the baobab tree. It's the defence of the West that allows you to do it. If the Nazis got here, my God, my friend you would be among the very first to be swinging from the nearest lamp-post. Don't you think you ought to bear that in mind? From time to time.'

Cilydd took his time to answer. They walked side by side in angry silence until they reached the mouth of the lane. Cilydd began to snap finger and thumb as if trying to remember a name.

'What do your English newspapers call people who collaborate with the occupying power, hm? A man's name they've made into a term of abuse. There's power in the press for you. Quisling. Now tell me Captain Meredith. Who is the occupying power in this little country you profess to love so much? And what shall we call our native people who collaborate so wholeheartedly with the occupying power?'

Their faces grew red as they confronted each other in the leafy lane. They would not come to blows but the things they found to say would prove more hurtful and the damage would last longer.

'That's what you are, Meredith. Like your father before you. A Quisling. A natural born collaborator. Professing undying devotion to your native land and climbing on to every government-propelled bandwagon in sight. Well I'm afraid I'm not going to collaborate. Not in the smallest degree. And it's no use dangling tempting little tit-bits in front of my nose. I don't give a damn if the world knows nothing about me or my poetry. And you damn well know it.'

Cilydd finished by looking pleased with himself. He had crushed the opposition so completely he could afford now to relax. He sauntered up the autumnal lane while Eddie took a nip at his hip-flask. There were several yards betwen them when Eddie called out.

'What about your wife? I hear Amy is on the list of potential Labour candidates. What do you think she's doing? Would you call her "Quisling" too?'

~ ii ~

Robert Thomas leaned inquisitively about the half-door of Uncle Tryfan's workshop. Tryfan Lloyd was absorbed in finishing off a pair of clogs for a small child. An afternoon haze cut off the warmth of a white sun. In the distance there was the noise of a threshing machine at work on a neighbouring farm, with dogs barking and children shouting. Glanrafon Stores was shut for early closing. Weeds were growing unchecked between the cobbles of the forecourt: a melancholy silence hung like faded sunblinds over the shop windows. Their frames needed painting. Watching a craftsman at work the molecatcher chewed respectfully. When he was moved to speak he first turned his head briefly to spit tobacco juice over his right shoulder.

'The falling leaves, Tryfan Lloyd,' he said.

This was an anodyne prologue that did not require any reply.

'The glories of the past,' Robert Thomas said. 'That's the way it always strikes me. Sweet sad days when the mists rise and the leaves fall. As I call here, this honoured hearth and hub of commerce, I think to myself, and you'll forgive me for saying this Tryfan Lloyd, it's never been the same since your dear mother passed away.'

Uncle Tryfan examined a clog more closely. There was a sufficient trace of approval in the autumn air to encourage Robert Thomas to continue. He drew a deep breath.

'If the rulers of the earth had half or even a quarter of that good woman's common sense, this world would not be in the mess and turmoil that we find it in at present.'

The smile Tryfan gave was only a pale shadow of the cheerful grin he used to bestow on all and sundry before the war, when his mother was still alive. The view of the world from the cobbler's workshop had darkened irreversibly. There was little room left for the old light-hearted singing and laughter.

'Do you understand what's going on, Tryfan Lloyd?'

Robert Thomas sounded more baffled than annoyed. It was his habit to point out that he had left school at the age of twelve and his attendance had never been regular, and that therefore he had a certain right, verging on a privilege not to follow the intricacies of great affairs that did not impinge directly on his diurnal course. Nevertheless the steady increase in the volume of incomprehensible events and occasions was something of an affront to a naturally enquiring mind.

'I try,' Tryfan said. 'John Cilydd gives me *Cwrs y Byd* to read every week. To be honest with you, I find it heavy going.'

'I'm rather glad I can't read English,' Robert Thomas said. 'God knows what additional sorrow such an accomplishment would bring.'

'It's not English, Robert Thomas,' Uncle Tryfan said. 'It's Welsh. If you read it you'd be a wiser man. But I can't say you'd be a happier one.'

'You've heard about the English Sunday papers reaching the highest villages,' Robert Thomas said. 'And people lying in bed reading them instead of going to chapel. That's the kind of world we've come to. And do you know what puzzles me, Tryfan Lloyd?'

He waited for Uncle Tryfan to take full cognisance of a worrying question.

'What information do they acquire from those pages? Does it make them wiser do you suppose? Does it bring them satisfaction? Wouldn't they be better off washed and dressed and in their pews singing a decent hymn?'

Robert Thomas examined the palms of his hands and picked at drying blisters. They had arrived at that measure of accord that allowed them to drift into calm silence. It stretched between them like the cobwebs that reached from the rafters of the open coach-house to the lamps and shafts of the governess cart that had not been in use since Mrs Lloyd took to her bed for her last illness. It lasted until Robert Thomas raised his head to detect the screams of a child in the distance.

'Do you hear what I hear Tryfan Lloyd?' he said. 'A child screaming in the house?'

Tryfan put down one clog and picked up another, barely pausing to listen.

'I wouldn't be surprised,' he said. 'Little Gwydion is given to crying, especially when he doesn't get his own way. Good pair of lungs.'

A hen squawked and flew out of the way as a bicycle approached. Cilydd was trying to avoid the potholes in the road. A briefcase dangling from the handlebars made his balancing act more difficult. Robert Thomas straightened in the hope of being seen. Cilydd was preoccupied. His face was flushed with the exertion of the long ride. To gain his attention, the molecatcher had to hurry across the cobbles, his knees bent with the need to make rapid strides.

'John Cilydd More! I am here to give a true account of my stewardship.'

Cilydd held on to the handlebars and gazed warily at Robert Thomas. He did not appear to be in the mood to relish the mole-catcher's fondness for home-spun eloquence.

'What is the trouble, Robert Thomas?'

'You know I am not a man to complain. And I have nothing against conscientious objectors as such, unlike many people in these troubled times. But I must admit you have the messiest lot I ever remember in Cae Golau these days. They may all be BAs and MAs but they don't know the first thing about shutting gates. I have serious news for you, John Cilydd More. The sheep have eaten the cabbages and cauliflowers in the kitchen garden. And there isn't a single Brussel sprout left. All my labour in vain. And all because a lazy good-for-nothing conshie left the gate open. Can you imagine that? A child would have more sense.'

'What do you expect me to do, Robert Thomas?'

The molecatcher was disappointed. He had expected Cilydd to echo his righteous indignation.

'There are two of them there, John Cilydd More, you could only describe as disgracefully idle. They have a corner between the garden and the old orchard where they hide every chance they can get. I've caught them there more than once. Reading little books no bigger than the palm of my hand and scribbling in secret note-books.'

Renewed screams from inside the house curtailed Robert Thomas's complaint. Cilydd had made for the shop entrance. He was banging impatiently on the frame of the double doors. He shaded his eyes with one hand and tried to peer inside the shop between the old-fashioned advertisements for Colman's Mustard and Mazawattee tea. Dimly he could discern the figure of his sister in her cleaning clothes kneeling in front of a sagging sack of dried fruit with dust-pan and brush in hand. When he banged on the door again she rose stiffly from the floor to let him in. He edged through the half door without speaking. They were both aware of the figure of Robert Thomas like a question mark lurking on the forecourt. Nanw occupied herself with bolting the door. Cilydd listened rigidly to Gwydion's muffled howls rising and falling in the interior of the house. The boy would conserve his energies with a wail that came as easily as breathing in order to give off piercing screams at regular intervals.

'What on earth is the matter?' Cilydd said. 'What on earth's going on!'

'Can't you smell it?'

Nanw was already on the offensive.

'Can't you smell it then? We can only thank God the whole place hasn't gone up in flames.'

'Just tell me what happened.'

'All this rationing business. And the Post Office section. I have to do it all myself. All the forms. The Ministry of Food. Everything.'

Nanw was back on her knees with the dust-pan and brush sweeping spilt flour and sugar in a bucket to be carried away. A sack of dried fruit had been toppled over and its contents spread over the floor.

'As if I didn't have enough to do.'

'What happened?'

'The minute my back was turned. I haven't got eyes in the back of my head. And he had matches in his pocket. A box of matches.'

'What did he do?'

Nanw was incoherent with what might have happened. The entire order of the universe had been endangered by the caprice of a wilful child. She was trembling so much as she contemplated the catastrophic consequences of irresponsibility that she was forced to bend double and contain her arms in her lap. Cilydd bent over her, concerned for her distress and even ready to console her.

'You know the trouble as well as I do,' Nanw said. 'But you won't face it.'

All the blood had drained from her face as she looked up at him.

'What did he do?'

'He said he was mixing flour and sugar with paraffin to make mintcake.'

Cilydd smiled in spite of himself.

187

'Go on, laugh at him. And laugh at me. The boy is thoroughly spoilt. His mother never says "no" and never has. And the more she goes away, the more she spoils him when she comes back. Anybody can see it. It's not just my opinion. And you don't do anything about it. And I just have to keep my mouth shut and watch.'

'If he's too much for you, you should say so,' Cilydd said.

He was ready to be agreeable.

'We can always leave him with Menna and Flo Cowley Jones. I just thought it would be good for him here. The atmosphere and so on. The old place. The old style. He's not too young to feel the influence. To sense his inheritance.'

'He's not your son.'

Nanw was hoarse with desperation. Her shoulders shook and she lowered her head until it almost touched her knees as she began to cry.

'He's not your son. Pen Lewis was his father. You've only got to look at him. You must know as well as I do. I can't bear to see you deceived and betrayed. I can't bear it. That man out there saw them together in the garden at Cae Golau. The day the new hospital was opened. He came in here when he was drunk to collect his pension. He tried to put his arm around me. "Come on," he said. "Nobody will notice a thin slice off the loaf." The molecatcher daring to talk to me like that. That's why I turned against her if you want to know. You may have decided to forgive and take the boy as your own. I don't know do I? You don't take me into your confidence. I'm not worth it. You prefer to treat me as if I were the one at fault. I've always been loyal to you all my life. You know that.'

'Where is he? What have you done with him?'

'The cupboard under the stairs,' Nanw said. 'What else could I do?'

She raised an arm imploringly as her brother stalked off down the passage to the old house. Hearing his father's footsteps in the kitchen incited Gwydion to an effort in howling that outdid everything he had previously achieved. When he unlocked the door of the stair dispensary, Cilydd saw a small white face streaked with tears and distorted with fright. Gwydion was squatting on a box filled with dried earth intended for plant cuttings. His arms when he raised them imploringly towards Cilydd were covered with dirt and dust. As if to make double certain of parental sympathy, Gwydion began to cough. His face began to turn purple as his father bent to pick him up. He was rubbing the boy's back when Nanw appeared in the doorway to the kitchen.

'Raking up the past,' she said. 'I suppose that's what you think I'm doing. A bitter old maid raking up the past and your loyal friend Pen Lewis gone to a hero's death in Spain. And you perhaps feeling guilty about it and still doing penance. Forgiveness is all very well and so is repentance I dare say as long as you're still alive to repent. But what I ask you is, just what is she up to now? Have you thought about that? Robert Thomas saw her with the Jewish painter, Hans Benek. I suppose you know that too. Does forgiveness mean she's given a blank cheque for the future, to do just whatever she likes? And how much loyalty has she got left to Wales, may I ask? Swept away by the war effort no doubt and I'm afraid her loyalty to you has gone with it.'

'Just shut your mouth.'

His own mouth barely opened as he pushed past his sister with the boy in his arms.

13

~ i ~

AT THE BUS STATION A UNIFORMED BUS CONDUCTOR CARRYING A load of chromed ticket punches directed Cilydd to a bus shelter on the opposite side of the road. The roar of an engine reverberated so loudly among the stays and struts of the metal roofing that Cilydd had great difficulty in making out what the bus conductor was saying. His accent, too, was unfamiliar. He spoke at great speed as if whatever he had to say was so self-evident that he should not be expected to waste time in saying it.

'It's not worth the company's time to bother with out-of-the-way villages.'

The bus conductor shouted while waving to attract the attention of a colleague in the depths of the bus station.

'It should be along soon. Not that you can depend on Noah Jenkins. He's a bit of a law unto himself. You better not stand where you're standing, friend. You might get run over.'

He glanced at Cilydd, noting he was dressed in black and wearing a black tie.

'Funeral is it? Let's hope Noah gets you there on time. The Ark they call it. You could get there quicker walking. Today you could be lucky. Here he comes. Better get across there quick if you want a seat.'

The bus was an old model, high off the road. It rattled and shook as it chugged down the wet street to the people waiting at the shelter. It was painted blue and the words JENKINS MOTORS CANTRE were blazoned on the side in large white capitals. Cilydd walked across the wet forecourt and avoided the puddles on the wide road. In the warm drizzle the buds on the young plane tree next to the shelter looked ready to stretch into leaf form even as the bus was still moving.

Inside, the passengers were already engaged in establishing comfortable and neighbourly relationships. This was their territory: an extension of their familiar world. The bus served their village, their parish, and once they were on it it was as much a part of their natural habitat as the chapel or the village hall. And it had the additional virtue of being mobile. They accepted Cilydd's presence with friendly waves and an assurance that there was ample room in the chariot. The village wag had already placed himself in a key position in the centre of the back seat. The grin on his moon-shaped face showed he was ready to pipe out amusing remarks whenever the company was inclined to listen. His oval spectacles fitted so closely above his gleaming cheeks it was difficult to imagine how they ever came off. He raised two fingers in an episcopal gesture to gain Cilydd's attention.

'Welcome to Noah's Ark,' he said. 'Where there's room for one there's room for two. Half price if you're willing to go backwards.'

The women particularly responded with encouraging laughter. They turned to look expectantly for further witticisms from the wag's repertoire. It wouldn't matter if they had heard them before: the delivery and the apposite moment were more diverting than the content.

'If you've not been here before, stranger,' the wag said. 'Welcome to the city of Cantre where every cockrel believes the sun comes out to enjoy his morning song.'

The women looked at the solemn newcomer in black to make certain he was capable of entering into the spirit of the occasion. When he had smiled and nodded his tribute, they vied with each other in showing him where he could find the best seat. He sank down to enjoy his limited privacy. The noise level in the bus would be sufficient to allow him to keep his own counsel. The driver mounted the step of the bus. He raised his battered hat to air his balding head and study the passengers as if he were counting them like sheep. The wag at the back was quick to respond to the driver's presence. He recited a home-made epigram in a falsetto voice that made everyone laugh.

> 'Into the ark the animals rush
> While the humans all get out
> and push.'

The driver ran the coins in his leather bag through his fingers, lifted and lowered his hat and made pointed reference to Ianto-the-wag's aversion to any form of exercise except talking. Even as he spoke his glance darted among the passengers gauging their willingness to have their departure delayed by cross-talk, however entertaining. There were still seats to be filled. The older women were cackling and ready for further badinage: but they were always the passengers in the least hurry. For those inclined to insist on adhering to the advertised timetable, an item of news would be more acceptable.

'A land mine,' he said.

The English phrase sounded ominously technical. Everyone stopped talking to listen. The driver looked through the window and swallowed hard before he went on.

'That's what they said it was. I saw a whole row of houses in the middle of the country split open from end to end. Two killed. I knew one of them by sight. There were clothes still hanging from the top of the trees behind the chapel. I took it they were clothes, not skin and flesh. I couldn't stop to look. They waved me on. The crater was big enough to bury two buses in it.'

The war hung in low clouds over their heads and they could never escape it for long. Bad news was like bad weather.

'They found his leg in the garden,' the driver said.

He was pleased with the awed reception.

'I heard that,' he said. 'And they found his old father sitting on a bed, staring at a crack four inches wide in the wall and nursing the face of a grandfather clock in his lap as if it were a little baby.'

The women who had laughed were now murmuring their distress and sympathy. The driver became aware of someone prodding him in the back. A new arrival wanted to mount the step and enter his bus.

'Is there room for one more little one?'

Tasker Thomas was smiling in the most benign manner at everyone. But the mood of the company had changed. Ianto had lapsed into moody silence. The newcomer's large presence was disturbingly unconventional. He had the penetrating tenor and the cadences of a preacher, but he looked like an alien, some kind of tramp with the spring rain clinging like dew to the fringe of ginger hair around his sunburnt pate. His long mackintosh buttoned at the neck reached to his brown walking boots. He carried a khaki rucksack over one shoulder, his mouth was open wide and his pale blue eyes shone with an eagerness to share his perceptions with everyone in equal measure. It was this avidness as much as anything that put them on their guard. The driver sank into the broken-sprung seat behind the large steering wheel. Tasker shuffled down the bus and threw up his arms with delight when he saw Cilydd sitting alone next to a steamed-up window. The women sitting near were interested to witness the encounter of what could have been long-lost brothers.

'Dear friend,' Tasker said. 'Dear friend.'

Cilydd looked quietly embarrassed at Tasker's ineffective

attempt to restrain his joy. The driver half stood up in his seat to ask Tasker to store his rucksack on the sagging luggage rack and not on the floor. Tasker obeyed, giving the driver a beatific smile.

'We are going on the same pilgrimage!'

As he called out, the passengers looked at him with renewed hope. He could have been a travelling entertainer of the old sort, now in reduced circumstances, capable of enlivening the journey home with a more extensive repertoire than Ianto-the-wag. The driver revved the engine to show that it was his intention to begin the journey. Tasker extracted a large brown handkerchief from his mackintosh pocket to blow his nose before sinking down to sit alongside Cilydd who pressed himself against the side of the bus to give the large minister more room.

' "The men I love are dead musicians . . ." '

Tasker was quoting one of Cilydd's early poems: an elegy for the fallen of an earlier war. His tenor voice was sharp enough to pierce the noise of the engine.

> '"My image cannot live in empty sockets . . .
> Each one had stronger title to exist than mine . . ."'

Tasker shook his head and gave a deep sigh.

'It seems unbearably sad,' he said. 'The warp and the woof of it. When we look back and think of his heroic figure on that platform. Dear Val. A young Arthur come to judgment. Defying the cohorts of Lloyd George placemen lined up like a wax-works on the platform behind him. It seems so sad, so bitterly sad. But we mustn't give way. We mustn't.'

'Why not?'

Cilydd muttered rebelliously.

'His message was simple. All embracing. Organic as they say.'

Tasker clenched his fist, determined to be positive. The bus moved off, rumbling and shaking. The driver raised a magnanimous hand to greet a cluster of employees of the company that owned the new bus station. His ageing bus would plough through the rain puddles and he would rise above their disparaging jeers.

'To me he was an inspiration,' Tasker said. 'Right to the very end.'

His voice rose to spell out the simplicity of Val Gwyn's message as well as overcome the grinding noise of the engine.

'God the source of creation, Christ the sacrifice of reconciliation, the Holy Spirit the sustaining power of a better social order. So simple. How could anybody fault it? All he wanted to do was apply it to the little world of Wales.'

'And he failed.'

Cilydd was uncompromisingly morose.

'He failed completely.'

'Who are we to say that? We may have failed him. That is likely enough. But the message lives on. And that is the strength of a message and the test of truth, John Cilydd. The ability to live on. Like your best poems, old friend. Like every good deed, small or large. Part of the creative capital of mankind. The bulwarks against the storms and stresses of destruction.'

Faced with a hill, the driver slammed into a lower gear. The roar of the engine blotted out Tasker's voice. He sat back and shook his head and smiled. At the first opportunity he would say something to cheer Cilydd up. A poet was a sensitive plant in need of a basic quantity of care and protection. An amusing thought had occurred to him that would not keep. He leaned sideways to shout in Cilydd's ear.

'Seize every day as if it were the last bus to salvation!'

His body shook with the bus. His smile was sculptured with imperishable goodwill. The moment the engine noise subsided, he was ready to give an account of himself.

'I doss down with the Christian Pacifist Unit in the docks,' Tasker said. 'We've been bombed twice and nobody hurt in that big old house. Every window blown out. "Guy Fawkes, thou shoulds't be living at this hour," says little Les from Cardigan. He left a message with Sister Emmanuel, about the funeral. The time and the place. So off I went and one of the surgeons who hates conchies and Germans in that order asked me where the hell I thought I was going. And I told him, "I was a padre in the last show as they call it and I'm a reverend conchie in this one. A conchie volunteer." He didn't like it. So off I went like a latter day version of Bunyan's pilgrim pretending to be George Borrow. To keep me company on the way, I decided to meditate on suffering. With so much of it in the world, how in God's name can we cope?'

It was a rhetorical question. Like a man who has solved a crossword puzzle, he waited a decent interval to give his companion time to ponder the clue. Cilydd wiped the film of condensation off the window with his sleeve and peered out at the fresh green countryside they were passing through, even in the lumbering bus, too quickly for him to reduce to a recognisable pattern. Tasker's voice was strained with urgency.

'We need a new definition of courage,' he said. 'I know that much for certain. And yet it's not new at all. I realise that. To confront persecutors and torturers and to do it on your own, alone, what is that except a modern version of martyrdom? Doing it alone is the most frightening part. You don't join the noble army of martyrs until you've been through the fire and come out on the other side. In a day and age like this such a notion seems so absurd and incongruous. No part of modern living. The queues outside the football grounds and the picture houses. The holidays by the seaside. Fishing off the pier. The day has dawned and we still don't know it. The time when the intellectual is called to withstand pain and imprisonment with the patience of a dumb animal. To tell you the truth, dear friend, my meditations went clean against my happy-go-lucky nature.'

He winked at Cilydd. He was enjoying being in the company of an old friend to whom he could unburden whatever passed through his mind without feeling unduly wrong or foolish.

'You'll never guess where I spent last night.'

He nudged Cilydd to show how jovial he felt.

'In the barn at Caerhen Uchaf. As snug as a bug in the hay. I lay there listening to the dawn chorus and I thought for one blissful moment I was in heaven or at least in the earthly paradise. I waited until seven o'clock before knocking the kitchen door and opening it and calling out, "Do we have people?" What a place! What a refuge. Do you remember dear old Gomer Owen, Caerhen? Up there nothing changes. A green citadel. The last fastness. You can look down on the village and you can see it nestling there, a sweet undamaged toy town . . . And there was buttermilk and a loaf as big as this seat. And those hills fit for the gods to walk on. And I thought, "how beautiful upon the mountains are the feet of him that bringeth good tidings, that publisheth peace . . ." '

Words failed him at last. He leaned his forehead against his fingertips as though the weight of his thoughts was too heavy to bear. In the back of the bus some of the passengers had begun singing. Ianto on the edge of his seat made gestures that implied their voices would help the bus on its way. A Sunday School hymn grew into a rousing chorus. Under the impact of the sound Tasker's mood changed. He was ready to join in the simple pleasures of country folk. He even waved an arm encouragingly.

' "For each one that stays faithful under his banner, Jesus has a crown prepared . . ." '

He failed to persuade Cilydd to sing. He sought an explanation for the poet's withdrawn condition.

'Where is Amy. Dear Amy?'

He shouted above the singing.

'In London,' Cilydd said. 'As far as I know.'

It was as much as he was prepared to reveal. Tasker was nodding approvingly.

'A practical woman,' he said. 'A woman of great ability. A great heart. Seeking every chance to alleviate suffering.'

The bus stopped outside a chapel and a row of houses. There were cheerful exchanges as a portly woman wearing a man's cap descended with her basket on her arm. Tasker was restless in his seat, showing the keenest interest in everything going on around him. He made out the name of the chapel.

'Peniel,' he said. 'Dear me. Peniel. I preached here once what seems like a century ago. It was one of a pastorate of four churches. Baptists thin on the ground in this corner of the country. Very daring and ecumenical as they say now, for a Methodist like me to ascend a Baptist pulpit. Old Elis Prys, you see. A man ahead of his time. Full of pithy sayings, dear old Elis Prys. A man for long pastorates. Do you know what he said to me? "Never miss a funeral, my boy," he said. "At any cost. In this part of the world they are a way of life, and have been since the megaliths." Peniel. Where Jacob wrestled with the angel.'

Tasker sighed and shook his head, stirred by memories that could make him smile and make him sad. The bus back-fired as they resumed their journey. As it rumbled downhill Tasker appeared to be attempting to reconcile the young minister he had been with his present condition.

'We have to hold on,' he said. 'Like Jacob did. Hold on and demand a blessing. That will be our reward. I am more a tramp and a down-and-out than a minister, but I would like to take part in Val's funeral rites. I hope they will allow that. Just to tell them something of his vision, for a better Wales and a better world. Charity begins at home. Of course it does. But you can't have one without the other.'

On the hillside the light seemed to lift the fine rain and thin cloud to one side to reveal in detail fields of young corn with a brilliant lustre on the green shoots. On its way up a steep hill with a grinding of gears the bus came to a halt. This was not entirely unexpected. Ianto called out, "All hands off deck!" and invited ladies obviously unsuited to the task to get out and push, assuring them their fares would be returned if they got the vehicle to the top of the hill. The driver did not take kindly to his banter. He lifted his hat on and off and stared stonily through the windscreen while the passengers gave out a variety of good-humoured protests and shuffled cheerfully off the bus. Tasker listened attentively to their chatter. He wanted Cilydd to share his enjoyment of the poetic element in their dialect. It was such a rich and expressive reflection of the particular qualities of a people whose way of life had altered little over the centuries.

'"The taste of the rich earth," dear Val used to call it,' Tasker said. ' "As much part of the landscape as the sunsets that give the sea its repertoire of colour." Dear Val. I can't listen to their voices without hearing him and feeling his presence.'

Tasker raised his eyebrows and held out his hand as delicately as an orchestral conductor as he listened to the outpouring of a farm wife smelling of hay and camphor balls temporarily stuck in the narrow aisle. He offered to relieve her of her basket. She barely interrupted her canticle to decline the offer.

'You think I'm glorifying the commonplace,' Tasker said.

He paused in his effort to get to his feet to put the candid question to Cilydd. He answered his own question before moving into the aisle.

'Perhaps it is only when such things are threatened with extinction we recognise their true value.'

After the rain, the countryside was so fresh the people from the bus looked around as if they had never seen the place before. Under the warmth of the sun, heady scents crept out of the hedgerows. At the top of the hill larks were ascending. Tasker held up a finger to show he was listening to a cuckoo calling from a distant wood. A shaft of sunlight picked out a white-washed farmhouse on the hillside in minute detail. In the hedges behind the straggling passengers, chaffinches began to chirp among the wet leaves. Tasker could not resist making apt quotations. Cilydd lowered his head as he listened. The bus waited until the passengers had reached the top before beginning its own crawl up the hill.

A black Morris Eight hooted vigorously as it overtook the bus. Everyone turned to witness the manoeuvre. At first Cilydd and Tasker did not recognise Amy at the wheel. She was wearing a blue forage cap and an unfamiliar uniform with epaulettes edged in red. At the top of the hill she waited for them with a triumphant grin on her face.

'Did you think I wouldn't get here?'

She was pleased with herself and therefore they should be pleased with her too. The back seat of the little car was covered with forms and files and leaflets. While Amy was shifting them to one side to make room for him, Tasker raised a hand in solemn farewell to passengers getting ready to remount their bus. Cilydd was still puzzled by the car in Amy's possession as he sank into the front passenger seat. A black arm-band was conspicuous on her uniform sleeve.

'Where on earth did you get this?'

'Requisitioned.'

Amy's voice was as bright as a child's enjoying a game she has improvised for herself.

'To be more precise,' she said. 'It belongs to a Lady Arnold and it's on loan to the Red Cross. And now it's on loan to me. I worked it all out. We have this weekend conference in Plas Iscoed. *The Battle For Full Employment*. I signed myself out for the afternoon. I've told Eirwen you'll be coming back with me tonight.'

She turned, raising her voice to extend the invitation to include Tasker. She spoke in a teasing fashion.

'Old haunts,' she said. 'Old flames even. What do you say Reverend Tasker?'

Tasker crouched forward.

'Oh no,' he said. 'I don't think so. It's not for me. I tried in the past to move among the influential of this world. But it wasn't a success.'

'Maybe you gave up too easily.'

Their exchange had an edge, but it was amiable enough. Amy had to concentrate on the route. All the fingerposts had been removed. Tasker should have been more familiar with the route than either Amy or Cilydd, but he found it difficult even to distinguish between farm lanes and the country roads and was obliged to confess himself confused.

'We mustn't lose our way,' Amy said. 'That would never do.'

Her mood of exaltation evaporated as they peered from one hillside to the other and found them all alike. Tasker tried his best to be helpful. He laid an arm across a heap of Ministry of Health leaflets to stop them slithering to the floor.

'I don't remember what the farmhouse looked like,' Amy said. 'Well enough to distinguish it from other farmhouses around here. But I do remember the chapel. It had stables underneath it. Val asked me if I'd like to be married there. I was so taken with the stables I said yes. And now here I am on the way to his funeral. Sad of course. Terribly sad. But completely dry-eyed. Isn't that shameful?'

She looked at Cilydd inviting his rebuke.

'Something in us always dies when those we love die,' he said.

He spoke so sympathetically, she reached out her hand to touch his in a token of silent gratitude. Tasker leaned forward to pat her shoulder and raise a hand in a gesture of benediction.

'What I want to get across, you know, in as few words as possible . . .'

199

Tasker cleared his throat in an effort to control his emotions.

'. . . is why he meant so much to us. Why we loved him so much if you like.'

He sighed loudly.

'It's very difficult,' he said.

Amy's voice sounded hard and bright.

'Well, what do you think of me?' she said. 'You could start there. What does the Reverend Tasker Thomas say about a wife and mother who neglects her husband and her children in her reckless pursuit of political power? What does he say about that?'

Tasker shook his head disapprovingly.

'You mustn't torment yourself,' he said. 'No good at all will come of that. Especially now.'

'Now?'

Amy snapped out.

'Now. As good a time as any other.'

They slowed down at a crossroads uncertain which way to take.

'I'm sure we should turn here,' she said. 'I'm almost certain of it.'

Tasker waved an arm to signify the whole district.

'This is such an enclosed traditional community,' he said. 'You can quite see why he loved it so much. As old Elis Prys used to say it's like a Welsh Outer Hebrides, landlocked in its own delightful language.'

'And I'm completely lost.'

Amy sounded exasperated. Tasker remained resolutely calm.

'What I want to say in as few words as possible,' he said. 'Is why his life was such an inspiration to each one of us. What his essential message was. It could be quite hard for them to understand. What Val meant in the wider world.'

'If we don't find the way, we'll be too late for you to say anything,' Amy said. 'Perhaps we should have followed the bus to Cantre and taken it from there.'

She leaned over the steering wheel and made a decision to turn right instead of going straight on.

'I know what I've been wanting to ask you,' Amy said. 'The phrase kept repeating itself in my head as I drove along. What does it mean. "Let the dead bury the dead"?'

200

Tasker gave a friendly chuckle. This was the sort of Sunday School class dispute he was adept at resolving.

'Aha,' he said. 'That's a difficult one.'

'Tell me,' Amy said. 'I'd really like to know.'

'I can start by telling you what it doesn't mean.'

'What does it mean? That's what I want to know.'

'It could mean several things,' Tasker said.

'That's just what I was afraid of.'

'What it doesn't mean, my dear, it doesn't mean we have to set aside our basic human obligations. What we are trying to do now . . . Isn't that the chapel? Just up there. With the burial ground on the hillside behind it.'

Amy slowed down so that they could study the site more carefully.

' "Let the dead bury the dead".'

Tasker resumed his exposition of the enigmatic phrase.

'An absolute priority of the call of the Kingdom,' he said. 'In my view, that's what it means. Such a harsh injunction. Asking the impossible.'

'What's the point of that?' Amy said.

Tasker waved a finger excitedly as if he were indicating a chink of light at the end of a tunnel.

'Take his case,' he said. 'Dear Val. Ready to give up everything for the sake of his mission. You can bear witness to that. Even the closest warmest most comforting human relationships. Even life itself. Yes. Giving that up. The most precious possession.'

Cilydd drew their attention to the chapel.

'People in black,' he said. 'You can see them up there. Assembling outside the chapel. That must be the place.'

Now that the way was clear, they travelled on in silence.

~ ii ~

Hans Benek clasped his hands together with his thumb knuckles pressed into his lips. He leaned out of the window of the studio on the second floor of Plas Iscoed to attempt his imitation of a cuckoo call. He was rewarded for his efforts when Amy and John Cilydd paused in their measured pacing of the terrace to look up. He waved and spread out his arms to share with them his appreciation of the terraces and the gardens and the brilliance of the morning sunlight playing on the water of the ornamental lake.

'What's he doing here?'

There was no disguising the trace of suspicion and distrust in Cilydd's voice. He was still dressed in black after the funeral. He had to resist the attractions of the place until they could escape from it. The slopes of the woodland beyond the gardens were alive with birdsong. In so much lavish sunlight everything out of doors was brimming over with potential for pleasure and joy. He gripped his hands behind his back and watched Amy and Hans wave at each other. Hans began a series of triumphant gestures, in order to bring their attention to a particular camellia bush and more importantly his own unique aerial view of the rose-coloured petaloid structures nestling in the security of the dark shining leaves as if they had achieved the capacity to live for ever.

'Painting as he never painted before apparently,' Amy said. 'Eirwen has been marvellous. Handing over her studio. And he's so relaxed now. Doesn't have nightmares about Nazis coming to collect him.'

The critical expression on her husband's face made conversation difficult.

'We must talk,' Amy said. 'We really must.'

'How did he get here?'

Hans hung out of the window expecting more attention. Cilydd moved away as he murmured his question.

'Eirwen said he could stay here as long as he liked, so long as he exercised his art to the top of his bent,' Amy said. 'You can't call that anything except enlightened patronage. He was employed on Air-Force camouflage until he got some toxic infection of the lungs. That got him his discharge. And now here he is painting away and happier than he's ever been in what amounted to a pretty miserable life from all I hear.'

'You seem to know a great deal about him,' Cilydd said.

'Well of course I do. And so would you if you paid a little more attention to what was actually going on in the world.'

They followed a path between smooth columns of beech trees towards the small pavilion with the Latin inscription on the stone lintel obscured by the star-shaped flowers of the white clematis trained to grow over the portico. With such a southern aspect there was a trace of truth in the boast of the inscription that this refuge would provide perpetual spring and long summers. A pair of chaffinches, their tails tipping up and down flew up from the steps as Amy approached. Cilydd stood still to watch their flight. Without going further than an azalea bush about to break into flower, they looked at each other and looked at him before flying further away.

'It's ironic,' Cilydd said.

'What is?'

Amy turned to look down at him from the highest step.

'To be here on the day after Val's funeral,' he said. 'These people did their best to destroy him.'

'Really John Cilydd. That's nonsense. Absolute nonsense.'

'They dangled the promise of being Warden of the Adult College and then snatched it away. That Lord Iscoed made sure he wouldn't get a fellowship. Everything they ever did militated against everything he ever stood for.'

'I probably did him more harm than they ever did,' Amy said.

She sat on the segment of the wooden seat warmed by the sunlight. Behind her the shadowy interior of the stone structure was as uninviting as a damp cave. With the palms of her hands against the seat she brooded over her own shortcomings, momentarily as rigid as a funerary monument. Cilydd could not resist pressing home his advantage.

'The last time I came here was with Pen Lewis, to picket their pompous garden fête,' he said. 'He borrowed one of my suits to look respectable enough to get in. Poor old Pen. "Aid for Spain". Poor Spain. That's what kind of a place this is. A bastion of privilege. Built on the blood and sweat of Welsh workers. I tell you I can't wait to get away from here.'

He stood on the path like a nervous animal ready to turn and flee at the slightest sign of danger.

'We should talk,' Amy said. 'We really should.'

In the gap between them there were barriers of distinct and separate cares and preoccupations as heavy as dolerite boulders that had to be shifted before they could begin to communicate freely.

'I wasn't much use to Val,' Amy said. 'If I didn't know that at the time, I certainly know it now. I haven't been much good to you either, have I? If you wanted to get rid of me, I wouldn't blame you. You'd be better off without me.'

Cilydd went pale. Suddenly he was unsteady on his feet. His arm reached out for support.

'Mind you for my own selfish reasons I'd prefer a separation,' Amy said. 'To keep up appearances. To avoid damage to what they call my public life. Ridiculous expression. Not so ridiculous either. I don't appear to have much talent for personal relations. I seem to let everybody down. Maybe I'll be better in public life. They say people who devote themselves to politics are often deficient and inadequate on the personal level in their private lives. Why don't you come and sit here? I feel as if I'm rehearsing for addressing a public meeting.'

He was unable to smile at her attempt at a joke. He moved up the three steps with the somnambular care of a convalescent still unsteady on his feet.

'We must be honest with each other,' Amy said. 'It may be all we'll have left in the end. It's no use going on and on about Val and Enid or Pen. We loved them. We both loved them according to our fashion. Loved them to distraction. But they're dead and buried and rotting in the grave. And we are still here. We can only build with what we've got left.'

'I love you.'

He was choking with so much emotion he could only whisper the endearment. Amy frowned with the effort of concentrating on her thesis.

'We can start again,' she said. 'If there is such a thing as a fresh start. I know you don't approve of my Labour connection, or whatever I should call it. But I've made my mind up. I've got to try and change things and as far as I can see the only effective way is to attempt it from the inside. My views haven't changed. The aims are exactly the same. The same as yours unless you have changed. We've spoken so little of these things lately. I haven't wanted to give you unnecessary offence. Perhaps I should have been franker. Much more forthcoming. But I became so wrapped up in the War Effort and you did exactly the opposite. And now I'm obsessed with the whole concept of building a new Britain and a different world altogether after the war. I've just got to see how far I can go. Do you understand that?'

Cilydd nodded miserably.

'You'd be perfectly justified in insisting on a divorce,' Amy said. 'I wouldn't contest that. It's not what I want. All I ask for is freedom of action.'

'Of course,' Cilydd said.

He found the strength to speak.

'You're absolutely entitled to that,' he said. 'I've always said so.'

She smiled at him affectionately.

'I mustn't weaken,' she said. 'What we are doing now is renewing a contract. Negotiating a new bargain.'

Cilydd hung his head.

'You can have whatever you want,' he said. 'So long as you don't leave me.'

Amy took his hand. She was ready to comfort him and take some account of the emotional strain he was under.

'I'm a wife and mother,' she said. 'I know that. Responsibilities and so on. But in the new world after the war, women must come out and take their proper share of power. Take their place in the machinery of government. They are more balanced and more mature than men in all sorts of ways. If we're going to avoid the threat of more wars in the future, it is absolutely essential that women have a voice, a decisive voice, in the way the affairs of the world should be run. You agree with that, don't you, John Cilydd?'

'Yes of course I do.'

He sounded ready to agree with anything she said so long as she smiled at him. She spoke more confidentially as she revealed her plans for the near future.

'The boys are growing fast,' she said. 'If I were chosen as the Labour candidate for North Maelor, I would have to spend time nursing the constituency. I could ask my Aunt Esther to come and live with us. Or Connie Clayton. Or both of them. We have enough room if you were willing to have them.'

She caught the expression of misery on his face and hurried on.

'We have to look ahead. Connie is a super cook. Esther adores the boys. Handles them beautifully. And they could spend more time at Glanrafon. Your sister Nanw would like that. I'm looking far ahead of course. But one has to. And it's far healthier I'd say than dwelling for ever on the past. What's the matter?'

'My sister! She can't look after the children. She's unbalanced.'

He was so vehement Amy gave up outlining her design for their future.

'Absolutely unbalanced,' Cilydd said. 'She says Gwydion isn't my son. She says Pen Lewis was his father.'

In the silence every sound in the world was enlarged, even the sound of a wireless through an open window in the Plas. In the distance someone was chopping wood. The thuds reverberated with painful regularity. A sparrow alighted on the steps and its eye looked bright with a malevolent intelligence.

'She's right.'

She spoke so quietly the bird was undisturbed. It took its time to demonstrate how quickly it could move its feathers and vanish from their sight.

'I thought you knew,' Amy said. 'I thought you accepted it.'

Cilydd's shoulders were stooped under the weight of his misery.

'In the garden at Cae Golau,' he said. 'Robert Thomas saw you.'

'It's true,' Amy said. 'I gave way to him. I wanted him. I used to long for him. Physical longing. They call that love. I let him down too. There's your reason for a divorce if you want one. They're dead John Cilydd. They're safely dead. And we are left to grow older.'

Amy's arm stole over his shoulders to comfort him. He turned to seize her in a fierce embrace muttering her name like an incantation, swearing his devotion over and over again. She responded to his kisses. They had their grief in common. They could find some consolation in each other if they made the effort. Ready as she was to abandon herself, the sound of voices on the path and the squeak of a wheelchair made her thrust Cilydd away. He was still close to her when the wheelchair stopped on the path below. Sir Prosser Pierce raised his flat black hat. In his lap was a large bunch of bluebells freshly picked, and across the arms of the chair his ornamental walking stick. The invalid chair was being pushed by a sallow-faced man with a sharp nose and black hair brushed across his head to disguise premature baldness.

'Forgive the intrusion!'

Sir Prosser raised his hat a second time in case John Cilydd had failed to notice the old-world flourish.

'The merry month of May,' Sir Prosser said. 'Let an old man announce his gratitude for being allowed to witness the miracle once again. D. I. Everett! Staunch colleague, Apostle of Progress. Grey Eminence-in-waiting! Why don't you present the beautiful Mrs More with a posy of bluebells? A true token from an old admirer.'

Sir Prosser chuckled and sat back in his wheelchair like an actor-manager, temporarily incapacitated, directing a recalcitrant group of actors, uncertain that their efforts would be properly rewarded. D. I. Everett grasped the cool stems of the bluebells and ascended the steps to present them to Amy who blushed and laughed before she accepted them. She introduced Everett to her husband. Sir Prosser observed the minimal ritual with undisguised delight.

'It's quite wrong of me I know,' he said. 'But I can't resist the flavour. Little known facts, unobserved coincidences, the grace notes of history, shall we call them? Well now then, John Cilydd More, how does it feel to be married to a woman of the future? To be the consort of a superior being so obviously marked out for greatness.'

'Sir Prosser!'

Amy spoke in a loud voice that would mask her husband's withdrawn taciturnity as well as demonstrate her readiness to join Sir Prosser's game.

'You are a shameless flatterer,' she said. 'Quite shameless.'

Sir Prosser responded with a burst of operatic protest.

'Indeed I am not,' he said. 'Sincerity is my hallmark.'

He smiled before becoming serious and inviting Cilydd's close attention to a finely wrought apologia.

'I have been converted,' Sir Prosser said. 'By a heady combination of revolutionary fire, feminine charm and the Beveridge
Report! Mark you, these ingredients are not so incongruous as
they may sound. Not so much the road to Damascus as the road to
Wigan Pier. My whole world has made a decisive shift to the left
and if I didn't move with it, where would I be? Hanging in mid-air
like an improvident balloon awaiting inevitable deflation!'

He was so amused by his own invention, he could only improve
upon it by a further bout of daring frankness. He kept an eye on
each member of his small audience to reassure himself that they
tasted the trace of salt in his sallies.

'There are unkind observers who say I know which way the wind
will blow before I get up in the morning. So be it. My public skin is
hardened and impervious to insult. A man who sits in a wheelchair is safe from the white feather. I know this much. We must
not win this war, only to lose the peace. Is that not so, brother
Everett?'

Everett agreed and then moved behind the wheelchair so that he
could wink and smile sheepishly at Amy and Cilydd. Sir Prosser
had more to say and every intention of saying it.

'As one who has done the State some service, I can claim that all
along, the great dynamic behind my efforts has been the drive
towards the elimination of poverty and loathsome inequalities. Not
for nothing was I born over a shop in a South Wales mining valley,
eh Everett?'

He narrowed his eyes and stared accusingly at Cilydd.

'Do I sense that our efforts are not meeting with your whole-
hearted approval, John Cilydd More? If I may be totally frank, and
what else is old age good for, you seem a little withdrawn and out
of sympathy with our enthusiasm.'

'I don't hear much about Wales and Welshness in your pro-
gramme,' Cilydd said.

His arms were tightly folded as if at least for his wife's sake he
was resolved to keep his dissent within bounds. Sir Prosser fondled
the ornamental handle of the walking stick. Now the bluebells were
no longer in his lap there was a repertoire of gestures he could
make with the stick if he had a mind to.

'Beware of poets, Everett,' he said. 'They are worse than the Ides of March.'

He raised the stick to underline his jovial warning.

'Plato was quite right, you know. Poetry is inimical to the pitiless art of politics. Remember I said that when you come to collect my *obiter dicta* as I am sure you will. As a minimum act of piety. D. I. Everett and I come from the same valley, Mrs More. Were you aware of that fascinating fact? While your good husband and his friends were waiting for a telegram so to speak from Owain Glyndŵr, my friend here was listening to the music of Karl Marx.'

There was no response to be conjured out of John Cilydd: not even a smile. Sir Prosser's interest and his pleasantries were simultaneously exhausted.

'We must leave this pair of married lovers in their bower of bliss, Everett,' he said. 'Drive on, there's a good chap. Let us seek a little more inspiration in the murmurs of bright Spring before we settle down to more gruelling business.'

Cilydd began to protest before the wheelchair was out of sight.

'What a repulsive pair,' he said.

Amy looked angry and embarrassed.

'Shut up,' she said. 'Keep your voice down.'

Obediently he kept his mouth shut. There was sufficient breeze to make the young leaves on the beech trees tremble and create a dapple of quivering shadows on the sunlit slope. The sky above them was a brilliant cloudless blue.

'I don't know how you can bear to mix with such people,' Cilydd said.

There was no reproach in his voice, only puzzlement. This seemed to irritate Amy even more.

'My goodness,' she said. 'I had no idea you were so pure.'

'Sir Prosser passes,' Cilydd said. 'And all the invisible strings of power pass in silence from Liberal to Labour. That's what's happening in the Welsh rabbit warren. And in the world outside the Anglo-Americans are bombing and blasting their way to unconditional surrender.'

'If there's one thing I can't bear John Cilydd,' Amy said. 'It's the way you over-simplify things. I mean it might be a method for

209

shelling out lovely lyrics: but in practical life, I can tell you here and now it's utterly useless.'

Cilydd showed how unwilling he was to deepen any rift between them by disagreeing with her. Each involuntary gesture, the note of pleading in his voice, made his devotion and attachment to her manifest.

'You said we had to be honest with each other,' Cilydd said. 'We've known all this for years. When Val was alive we called him the Puppet Master. Pen used to call him a "Fascist lackey". He's part of the way the system works, which ever party is in power. Not even a revolution would dislodge him.'

Amy looked grim and determined.

'I'm not his puppet,' she said. 'I can tell you that much.'

'So why do you have to please him?'

'That's simple enough.'

Her answer was blunt.

'He's still a power in the land. He's written on my behalf to Griffith Pike. To please Eirwen I think, more than to please me. I wouldn't claim to be able to fathom his motives. Anyway he wrote. And so has Die Everett. So there you are. I am in their debt.'

'Who is Griffith Pike?'

Cilydd was making an effort to show tolerance and interest. This was reinforced by the way he gazed at her face like a parent unable to stop doting on the beauty of an only child.

'Chairman of the constituency party,' Amy said. 'Chairman of the County Education Committee. Trade Union boss. I'm surprised you haven't heard of him.'

His open devotion drew her closer to him.

'I'm sorry, but it's the game you have to play. It's no use going in for politics in this country unless you are prepared to play it. You understand these things better than I do really, except that you've deliberately turned your back on it all. Sulking in your Welsh poetic tent.'

She was smiling at him and the sign of approval raised his spirits.

'This is the only avenue open,' Amy said. 'Val used to say that when he was arguing with Pen down in the Settlement. If you can't bring about a religious revival or a bloody revolution, this is the

210

only way. I'm not stupid you know. At least not as stupid as I look.'
They sat side by side as decorously as an old couple enjoying the glory of the May morning together.

'I don't know what they'd think,' Amy said quietly. 'I suppose they'd both hate what I'm doing. Even more than you do.'

They listened to voices coming through the open windows of the great house. A field ambulance drove into view beyond the trees.

'It's a strange feeling,' Amy said. 'To see those rows of empty beds. So white and clean. Ready for the first casualties when the Second Front opens. And we're sitting here enjoying a private view of the Garden of Eden. It doesn't seem right, does it? This world was never designed for total war. You don't hate me, do you? Even if you hate what I'm doing.'

Cilydd spoke as simply as a child as she took his hand.

'I love you,' he said. 'I couldn't live without you.'

14

~ i ~

GRIFFITH PIKE HAD SOME DIFFICULTY IN LIFTING HIS BULK OUT OF the depth of the leather armchair. As if not to embarrass him by observing the process too closely, Amy turned her head to study the view of the waterfall through the bay window of the hotel lounge. At a distance it was picturesque rather than awesome. The white foam seemed as stationary as oil paint and the noise was no more than traffic in a distant street. The slopes above the falls were covered with regimented plantations of spruce that exuded a misty power to draw down rain-bearing clouds. Nearer at hand, stunted oaks shared zones of moss and lichen with the rocks out of which they had struggled to grow. Griffith Pike cleared his throat. Speaking English for the benefit of D. I. Everett his Welsh accent was tinged with an aggressive Liverpool twang.

'Now you'll have to excuse me for a minute.'

The way it rumbled out sounded more like an accusation than

211

an apology. Amy raised her head as if she were considering rising respectfully to her feet. Everett, his chair placed so that he could divide his attention between the chairman and Amy and keep them under equal surveillance, considered the tips of his fingers which he had already brought together in a pyramidical formation that he could contemplate while he gave the problems confronting them concentrated consideration. Yellow crumbs from the slice of sponge cake Griffith Pike had just finished eating hung in the crevice that divided his chin from his cheek on the left side of his face. His chest rose and fell like a defective bellows as he stood erect and eyed this attractive woman who needed to pay him court in order to further her candidacy. His pale eyes floating in a transparent liquid looked for the appropriate combination of sympathy and respect. Amy was dressed in a blue-grey tweed suit and wore a dark blue hat tilted forward at a fashionable angle. Griffith Pike stared at her as if every detail of her form would be stored in his memory.

'I wasn't always like this.'

The complaint bubbled in his throat defying the constriction of emphysema.

'I wasn't always a wreck and a ruin,' Griffith Pike said. 'I was something worth looking at in my younger days.'

Amy rewarded him with a brilliant smile.

'You are still a fine figure of a man, Mr Pike,' she said. 'And in any case, there is nothing more impressive than an older man who has wisdom as well as experience. You ask any woman with an ounce of common sense.'

A slow smile lifted his long face. He wagged a finger to draw D. I. Everett's attention to Amy's display of tact and grace.

'You watch her lad,' he said. 'Pick up a few tips. Like one of them charm schools. That's the way to handle people.'

He moved away slowly as if he were listening to the softness of his own footfall in the carpet pile. By the door he looked first one way and then the other waiting to be directed to the men's toilet. Everett bent his wrists in Amy's direction without detaching his fingertips from each other.

'Gwenda was so sorry she couldn't come,' he said. 'Sends her love. Wants you to be sure to come and stay with us, next time you come to London.'

Amy found it difficult to reply. She was confronted by a former admirer without his wife. Griffith Pike's fulsome compliments still hung about like a deodorant in the hotel lounge. It was difficult to revert instantly to the blunt and forthright manner of undergraduate contemporaries.

'Did you hear about Frankie Yoreth?'

Everett had sensed her difficulty. To talk about a mutual friend would be a way of narrowing the distance between them.

'Poor old Frankie,' Everett said.

'What happened to him?'

'Stationed somewhere in Cornwall. Drowned trying to rescue a dog.'

'Oh no. How terrible . . . Poor Frankie.'

He watched her reaction closely before he mirrored her sad smile.

'Such a clown, wasn't he?' Everett said. 'Set on being the life and soul of every occasion. All he wanted to do was sing and dance. He used to write to Gwenda. Hoping to get transferred to ENSA. Too late now of course. Gwenda likes to keep in touch. Wants to know what's happened to everybody.'

He plunged his hand into his jacket pocket and drew out a small sapphire brooch on a thin gold chain. He let it dangle from his bony fingers so that Amy could see the stone catch the light.

'Remember this?' he said.

Amy shifted uneasily in her chair. She stared at the brooch and at the dark intense figure of Die Everett.

'I brought it to prove my soul was not devoid of poetry,' he said. 'Amazing isn't it? I've kept it all these years. Hidden in my heart as they say. I wanted you to see it.'

'Dan Ike.'

She was awarding him the name he used to prefer.

'Emblem of devotion,' he said. 'That's what it was. And that's what it will always be. I didn't get you. Never had a hope. And I didn't get my Revolution. But I'll be faithful to both, in my fashion. That's what I wanted to say. A secret seal. A pledge. I'll keep it.'

He slipped the brooch back in his pocket.

'Can I ask you something,' he said. 'I know I shouldn't. One little favour to a loyal retainer. And I am loyal. You know that don't you, Amy?'

He was studying her face with a worshipful intensity.

'Why did you marry him?'

Once he had put the question he looked startled by his own daring. Amy laughed. She did not appear to be displeased by his curiosity.

'He rescued me from the classroom,' Amy said. 'For that a girl has to be grateful.'

He leaned so far forward he almost knelt in front of her.

'The real reason,' he said. 'I'd like to know.'

His sharp face was strained like a man in the throes of a romantic torment. Infected by the intensity of his mood Amy contemplated the view of the waterfall through the hotel window. Seagulls had flown inland in anticipation of rough weather.

'Why do we do anything?' she said. 'I think sometimes we ourselves are the last to know. For Enid's sake. Because I loved her so much. For Bedwyr's sake. Her lovely little boy. For security. Because he loved me so much.'

She pulled herself up abruptly as a casual visitor entered the lounge, looked around and walked out again.

'You mustn't ask me such questions,' Amy said. 'Really you mustn't.'

Everett's elbows pressed into his sides as he clasped his fists under his chin like a man prepared to bare his soul.

'He may be a poet,' he said. 'But you mustn't hold it against me when I say he's not worthy of you. Let's understand each other, Amy. I'm at your service. Always. That's all I wanted you to know.'

In an interval of respectful silence Amy accepted his homage. She rewarded him with an affectionate smile. He was her political mentor. The idealogue who would provide her with the substance and structure of a campaign: guide her through the dangerous waters of party practice, instruct her in the arcane skills of the great game.

'Look,' Amy said. 'Who's this fourth candidate? Sergeant Roberts of the Pioneer Corps. Where did he spring from?'

Everett lay back in his chair, ready to display his intelligence.

214

'Local lad,' he said. 'Father, ex-miner's agent who keeps a tobacconist's shop in the High Street. Not very popular for reasons I am still trying to ascertain. Some rumour about misappropriation of Welfare Funds. But nothing proven. Stigma unlikely to damage the son who has made a lifelong habit saying "hello" to everybody. Under his mother's instructions. "Don't you ever pass anybody, my boy, without asking how they are."'

They allowed themselves a brief laugh before Everett embarked on a brisk critique of Amy's progress.

'So far you've done extremely well. What we have to concentrate on is damping down the prejudice against women politicians and playing down the influence of your nationalistic past. That's where I can help. I bring you Red credentials. In our own quiet way we're going to move North Maelor half-way to Moscow.'

'I don't know,' she said. 'It is disturbing. Prosser Pierce was so definite about there only being three horses in the race and me being the favourite and that sort of stuff.'

Everett resumed a calm, meditative pose, brushing his fingertips with his lips.

'We have to look out for him,' he said. 'That's something I needed to tell you. We need to be frank and open with each other.'

Amy nodded her approval.

'He's not just a trimmer,' Everett said. 'He's got a twist in his tail. He doesn't really believe in anything except his divine right to partake in the more refined processes of government. We have to make use of him. All well and good. Of course we do. But never rely on him. Never. And we have to watch out for the perverted psychology of old men. I'd say they get spurts of perverted sexual pleasure from dealing out deception and disappointment. It's a kind of lust we have to watch out for.'

He raised his eyebrows to gaze more intently at Amy and gauge the extent to which she appreciated his advice and was likely to rely on the cutting edge of his analysis.

'It's a complex game,' he said. 'Introducing revolution by stealth. But I think we can play it. And it's worth the trouble, Amy. It's almost certainly the most effective way of transforming society. Superior in the long term to war or civil war or open class warfare.'

215

Griffith Pike was returning to join them. He had washed himself and his grey locks were streaked with water. He smiled at Amy and gave an involuntary groan as he resumed his seat.

'Well now then, young lady,' he said. 'The time has come for me to give you a word of advice about your speeches. You've got to warm them up a bit.'

Amy sat up as attentive as a model pupil listening to a teacher. Griffith Pike relished her response.

'I don't know what young Lenin here has been trying to stuff down your pretty throat, but I can tell you this, here and now lass. Karl Marx does not cut any ice in North Maelor. Go for the simple issues. One at a time.'

Griffith Pike roughed out a straight left with his large fist. Flecks of saliva appeared at the corner of his mouth. In an obscure way the motions he was going through were a tribute to the compelling beauty of Amy's presence. Somehow the effort he made would tear aside the layers of custom and costume and reveal the irresistible radiance of the naked woman to his eager gaze and the miracle would renew his own fading power.

'One point at a time,' he said. 'And slam it home. Warm them up. Drive it home. Again and again. In a dozen different ways with lots of comfort and seduction thrown in. Like Lloyd George used to do. But this time in the Labour cause. That's the ticket. That's what we need.'

Amy crossed her legs and straightened her skirt.

'Well I'm not sure I've got a gift for that kind of thing,' she said. 'I'll try of course. I'll do my best.'

'Course you have.'

Griffith Pike leaned back to recover his breath after the effort he had, made.

'You've got to harden yourself, girl,' he said. 'Get used to the public gaze. If you're a politician, a practical politician, you've got to be prepared to wash yourself in people. And that means you've got to toughen your skin.'

He mumbled these ultimate truths into his chest, glancing malevolently at D. I. Everett.

'And don't get your pretty head stuffed with too much theory.'

He raised a finger and waved it feebly.

'I'll tell you what my wife says. And she's a woman with her head screwed on the right way if ever there was one. It's the wrong people that have got the money. And that's the long and the short of it.'

He gave time for this summation of a lifetime's experience to sink in. There was an outburst of raucous laughter from a group of officers in the bar. The noise did not meet with Griffith Pike's approval. There were other points he wanted to make when his breath was fully recovered. His glances warned Everett to keep silent.

'There's one other thing,' Griffith Pike said. 'Don't go making a fuss about this Welsh business. We don't bother much in North Maelor about who's Welsh or who's not Welsh. That's something you can safely put to one side . . .'

Amy went red. He had touched a raw nerve and her reaction was fiery.

'Do you expect me to say I'm not Welsh?' she said. 'And proud of it. If you do, you'd better start looking for someone else. I can tell you that now.'

Griffith Pike shook with quiet laughter. He had penetrated her defences. She had been stung. Her self-control had been pierced. He was delighted.

'That's the spirit we want to see,' he said. 'That's what's needed. You've got it all there to give, lass. The trick is to make other people see it. As big as a billboard. You know what they want? I'll tell you what they want.'

He made a great effort to take them both into his confidence. His chest wheezed as he spoke.

'More than anything else what people want is a leader. Some-body to look up to. Now what we've got to convince them is that that "somebody" in this day and age could very well be a woman.'

~ ii ~

Cilydd leaned his bicycle against the dry stone wall. The stones were hot in the sun. He peered at white and yellow lichen before

217

removing his spectacles to wipe the sweat off them. The sleeves of his cricket shirt were rolled up. His grey flannel trousers looked too thick for such a hot day. Amy took her time to push her bicycle up the hill. He studied the landscape as alertly as a traveller taking in his first view of a strange continent. When Amy caught up with him he had prepared his comparison. He made a sweeping gesture to include the whole length of the broad valley below them.

'It lies there like an old sheepdog,' he said. 'Panting for breath. Too fagged to crawl into the shade.'

Amy drew his attention to the chapel behind them, built on the steep hillside above the white road.

'Here it is,' she said. 'Siloam. And the chapel house stuck on to it. The iron gates. The slate steps.'

She was wearing a light summer dress of red and white check and leather sandals on her bare feet. Her white cardigan was stuffed into her saddle bag with a towel and a bathing costume. He stared at her with unconcealed admiration as though he were unable to decide on the degree of apotheosis. Was she human on the way to becoming divine; or a goddess condescending to wear a supple youthful human form? He also had to establish a meaningful connection between the stone chapel of her childhood and this sun-tanned woman who by some remarkable chance was also his wife.

'I had a kite,' Amy said. 'Made of brown paper. And an old tennis racket. And a worm-eaten lacrosse stick. They were my most precious possessions.'

He shook his head in so much wonder that she had to laugh at him.

'So here we are,' she said. 'Do we really need to go any further?'

'Whatever you say.'

He was disappointed by her apparent reluctance to explore the landscape of her childhood in his company: but more eager to display his willingness to abide by her wishes.

'I mean, if it makes you miserable,' he said.

He was ready to collect and classify and cherish every fleeting fragment he could glean about those early years of which he possessed no first-hand knowledge. But any investigation into the

218

secret and mystery of her unique existence, however scientific, had to be set aside if it threatened her present well-being in the slightest degree.

'Oh, it wasn't that bad,' Amy said. 'I was quite happy here. Spoilt in a way. As far as Esther and poor old Lucas had the means to spoil me. It's quite interesting. Coming back after all these years. Or at least it's up to me to make something of it. An exercise in self-examination. Not that I am very good at that. As you well know. Now then, Mr More . . .'

He was grateful for her smile.

'Today we are going to do whatever you want. That is agreed. A minute miniature holiday. Politics, the war and everything else can wait. This is one of our little exercises in give and take. What do you think?'

'Swyn y Mynydd,' Cilydd said. 'I'd like to see it. Or whatever's left of it. If you don't mind.'

Amy was looking at the plain facade of Siloam. The lower half of the long windows were filled with opaque glass that looked like algae on the surface of a stagnant pond on this summer's day.

'I think I quite liked it in there,' she said. 'Especially in winter. The smell of the paraffin lamps. The wheeze of the harmonium. Esther popping a mint imperial in my mouth to keep me quiet. Saying my verse standing on the red felt on the seat of the deacon's pew.'

'It's well built,' Cilydd said sagely. 'Stone quarried from the same hillside. Very solid. Very safe.'

'Come on then.'

She pushed her bike to the top of the hill. He watched her mount and gather sufficient speed down one slope to reach the top of the next incline without dismounting. He gave her a start so that he could set out in hot pursuit and they could both enjoy the chase and the breeze they created as they sped uphill and down dale. When he caught up with her she complained that she was laughing so much she had no strength left to pedal and keep ahead of him.

'Isn't it marvellous?' she said.

As if to celebrate their freedom and the complete absence of any form of traffic they zig-zagged from one side of the country road to the other.

'Politics,' Amy said. 'Seem so far away on a day like this. Maybe I'm not qualified at all, John Cilydd?'

'Of course you are,' he said loyally. 'If you want to be.'

'Yes, but do I want to be? There lies the question. All that pushing and shoving. Like an unholy mixture of a jumble sale and a cattle mart. Having to sell something to people I don't really like. I don't really like it. Maybe I want the prize without the effort. Maybe I'm not really the competitive type. In spite of eisteddfodau.'

He was looking at her so sympathetically, she had to show some gratitude. She gave up butterflying from one side of the road to the other.

'You are so much nicer,' she said. 'And so much better in every way. Don't think I'm not aware of that. Don't whatever you do. Or whatever I do, which is more to the point. We turn up here.'

The farm lane was so stony it was easier to walk than ride. They both leaned over the handlebars to steer between holes, stones and dry cart ruts as they confided more closely in each other.

'I think the cause is good,' Amy said. 'I really think that. Whenever this war comes to an end, Labour has to inherit. If that doesn't happen, it will be just sinking back to the bad old days, poverty, unemployment, slums, malnutrition, TB, domination of the City of London, neo-imperial follies, the whole lot. And it will be better for Wales. I honestly believe that. And for you, John Cilydd. You are the civilisation we are fighting to protect. I am fighting to protect anyway.'

Cilydd lowered his head until his chin touched the handlebars.

'Pilgrim's Progress,' he said.

'Now, you mean?'

The lane narrowed. The high hedgerows blocked out the view of the undulating hills around them. They also provided a ribbon of shade from the hot sun. A small bird darted across in front of them from one hedgerow to the other. The momentary turbulence emphasised the sheer weight of the heat.

'I mean the Labour Party,' Cilydd said. 'The road to the Celestial City. That sort of thing.'

Amy had become too hot to argue or enquire further into what he meant exactly. She let her bike sink to the ground. She lay back smiling among the grasses and wild flowers growing in unchecked profusion along the bank. Above her a thorn bush run wild offered additional shade. She yawned, stretched herself and purred in imitation of a cat preparing to sleep out of the sun.

'Forty winks', she said. 'Why bother to go any further?'

Cilydd laid his bike against the opposite bank. He was eager to come close to her.

'If there were a goddess of summer,' he said. 'This is what she would look like.'

She placed her hand on his chest to prevent him lying on her.

'Well this particular goddess is too sticky and sweaty for human contact at this moment. Thank you all the same.'

He moved back to squat on a large stone in the sun. He contented himself with studying her as closely as a model for a picture. Buttercups grew large out of the damp earth where she had anchored her heels. Their burnished petals responded to the sky like mirrors, each reflecting its own miniscule sun. Wild flowers were hidden in the long grass, leaving only pink and white and purple traces of their presence.

'You look so young and beautiful,' he said.

His voice was soft with adoration and happiness.

'Rubbish.'

Amy spoke without opening her eyes.

'What you see is an ageing wife and mother.'

He was ready with his answer.

'A Celtic goddess was always a mother,' he said. 'And a politician too. They were the real rulers of the old world.'

'That's nice,' Amy said.

With studied care she plucked the hollow stem of a dandelion and raised its trembling clock to the level of her lips so that she could blow it apart with one long steady breath.

'Do you remember doing that?' she said.

He was pleased to remember with her.

'Little simple pleasures,' Amy said. 'Perhaps I was much happier than I thought? Of course I was. We always are. This lane was the

221

highroad to freedom. I used to bump down it on my precious old bike. Lucas always had letters to post. That was a blessing.'

Cilydd shifted a large stone with his boot. It was the roof of an ant's nest. He saw the population scatter in a gust of unbridled terror. He knelt down to examine the turmoil he had caused more closely. The disjointed individuality did not last. The jostling and running over each other was overcome by the pressing need to protect and preserve the white eggs and nymphs that lay exposed. The open air which had replaced the shelter of the stone was bright with danger. Amy murmured her content under the shade of the thorn tree.

'This is the life,' she said. 'There is no other. No war. No politics. You go and look at the place. I'll just stay here. Like a bird under a leaf.'

Cilydd allowed the stone to fall back at a different angle. The ants were all resource and determination, lifting and shifting in pairs and in bands driven by a code that excluded any form of unsocial behaviour, devoted to rebuilding their polity on a parallel site, concentrating on surmounting insuperable obstacles, dedicated to survival.

'They can manage,' Cilydd said. 'They will always manage. So why can't we? We'll divide the world between us. You are in charge of the future and I'll rebuild the past.'

She stretched out a lazy arm to point at him accusingly.

'What about that book you should have written?' she said. 'Margot was asking about it. In that funny way of hers. Apropos of nothing at all. Making an omelette from dried egg in that dismal basement flat she's rented in Holland Park. "What about that book John Cilydd was supposed to be writing?", she said. She must have been thinking of Hetty. And that made her think of you. Not that you can ever really tell what old Margot is thinking. What are you laughing at?'

'I gave that up ages ago,' he said.

'And I suppose I should have known that,' she said. 'If I weren't so absorbed in furthering my brilliant career. It was an important book. You should have finished it. Why haven't you?'

Her question was intended as an encouragement. He gave a considered reply.

'I suppose what it amounts to is that I don't really care what the English think,' he said. 'About our poetic tradition or anything else really.'

'It's more than the English, isn't it,' Amy said. 'It's the English-speaking world now.'

'Well I'm only concerned with the Welsh-speaking world. That's all I've got the strength left to care about,' Cilydd said. 'Making the natives more aware of their heritage. Make them adhere to it. Make the swine cherish it.'

'Huh.'

Amy stood up and began to rub her back.

'What's that supposed to mean?' Cilydd said.

'Just thinking about what I've heard you repeat on occasions too numerous to mention,' she said. 'The Welsh never know what to think until they pick up the signs and signals from London. May as well leave the bikes here. Bring my cardigan perhaps. It's always chilly up there.'

They moved up the lane with the hesitant steps of the first pair to return and investigate the deserted site of some obscure disaster: it was instinctive to look around for the comfort of the familiar, for likenesses that would reassure, signs that the area had reverted peacefully to the unstinting benevolence of the natural order. A green woodpecker rustled out of a tree and fled squawking across the bracken and gorse towards the safety of the wood. Amy had become conscious of the details of their surroundings as if every-where, even between the wild flowers of the hedgerow, traces of her childhood lurked waiting to be rediscovered.

'I hated the place,' she said.

Cilydd found it difficult to believe her. He waved his arms in a gesture suggesting that they were walking through the earthly paradise. Every flower and every stone a revelation. The world about them breathed through trees and fields and all they had to do was respond like children or lovers to the sentient being of creation.

'Look at that,' Amy said.

She was pointing to a piece of ancient piping that diverted the water of a streamlet into a ditch choked with yellow water lilies.

223

She seemed to take exception to the thick fleshy rootstock creeping in the mud. The water through the pipe was reduced to a feeble trickle.

'That's where I had to go for drinking water,' she said. 'One of the places anyway. In all weathers. I was the one who had to clean it all out. That was my job. I never wanted to come here. Did Esther never tell you that?'

It was clear that she was aware how often her husband and her aunt talked about her. It was she they chiefly had in common.

'I wouldn't come out of my room in the chapel house,' she said. 'The day we moved. Even when they took the furniture away. I sat on the window-sill in my bedroom clutching my old tennis racket and hating and resenting everything they did. I must have been eleven years old. A little horror I can tell you. A difficult little horror. Much worse than Gwydion.'

However vehemently she tried to condemn herself she could not diminish the glow of unstinting admiration that shone out of his face.

'It's not a good thing to spoil children or wives, John Cilydd,' she said. 'You remember that. Goddesses or no goddesses.'

'It's my ambition to spend the rest of my life spoiling you,' he said.

They held hands as they approached the ruin that had once been Amy's home. The roof had fallen in. Brambles and thorn grew as high as the gable ends, climbing through the blind window spaces to choke what was left of the interior. Nettles grew higher than any flames in an open fireplace. A straggling elderberry grew out of a long crack in the wall. Sheep and calves had been sheltering inside. Prints of their hooves were drying in the layer of mud and dung that rolled out of the collapsing doorway to cover the flagstones of what had once been a modest front garden path.

'I'm glad Esther can't see this,' Amy said. 'I expect it would break her heart. Well it's not going to break mine.'

The outbuildings were in better condition. They were still in use for feeding and sheltering store cattle in winter. They were less depressing than the ruined dwelling. Part of the half-door of the small barn hung rotting from a single rusting hinge.

'This is where I kept my bike,' Amy said. 'Very elegant ladies model pre-last war. It still had faint yellow lines painted on the chain case. And the rear mudguard was stringed like a harp.'

Cilydd trod down nettles and brambles as they pushed their way through straggling bushes to where the back garden had been.

'So much decay in so short a time.'

Amy muttered to herself.

'It's worse than a bomb site, somehow. I don't know why.'

The sound of insects intensified the silence. The simple design of the rear of the house was more recognisable than the front. Amy pointed out where she had slept as a young girl.

'There's my little window,' she said. 'Or what's left of it. There were three bedrooms. Separated from each other by wooden partitions. Have I been on this earth so long? Or was it someone else who lived here? I can still smell that little bedroom. So stuffy in summer, so cold in winter. I can smell the wool and the mothballs. No bathroom of course. The wash-stand was in the spare bedroom as Esther called it. The ewer filled with rainwater. Dark. Like ditch water. The earth closet down there at the bottom of the garden. I was obsessed with keeping myself clean. The highlight of my existence was staying with Beti Buns or Enid at Llanelw and switching electric lights on and off and flushing water closets. There's the past for you John Cilydd. Try rebuilding that.'

The bottom of the garden was overshadowed by tall sycamore trees. Amy shivered when a wood pigeon broke out of the heavy leaves and flew away.

'Are you cold?'

Cilydd placed her white cardigan over her shoulders. She shook her head.

'Somebody walking over my grave,' Amy said. 'This place I expect. Change and decay. Brambles where majesty and misery once were. Misery anyway. An absolute economic non-starter. Even I could see it. But once the step was taken their pride wouldn't let them turn back. The illusion of independence. It's a disease. I've got it too.'

Amy could no longer bear to look at the ruin. She led the way across a thistle-infested field, determined not to look back. Cilydd was taken with the sight of a bumble bee disappearing into one of the flowers of a large foxglove. It was like a train shunting noisily into a workshop. The purple flower strained away from the stout stalk that had grown out of a heap of white stones of a collapsed wall. He called out Amy's name, but she had already begun to scramble between trees and saplings down a steep slope to the point where rocks had held up the stream long enough to create a pool deep enough to swim in. She undressed while Cilydd hung on to roots and branches as he slid down the slope.

'The cleansing stream,' Amy said. 'I'll come out younger on the other side. Here I go. For old time's sake.'

She stepped carefully to the rock from which she could make a shallow dive into the water. Like a servitor Cilydd bent to pick up her clothes and sandals. She lifted her face to the sun, remaining as still as a white statue before plunging into the water. She gasped as she called out.

'Heaven! Heaven! It makes you feel so fresh and clean.'

The water was too cold to endure for long. He watched her emerge dripping on to a rock surface covered with a carpet of bright green moss. Behind her a slanting oak was black against a silvery blue sky. She waved to him to join her. Carrying her clothes he scrambled sure-footedly across the rocks without looking at the small waterfalls under his feet. Amy was shivering.

'Lie on me,' she said. 'Keep me warm. And keep still.'

Willingly he obeyed her. They laughed as the water from her body soaked into his shirt and trousers. With her cold fingers she removed his spectacles and set them carefully to one side.

'You are such a kind man,' she said. 'My husband.'

He kissed her gently. She let her wet head fall to one side on the moss as if it was a pillow.

'What are you writing now?' she said. 'Rebuilding the past, are you? Must be much nicer than living in it.'

'I'm living in the present.'

He murmured in her ear as he nibbled it.

'And loving every second of it.'

Amy held his head with both hands, her blue eyes wide open with urgent curiosity.

'Tell me,' she said.

With her hair wet her head looked sculptured and as defiant as a warrior queen.

'The remote past,' he said. 'Where the fawns gambol and the trout leap. And humans are few and far between.'

'Tell me,' Amy said impatiently.

'Trying to make it all as recent as now,' Cilydd said. 'Making an old myth new. A lover engaged in an everlasting struggle for the hand of a heroine held just out of his reach.'

'Really.'

Amy's dimples appeared in her cheeks and she smiled and he lowered his lips to kiss them.

'What kind of a man?' she said.

'Oh, a king of course. In the legend that is. Every man is a king in his own imagination.'

'You are a poet.'

Amy stroked the back of his head.

'It isn't so bad,' she said. 'Being married to a poet. Even a wet one.'

As she laughed, he stood up to remove his wet clothes. Amy shifted more directly into the sun's rays. As she did so a kingfisher streaked downstream in a flash of sapphire that made her cry out like a child with delight. Lovingly Cilydd used his shirt to dry her back. It was an excuse to trace the outline of her whole body with both his hands. He whispered in her ear. Obediently she moved so that he could lie on her.

'Ah well,' she said. 'The king must have what he is entitled to.'

She placed her hands on his shoulders to exercise some control over his movement. She seemed to talk to disguise a state of uncertainty and unease.

'I used to lie here for hours looking up at the sky through the leaves. Thinking how to escape I suppose. How can we remember what we used to think? Or what we used to be if it comes to that. We can say it's only "now" that matters. But what is now except something that escapes us?'

She put her hand under his chin to lift it and make him look her in the eye.

227

'Can you tell me, poet?'

Whatever she said only served to excite him more.

'This is now.'

He mumbled fervently about their past and future meeting, about trust and understanding and the ultimate overriding need of belonging to each other, being part of each other. Her hands gripped his shoulders to urge him to be gentle and restrained.

'Be careful,' she said. 'I don't have any precaution. Be careful. Be gentle. I'm at your mercy. Be gentle with me.'

~ iii ~

D. I. Everett had to stretch to his full height to peer through the glass panels of the double doors of the Reading Room. He saw Amy sitting in a corner between two glass-faced bookcases. There was a magazine lying face downwards in her lap. In such a large chair she looked demure and defenceless. Her golden hair was tied back by a blue ribbon. There were candidates in each of the four corners of the room. The tables and reading lecterns were varnished dark brown. Now they were not in public use their only function seemed separating the candidates: preserving them in a state of temporary inanimation. Behind him, across the puddled floor of the vestibule he could hear the comforting click of billiard balls and the occasional youth giving an unintelligible shout. Outside it was raining hard. The tyres of heavy vehicles sizzled on the wet High Street of Maelor and shoppers scampered from one awning to another clutching their baskets and their ration books close to their persons. Everett entered the Reading Room.

'Bit like a visit to the dentist's?'

His harsh voice reverberated in the solemn silence as he shook the raindrops from his pork-pie hat.

'Or should I say a funeral parlour? Cheer up, comrades, we're all in this together. We're all on the same side I hope.'

With his hat he pointed at the door which led to the hall where the delegate meeting of the Constituency Party was still in session.

'Still at it?'

None of the candidates answered his query.

'That's the democratic process,' Everett said. 'Has its drawbacks, but it's what we're fighting for after all, Sergeant Roberts.'

Everett greeted first a pale intense man in uniform. Sergeant Roberts was reading an old copy of the *New Statesman and Nation* and biting his finger-nail. He smiled at the newcomer while wondering openly at his presence. Everett turned to the thin figure lurking in the opposite corner.

'Iorrie Coram isn't it? Special constable and lay preacher. Is that the right order?'

Coram gave a bird-like cry of welcome which he quickly suppressed by clapping a hand over his mouth. His large eyes rolled as he brought himself to order.

'Recognised your photograph,' Everett said. 'We've corresponded but we've never met. Better late than never. I'm Everett from Transport House.'

Coram's mouth was open like a beak. He would have liked more information and attention. Everett was already addressing an older man almost hidden behind a newspaper.

'And Colonel Hobbs. Back on the campaign trail. Good to see you.'

The colonel in mufti barely lowered his copy of the *Manchester Guardian* to acknowledge the new arrival. Everett was soon able to give all his attention to Amy.

'How did it go? Bit of an ordeal, isn't it?'

She shrugged her shoulders. She was still glassy-eyed.

'There must have been at least sixty people in there,' she said quietly. 'I kept wondering where they all came from.'

'How was old Pike?'

Everett's voice dropped to a conspiratorial whisper.

'Got it all in hand?'

'He was downright rude.'

Amy's cheeks flushed slowly as if she were coming to after an anaesthetic.

' "Short and sweet, Mrs More," he said. Before I'd opened my mouth.'

'That's his way,' Everett said. 'Cunning old bugger.'

'There was a woman in the back,' Amy said. 'With a face like an uncooked sausage. "Would the applicant tell the committee what experience she has, if any, in factory catering and canteen management?" And there was a little man in the front who said he was on the staff of the *Maelor Observer*. I'd never seen him in my life before. And I've been shown around their offices. "Just wanted to check, Mrs More, whether you've passed your Matric. This is a question I put to all the candidates. Fair's fair, isn't it?" '

Everett laughed.

'So it wasn't too bad then. The democratic process.'

Iorrie Coram was creeping towards them between the tables, keeping his head down like a man under siege in a wild west film. He smiled ingratiatingly at D. I. Everett.

'I can see it's thumbs down,' he said. 'But I wanted you to know I'm not a bad loser.'

Everest protested. He spread out his hands in a gesture of total disinterest.

'It's nothing to do with me, comrade,' he said. 'I'm only a paid servant of the Party. It's the folk in there you want to worry about.'

'If at first you don't succeed . . .'

'Exactly. That's exactly it.'

Iorrie transferred his smile so slowly to Amy it seemed that it left its ghost behind fixed on D. I. Everett.

'I've been wanting to tell you, Mrs More,' he said. 'All the time I've been over there in that corner like a cat on hot bricks I've been trying to remember where we've met before. It was in Cardiff. Aid for Spain Rally. You were with the late Pen Lewis. Now there was a real hero.'

Amy's face was guarded and impassive. Iorrie returned his attention to the man from Transport House.

'I don't have any connections with London social life,' he said. 'I'm just a working-class lad from the valleys. But that's what counts, isn't it? In the long run. I mean the trouble with some of our lost leaders was losing touch with their constituents. Losing touch with the people they represent. That's how I feel about it anyway. And we have to speak our minds, don't we? It's no use being less than completely honest. That's what I feel anyway.'

'Quite right,' D. I. Everett said.

He had no means of resuming his tête-à-tête with Amy. Iorrie Coram was smiling at him with undetachable affection.

'What did you say to them? Inside there,' Everett said.

Had he directed the question to Amy alone, he would have laid himself open to the suspicion of favouritism. Iorrie Coram pounced on the opportunity to display his thrustful grasp of political realities.

'The Beveridge Report,' he said. 'I hammered that one home. Nineteen out of twenty people had heard of it within a month of its publication and nine out of ten believed that its proposals should be adopted. What could that mean in electoral terms if we went about our business in the way we should. What could it mean except a thumping Labour majority?'

His wide smile demanded nothing less than wholehearted approval. Amy watched him with the close stare of an amateur observing the fingers of a virtuoso at work.

'That was good,' Everett said.

Before he could return his attention to Amy, Iorrie Coram was recapitulating further points from his address.

'I told them they were all students of politics now. And our task as a great nationwide movement was to transform the trappings of ostensible democracy into genuine government of the people, by the people for the people. That went down rather well.'

'I'm sure it did,' Everett said.

'And I pointed out how the present system was based on collusion between a self-perpetuating political hierarchy and the mandarin system at Whitehall. And the one weapon in our hands, we the people, was a positive majority in the House of Commons. Propaganda is the cutting edge of the educational process, I said. I know, Mrs More, as a former school teacher, would agree with that.'

His smile now indicated he was stepping aside graciously so that the decorative lady in the bardic chair could take the floor and address the meeting. There was also the hint of a challenge. If her talents for political exposition and public speaking were manifestly inferior to his, the man from Transport House could take note of the fact and add a suitable number of asterisks of approval to Iorweth Coram's name on the list of potential parliamentary candidates. Amy made a face to suggest physical discomfort.

'I feel sick,' she said. 'That awful rabbit pie we had for lunch . . .'

The door of the passage to the assembly hall swung open. A diminutive secretary in his Sunday suit with a wing collar barely had time to smile at all the candidates before Griffith Pike pushed him to one side. A noise swept down the passage behind him as if the top had been taken off a hive.

'Shut the door,' Griffith Pike said.

He wanted silence before he spoke. The candidates all stood. The Reading Room was quiet enough for their hearts to be heard beating in unison. Griffith Pike consulted the scrap of paper in his hand.

'Very close,' he said. 'Excellent candidates. Very good speeches. We are all agreed about that. Colonel Hobbs and Mr Iorweth Coram were eliminated on the first ballot. The final votes were cast as follows. Sergeant Roberts, 28, Mrs More, 32. And for some unknown reason four people abstained on the final vote. I didn't need to vote. So I have to declare Mrs More our chosen candidate for the next parliamentary election in this constituency, whenever it comes. And I can tell you this much now, it will be a damned hard seat to win. Anything wrong Sergeant Roberts?'

The Sergeant could not conceal his dissatisfaction with the result. He was also unable to control his jaw. It was jerking about under his mouth. He put his hand on it to hold it still and to assume a pose of judicious thought.

'I was just wondering,' he said. 'About a recount. That is if four abstained . . . The result could be different. I'm only thinking ahead. To the election. I'm a local man. I don't want to be personal, but we have to face facts. Mrs More's husband is well known or should I say notorious as a Welsh nationalist. What I'd like to know is, was that fact and other facts put before the committee before the second ballot?'

Griffith Pike glared at the sergeant. His chest rumbled like thunder before the storm.

'Poor loser is it? Second past the post never wins, Sergeant. And there's damn all you can do about it. Am I right, Everett?'

'Afraid so.'

Everett was about to say more, when Amy began to sway as she stood alongside him. Iorrie Coram reached out his hand ready to congratulate her. He helped to break her fall. He looked around in alarm and desperation.

'A nurse,' he said. 'A doctor. She's fainted.'

15

~ i ~

IN THE MIDDLE OF THE AFTERNOON A NOISY PARTY WAS IN PROGRESS IN the house directly opposite. The windows were open. A high pitched well-bred babble almost completely submerged a raucous gramophone version of "I can't give you anything but love, baby". A blue plaque proclaimed that the house had once been the residence of a distinguished person: but the street was too wide for Amy to be able to read the name or even make out the dates of birth and death underneath it. Erika stood beside her on the balcony of the second floor drawing room of 59 Oakley Street. She wore a khaki uniform of superior cut but without any recognisable badge of rank. She offered Amy a cigarette. Amy shook her head regretfully as she refused.

'Rackety lot,' Erika said. 'But I suppose if it were not so quiet and peaceful in the street we would not hear them.'

On a traffic island on the Embankment a woman in a blue uniform was on her knees removing dead leaves from the red geraniums growing in concrete pots. They had been placed there to soften the grim windowless exterior of the Police and Civil Defence Post that stood on guard in front of the Albert Bridge. Above the trees lining the road they could see a solitary tug fussing in elderly fashion on the slow moving river and beyond it the chimneys of the Power Station belching smoke decoratively into the blue sky. Erika smiled to show how happy she was to have Amy at her side.

'Idyllic,' Erika said. 'Calm before the storm no doubt. Before that maniac launches another Terror Weapon. This would be such a good time to stop.'

Amy shivered. 'It can't stop now, can it?' she said.

'London is so delightful when it is half empty,' Erika said. 'I have more theatre tickets than I could ever use.'

Figures of young women and men in uniform appeared on the narrow balcony of the house across the street. They were coming out for air. A young woman waved at them and Erika waved back.

'Do you know them?' Amy said.

'Sort of,' Erika said. 'All in it together is the thing I suppose. Some of them came over when we set up shop here as a hostel for Foreign Relief Workers. They couldn't make Margot out. Found her very austere. She tried to make them think of the great famine that will sweep across Europe. They were not amused. I heard one of them say. "She's not a foreigner and she's not a Quaker. So what is she?" '

The figures on the balcony were waving at them, inviting them to cross the road and join the party. An airman leaned over so far as he waved, he was in danger of falling. A girl gave a merry shriek as she pulled him back. Another party-goer emerged with a pair of binoculars and trained it on Amy as if she were an exotic bird on migration.

'They get Algerian wine from the Free French,' Erika said. 'Would you like to go over?'

'I could do with some gin,' Amy said.

'Let's go then,' Erika said. 'I will leave a note for Margot on the kitchen table.'

'I need gin,' Amy said. 'Lots of it. And quinine. And Penny Royal. Anything. Anything.'

Erika was taken aback.

'What is it? What is the matter?'

'I'm pregnant,' Amy said. 'That is the matter.'

The thought itself was so heavy that she could only drag herself back into the room to sit in the middle of a settee with worn springs and blue covers. She lay back and stared at the oil painting of Mediterranean red-tiled roofs that hung over the fireplace.

'It's awful,' she said. 'How it changes your view of the world. Of absolutely everything.'

Erika came to sit alongside her. Amy waved away the cigarette smoke with an irritable gesture. Erika hastened to put the cigarette out in the brass ashtray inside the fender.

'You can feel your whole personality changing,' Amy said. 'And there's nothing you can do about it. Another being, another person is taking possession of you. And I don't mean the foetus or whatever you call it. I mean your own self. It's being replaced by another self and there doesn't seem to be a damn thing you can do about it.'

She held out her hand and Erika grasped it and stroked it.

'It's such a relief,' Amy said. 'To have somebody to talk to. Somebody who can understand. Somebody who can sympathise. I want to get rid of it.'

She stared defiantly at Erika, prepared to divide her entire acquaintance of friends and relations into two opposing camps: those in favour of her freedom of action and those against.

'You must do what you think best,' Erika said.

Amy raised her fist to show her determination.

'The moment this war comes to an end there will be a general election,' she said. 'We'll have to get that old man out of Downing Street. It's absolutely essential. The first step. Why are you shaking your head?'

Erika sighed.

'It won't end just like that;' she said. 'That's the trouble. Those bloody Germans won't give in so easily. I know. I'm one of them. The ones who would talk or negotiate are dead or in prison. Don't count. It would be nice of course if one could seal up Grendel in his lair. Let him devour his own. Or let them devour him. That sort of thing. But that won't happen. The next act will be all Wagner. The twilight of the Nazi gods. A great splurge of sacrifices and suicide. The Halls of Valhalla on fire. The sewers of the Reich running with blood. An abattoir with recorded music . . . and then? And then what? European Soviets or Pax Americana?'

Amy curled into a despondent posture in the corner of the settee.

235

'You think I'm making a fuss about nothing,' she said. 'One pathetic little female obsessed with her own fate.'

'Of course not.'

Erika seized Amy's hand and raised it to her lips. 'You must tell me what you want,' she said. 'You know that I will do anything for you. You know that.'

'I am a parliamentary candidate, for God's sake,' Amy said. 'I have a good chance of getting in. When the time comes. And what a time! The moment of melting. The one and only time in the history of the country when it might make a bit of difference. Just might. We have to look ahead. We have to be optimistic. Otherwise what has all the sacrifice been for?'

Amy flushed with enthusiasm and conviction. Erika gazed at her with open-eyed longing.

'I know I'm not capable of setting the Thames on fire,' Amy said. 'I know that. But I want to be here to help because this is where all the decisions are made. I could even hold one of the candles while somebody else blew up that Gothic monstrosity . . . that temple of mealy-mouthed neo-imperial hypocrisy . . . that . . .'

They both fell back laughing in the deep settee when words at last failed her. Amy's spirits sank as rapidly as they had risen. Her eyes filled with tears.

'We don't have to be such puny creatures,' she said. 'We have the right to exercise some control over our own destinies, surely? Otherwise, what are we except helpless and hopeless? Don't you agree, Erika?'

'Of course I do,' Erika said. 'Otherwise I would not be here.'

'Well you will help me then? Can you get me some quinine? And the sooner the better.'

'Are you sure?'

'Of course I'm sure. Why do you ask? But I must be quick. Before I change my mind.'

Amy clapped her hands over her ears. The air raid siren on the Albert Bridge was sounding. The face she pulled suggested the noise prevented her thinking as well as talking. Across the street the party continued in full swing. Erika smiled and shrugged her shoulders. She did not bother to close the French windows. She spoke as soon as the piercing wail of the siren began to subside.

'Margot's the one', she said. 'We have a training intake next week. Under canvas. Learning to make field ovens out of oil drums. That sort of thing. Margot will be organising the course at the Army Medical College. She's well in with the staff there at Millbank. She's the one.'

Amy jumped to her feet. She leaned her hot forehead against the marble of the mantelpiece.

'Men,' she said. 'You try to humour them and this is what happens.'

'Does he know?'

Amy shook her head.

'Why should he?' she said. 'He's no idea what he's done. They're so far removed from reality. That's half the trouble with the whole world it seems to me. It's their fantasies that are responsible for the mess. They are good at inventing. Good at destroying. Basically irresponsible. Like children. Dithering like this is not my style at all. You know that, don't you?'

'Of course I do.'

Erika was ready to give her any comfort she could.

'Usually I make up my mind and get on with it,' Amy said. 'I can't bear being like this. I really can't.'

Both raised their heads to register the engine hum of a flying bomb grow into a more sinister splutter as it drew nearer and nearer.

'Damn things,' Erika said.

She could have been speaking of a particularly virulent strain of wasp or mosquito.

'I've got into the habit of counting the moment the engine cuts out,' she said. 'Not that it helps at all. Morning, evening, noon or night. It doesn't make the slightest difference. I don't know why they bother with that siren. There's nothing we can do except carry on as usual. Let's go downstairs and have some tea.'

The engine cut out just as she made the suggestion. Simultaneously the noise of the party across the street broke off. The woman in uniform tending the geraniums slipped into the Police Post. Erika took Amy by the arm and drew her across the room to face the bookcase. There was a row of novels in French and Italian at their eye level. Erika's arm grew rigid. The explosion when it came was half a mile away. An ironic cheer went up among the party-goers across the way. Amy and Erika could hear the gramophone being wound up with the needle still in the groove. Some of the men were so amused by the bass distortion they began to imitate the noise and even improve on it with siren-like variations. Erika herself hummed the tango melody about jealousy as she escorted Amy downstairs for tea in the basement kitchen.

They were surprised to find Margot there already. She sat alone at the large table with a mug of tea in front of her. She was still wearing her khaki overcoat and cap. She was thin and pale to a point of emaciation. She greeted Amy with a warm smile.

'No idea you were down,' she said. 'How nice.'

'I've brought you two half a dozen fresh eggs,' Amy said. 'Thought they'd never survive the journey. Especially two hours on Crewe station in the blackout. So you jolly well eat them. You look in need of nourishment.'

'Any more tea?'

Margot held out her mug for Erika to fill.

'Your Labour people,' Margot said. 'They're much too quiet.'

'They're your Labour people too,' Amy said. 'Before they were mine if it comes to that.'

Margot shook her head.

'I'm out of politics. From now on relief work is all. Isn't that so, Tornago? There she is. Our interpreter. Working night and day on her Serbo-Croat. You tell little Everett from me that before this business is finished Europe will be a desert. Get that message through at Transport House. And it will take decades to recover. If it ever does. You tell him these thousand bomber raids have got to stop. They are not doing any good at all. Barbaric and senseless. Only prolonging the war and destroying the very sources of recovery. Those are people out there. Not vermin. You tell them that.'

'You must have something to eat,' Erika said. 'You really must.'

Margot shook her head.

'I've had the most depressing afternoon,' she said. 'New Scotland Yard of all places. Moral Welfare section. I didn't even

238

know they had one. Girls from the suburbs, girls from nice families as they say, sitting glued to their seats, verminous and covered with cosmetics. Rounded up after spending God knows how many nights in the shelters with foreign soldiery. Yanks mostly. So resentful. No fear of bombs or men. Only pregnancy and VD. And maybe dying from abortion. A woman brought in a girl of fourteen. Pregnant. I watched the interview. "Who's responsible?" the policewoman said. The girl herself produced a little book with forty names on it. "Any one of these," she said.'

'Fourteen!' Amy said. 'What did they do with her?'

She was fascinated by the case. The air hummed with the approach of another flying bomb. Margot's grip on her mug tightened.

'I hate those things,' she said. 'I really hate them.'

'The girl,' Amy said. 'What did they decide to do with her?'

'Let her go the full term,' Margot said. 'Just like her mother before her. Probably a Caesarian. Very jokey the moral welfare lady. She knew the mother. "History repeating itself," she said. "And the grandmother." So she said. "Either I'm getting older faster," she said. "Or the generations are reproducing faster. Or both . . ." Plump, pleasant old body she was.'

The engine of the flying bomb cut out. Erika turned to the wall and began to count under her breath. The crash when it came was near enough to make the crockery dance and bring lumps of plaster off the wall. Margot pushed back her chair. She was no longer tired. Her eyes glittered, ready for action.

'Come on Tornago. That one was near enough. We've got to help. It's what we're good for.'

She paused in the doorway and turned to look back at Amy as if the unexpected visitor had called out her name. Amy held on to the back of a chair to conceal the fact that she was trembling.

'Was there something you wanted to ask me?' Margot said.

Amy shook her head.

'It can wait,' she said. 'It's not important.'

239

Esther Parry and Connie Clayton sat in one of the shelters on the promenade at Pendraw. They were well wrapped. There was sufficient space for a third person equally well wrapped up to sit in comfort between them. They were not obliged to talk. The weather was fine enough to make them smile for no other reason. The sunlight was so dazzling on the shifting tide they could only look at it through half-closed eyes. A stout woman urging her dog to retrieve the stick she had thrown into the waves was like a blurred pictograph marking the empty expanse of the shelving shore. Esther shifted sideways so that through the plate glass of the shelter she could keep an eye on the three small boys on their bicycles. Like birds in a breeze they explored and exploited the length and breadth of the deserted promenade. Their motion was random and yet predictable: freedom within limits. When they encountered a serviceman and a woman walking hand in hand with their backs to the east wind the boys wove patterns around them that were only discernible from a distance: the man and woman seemed unaware of their manoeuvres.

'I think Bedwyr wants to be a sailor,' Esther said.

She spoke of the boy with a lingering fondness.

'"What are you doing zig-zagging like that?" I said to him. "Tacking," he said. "That's what I'm doing. Tacking."'

Esther repeated the word to savour its revelatory power: one word, enough to throw a beam of light into the depths where embryonic yearnings clung to the core of a growing boy's existence.

'They keep you going, don't they?' Esther said. 'In a funny sort of way.'

Connie clasped her hands inside the fur muff she still used as a memento of gentility. It had been a gift from Lady Violet many Christmasses ago. She cleared her throat to make a prim pronouncement.

'They are very fortunate boys,' she said. 'A seaside resort out of season is a very nice place to grow up in.'

She shaded her eyes to gaze at an aeroplane on a training flight high above the bay.

'Lady Violet is in Vancouver,' Connie said. 'She doesn't plan to return to London for another year. She just can't face the journey.'

Esther turned her head to raise her eyebrows and made no other comment. Connie was about to embark on one of her favourite topics.

'The family scattered to the four corners of the earth,' Connie said. 'It makes one wonder. It really does. Will it ever end. Will anything ever be the same again? Miss Margot somewhere in Italy. Master Nigel in Burma. On the road to Mandalay. Do you remember that song, Esther?'

Connie's voice quavered in the breeze as she attempted the familiar melody.

'We had a footman at Cranforth Royal who used to sing it beautifully. By special request at the Christmas concert. We all used to troop up in our Sunday best to join the family in the music gallery. Wonderful times we had. I don't expect we shall ever see those days again.'

The boys shot past the shelter in convoy. Bedwyr was in the lead, his pale face as intent and single-minded as his father's until it changed to give Esther and Connie a bright smile that gave them a thrill of pleasure. He was followed by Clemmie all curly hair and spectacles and bad teeth, with legs thin enough to snap as he pedalled along. Gwydion came last, so much smaller and younger than the other two, but trying to keep up and ignoring Connie as she called out his name.

'There goes our fallen angel,' Esther said. 'Let's hope he doesn't fall. He's quite a handful I must say. And I don't at all know why. I know Amy worries about it. She really does. And she blames herself. For neglecting him by being away so often. And then spoiling him to make up for it. But I don't think it's that. I really don't.'

Esther gazed at the sea as she pondered the mystery.

'You brought her up beautifully, Esther,' Connie said. 'Amy is a great credit to you. I've always said so.'

Esther accepted the compliment. It had been made before, but it still had a soothing quality capable of taking the edge off a fresh anxiety.

'She's had a disappointment now,' Connie said. 'Of course she has. But who knows what consolation a new baby will bring?'

The pious hope sounded hollow the moment it was put into words. The burly woman on the edge of the sea gave up throwing sticks into the water. Her heels sank into the wet pebbles as she trudged along with her dog trailing behind her.

'You can't alter things,' Connie said. 'It is a man's world after all. Always has and always will be. There never has been much room for women in politics. When I was at Cranforth Royal, Lady Anne was that way inclined. Quite the suffragette. But Lord Cranforth put a stop to it. He could be very stern Lord Cranforth. And I must say Lady Violet used to worry terribly about Miss Margot. She was her guardian after all. It used to upset her so much when Miss Margot called herself a socialist.'

Esther might have liked to argue: but detailed criticism would have developed into disparagements. She had to content herself with a generalisation.

'Just because they have always been that way doesn't mean you can't alter things,' she said.

This brought their conversation to an impasse. There were tracts, whole territories of discussion, out of bounds because they were so heavily mined with explosive subjects. Nothing had ever been laid down or spelt out. But sighs and silences marked off these treacherous areas with unmistakeable clarity. In the interests of living together and daily co-operation, both women kept as clear of them as they could.

'This awful war,' Connie said at last.

This was a topic on which they could arrive at tolerable agreement.

'It drags on and on,' Connie said. 'I mean we are saved they say. So when will the boys come marching home? Does it have to go on for ever? So many young men went away and died to save us. In the flower of their days. When you think of the sacrifice . . .'

Esther was moved to utter a more personal complaint.

'They managed to kill my Lucas as well,' she said. 'There was absolutely no need for it.'

Connie sighed and lapsed into a tactful silence. The boys swept by again in the same ragged formation. Clemmie managed to call out as he passed.

'What about my cake?'

Connie flung up a hand.

'Oh my goodness,' she said. 'I quite forgot.'

Esther shook her head. Her reaction to Clemmie's behaviour was equally divided between amusement and disapproval.

'Poor creature,' she said. 'He can't help it. Doesn't mean any harm. An orphan thoroughly spoilt by a pair of foolish aunts. I may as well say it.'

Their interlude of leisure was at an end.

'No peace for the wicked,' Esther said as they made their way across the promenade.

Connie was muttering about the ingredients of the cake she had promised Clemmie when she was told he had just celebrated his tenth birthday. 'Double figures,' she said. 'Double figures now. I must make you a double figures cake. Like the ones I made for Lady Anne and Lady Diana. If only we could get half the ingredients.'

Her vaguely expressed intention had galvanised Menna Cowley Jones into action. Delighted with the excuse she made a tour of farms where distant relatives could be persuaded to part with a few eggs and a little fresh butter: all for Clemmie's sake. And it gave her a pretext to drop in at Amy's, test the variable atmosphere while sitting in the kitchen over protracted cups of tea giving lively accounts of her adventures.

'I must keep my promise,' Connie Clayton said.

The breeze from the east made her large eyes water.

'I really must. Or what will those sisters think of me?'

Esther waved energetically at the boys. Bedwyr and Clemmie raced across the promenade to be first to reach her. Gwydion brought up the rear. He threatened to cry for being last. Bedwyr and Clemmie watched him with the impartial interest of students of his unpredictable behaviour.

'You weren't last,' Esther said smiling comfortingly. 'He was first of the under tens, wasn't he boys?'

Bedwyr conceded the justice of the verdict. Clemmie was more enthusiastic, excited and impressed by its ingenuity.

'You are a good one, Mrs Parry. I have to admit it.'

His old-fashioned way of speaking never failed to amuse Esther Parry. He was capable of saying something quaint every time he opened his mouth. The chain came off the rear wheel of Gwydion's bicycle. Esther chose to carry the bike rather than attempt to get the oily chain back on the cogwheel. Clemmie engaged her in solemn conversation. Gwydion trailed behind uncertain whether to prolong his sulk or take advantage of being unobserved to indulge in some calculated misdemeanour. Bedwyr rode ahead. He was the first to see his Aunt Nanw sitting on the weather-worn garden bench outside the lean-to glass conservatory that stretched the width of the tall terrace house. He braced himself at the prospect of her excessively affectionate greeting.

'Bedwyr,' Nanw said. 'My darling! How are you my lovely boy?'

There was a shopping basket beside her on the bench.

'I've made you some flapjacks,' she said. 'I know you like them. Are you going to give me a kiss?'

When Bedwyr hesitated his aunt rose to her feet and enveloped him in a tight embrace. His best protection was to become limp and unresisting.

'Why don't you go inside?' Esther said. 'The door is open.'

She stood on the narrow garden path holding Gwydion's bike, smiling to show that she found Nanw's reluctance to enter the house quite unaccountable.

'I don't think my brother's back,' Nanw said.

This could only mean that she did not wish to find herself alone with Amy. Her face flushed when she saw the same understanding reflected in Esther's face. She had to provide a more plausible reason for remaining outside.

'I thought she might be resting,' Nanw said. 'I didn't want to disturb her.'

This was an attitude that Esther could accept. She warmed towards Nanw's visit and began to show polite interest in the contents of her shopping bag. She pricked up her ears like a startled mare when the peace and quiet of the afternoon in the back gardens was rent by a shriek that even managed to disturb sea gulls strutting in the sand dunes and send them wheeling above the slates of the tall terrace roof.

'Gwydion,' Esther said. 'Now what has he done?'

Clemmie knew. He stood under the stone archway of the garden door. His teeth stumps showed as he grinned engagingly at Esther and Nanw. He waved Esther back.

'Fallen off our wall,' Clemmie said. 'Don't worry. Auntie Menna is on her way to the rescue.'

He wagged his head admiringly.

'Gwydion,' he said. 'Never knew anybody like him for screaming. He could win medals for it.'

Bedwyr looked first at one aunt and then the other, ready to obey any instructions they might see fit to give him. In the last resort he was always responsible for his younger brother. Nanw's face was tight with distaste and disapproval.

'Where is his mother?' she said.

Esther was momentarily confused.

'He does cry a lot,' she said. 'For nothing sometimes. Connie Clayton's there.'

She sounded as though she were finding excuses for her own inaction.

'She is a splendid cook,' Esther said. 'Those big people know what's what as far as their bellies are concerned.'

In the garden doorway Clemmie shifted his bike to make way for his Aunt Menna and the sobbing Gwydion. Menna's dimpled hands hovered between closing the overcoat she had hastily put on over a greasy skirt and jumper and touching Gwydion on the shoulders to comfort and even guide him homewards. He moved stiffly to show he had grazed both knees.

'Is it a molehill, or is it a mountain?' Auntie Menna said. 'You're not too bad now are you Gwydion, love?'

Her plump cheeks quivered as she tried to smile and at the same time continue her sympathy and concern and even apologise mutely for being out in carpet slippers. Gwydion stopped howling when he saw the stern figure of Nanw watching him. Esther bustled him through her shadow into the kitchen.

'It's not serious,' Aunty Menna said.

The expression on Nanw More's face in some way allowed her to take the matter lightly. The noise subsided. Fresh from her

245

afternoon rest, although still unwashed, Menna was ready for a chat. She wriggled inside her coat in anticipation of the pleasure.

'Well how are you?'

She peered at Nanw with prolonged benevolent interest.

'Haven't seen you for ages.'

'Extra sugar,' Nanw said. 'In exchange for Mrs Esther Parry's jam ration points. As promised.'

'You are kind. How very kind. . .'

Menna summoned Clemmie and Bedwyr to witness. They were charged with transporting the blue bags of sugar with special care to the Cowley Jones's kitchen where even now, Aunt Menna assured them, Mrs Connie Clayton was assembling the ingredients for Clemmie's double figures cake-to-be.

'It's like gold,' she said. 'So you be careful.'

She turned to Nanw smiling.

'The world of children,' she said. 'There's nothing like it is there? Outside the world of tragedies, great and small. I was telling my sister Flo about that terrible case in Denbighshire. Did you read about it?'

She was ready to sit on the garden bench and enjoy a chat.

'About the tanner's wife and the Italian prisoner-of-war. He was the trouble really. Always combing his hair and looking at himself in a pocket mirror.'

Menna pressed the palm of her hand against her hair, suddenly conscious of her own appearance.

'Don't I look a mess,' she said. 'I think I'll take a seat. My nerves are all a-jangle. I thought at least the world was coming to an end. Or the war at any rate.'

She raised her face to the sun and drew her coat more tightly around her ample frame. The garden faced south-west and the height of the terrace gave protection from the sharp breeze. She smiled when Nanw moved her basket to sit down beside her.

'I'm overweight and I'm a disgrace to be seen out of doors,' Menna said. 'That's what's so nice about being among friends. They take you for what you are, not how you look. Beauty is only skin deep.'

This was something they could accept with equal satisfaction.

246

'My sister Flo knew the woman slightly,' Menna said. 'They were in training college together. Or her sister was. She couldn't be quite sure. Brought it closer home somehow. The tragedy. You hadn't heard about it?'

'I never look at the papers,' Nanw said. 'Or hardly ever. There's so much to do at Glanrafon. We're always shorthanded. And the news from the war. Pouring out like poison day and night. I don't think I can bear it much longer.'

'Oh I know,' Menna said. 'Little tragedies get lost. Ignored.'

Howls and squeals issued from inside the house as Esther washed Gwydion's scratches with warm water and antiseptic.

'All the same it is terrible to those involved. I wanted to tell your brother about it. He should know the people. I'm almost sure I've heard him mention the family. There was a case a few years ago. An accident with cattle on the road. Do you follow his cases?'

'I don't have the time,' Nanw said.

'In any case, this is what happened. They used to meet in a barn away from the house to make love. If that's what you call it. The husband got to know. You can just imagine it, can't you? Like fire on his skin. Maybe that's what gave him the idea. He followed them you see. Like a bloodhound. Like a ferret. And when he knew they were in there, he barred the doors and set the place on fire. Then he went home and hanged himself. Wasn't it terrible?'

In the basement Gwydion had started crying again. He was making lusty demands to be allowed to go up to his mother. Esther was firm. They could hear her repeat that on no account would she allow him to disturb her.

'The awful thing is, they got out,' Menna said. 'When I say awful what I mean is the husband, poor man, hanged himself for nothing. They got out. Scot-free says my sister Flo and not even scorched. It's not a thing to laugh about. But I wanted Mr More to know there are signs of litigation on a large scale and Flo and I are pretty sure the family are related to the Bryn Eryr people and if that is the case they will almost certainly have a finger in the pie and need to be represented. Do you know what I mean?'

Menna was looking for some subtlety of understanding. Nanw after all was a lawyer's sister. It was reasonable to assume she would have an instinct for such matters, some inkling of a legal response.

'Will the woman hang on to the property and to her lover? His family are up in arms. There is a great deal of property involved. Two or three farms. Rows of houses. Will it all drop in her lap? They want her punished of course. But punished for what? It's a very interesting case.'

'Justice is blind,' Nanw said. 'Or if it sees, it only sees what it chooses to see.'

'I know. Exactly. My sister Flo says I should have been a lawyer.' Menna chuckled at the notion.

' "Always with your nose in other people's business," she says. Which isn't a very kind way of putting it. But I said to her what I'm saying to you now, my dear. This is the kind of case Mr John Cilydd More should be involved in. It's none of my business, I said, but when you consider all the good causes he gives so much time and trouble to without any reward . . .'

She paused briefly for some support from Nanw. When it was not forthcoming she was obliged to strengthen her own case with a show of even greater oratorical emphasis.

'Where is he now at this very moment? In London. At the High Court. At his own expense. Fighting the Admiralty and the powers of financial darkness to stop them turning that Naval Training Centre into a holiday camp that will ravage the life of this district. Working for the All-Party campaign to defend our little land . . . All-Party indeed. He does the donkey work. And if he wins they take the credit. If he loses he gets the blame. And not a penny piece for all his trouble.'

Menna's indignation had burnt itself out. Nanw was listening to Gwydion's renewed howling.

'How can she stay up there?' Nanw said. 'Why doesn't she come straight downstairs and smack his bottom? He's her responsibility. Why should Esther Parry have to worry?'

248

Undeterred by her pregnant state, Amy climbed on a chair to reach the shoebox crammed with old letters on top of one of the floor-to-ceiling bookshelves in John Cilydd's study. She carried her baby high. The swelling belly lent a new strength to her figure: her loose nightdress and dressing-gown were like regal robes. She blew the dust off the box before descending with steady care from her perch. There were two desks in the study representing the division of her husband's labours: one in the bay window for his creative work and the other in the shadow for matters connected with his practice and public affairs. Amy laid the box on the desk by the window. She sat down in the mahogany swivel chair before opening it with a certain reverence. Far across the harbour there was a view of the mountains that extended the length of the eastern horizon. They were surmounted now by stacked coloured clouds that were spectacular enough to command the world's attention and yet so familiar that their perpetual shifts and manoeuvres rolled on unobserved.

The letters were written by Enid, Cilydd's first wife. Amy was familiar with the contents. She stared now at the handwriting as if its shape in itself concealed a secret she longed to share. The writing was Enid. All that was left of the unique personality of the girl who had been her best friend. Merely to look at the hastily written script would renew the elusive tie that had bound them so closely together: given peace and quiet, the trace of Enid's hand was a fixed line she could contemplate with a mystical intensity capable of releasing her spirit from the bondage of that place and time.

The tap on the study door was so quiet the first time Amy didn't hear it. Amy turned to face the door with one of Enid's letters in her hand.

'Come in!'

She spoke in a gentle tone, a smile already on her face as the door opened and Nanw walked in. She was still wearing her hat and coat: a reluctant caller, not inclined to be the first to speak.

'I was looking at Enid's old letters,' Amy said. 'We should really do something about them.'

The expression on Nanw's face suggested it was not her responsibility.

'The trouble is they sound so innocent and naive sometimes,' Amy said. 'And then you come across whole strings of pearls of wisdom. That's how she was of course. You couldn't have one without the other. And she was so young . . . From the point of view of a book they would need editing. With notes and explanations every other line. But it ought to be done. As John Cilydd says the world has changed so much. Out of all recognition. And I suppose we've changed too.'

The last phrase verged on a challenge. She stared calmly at her sister-in-law.

'I've been thinking,' Amy said. 'I wanted to tell you this more than anything. If we both want to help him, we must meet each other half way.'

Being in the open doorway meant Nanw was at least prepared to negotiate. Amy encouraged her to close the door and come and sit down. When she eventually spoke, Nanw touched on a topic of mutual concern.

'I called to see Nathan Harris,' she said. 'There's hardly anything left of him. He'd like to see you.'

The subdued hint of censure was drowned by Amy's vigorous self-reproach.

'I'm at fault,' she said. 'I know I'm obsessed with my own concerns. Everett says that Sergeant Roberts has been adopted and is bound to get in. Every test-poll they take suggests a thumping Labour majority. I'm sorry. But you see how I am. Infected. It's like a temperature. We'll go to see him together, shall we?'

Amy showed her sister-in-law how eager she was to please her.

'He said he was ready to pass into the cool arms of death,' Nanw said.

She spoke impassively.

'He was smiling as he said it. He said how wrong we were to fear it. He said we should fear our own death far less than the death of others.'

'We must go and see him,' Amy said. 'We really must. I ought to get out and about far more than I do. I wanted to tell you about my scheme. I'm so grateful to you for coming.'

Nanw's attention fastened on the word 'scheme'. She appeared less aware of Amy's softening smile and eagerness for reconciliation.

'We both want to do our best for him,' Amy said. 'That's the important thing. I admit I felt trapped by this pregnancy. Out of the race. High and dry or whatever the expression is. And I was disappointed. Bitterly. I admit it. I must have imagined troops of important people beating a path to my door! I must have imagined a whole host of things I could do with just a little power in my hands. The principle remains. Pregnant or not. There are things I can do. And it is a race against time. There's a new world taking shape. Every day. Every hour. The Russians within forty miles of Berlin. The Americans over the Rhine. The last stand in the Apennines. And what is happening here in this tiny patch of ours, it's all a part of the same great terrible pattern. Great is small and small is great. If it isn't, we count for nothing at all. Do you know what I mean?'

She had to prove she had no ulterior motive. She gazed at Nanw with the wide-eyed earnestness of a merchant disguised as a missionary pressing a gift of blankets and glittering beads on a suspicious native chief.

'At the grass roots,' Amy said. 'It's the same old story. We need a fighting fund and we need a petition signed by every adult in the whole area. The old united front business all over again. As it was in the beginning is now and ever shall be . . . oh dear. But we mustn't give up. I've got petrol coupons and I've got the right to use them. As far as I can see there is no worthier war effort and peace aim in this little corner of the globe than preventing a nasty commercial exploiter grabbing that Naval Training Centre and turning it into a horrible holiday camp. When the County Council could perfectly well use it as a teaching base and a first class emergency training college, et cetera, et cetera. What I suggest, Nanw, is that you and I start working together. House by house and farm by farm, collecting signatures and collecting money.'

Nanw nodded her head in the direction of Amy's swollen pregnant state.

'Doesn't matter,' Amy said. 'Might help to increase support and

251

sympathy. I need the exercise. I'm an actor by temperament. Active I mean. I need to be occupied. Passivity doesn't suit me. And when they see us together that will scatter any rumours about division in the family. I'll say I'm still a socialist and you'll say you're a true Welsh nationalist or whatever: but that we are united and determined to defend our corner and our culture. And we'll win! You mark my words.'

At last Nanw was caught up with the same enthusiasm. She even ventured to smile. Amy clapped her hands and then restrained herself so as not to put Nanw off with excessive display.

'John Cilydd will be so pleased,' she said. 'I can't tell you. I'm going to telephone him from the office late in the afternoon.'

Nanw was distracted by the sound of the front door bell ringing. Amy waved her concern to one side.

'Don't worry,' she said. 'Esther or Connie will answer it.'

It was understood that they would. Esther and Connie had consented freely to translate themselves to the terrace house in Pendraw for an indefinite stay. Cilydd was preoccupied with his practice and his causes. Everyone around her forfeited at least a tithe of their independence in order to conform with Amy's wishes. Their devotion made it possible for them to drift easily into servant roles. Advancing pregnancy allowed Amy to elevate her own status into that of a mistress controlling a large and busy household.

'I should need to have someone look after the Stores,' Nanw said. 'I can't possibly expect Auntie Bessie to do everything. She has far too much to do already.'

Amy was quick to show how well she understood Nanw's problem: that she had in fact already given some thought to it.

'There's a family called Huskie,' she said. 'Photographic studios, junk shop. Second-hand furniture. Buying and selling. Goodness knows what. Very ingratiating in an odd sort of way. Eager to please. One of the girls could do with part-time work. Very good with the WVS. Very hard working.'

'English,' Nanw said. 'Wouldn't have them near the place.'

Esther was calling Amy's name as quietly as she could. She leaned on the door-knob to regain her breath.

'These stairs,' she said. 'They'll be the death of me. There's a man called. I've put him in the parlour. He is wearing uniform. A foreigner.'

Amy frowned long enough for Esther and Nanw to see she was momentarily puzzled.

'Hans,' she said. 'It must be Hans Benek. Should I go down like this?'

She became concerned about her appearance.

'Does it matter? Of course it doesn't. It's only Hans for goodness sake.'

In the parlour Amy and Hans stood at a distance from one another sharing an equivalent disbelief in the change in their condition. The awkward silence was an embarrassment. Amy spoke first.

'Hans,' she said. 'You've put on weight.'

Only when she noticed his polite attempt not to laugh did she realise how much more the remark applied to herself. She placed both hands above her swollen belly with a delicate precision that gave him obvious pleasure.

'Let me tell you,' he said. 'You are more beautiful than ever.'

Nanw lurked in the gloom of the passage, uncertain whether to leave or maintain a watching brief on her brother's behalf. Hans Benek in uniform was no less odd and unpredictable than he had been as the Bohemian painter in the stable at Cae Golau.

'You must let me paint you,' Hans said. 'You really must.'

'Goodness,' Amy said. 'I'm distorted enough already. You remember Nanw. My sister-in-law. You remember Glanrafon.'

Hans made a dramatic gesture.

'I remember everything,' he said. 'It is all stamped on my consciousness. For so little time I was here in my life but it was a big experience. Maybe I think sometimes it will be a major theme for me. A nightmare and a dream.'

Nanw's immutable presence imposed a second phase of silence. No more than a foot or two inside the open door, with a pulse throbbing in her pale cheek, she continued to remain rooted to the spot. Hans plunged his hand excitedly into his overcoat pocket. He explained the uniform with rapid insistence.

'Free French,' he said. 'I am attached to. Accredited. War Artist.

I have simulated rank. Captain. I am Captain Benek. War Artist. This is very good for me. I bring you a precious gift. From Erika. Part of her Tornago treasure.'

He held out a small leather bag. Amy was reluctant to accept it, conscious possibly of Nanw's disapproving stare even when it was directed against her back. She loosened the thong and spilt a pair of diamond ear-rings on the sideboard. She stared in fascination at the fiery refractions of white light.

'They did exist . . .'

Amy shifted to one side so that Nanw could view the brilliance of the diamonds. Hans was excited.

'She got them all back,' he said. 'In spite of the Germans. In spite of the wild Moroccans. They came through and took everything. She says there are more for you whenever you want them. She was in Paris only for three days. She had a place in a Dakota. She says this is a small repayment. You took us in when we had nothing. You fed us when we were hungry.'

He stretched out his arms, ready to embrace Amy: but restrained by respect for her pregnant state, or the rigid figure of Nanw standing behind her.

'I couldn't possibly take these,' Amy said. 'They are much too valuable. Really.'

Hans shook his hands in the air, signifying he had delivered the diamond ear-rings, was relieved to be rid of them and would on no account take them back. His responsibility had been discharged.

'I have been in the studio of Georges Braque,' he said. 'Brown is the colour. Miracles in brown and black and dull white. Colour where there is no colour. That is the secret.'

He grinned triumphantly at Amy.

'The jug. The chair. The table. The pregnant woman. Matisse taught him. Now he teaches me. I have my message. I have my revolution.'

He was anxious to be understood.

'A new age. A new sky,' he said. 'Out of the hot ashes of the old Europe new flowers will grow.'

He pointed at Amy's belly.

'He will be born into peace, that one,' he said.

'Or she,' Amy said.

'Better she,' he said. 'More like you.'

Amy could not respond adequately to his admiration while Nanw was watching. Even common politeness was made difficult by her silent presence.

'You are on leave?' Amy said. 'How long?'

'It is not good that I stay?' he said. 'Not convenient?'

Amy became suddenly decisive.

'Of course you can stay,' she said. 'You can stay as long as you like. Of course you can. You can have the boys' room. Bedwyr and Gwydion can sleep in Clemmie's house. The little boys will love it. And I know Menna and Flo won't mind one little bit. It's only next door but one.'

Amy's face was radiant as she included Nanw in her plans.

'He can come with us,' she said. 'Can't he Nanw?'

Nanw said nothing. Amy was not deterred.

'I want to hear every tiny detail about everything,' she said. 'Everything that's happening in the Big Wide World. Will you tell me everything.'

'Of course,' Hans said. 'Of course I will.'

'And in return,' Amy said. 'You can renew your inspiration. Celtic magic. That's what John Cilydd calls it. There is no springtime anywhere in the world more beautiful. And you know it. "Too much green!" Do you remember?'

Amy raised her fingers in front of her face to invoke his old vision of bars of light.

'I must get dressed,' she said. 'The minute the sun comes out we'll set out on an expedition. A return journey.'

iv

Inside the walls of the ruined castle the ewe with twin lambs looked up at the intruders. Spring sunlight polished the short grass she was cropping. Her lambs jumped about in disjointed ecstasy before thrusting their muzzles into her udder and sucking with the relentless concentration of a demolition squad.

'There you are, Benek,' Amy said. 'A genuine Welsh castle. Old as the hills.'

Enveloped in a dark cloak she could indulge in vatic gestures. Her declared mission was to immerse the painter and his Free French uniform in the healing stream of Welsh atmosphere. He was to be restored and made whole again as rapidly as a sick Indian sealed in a sweat house. He was more than willing to submit to the treatment. Through the gateway of the castle they could see the roofs of the little town. Nanw had been drawn into a terrace house next to the bakery to be given tea and sympathy by an ardent well-wisher of the campaign to defend and preserve the integrity and well-being of the district. Showing Hans Benek the castle hill gave Amy the excuse to wander off with him.

'There isn't much to see,' Amy said. 'It means more to some than to others. But the view is fantastic. In any weather. Cilydd should be here. It means so much to him.'

She spoke in a loud public voice although only Hans and the ewe were close enough to hear her. The ewe stamped a foot to warn off too close an approach. Amy crossed fallen stones to a gap in the wall where she adopted a commanding posture. The bay and the mountains, the land and the sea for a radius of seventy miles at least seemed to belong to her: she was the queen in her castle able to survey her territory and find it good.

'He has a poem,' Amy said. 'About the city under the sea . . . And he has another one. About Merlin in his glass prison. That's more fanciful. But I like it.'

'He has you,' Hans said.

Now they were alone, he was intent on paying court to Amy. He offered her his hand so that she could step carefully over the stones and move down the slope to a sheltered shelf on the headland. Bushes of hawthorn and hazel gave some protection on one side and a shoulder of rock on the other. It was a place where they could be alone and talk freely without fear of being overheard.

'Her letters don't tell me much,' Amy said. 'And Margot doesn't write at all.'

'A piece of metal, . . .'

Hans raised his hands to indicate the size.

'Went right through her truck,' he said. 'A great explosion in the harbour. She is lucky to be alive. And she works day and night. Always moving. Erika is different. Something has happened to her. The fire storm at Dresden. People and places she knew. She has lost her heart. Lost confidence. You should go to her.'

'I wish I could,' Amy said.

She made herself comfortable on the cropped sward, able to rest her back against an outcrop of rock.

'They mention places like Perugia and Assisi and Florence and all I want is to be there with them. And instead I'm tied to this place like a pregnant goat on a tether.'

His admiration for her was so apparent she could afford to be petulant. She clenched her fist.

'I am,' she said. 'Tied. Bound. That's what it amounts to.'

Hans knelt alongside her.

'You should have whatever you want,' he said.

Amy frowned.

'That's just silly,' she said.

'Perhaps politics was wrong for you. How can I explain . . .'

His neck sank inside the collar of his khaki overcoat with the effort of being solemnly concerned.

'Before in the old days you could only have freedom if you had power,' he said.

'What "old days"?'

Amy was demanding, sternly critical.

'The life that was,' Hans said. 'Before the war. This tranformation of the world. Only the powerful could do just as they liked. You know. Kings with many palaces, many mistresses. A millionaire would want to be like a king. But now it is perhaps the one good thing of this war. You can have freedom without power. You can do what you like.'

'That sounds very dubious to me,' Amy said.

'You listen to me,' Hans said. 'It is like a new primary colour. You can add it to what is there already and create a new form of expression, live in a new world.'

Amy stroked her folded hands with her chin and gazed dreamily at the sea.

257

'It would be nice,' she said.

'That is what I mean,' Hans said. 'The life of a free artist is to make dreams become reality. I always said that. But there were obstacles. Hideous frightening, nightmare obstacles. Now these will be swept away. You find the will in yourself, you find the means and you are free. You have freedom.'

Amy straightened her back determined to be sceptical.

'It's quite obvious you haven't got a family,' she said.

Hans's optimism evaporated.

'I had,' he said. 'I have no more.'

He lay limp on the ground alongside her, overcome by a sudden weight of depression and apathy. Amy reached out to touch his head. She was full of apology.

'How thoughtless of me. Oh Hans, I wasn't thinking. I am sorry . . .'

He seized her hand and pressed it against his lips.

'You are all I came back for,' he said. 'The only thing of worth out of a miserable experience.'

He was blinking at her in such a childlike way, it made her smile.

'Was it that bad?' Amy said.

He closed his eyes and shrank inside his overcoat like a small animal trying to hide.

'I was walking to the Art School,' he said. 'Nine o'clock in the morning. I had to pass the police station. I prayed to become invisible. That morning I was praying I was so afraid. They got me. They snatched me off the street. I was in the cell. They were kicking me. I was terrified. I was bruised and shaking. Frightened to death. And I saw him pointing at me. In the doorway of the cell. In some uniform I had never seen before. A man with grey hair and a decoration on his chest. This was my miracle. Erika's uncle. He saved me. He was burnt alive in Dresden.'

'Poor Hans, my poor Hans.'

She was intent on bringing him comfort. She stroked his head like a mother consoling her child.

'We don't know anything, do we?' she said. 'In a place like this. We have no idea. No conception.'

'You come with me.'

His voice was muffled as he pressed his face against her breast.

'You will have everything,' he said. 'I can say this. Jewels. Sunshine. Lovers. I am not selfish. You will be the model I worship.'

'You silly boy.'

He sat up when he realised she was laughing at him.

'After what we have been through we do not make pretence,' he said. 'We could be somewhere together in the sun. You. Erika. Me. We offer you this. You live with us and be our love. We serve you. Worship you. We give you the fruits of the earth.'

'I'm sorry,' Amy said.

She made an effort to stifle her laughter.

'What do I do with my husband?'

Hans spread out his hands in a gesture of incredulity.

'Why should you belong to him? You belong to yourself. And whoever you want. Why should you humour him? You should have many lovers. It is your right. You should be fulfilled. You are not fulfilled here. I know. Unhappy women run away. Even when they are pregnant.'

'Who says I am unhappy?'

'I do.'

Hans was so positive she took his answer seriously.

'You are deprived,' he said. 'You have sexual needs, sexual drives that have never been fulfilled. You have lived in this cloud-covered cold wet corner of nowhere. You should let me lead you to the sunlit freedom of full living, to the riches of art. This Erika wants. She will have the wealth. What else is it for?'

'We should talk much more seriously,' Amy said. 'We really should. Don't you want to go to Palestine? I honestly thought you did.'

Hans shook his head vigorously.

'I have got rid of one burden,' he said. 'I don't want to lift up another. I want to be free. Don't you understand?'

She was thoughtful and silent. He moved closer to her so that he could bring his lips against hers. Amy was curious and unresisting, as though the process of kissing would possibly give her a clearer notion of what Hans was talking about than the words he was using. He murmured endearments she could barely understand.

259

He was gentle, responding to any restraining pressure from her hand. She even ventured to close her eyes. When she opened them she saw Nanw standing beyond the hawthorn bush as still as a figure turned to stone. She pushed Hans away from her and struggled to her feet. By the time her face was composed and smiling with some form of explanation on her lips, Nanw had gone. Hans rolled over to look up at Amy puzzled by her behaviour.

'What is it?' he said.

'You fool. You idiot. You fool!'

Her spurt of uncontrollable anger was inexplicable. Was she talking about him or about herself. He gazed in amazement at her flushed face. He uttered the first consoling remark that came into his head.

'It will be wonderful,' Hans said. 'When you come with us.'

'You idiot!'

There could be no mistaking that it was he. Her voice had the wail of a bereaved woman. There were tears in her eyes.

'I'll never hear the end of this,' she said. 'Not till the end of time. Why didn't you leave me alone? Why did you have to come here? Look what you've done to me.'

'But I have done nothing.'

Hans protested his innocence. Amy began to scramble back up the grassy back to the castle wall. To prevent herself from slipping she was obliged to scramble on all fours. She muttered to herself in a state of panic as she rehearsed whatever she would say to Nanw when she caught up with her. The rest of the day was a prospect too unpleasant to contemplate. She could no longer bear the sound of Hans's central European accent as he followed her still protesting his innocence and devotion. In the castle grounds she turned on him and stamped her foot.

'Will you just shut up,' she said. 'I don't want to hear any more of it.'

16

Mrs Rossett was in deep mourning. She sat in the Windsor-backed chair which had always been her brother Nathan's when he was alive. In her lap she nursed a baptismal bowl. The glaze of the bowl glowed in a blue halo against her black dress. She smiled sadly when her cat purred and rubbed her fur against her leg.

'Beauty Puss!'

Mrs Rossett's voice was no more than a murmur.

'She thinks this is a bowl of milk.'

Her house was filled with people but only subdued voices broke the silence. The door of every room was open so that Tasker Thomas could move about to make any whispered explanations that were necessary. In the front room under the enlarged tinted photographs of Mrs Rossett's husband and father in uniform, Simon Lloyd and Gwilym Lloyd sat as still as graven images in their stiff Sunday shirts. Their wives made do on smaller chairs in the bay window. Tryfan Lloyd was content to stand up or lean against the sideboard. He gave up his contemplation of the oil painting of Mrs Rossett's father's merchant ship on a stylised rough sea when Tasker passed close enough for him to clutch his arm. Tasker bent so that Tryfan could whisper in his ear.

'Nanw is not well,' Tryfan said. 'Not well enough to come. I said you would understand.'

Tasker nodded slowly and smiled to show that understanding was his *métier*. He was wearing a clerical collar and a neat grey suit. In his large right hand he carried a slim bilingual service book with his index finger keeping the page of the Welsh order of baptism which allowed the sacrament to be celebrated in a private house under exceptional circumstances. On the table in the centre of the room the food prepared for those needing refreshment after the funeral of Nathan Harris, which was to take place later, was covered with an immaculately laundered white damask table cloth. The arrangements were complex. The undertaker was kept in the

261

background. Tasker had much to think about. He whispered back into Tryfan's ear the substance of what he had already managed to convey to his brothers.

'If you wish to see him for the last time, there will be an opportunity after the baptism, upstairs. Before the lid is screwed down.'

The baby was asleep in the middle room which had been Amy's when she was a teacher lodged at number seven Eifion Street with Mrs Rossett and the late Nathan Harris. The baby boy lay in Esther Parry's lap, wrapped in a voluminous white shawl. Esther sat on the edge of a mahogany chair with her elbow raised to protect the baby's head from the grotesque carving of the chair arm. Connie Clayton sat near her on a lower level, her neck frequently stretching forward to marvel in gratitude for the infant's uncharacteristic silence. Clemmie, Bedwyr, and Gwydion sat with their backs to the window that overlooked the back garden. They were so neat and quiet in their Sunday clothes they could have been sitting in a chapel pew. Behind them, in the small garden, drizzle settled on the burgeoning apples of the single tree and on the elephantine leaves of a rhubarb patch run wild.

Tasker faced Cilydd and Amy who had placed themselves in the open doorway. Dressed in black, Amy looked pale and thin. She leaned heavily on Cilydd's arm, disinclined to move closer to her baby and yet wishing to keep it within sight. Tasker brought his benevolent smile as close as he could to both of them.

'I'll say it again,' he said. 'I'm so honoured. And so grateful to you both: to allow us to do things in this fashion. I know how difficult it is for you.'

His murmur went even lower so that they could barely hear him.

' "Help Thou mine unbelief" . . .' Tasker said. 'Think of it as a gift. It was given to you. Now you are giving it to him. He will decide what use he will make of it in the fullness of time. But you will not have withheld the opportunity from him. Bless you. Bless you both. In the name of love and friendship.'

He closed his eyes momentarily and almost winked when he open them again.

'I like the name,' he said. 'I really do. Peredur Cilydd More.'

He stared at Amy so closely that she sighed with the weariness of a long distance runner in the course of a race she could not hope to win.

'Perhaps he'll learn to sleep at night.' she said. 'Once he's been baptised.'

Tasker moved about making signals that those present should assemble in the kitchen where he would celebrate the sacrament of baptism. Like a policeman he made way for Esther Parry who carried the child in the white shawl that almost swept the floor. Amy and Cilydd followed her. Tasker seemed capable of solving problems of precedence as they arose. Everybody obeyed his gestures without question. When Mrs Rossett rose to hand him the baptismal bowl he held it up so that everyone could see it.

'Simple and sacred,' Tasker said. 'In a sense this bowl is an important part of the reason of why we are gathered together in this house. It has been in this family for two hundred years. Saints of the eighteenth century used it when they still met in secret in each other's houses. This was the bowl used to baptise our friend and teacher who now lies upstairs in the final peace which passes all understanding.'

When the bowl contained water, Tasker set it on the corner of the table as reverently as though he were handling the Holy Grail. The baby stirred in Esther's arms as she brought him before the minister. Amy shivered inside her black costume in spite of the warmth of people standing close together behind her. Esther's hat was balanced precariously on the bun at the back of her neck. The steel hat-pin with a black head looked loose. If it fell to the ground there would be nothing she could do about it. Tasker clutched the service book in both hands but had no need to refer to it. His eyes closed when he prayed. He opened them again to address his small congregation. The blue eyes shone with the triumph of conviction in what he was saying.

'Under the shadow of the ministry of death, we give thanks to the God of the universe for this new life . . .'

The baby uttered its first grizzled yelp. Amy closed her eyes. Cilydd could feel her whole body stiffen at the sound.

'In our church,' Tasker said. 'God through his only begotten son claims each child as his own. "Suffer little children and forbid them not to come unto me: for of such is the Kingdom of Heaven." This is a profound mystery which through the centuries has laid on Christian parents the obligation and duty to bring up their child, "in the nurture and admonition of the Lord".'

The baby's intermittent mewling was making the immediate family anxious . . . Tasker gave young Bedwyr a particularly reassuring smile. He put down his service book and held out his arms with dignified slowness to receive the child. The transfer took the infant by surprise. For the moment it stopped crying. Tasker stepped closer to Cilydd and Amy.

'Now I must ask you,' he said. 'Do you promise to bring this child up in the nurture and admonition of the Lord and train him to become a disciple of the Lord Jesus Christ?'

The answer was slow in coming. Amy and Cilydd looked at each other with a degree of alarm which suggested they were now regretting not having given more thorough consideration of a question that was such a lot to ask. One or other of them had to make a public promise. They were surrounded by witnesses of all ages quite capable of reminding them of their promise for the forseeable future. It may have been to please the family or merely the line of least resistance that had brought them to this confrontation. To speak now would be like opening a forbidden door: two words and the world around them would be invaded by ghosts.

'I do.'

It was Cilydd who spoke. Once again Amy squeezed his arm to show how much she relied on him. Tasker Thomas nodded his approval: it was like a pat on the back for a novice who has just cleared a hurdle.

'And how shall he be named?'

'Peredur Cilydd.'

John Cilydd murmured the Christian names.

'In the name of the Lord Jesus Christ I receive this child into the Christian Church and as a token of that I baptise him with water.'

Tasker was obliged to turn away from the parents in order to dip his fingers with awkward grace into the water in the blue bowl.

'Peredur Cilydd, I baptise thee in the name of the Father and of the Son, and of the Holy Ghost . . .'

He raised his voice to pray in competition with the baby's coarse howl. He had things to say and he was determined to say them.

'Then will I sprinkle clean water upon you, and ye shall be clean . . . and ye shall dwell in the land that I gave to your forefathers: and ye shall be my people and I will be your God . . . Father of all mercies, we most humbly give Thee thanks for the privilege of doing that which we believe is in accordance with Thy will . . . Surround him in the days of infancy and childhood with Thy loving care: mercifully preserve and protect him and grant that growing in stature, he may grow in wisdom and grow in Thy divine favour . . .'

The baby's scream made all the women present restless. Esther saw that Amy was trembling with distress. She stepped forward in the mother's place her elbows jerking as she touched Tasker's sleeve to show him her arms were ready to hold the child. Her intention was to take him home without delay and feed him. Small as he was he had a vigorous appetite that could not be satisfied by his mother. At five weeks Amy had given up breast feeding and Esther had begun to prepare bottles of National Dried Milk for him.

There was an interval between the baptism and the first stages of Nathan Harris's obsequies. The older mourners were observing the tradition of trooping quietly upstairs to pay their last respects to the body before the coffin was closed and carried down to the hearse now waiting patiently in the street. Pendraw had always admired Nathan Harris's fortitude in spite of what most regarded his extreme views: now there were many on the streets ready to pay him their form of homage. Mrs Rossett sat in the Windsor chair, a white handkerchief in her black gloved hand. People approached her to sympathise. She was calm and resigned with a variety of observations to make to those who were prepared to listen and understand.

Her brother had been lucid to the end. Quite lucid. It convinced her that some invisible source of strength had enabled him to subdue his will so that the wasting away became a path of spiritual release.

They had both understood this with equal clarity. There were other things he had said which she could not follow. He said the slow process of dying, the process he suffered, was a form of purge and purgatory that eased his way to the perpetual night that was perpetual light. All his life Nathan had been fond of paradox and he kept it up to the very end. Mrs Rossett applied the clean handkerchief to a corner of her eye. When the tears came she said they would be more for herself than for him; the prospect of loneliness and solitude; the absence of his ringing tenor voice; the consolation of sharing those thoughts that were so often only barely understood: but most of all the absence of his need for her attentive care.

Amy looked pale and on the verge of fainting. Cilydd made her sit in the mahogany chair of her former private room. It disturbed him to see her so uncharacteristically helpless and unnerved. She was no longer a centre of attention. She no longer had a major role to play in any ceremony or ritual.

'I should take you home,' Cilydd said. 'Right away. The boys have gone. There's a car here. You're not well enough to go to the chapel and the graveyard.'

Amy rubbed her gloved hand against the carved arm of the chair as if it were a mute memorial of how attached she had been to Nathan Harris. She shook her head repeatedly.

'No. I must go,' she said. 'I must go.'

He knelt down so that she could look directly into his eyes and see his concern.

'I feel so guilty,' she said.

He grasped the carved ends of the arms of her chair and moved closer so that his body would muffle whatever she wanted to say. There were still people standing about ready to pick up things it might be better they should not hear.

'I feel nothing towards that child except resentment,' Amy said. 'Nothing.'

He glanced over his shoulder to check that no one appeared to be listening.

'I'd sooner stand in the graveyard in the rain than sit listening to him gripe and whine. Isn't that terrible?'

She was inviting him to blame her like a penitent longing to be punished.

'It's natural,' Cilydd said. 'You've had a difficult time. Your nerves are shattered. You mustn't blame yourself. Not on any account.'

He restrained himself from being too intense as he saw her stare wild-eyed at him. It was better to smile in preparation for a quiet joke.

'Can't say I'm any too pleased with the little blighter myself,' he said. 'I don't know how we would have managed if Esther hadn't been with us. I can't tell you how much I admire that woman.'

Amy tried hard to respond in kind.

'Perhaps you should have married her,' she said. 'You'd have been much better off.'

Cilydd pulled up a dining chair so that he could sit close to Amy and express himself close to her ear.

'We'll go away,' he said. 'As soon as you feel well enough, we'll go. No matter how much it costs. A proper holiday. To take stock. Talk things over. See them in perspective. At least the war is over. We can move about. We could even go abroad if that was what you wanted. We'll do whatever you want.'

She gave a wan smile and patted his hand. He seized it and held it. They looked up to discover they were both under the beam of Tasker's benevolent smile.

'I have to thank you both,' he said. 'You allowed it to happen. I am grateful. And so is Mrs Rossett. And I believe so is Nathan. Nothing would prevent me being here today. Nathan was such a saint. He even died at the right time. A week today I shall be on my way to Poland. For the Save the Children Fund. And I'll tell you something miraculous! Your good friend Margot. In Assisi of all places under the sun. Brother Sun. You know what went through my mind when I dipped my fingers in the water and made the sign of the cross on little Peredur's forehead. "Praise be my good Lord, for Sister Water which is so useful and humble and precious and pure." This is what I want to say about Nathan today. What the world needs is soldiers transformed into saints. And he is a most precious example. He moved on this earth to bear witness through suffering and to humble our proud spirits. His spirit was useful, it was precious, it was humble and pure, just like Francis's Sister Water. And when he died the larks sang outside his window.'

His enthusiasm made Amy and Cilydd so uncomfortable it was a visible effort on their part to go on looking at the fervent smile on his sandy face. It was a relief when they saw the large calloused hand of the carpenter-undertaker tap Tasker Thomas firmly on the shoulder.

'Mr Thomas,' the undertaker said. 'We are ready now if you are.'

~ ii ~

Uncle Tryfan emerged from his workshop still wearing his shiny leather apron and carrying a hammer in his hand. He stood away from John Cilydd so that he could study his reaction as well as observe the dingy facade of Glanrafon Stores. Down the lane near the deserted smithy, pigeons and crows drifted over the hedge from the cornfields weighed down by the fullness of their crops. They sauntered along the road as if they had adopted it for their private use. Apart from the peeling paintwork, John Cilydd was staring at a conspicuous tear in the sunblind lowered half-way down the left hand window without concealing the dummies and cardboard displays of products that had not been available for four or five years. He waved a hand to draw Tryfan's attention to the tear. Tryfan was ready to see the place through his nephew's eyes.

'It looks bad,' he said. 'It looks as if the place is going to rack and ruin. I quite agree with you. But what can I do about it?'

'That tear,' Cilydd said. 'It's like a symbol of neglect. It says everything.'

'You talk to her,' Tryfan said.

He seized the chance to press the point.

'She won't listen to me. But she'd listen to you. I know that.'

Tryfan waved his hammer as he moved closer to address John Cilydd in greater confidence.

'She puts people off,' he said. 'You can't keep a country store without being nice to people. I don't know how many ways I've tried to tell her. Poor Bessie is run off her feet with work indoors and out. Nanw won't let her put things to right in the shop. And she won't have any paid help. Hasn't got the money, she says. Hasn't got the turnover. Well how can you have the turnover if you turn people away with the sharpness of your tongue? That's what I want to say to her. But I can't of course. It's not my part to say it, is it? But it goes to my heart and through my heart to see the place going downhill. Every day I say to myself what would my mother say if she could see it now.'

He paused to allow John Cilydd to make some useful comment. A sheepdog slept on the warm threshold stone in front of the double doors apparently certain of not being disturbed by the ringing of the shop bell or the feet of customers making entrance and exit.

'I know she's got principles,' Uncle Tryfan said. 'And I know she gets most of them from you. But it's no use thrusting them down people's throats every time they come in to buy half a pound of tea. They take their ration books elsewhere and that's the end of it. I don't know. Even Robert Thomas doesn't bring his pension book here any more.'

'I should think not,' Cilydd said grimly.

'What is it?'

Tryfan demanded to be informed. His business too was suffering: and his social life diminished when familiar figures ceased to drop into the cobbler's workshop for a chat. The harsh sequence of disruption caused by the war showed no sign of abating now the war had come to an end. Hardly a day passed without its unpleasant surprise.

'He's a bad man,' John Cilydd said. 'A scavenger without any conscience. He and that family of his have looted Cae Golau. Literally robbed the place and ruined it. Bit by bit. All the time blaming the conscientious objectors. They saw their chance, I suppose you could say, and they took it. Imagine taking a door off its hinges! Perhaps I'm at fault. Letting them get away with it. But one can't be everywhere at once.'

'Too many irons in the fire,' Tryfan said.

He offered the platitude as if it were a helpful suggestion.

'Low cunning,' Cilydd said. 'He has enough of that to make a first class politician. It wouldn't be worth my while trying to prosecute. No real evidence to pin him down.'

'This world can be too much for us,' Tryfan said.

Cilydd was moved by the note of wistful pessimism.

'A breed like ours,' Tryfan said. 'One layer less of skin than most people. Tell me, John Cilydd. I've been wanting to ask you. This atom bomb. I've been sitting there in my little hovel and tapping away and I've been thinking. Is this the end of the world?'

'Who can tell,' Cilydd said. 'The end of one world certainly. The end of war altogether. Or the end of the world. That seems to be the choice.'

Tryfan shook his head. He did not appear optimistic.

'Very difficult thing, I should think,' he said. 'To change human nature.'

'I'll go in and have a word with her,' Cilydd said.

'Yes, indeed.'

Tryfan was eager to encourage him.

'She'll listen to you. You take it tactfully. Put her back on the right road. That's just what she needs. She'll listen to her brother. She always has.'

The interior of the Stores was dim and melancholy. The remedies in the tall glass-fronted medicine cupboard looked too antiquated ever to be taken. The label on the cupboard key was shrivelled with age. Behind the food counter most of the shelves were empty. The domestic utensils hanging from the ceiling, brushes, buckets, ropes, wooden rakes, festooned with cobwebs, looked like a display of things nobody would ever want. Only the strong smell of paraffin from the side warehouse suggested a commodity still in general demand. Nanw emerged from the shadows, wraithlike in her brown overall. She stood in front of the drapery counter and waited for her brother to speak. Their closeness had always dispensed with preliminary formalities: so much was understood between them, with or without sympathetic agreement.

'Uncle Simon is the answer,' Cilydd said. 'He could provide you with a mortgage loan. I'm sure he'd jump at the chance.'

Her staring was unwavering.

'I don't want to ask him,' she said. 'He comes in here, holds out his hand for a bag, helps himself to the best biscuits and never dreams of paying. I couldn't bear to be in his debt.'

Cilydd strode about the stores, his hands clasped behind his back.

'What this place needs more than anything is a proper injection of capital,' he said.

'Do you think I don't know that?'

'You won't listen to anybody,' Cilydd said. 'You've let the place run down. You won't employ anybody.'

His arms flapped in a despairing gesture.

'It's all my fault then?'

Nanw's voice began to wobble dangerously.

'Well, who else?'

He appealed to her to be reasonable.

'And you won't lend me the money,' Nanw said.

'My dear woman, I haven't got it to lend. I would have thought that was obvious.'

'Oh it is,' Nanw said. 'It is. Only too obvious.'

Unable to stand still any longer she marched down the passage to the kitchen. She stared through the window that looked out on an overgrown garden. Someone had scythed the lawn, but had left the swathes of grass to rot. The kitchen was clean enough and yet the worse for the wear. The oilcloth on the table needed replacing. The corners poked through the material like a tramp's elbows.

'The whole place is falling to bits!'

Cilydd raised his voice as he entered the kitchen.

'And for one reason only. You refuse to learn to handle people. You prefer to attack them.'

'Who says that?'

She folded her arms and stared at the garden.

'I say it,' Cilydd said. 'You've just got to take yourself in hand and break the habit. Nobody can help you until you start to help yourself.'

'Esau's hand and Jacob's voice,' Nanw said.

'What's that supposed to mean?'

'I don't know how simple you both think I am.'

She turned to face her brother.

'Where has all the money gone? I'm not blaming you. You've made an heroic effort. All through the war. If anybody saves this district from the holiday camp it will be you, although I don't know how much thanks you'll get for it. But that's not where the money's gone. It's been thrown away on that silly girl's stupid ambitions. Nain's money. Trying to be an MP for goodness sake! No expense spared. Nursing a constituency instead of nursing a baby. Running backwards and forwards to London. And all for nothing and worse than nothing. Neglecting her children and neglecting her husband. Just to feed her vanity. Just to pander to her ambition. Her insatiable appetite to be this, that or the other.'

He shook his head and forced himself to smile in order to show how patient he was.

'You're just jealous,' he said.

'Jealous!'

The word choked her.

'It's you that should be jealous. Do you think I'm blind? I saw her with my own eyes. With that Benek creature. On the castle hill. I saw them.'

Cilydd was ostentatiously calm.

'A man who has lost half his family,' he said. 'I know all about it. She was only trying to comfort him. She's told me herself.'

'Is that what she calls it? Well I'm not blind. And I don't forget things.'

'That's something that might be worth learning to do,' Cilydd said. 'I'm going anyway. I've given you the best advice I can.'

She did not want him to leave. Her knuckles were white as she pressed her fists together against her breast bone as she approached him.

'What hurts me more than anything else is the way she deceives you,' Nanw said. 'And you can't see it. You believe every little lie she chooses to tell you. She collects men. Everybody can see it except you. She's ruining my brother. And she's poisoned you against me. What do they call a woman that collects men? Is she any better than a whore?'

272

It was a primitive challenge. The muscles of her neck extended as her voice rang through the house. He responded by striking her across the mouth with the back of his hand. She collapsed, a sobbing heap on the kitchen floor. He stood over her, white faced and appalled.

'Look what you've made me do,' he said.

He could hear Auntie Bessie's feet clattering down the oak staircase. It was plain that she had stayed out of the way to keep out of their row until she could bear it no longer.

'What's the matter with you two?'

She was their aunt and they were quarrelling children again.

'Screaming and shouting,' Auntie Bessie said. 'On the kitchen floor. What would my mother say if she heard you?'

Cilydd shook his head miserably.

'Auntie Bessie,' he said. 'Nain's been dead for nearly five years.'

His aunt was overcome with sudden weariness. She dragged out a kitchen chair and slumped down on it. She looked worn out with the daily struggle of trying to keep the place in order.

'She's not dead to me,' she said. 'I think of her every day. And I will do, until the day I die.'

~ iii ~

Cilydd had to bend his head as he entered the little church. The warmth of the afternoon penetrated no further than a few feet from the open door. There was little to see once his eyes grew accustomed to the chilly gloom. The brass eagle of the lectern was tarnished by the damp. The bible was open at the Book of Proverbs. He was drawn to the printed word. The black letters were stamped deep into paper thickened by the moist air. 'Sundry maxims and observations', announced the rubric. 'As a mad man who casteth firebrands, arrows and death so is the man that deceiveth his neighbour and saith, "Am I not in sport?"' The bright sunlight made the blues and reds of stolid stained glass in a memorial window more visible. Cilydd read the lettering underneath. The window had been installed to the glory of God and in

273

ever loving memory of a lieutenant who fell at the Pass of Madanpur on March 3, 1858. A smell of clammy sweetness oozed from the maps of discoloured damp on the plastered walls. It was pleasanter outside.

The porch had sagged under the weight of oak roof timbers and heavy rough hewn slate. The church and the old graveyard surrounding it stood in the middle of a large field overlooking the estuary. The corn had been gathered in. Sheep were grazing the new grass growing between the stubble. Cilydd sat on a horizontal tomb, rubbing a finger over the circles of lichen. The dead grass shed its seeds when he moved his feet. Through a gap in the thick periphery wall he saw a figure in uniform pass through the iron wicket and hurry up the narrow path to the church. His own car was parked off the road which ran along the foreshore. Cilydd raised his hand to ward off the insects flying about his head. A horde of winged creatures had emerged from soil he had trodden on between the tombs. The newcomer imagined he was being greeted with a friendly wave. He waved back and began to run up the slope so that by the time he had passed through the lych gate he was out of breath.

'Good old Cilydd,' Eddie Meredith said. 'I knew you wouldn't let me down.'

Cilydd gazed ironically at Eddie's uniform.

'Hasn't anyone told you,' he said. 'The war's over.'

Eddie grinned.

'Makes a good impression on the natives,' he said.

'"Captain" Meredith now is it?'

'Not for much longer.'

Eddie leaned against the edge of the tomb.

'Quite alarming in a way,' he said. 'Throws you back on your own resources, such as they are. You wake up demobbed, venture out and discover you are more or less a "has been".'

'Dear me,' Cilydd said.

He sounded objective but not unsympathetic. He folded his arms and lapsed into silence. This meeting was at Eddie Meredith's urgent request. He was under no obligation to initiate a conversation. He could attend to the breath of wind over the shorn field as it entered the little wilderness surrounding the church, ruffling the dead grass and the nettles. The overgrown weeds held what was left of warm air. There were butterflies he could watch hovering around melancholy headstones warmed with afternoon sunlight.

'Marvellous spot,' Eddie said. 'Just right for a poet.'

He was making a conscious effort to put himself in tune with what he assumed Cilydd's mood to be.

'The spirit of nature,' Eddie said. 'The sense of the boundless and all that. Matching the earth to the sky and the sky to the earth. I haven't forgotten, you know.'

'What was it you wanted to see me about? All so secret and hush-hush.'

Eddie stuck to his preamble, stepping delicately along a narrow path of reminiscence.

'It may seem long ago,' he said. 'Another world. Another exist-ence. But you presented me with the breath of life just when I most needed it. Through your poetry. You transformed the snotty little pimply son of the workhouse master into a breathless adolescent walking on air, let out of that prison, excited by everything: from the stars at night to getting up at five in the morning to run barefoot through the dew. I owe you the most enormous debt. You set me free. What I've done with my freedom is another matter. I know we can never get back to how we were. The war and so on. Changing the landscape. Building barriers bigger than the mount-ains between one period and another. But I don't want to lose your friendship. I want us to be friends.'

He grasped Cilydd's arm. Cilydd was prepared to be patient and amicable.

'I don't see anything against that,' he said.

Eddie's arms reached out to embrace him. Cilydd remained on his guard, resolutely unemotional.

'But why all the secrecy?' he said. 'Why drag me all the way out here?'

Eddie made refined gestures with the tip of index finger and thumb.

'There's someone I want you to meet,' he said. 'A first class person. A man of integrity and so on. English. But in love with Wales and her mountains.'

'Not George Borrow by any chance?'

Eddie burst out laughing and slapped Cilydd heartily on the back.

'Marvellous,' he said. 'The same old Cilydd. It is good to see you. On form as ever. Don't ever change whatever you do.'

'Well? Who is this mysterious stranger?'

'First I want to talk to you about "Urban Hordes". A cool dispassionate philosophical discussion. About urban hordes, labour camps, training camps, concentration camps, and holiday camps.'

'Ah.'

Cilydd looked down between his feet as if he had just caught a glimpse of a ferret being let out of a bag.

'Ah, nothing,' Eddie said. 'Just listen. Just give me a hearing.'

He paced about in front of Cilydd searching for the right words to convey his message with penetrating sincerity.

'The urban masses are on the march,' he said. 'It had to happen. Like the war had to happen. Nobody wanted it but nobody could stop it. Let me give you a brief insight into post-war politics.'

'I'm not sure that I want one,' Cilydd said.

'No. Just listen. The day of Labour has dawned for God's sake. Now that means something. The day of Labour, not the day of the Proletariat. It isn't socialism. It's nothing to do with the socialism poor old Pen Lewis used to dream about. It's just a minute shift in the load on humanity's back. I know what old Pen would call it. A secret pact between populist politicians and financial power. It's not the earthly paradise but it's going to have to do. And the shift in the load has got to make the people at the bottom more comfortable. You can see that?'

'I wish you'd just tell me what you're after,' Cilydd said.

'Of course I'm after something,' Eddie said.

He made an effort to appear angry, even outraged.

'What about Roberts MP for North Maelor?'

'What about him?' Cilydd said.

'Sergeant Roberts late of the Pioneer Corps and Iorrie Corman South Wales Salvationist, squashed together on the overcrowded Labour back benches. My God, that's a sight for you. Both of them

276

speaking out for the Carefree Holiday Camps. The common people of this country are entitled to their proper share of fresh air, relaxation, health and beauty. We cannot allow their welfare to be impeded by a self-appointed elite of linguistic culture snobs.'

Eddie appeared to be disgusted with the words he was quoting.

'Roberts will never forgive you and Amy for beating him to the nomination. Vindictive little sod. You'll have to watch out for him for years to come. He's well ahead in the sticky race to get his hands on the perks of power. Might even end up in the cabinet, God help us.'

It seemed a prospect Cilydd had not considered before.

'They are in and they mean to make the most of it,' Eddie said. 'There's damn all you can do to stop it. The train is moving. You have to get on it before it runs over you.'

'You sound quite envious,' Cilydd said.

Eddie was not willing to be teased.

'I'm not an idiot,' he said. 'I understand what you are on about. Of course I do. How could I not? But I also understand what's happening in the world a good deal better than most, and I can tell you it keeps me awake at nights. I tell you what it boils down to. The secret of post-war politics is the manipulation and management of urban hordes and if you want to save anything from the cataclysm, you'd better be on the side of those who know how to manipulate, manage and govern. It's as simple as that.'

Cilydd held his head to one side to put a falsely naive question.

'What about all those West End hits you were going to write?' he said. 'Don't tell me you've missed the bus. After going to such trouble to perfect your English.'

Eddie looked hurt.

'You don't mind kicking a chap when he's down, do you?' he said.

'You don't look a bit down to me,' Cilydd said. 'You look very smart. Very nifty.'

'I haven't got the talent,' Eddie said. 'I never did have. And you know it. My eye was bigger than my belly. Always biting off more than I could chew. I've got all my work cut out trying to be a decent journalist. If there is such a thing.'

'Come, come,' Cilydd said. 'You mustn't be too hard on yourself. Now what about the mysterious stranger?'

'Colonel Ricks,' Eddie said. 'Rollo Ricks. A great chap, honestly. I mean he was terribly impressed when I told him you were a friend of mine. His great hobby is tramping mountains. Absolutely loves it. Not so much climbing now because of his leg wound. But he gets up there and he says it's the nearest thing he will ever come to the Beatific Vision. Bit of a mystic in his way.'

'Why should he want to meet me?' Cilydd said.

'It's quite simple really,' Eddie said. 'He's been invited to serve on the Board of Carefree Camps.'

Cilydd's outburst of laughter sounded forced. He slapped his thigh and jerked his knee.

'I don't believe it,' he said. 'I can't believe what I'm hearing.'

'He'll accept of course,' Eddie said. 'He can't afford not to. It's not easy for chaps being demobbed. There isn't all that much choice. But he wants to hear the arguments against. He loves Wales. If he takes over in any capacity, he wants to do everything he can to soften the impact. I mean at least he is aware of a heritage to preserve. He wants to make contact . . . Why can't we co-operate?'

Cilydd continued to be unable to get over his amazement. He moved away to the oldest part of the burial ground. Eddie followed him protesting the innocence and purity of his intentions.

'It wouldn't do any harm,' he said. 'And it might do a lot of good. Rollo Ricks is a very reasonable chap. Cultivated. Not some vulgar fairground cheapjack. He's really civilized.'

Sycamore trees as profuse as weeds had tumbled the wall at the end of the consecrated ground. They cast long shadows over brambles advancing towards tombstones tilted at odd angles, like rolls of barbed wire creeping towards abandoned defences.

'Just a talk,' Eddie said, pleading. 'Just a chat. Make your voice heard where it really matters. They're bound to win in the end. A bit of an injunction isn't going to stop them. High Court or no High Court. They've got it tied up I can tell you. You can't win. You simply can't. Your local bigwigs are brought and bottled already.'

Cilydd had advanced too far into the brambles in an effort to read faint inscriptions carved on the headstones. The thorns clung to his trousers as he struggled to extricate himself. Eddie was sounding desperate.

'Alderman Llew, Davies DSO, my old man. The lot. They'll go on making pious noises, but they won't resist because they're already bought in one way or another. They'll rub their culture all over their chests like peanut butter: then they'll scurry off home to count their ill-gotten gains in secret.'

'And what about you?'

Cilydd was pointing at Eddie's chest.

'What's in it for Captain Meredith? That's what I want to know.'

'Just a chat over a drink. Or over a meal. That's all I'm asking.'

'Asking,' Cilydd said. 'But what are you getting?'

'The chance of a good job. And that's not something to be sniffed at these days I can tell you.'

'What job?'

Eddie took a deep breath.

'Assistant Press Officer to Carefree Holiday Camps Incorporated.'

'My goodness,' Cilydd said.

'It's a bloody good job. Real money. Plenty of expenses. Plenty of perks. And a chance to do a bit of good. Not to be sneezed at. Not to be despised.'

'What bit of good?'

Eddie flushed.

'Haven't you been listening to anything I've said?'

'Oh yes, I've been listening,' Cilydd said.

Eddie followed him as he walked back towards the lych gate. He was desperate to make him stop and listen.

'He really is keen to meet you,' Eddie said. 'I shouldn't anticipate whatever he's got to say but I'm pretty certain he'll want to make you some kind of offer.'

'Not thirty pieces of silver, surely,' Cilydd said.

'They'll need legal representation at this end of the operation. It's large scale stuff, for God's sake. There'll be Carefree Camps all over the United Kingdom. All over the bloody world I shouldn't wonder. You've got to adapt, damn it. You've got to adapt if you want to survive.'

'It's an interesting version of history,' Cilydd said. 'I'm afraid it's not mine.'

'Just come and meet him. For a drink and a chat.'

Cilydd shook his head. He was prepared to ruminate as he strolled down the path to the iron wicket. There was nothing Eddie could do to arrest his progress.

'There's one thing about lost causes,' Cilydd said. 'They have a certain dignity. I quite like that.'

'Look. I'm begging you. Just wait a minute. I haven't finished. I've got a lot more to tell you. Rollo Ricks has lots of confidence in me. He wants me to have the job. "I like your common sense, Meredith," he says. "It has the scent of infinite wisdom." He wants me there. Alongside him. This is the best chance I'm ever going to get . . . I'm not asking for anything really. Just meet him for a drink and a chat?'

Cilydd shook his head.

'I'm sorry,' he said. 'I only wish I could help you.'

The iron wicket was between them. Cilydd turned to see what birds were picking their way along the foreshore and the mud flats of the estuary. Eddie's voice was thick with frustration.

'You don't want me to have a chance,' he said. 'You just want to drag me down to your own miserable level.'

17

~ i ~

CONNIE CLAYTON STEERED HER SMOOTHING IRON LIKE THE PROW OF a ship over the crumpled surface of one of John Cilydd's white shirts. It was warm in the basement kitchen. Her long features were flushed with the concentrated effort she was making. Clothing already completed hung in precise order on the wooden clothes horse in front of the fire. But the clothes basket was full of items still to be done. Connie raised her head momentarily to catch the sound of voices upstairs. The house seemed filled from top to bottom with an atmosphere of bustle. Connie pushed the iron as if her arm were a piston in the engine room and the progress of the vessel depended on it. Three taps on the back door did nothing to break the rhythm of her labour. Menna Cowley Jones poked her head in. She was wearing a hat on what appeared to be a temporary basis: a thin excuse for scurrying from one terrace house to another. Her mouth turned up like the grin of a clown intent on invoking a friendly reception from the audience before parting the curtains and starting to perform.

'Here I am being a nuisance again!' Menna said. 'My goodness me, you look busy. So early in the morning.'

Connie muttered into the ironing board that there was a great deal to do.

'I won't keep you my dear,' Menna said. 'Not one second. I've brought the local rag. I thought you'd like to see it.'

'A bad night,' Connie said. 'Gwydion had toothache. And he woke Peredur up. We've been on our feet since five.'

'Dear me,' Menna said. 'So you saw the dawn breaking over the mountains. "Like a bright fan of mother-of-pearl opening in the eye of the sun". One doesn't always remember he's a National Winner. Look at this.'

Menna raised the paper to bring it to Connie's attention.

'He'll be so disappointed. Heart-broken I dare say. The County Council have voted in favour of Carefree Camps. That's what it amounts to. They refuse to raise the money to buy them out. Fifty thousand was well beyond them. And they wouldn't fight. So there we are. The battle is lost. We don't deserve to have such a good poet. As I said to my sister Flo, there's never any honour for a prophet in his own country. Not around here anyway.'

Connie frowned over her ironing.

'Lord Cranforth would never have allowed it,' she said. 'I know that much. They can say what they like about the aristocracy but they know how to get things settled. Lord Cranforth wouldn't have put up with their nonsense. Not for one second. He used to say, "if you want law and order, somebody's got to lay the law down. And that's the long and the short of it."'

When she saw a smile flicker across Connie's face, Menna

shifted closer to the fire. It was early in the morning but a sense of stolen sweetness would add flavour to Connie's rambling sagas about the great houses where she had worked. Even her sister Flo, who dared openly to disapprove of royalty and declare her republican affiliations, responded to the mythological lilt in Connie Clayton's tales of the great people and titled personages she had been privileged to serve.

'Lord Cranforth wouldn't have put up with all this Carefree Camps nonsense,' Connie said. 'Not for one second.'

She underlined her conviction with a thud of her smoothing iron.

'You iron beautifully,' Menna said encouragingly. 'I would call you a perfectionist. I really would.'

Amy clattered down the short flight of stairs. She looked busy. She was lowering her head to greet Menna, one hand on the bannister rail, when she heard the boys arguing upstairs.

'Listen to those boys,' she said. 'And we've only just got Peredur back to sleep.'

She turned on her heel and they could hear her hurrying up the two flights of stairs to the boys' bedroom and whispering dire threats.

'I had better be off,' Menna said without moving. 'I shouldn't be standing around here like a woman with nothing to do . . .'

She was suddenly struck by an idea.

'Unless I took the boys out,' she said. 'It's quite a nice day for a picnic . . .'

She gazed at Connie as she thought aloud.

'I couldn't take the baby of course,' she said. 'I wouldn't know what to do with him. Funny isn't it? My sister Flo says I'm deficient in the maternal instinct. You're a fine one to talk, I say to her. That's the way we are. Bickering all day. Think of little Clemmie saying, "Stop your bickering"! Telling us off you may as well say. He'd love to have the boys on a picnic. He thinks the world of Bedwyr, and Gwydion follows them like a little dog.'

Amy reappeared smiling on the last step of the stairs.

'At least they can't argue while they're eating,' she said.

Menna was ready with her suggestion.

282

'Mrs More,' she said. 'I was just saying to Miss Clayton. Would you like me to take the boys? It's quite warm today. Would they like a picnic?'

Amy was delighted.

'Would you really?' she said. 'That would be so kind. It really would.'

'I was thinking of Abercregin beach,' Menna said. 'It's so nice and quiet there. Not that it will be for much longer. Have you seen this?'

She raised her copy of the local paper.

'Oh don't mention it.'

Amy demonstrated her distaste.

'My poor husband is so depressed. The County Council! They don't know Queen Anne is dead, let alone Lloyd George. They are such idiots. Just fluff in the Alderman's pocket.'

Amy lowered her voice.

'Please keep this to yourself,' she said. 'I'm going to take him away. As far as we can get from this place. A proper holiday. Thanks to my Aunt Esther and dear Connie. They will be in charge. But please keep it to yourself for the time being. For all sorts of reasons.'

Menna was so pleased to be taken into her confidence she gave a faint but distinct purr.

'Flo and I will do what we can to help. I may tell Flo?'

'Oh of course.'

'Does your sister-in-law know?'

The question hung in the air while Amy decided how to phrase her answer.

'Er . . . not yet,' Amy said carefully. 'Not exactly. She does know we've been thinking about it. For some time. I expect we shall call there later in the day.'

'When are you think of going?'

Menna quivered with conspiratorial pleasure inside her coat, prepared to be astonished.

'First train tomorrow morning,' Amy said.

She was firm and decisive.

'The sooner the better,' she said. 'I don't believe in hanging about licking one's wounds. Off and away!'

'How exciting.'

Menna's lips were rounded by a spasm of delight.

'Where will you go?' she said. 'I know I shouldn't ask . . .'

'Over the hills and far away,' Amy said.

She stood above the clothes horse.

'Connie dear, may I take some of these?'

Amy made a point of asking Connie Clayton's approval and permission before carefully folding ironed clothes over her arm.

'A secret destination,' she said. 'Tell you all about it in great detail when we get back.'

In the back room of the ground floor, Esther was supervising the boys' breakfast. Amy stood over them with her husband's shirts on her arm. Her expression was full of gratitude to her aunt. To the boys she broke the news of the promised picnic. They began to swallow their food at great speed. Amy had to warn them not to eat too quickly. Observing their hearty appetites was pleasant, but she had packing to contend with. Suitcases were already open in her bedroom. She hummed to herself as she concentrated on the operation. Every drawer was left open as she pondered the problem of what clothes she would take. It was some time before she became aware that Bedwyr was standing in the doorway watching her. Wearing a Fair Isle sleeveless pullover and tubular short trousers that reached to his knees the boy looked infinitely patient and thoughtful.

'Bedwyr, darling. You are so quiet. I had no idea you were there. What is it, my precious?'

'You are going away.'

'Come here, my darling. We never get a chance to talk, do we?'

She encouraged him to sit alongside her on the edge of the unmade bed. She stroked his hair and remarked how soft it was.

'Little children are starving in Europe,' she said. 'You mustn't worry about it. I don't want you to worry. But your father and I want to go and see what we can do to help them.'

Bedwyr nodded gravely.

'While we are gone I know how good you will be. Helping Auntie Esther. Doing everything she asks as you always do because you are the best boy in the world. And I want to ask you something else . . .'

284

Amy placed her finger under his chin to tilt his face up so that they could look into each other's eyes.

'I'm relying on you to look after Gwydion. We know how naughty and silly he can be sometimes. He doesn't mean any harm, we know that don't we? It's just that he's been given that extra helping of high spirits.'

Amy smiled to remind the boy it was a joke they had shared before.

'All it means is we just have to keep an eye on him. What I want more than anything is that he'll grow up to be like you.'

Amy placed her arm over Bedwyr's shoulder to give him a hug. She was surprised by his response.

'He's not my real brother, is he?' Bedwyr said.

'Of course he is. Whoever told you that?'

'If you are not my mother, he can't be my real brother can he?'

'Oh Bedwyr darling. Your mother was my best friend in all the world. I loved her as much as I love you. When she died all I could think about was how to make you my very own. As you are now. The best boy in the world.'

She kissed him gently on the cheek.

'Mam.'

'Yes, my pet.'

'What do you think God is like?' Amy was amused.

'I only wish I knew,' she said. 'I've no idea.'

'Auntie Nanw says he's everywhere and sees everything.'

'Well I suppose that's what she believes,' Amy said.

Bedwyr looked up at her.

'Don't you believe it?' he said.

He was demanding an honest answer.

'I don't know,' Amy said. 'I really don't know.'

'That's what Dad said when I asked him. I haven't asked Auntie Esther yet.'

He stood up and looked more childlike, as if he had been able to shed a shadow of concern and shift himself back with ease to a more innocent state.

'Auntie Esther wants to go home,' he said.

'Does she?'

Amy was disturbed.

'She hasn't said anything to me,' she said.

'If she goes home, who will look after us while you are away?'

'She won't go,' Amy said. 'Of course she won't. She knows how much your daddy needs to get away. She would never leave until we got back. Of course she wouldn't.'

Amy became restless.

'I must go and have a word with your father. There's so much to be done today. Now you go downstairs, there's a good boy, and get ready for the picnic. Find the things you need. Your bat and ball.'

She watched Bedwyr descend the stairs before going up to Cilydd's study at the top of the house. He was still in his dressing-gown gazing moodily at the panoramic view across the harbour. A solitary swan was floating in on the shallow tide. Amy pointed at letters from Margot and Erika on the desk in the bay window.

'Have you read them?' Amy said.

Her tone of voice suggested she was making an effort to be patient and understanding. He had suffered a defeat. He had a right to brood. She was drawing his attention to the letters in order to take his mind off all the depressing implications of the County Council's decision.

'What are you thinking about?' Amy said.

'About the difference,' Cilydd said. 'Between then and now.'

'What difference?'

'It's the war of course,' he said. 'It's diminished everything and everybody.'

Amy picked up her friends' letters and put them down again. She made an effort to listen.

'There was a time when we believed we had some power to influence the way things were going. We could save Wales if we put effort into it. A little more effort and we could save the world. If anything, that would be easier. We believed that what we said and what we did would make a difference. So naive and childish it all seems now. I can't even save this little patch from desecration. I've no influence over anything. I'll end up an outcast even in my own country.'

'You've got to get away,' Amy said. 'That's all there is to it. You've got to take me on that holiday you promised. Except it won't be a holiday. Something much better. An adventure.'

She waved the thin paper of Erika's letter in the air.

'They came to us,' Amy said. 'Now we'll go to them. It will help to keep things in perspective. Help us to keep our balance.'

Cilydd smiled bleakly.

'My balance you mean.'

'Erika is a changed woman,' Amy said. 'There's no question about it. All that destruction and devastation. When I just think of her standing in front of that ruin in Berlin, knowing that the bodies of her sister and her Liesel-too-good-to-be-true probably buried under the rubble. Feeling like a ghost standing in front of her own tomb. "Dead already without knowing it." I was terribly moved.'

She waited for Cilydd to show some sign of having felt the same. It wasn't a time to be cautious and critical. She held up the letter to read out a sentence.

'I mean the proof is here,' Amy said. '"As for the diamonds, sell them for what you can get and buy an ambulance. What else are diamonds for?"'

Amy laughed delightedly.

'I think that's marvellous,' she said. ' "What else are diamonds for?" Such a marvellous spirit. We set off tomorrow Mr More, first thing. To buy an ambulance. I've never bought an ambulance before. And we stuff it with medical supplies and Margot's list of requirements and drive it right across Europe to Klagenfurt! And we'll meet up with them there. It can be arranged. There is absolutely no reason why we can't do it.'

Cilydd looked up at her admiringly.

'I don't know that you or I have the right to dispose of someone else's jewels,' he said. 'We don't know anything about jewels.'

Amy waved Erika's letter under his nose.

'There you are,' she said. 'Written and signed authorization. And who says I don't know anything about jewels? I know you get a better price in Brussels than in Amsterdam or London! I have my contacts in the Red Cross and the Relief Organisation ready and waiting.'

She was making a valiant effort to drag him out of his depression.

'You didn't know your wife was a bit of a pirate, did you? Get on your feet, John Cilydd.'

She pointed at the view of the mountains on the eastern horizon.

'Cross those, Hannibal More,' she said. 'And there'll be nothing between you and the Alps. You'll be free! Let out of prison. And you'll be able to compose an epic poem about the destruction of Europe. How men of science and intelligence perverted their gifts and brought down fire from heaven to destroy what they loved most. There you are. How's that for a theme. You can't say I haven't learnt something from you.'

He wanted to embrace her.

'I'm not good enough for you Amy,' he said.

Amy laughed.

'Now where have I heard that tune before?' she said.

'If only I had half your spirit . . .'

'We'll escape together,' Amy said. 'You'll forget about Carefree Holiday Camps and corrupt County Councils. And not just a jolly jaunt. We'll do some good. A lot of good in one way or another. Why don't you get out of that dressing-gown and get dressed? There's a lot to do.'

He made a show of humble obedience.

'You mustn't let them get you down,' Amy said. 'I met H. M. Meredith as I came out of the chemist's yesterday afternoon. He had the nerve to tell me we couldn't stand in the way of progress. So I told him to his face. "Exactly how much are they paying you and your brilliant son, Mr Meredith?" That was my parting shot. Poisonous little creature.'

Amy shivered dramatically.

'I can't wait to get away from this place,' she said.

The front door bell rang while Cilydd was getting dressed.

'I'd better answer it,' Amy said. 'Can't have Auntie and Connie running up and down stairs more than they have to. I think they both find them heavy going. It's no joke, getting old.'

She recognised the policeman. His bicycle was balanced against the kerb of the wide pavement behind him. He was sweating gently inside his tight uniform. He extracted a red cotton handkerchief with white polka dots to mop his face and wipe his moustache.

'Constable Pritchard,' Amy said. 'I expect you want to see my husband. Isn't it a lovely day?'

He seemed to have difficulty in responding to her cheerful greeting.

'Sergeant Lazarus should have come himself,' PC Pritchard said. 'But he's new here. So he sent me.'

He sounded resentful at being used as a messenger.

'It's something important?' Amy said.

She was looking at him with such enquiring innocence, he began to shake his head.

'Bad news,' he said. 'I don't know why it should be me to have to tell him.'

Amy asked the policeman to come in. He stood nursing his helmet in their front room and declining to say anything until Cilydd was present. Together they stood in silence listening to the noises in the house and in the street. A growing fear made it impossible for Amy to move her feet. Cilydd arrived at last, wearing one of the dark suits he wore to attend magistrates' courts.

'There's been a serious accident at Glanrafon,' PC Pritchard said. 'I can't tell you how serious. Your sister, Miss More, has been badly burnt. She's in hospital. They don't give much hope. But she's conscious. She's asking for you.'

~ ii ~

There was no warmth in the red sky. The sun was a vast disk floating beyond the black outline of the smithy. There was light to illuminate the cobwebs and fine dust covering the shop windows of Glanrafon Stores in some detail. John Cilydd was able to write meaningless hieroglyphics in the dirt with the tip of his finger and draw down cobwebs until they broke. He was a solitary figure stumbling about the forecourt. The doors of Uncle Tryfan's workshop were closed. A row of white poultry was perched like a ghostly court of enquiry on a cart frame in the coach house. There

289

was a chill in the autumn air and they had retired early. The whole place was stricken with the desolate silences that belong to disasters like war and famine and plague. John Cilydd stretched out his arms as if his strength were a torment greater than he could bear. He turned in a slow circle impelled to execute some obscure ritual on the threshold of the place where he had been born and brought up. Darkness grew out of the walls more powerful than the rosy elegiac light in the sky: a dense darkness that would last longer than any night.

He pushed open the door. The shop bell rang obediently over his head. The place was sinister and deserted. He had to feel his way across the length of floor towards the passage that led to the kitchen. He looked up fearfully at the brushes, buckets, ropes and rakes hanging from the ceiling. In a hostile environment he was lost and alone and ready to seek any refuge. He found his Uncle Tryfan sitting in his grandmother's chair: a small shrivelled creature not large enough to fill it. The fire had gone out. The red sky was a distant transparency outside the square window. When his eyes grew accustomed to the gloom Cilydd realised his Aunt Bessie was sitting like a graven image on the horse-hair sofa under the aquatint of 'The Broad and Narrow Way'. The crude colours of the picture were dead inside the frame. His aunt's hands were folded on the oilcloth of the table, whiter than he had ever seen them before.

'I woke and I could smell burning.'

The words of the litany had been put together in Uncle Tryfan's struggle to make sense of a catastrophe. There would be no end to the number of times he would repeat it to himself. His voice had become a worn echo of his familiar high-pitched tenor.

'It's a dream, I said to myself. A bad dream. I had been having bad dreams. One night after the other. But this was worse. The light was poor. I nearly fell down the stairs. And there she was on the cold stone floor, kneeling, her clothes and her hair on fire. Making this strange noise. I thought she was laughing.'

Tryfan sat up in his mother's chair to mime action. He stretched up first one stiff arm and then the other.

'There was an old blanket my mother used to use when she was plucking chickens. Or cutting my hair. It was hanging there from the tie-beam. I could just reach it. I wrapped her in that. I thought it would catch fire. And I was afraid of smothering her. She was so thin. We were less than three yards from the paraffin dispenser. The whole place could have gone up.'

Possibilities were infinite. They could be contemplated for ever. What she had done was a single fact; inexplicable, horrible. He needed an explanation.

'Why did she do it?'

He gripped the arms of the chair so that his whole body was an extension of wood twisted into the shape of a question. The muscles of his thin face were taut. His nephew was present and his function was to provide an answer.

'She died of shock,' Cilydd said. 'That's what the doctors said. They wrapped her in gauze and jelly. "Tulle gras" they called it. Sounded like a wedding dress.'

Cilydd moved to the window. The shape of the garden and orchard was unfamiliar in silhouette. The light of the setting sun illuminated a range of clouds with a deliberation that could have been meaningful if it had been less transient. A barn owl flew silently across the garden drawing out its own wavering border between evening and night.

'It was on her mind,' Uncle Tryfan said. 'I can tell you that much. People burning. That Hiroshima. Where is it? Robert Thomas said to me, "This Hiroshima. Where is it?" And he started singing that children's mission hymn about far away in China and far away Japan. "Can't be so far away then can it?" he said. My goodness he got on her nerves. She wouldn't have him near the place.'

'There will be an inquest,' Cilydd said. 'There was nothing I could do to prevent that.'

'Why did she do it?'

Tryfan's hands were like carved wood as he held on to the arms of the chair.

'Poured paraffin over her hair and shoulders with that measuring can. Striking a match. Why did she do a thing like that? She was always such a good girl. I don't remember her ever doing anything wrong. All her life. Not really. Never did anything out of place.'

They lapsed into a silence that threatened to last for ever. Uncle Tryfan struggled to speak.

'She worried about the war,' he said. 'Of course she did. We all did. She was a sensitive creature. My mother used to say Nanw has one layer of skin less than most people. Like you John Cilydd. She was always worrying about you.'

'You think it's my fault?'

Cilydd spread his hand over the surface of the kitchen wall. In the gathering dark, touch would be a more reliable guide to the appearance of the place than sight. There were unevennesses in the surface of the thick walls he could recall from his earliest childhood.

'You think I was unkind to her?'

Before his aunt and this uncle who had seen him grow up, who had watched over him, who remembered how devoted to him his sister had been, he could accuse himself with bitter forensic calm.

'You blame me,' Cilydd said. 'You think it's my fault.'

The shadows crowded into the kitchen like remorse. Auntie Bessie kept silent. Tryfan released the arms of his chair. His own arms hung limp and useless between his legs.

'We talk such nonsense,' he said. 'Nothing we say means anything. What will become of us?'

Cilydd's back stiffened. At least this plea was something he could respond to. There were responsibilities he could attend to on their behalf.

'We must give it some thought,' he said. 'Consider things calmly. List the alternatives. We could sell this place. If that was what you wanted. Not that it's a good time to sell. Country properties are going for a song. People flocking to the towns. Urban hordes. You could rent the shop. Let it for rent. You could live in Cae Golau. Or you could come and live with us. These are things we'll have to think out.'

Tryfan turned petulant.

'I didn't mean that,' he said crossly. 'That's not what I'm talking about.'

Cilydd sat on the low stool by the fire surprised by his uncle's uncharacteristic ill humour.

'What then?'

Tryfan was restless in his chair.

'What will become of us?' he said. 'I can't open a hymn book. The pages are stuck together. The words are all blurred. When they're blurred they don't mean anything. That's what I was talking about.'

~ iii ~

The blinds of the front room of the terrace house were lowered. Pin-pricks of light piercing the fabric did nothing to diminish the gloom of the interior. Amy sat on the edge of an armchair wearing her hat and coat like a passenger in a waiting-room. Her large valise was on the hearth rug. She relieved the tension of her inactivity by nibbling the hem of a white handkerchief. The silence of the house was oppressive. The voices of children playing in the sand dunes were as distant as the boom of waves on the shelving shore. Amy stuffed her handkerchief away as she heard Cilydd's footsteps coming down the stairs. He could not restrain his dismay when he saw she was ready to leave.

'You can't . . .'

The words escaped as he sat in the chair opposite. She responded immediately.

'I can, and I will,' she said.

His distress was beyond words. His hands made shapes in the air that were meant to outline elucidations: instead they gave the impression of a prisoner tightening the knots in his frantic effort to escape.

'We are contained,' he said. 'We are constricted by our families, by our commitments . . . we are never free to do exactly as we like . . . perhaps that is how it should be. I don't know. I only know that is how it is.'

Amy shook her head in violent disagreement.

'Words,' she said. 'That's all that means anything to you. What are they? You say one thing to one person and another to another. It's what you do that counts.'

She spoke with such vigorous conviction that he was forced to make some concession.

'Poor Nanw,' Cilydd said. 'She . . .'

She would not allow him to finish.

'Poor Nanw indeed. I'll tell you what I think of your poor Nanw.'

Amy restrained herself abruptly.

'You wouldn't be able to bear it,' she said.

They remained two hunched figures in identical armchairs. Speech had become dangerous. Silence was unbearable.

'She's stamped us with disgrace,' Amy said. 'She's dragged us down to her level. She's made sure you'll remember every single thing she ever said against me. For the rest of our life. That's what she's done.'

'That's not fair, Amy,' he said. 'That's not true.'

'I'm not afraid of the truth.'

She exulted in her own capacity for frankness.

'This is her triumph! And she did it at the very moment when you were unbalanced with disappointment. You can go on saying you don't know why she did it, but I know.'

Cilydd was shaking with disbelief and discomfort. He even held out a hand as though to protect himself from attack.

'You mustn't say such things . . .'

The prohibition was like fuel on her fire.

'You don't understand women, John Cilydd More. They are vicious dangerous jealous bitches. She was violent against herself because she couldn't be as violent as she wanted against me. That is a well-known psychological phenomenon. You ask anybody who understands these things . . . And why? And why? I'll tell you why. Because she was in love with you. Incestuous love. Thank God I never had a brother. No woman could ever love you as much as she loved you. And now she's proved it. She's destroyed herself so that she can move inside you and live in there for as long as you live, like a parasite feeding forever off a host.'

Cilydd's head and shoulders sank like a branch bent to breaking point by the force of a storm.

'You expect me to believe all that,' he said.

'It's what I think,' Amy said. 'You always want to know what I think.'

'And that gives you your excuse to leave?'

'I don't need an excuse,' Amy said. 'I am a free agent. I have the means.'

'They're not your means, are they?' Cilydd said. 'And it's no use pretending they are. Listen Amy. Listen to me. Don't let's quarrel. We have to think of others. There are rules. There are laws. There have to be. And there is deep sense in the idea that life is a ceremony. I don't mean a ceremony in any elaborate puffed up exaggerated sense. But there has to be an element of ritual observance in people's relationships with each other. There has to be.'

'Ritual?'

Amy voice was filled with contempt as she repeated the word.

'I must be honest,' she said. 'She has poisoned everything. I've got to get away from this place. I can't bear the idea of sleeping in the same bed as you. With her lying there between us. Can't you understand?'

He could no longer contain his misery. He turned in the chair so that he could bury his face in his hands on the upholstered arm. Amy rose to her feet and stood over him, a figure of strength looking down at a man in his weakness. She appeared undecided whether or not to attempt to bring him comfort.

'I've said more than I meant to say,' she said. 'That's how we are. Always saying things better left unsaid.'

His stifled sobs enlarged the silence between them. Her head shot up when she heard a scream from the back garden.

'Gwydion,' she said. 'What are they doing, back here already?'

The back door opened and the noise of several voices talking at once flooded into the basement kitchen. Gwydion continued to make sporadic efforts of screaming that sounded wholly artificial. Cilydd was on his feet wiping his face with a handkerchief. He had to assert his authority. He opened the door of the front room, moved into the passage and called out in a loud voice.

'What on earth is going on down there? What is happening?'

He heard a whispered consultation between Esther Parry and

Connie Clayton. The baby Peredur was sleeping in his pram. Esther couldn't leave him. It was Bedwyr who came dashing up the stairs holding a carving knife with a polished white handle.

'Gwydion had this,' he said.

His face was flushed with his exertions and a certain satisfaction with his own behaviour. Cilydd took the knife from him and stepped back into the front room. He held up the knife so that Amy could see it. Bedwyr came in. His gaze settled on the valise on the hearth rug and on Amy wearing her hat and coat in the house. He reduced the explanation about the knife to a minimum.

'He must have stolen it and carried it outside,' Bedwyr said. 'I took it from the toolbag on his bike. He started screaming it was his and that he'd found it. But I knew it was from the house. I did right, didn't I?'

He waited with his head raised for signs of his parents' joint approval.

'He could have hurt himself,' Bedwyr said. 'Or he could have hurt someone else. He could have got into trouble.'

Cilydd moved close enough to stroke the top of his son's head. He looked as if he would have liked to embrace the boy, but was under an obligation to restrain himself.

'Mam.'

Bedwyr addressed Amy urgently.

'You're not going away are you? It's the school concert tomorrow.'